Like many authors, Lesley started ~~writing~~ [. . .] chequered beginning, including jo[. . .] crew and nightclub DJ, she fell into feature writing for publications including *Business Matters*, *Which? Computing* and *Farmers Weekly*.

She progressed to short stories for the vibrant women's magazine market and, following a Master's degree where she met her publisher, she turned to her first literary love of traditional British mysteries. The Libby Sarjeant series is still going strong, and has been joined by The Alexandrians, an Edwardian mystery series.

Praise for Lesley Cookman:

'Nicely staged drama and memorable and strangely likeable characters'
Trisha Ashley

'With fascinating characters and an intriguing plot, this is a real page turner'
Katie Fforde

'Lesley Cookman is the Queen of Cosy Crime'
Paul Magrs

'Intrigue, romance and a touch of murder in a picturesque village setting'
Liz Young

'A compelling series where each book leaves you satisfied but also eagerly waiting for the next one'
Bernardine Kennedy

'A quaint, British cozy, complete with characters

MURDER BY MISTAKE

LESLEY COOKMAN

ACCENT

First published in 2022 by Headline Accent
An imprint of HEADLINE PUBLISHING GROUP

1

Cataloguing in Publication Data is available from the British Library

ISBN 978 1 4722 7835 7

Typeset in 10.5/13pt Bembo Std by Jouve (UK), Milton Keynes

Printed and bound in Great Britain by Clays Ltd, Elcograf S.p.A.

HEADLINE PUBLISHING GROUP
An Hachette UK Company
Carmelite House
50 Victoria Embankment
London
EC4Y 0DZ

www.headline.co.uk
www.hachette.co.uk

Dedicated to the NHS, all of whom have worked
so tirelessly over the last three years.

Character List

Libby Sarjeant
Former actor and part-time artist, mother to Dominic, Belinda and Adam Sarjeant and owner of Sidney the cat. Resident of 17 Allhallow's Lane, Steeple Martin.

Fran Wolfe
Former actor and occasional psychic. Owner of Balzac the cat and resident of Coastguard Cottage, Nethergate.

Ben Wilde
Libby's significant other. Owner of The Manor Farm and the Oast House Theatre.

Guy Wolfe
Fran's husband and father to Sophie Wolfe. Artist and owner of a shop and gallery in Harbour Street, Nethergate.

Peter Parker
Freelance journalist, part owner of The Pink Geranium restaurant. Ben's cousin and Harry Price's partner.

Harry Price
Chef and co-owner of The Pink Geranium. Peter Parker's partner.

DCI Ian Connell
Local policeman and friend. Fran's former suitor.

Flo Carpenter
Hetty's oldest friend.

Hetty Wilde
Ben's mother. Lives at The Manor.

Lenny Fisher
Hetty's brother. Lives with Flo Carpenter.

Jane Baker
Chief reporter for the Nethergate Mercury.

Reverend Patti Pearson
Vicar at St Aldeberge.

Anne Douglas
Librarian and Reverend Patti's friend and partner.

Edward Hall
Academic and historian.

Alice Gedding
Sheep Farmer and friend of Edward's.

Colin Hardcastle and Gerry Hall
Steeple Martin's newest residents.

Cassandra
Libby's cousin.

Mike Farthing
Owner of Farthing's Plants and partner of Libby's cousin Cassandra.

Tim Stevens
Landlord of the Coach and Horses, Steeple Martin.

Michelle Wells
Hairdresser and friend of Libby's.

Neil Barton

Joan Barton
Neil's mother.

Sylvia Cranthorne
Estate Agent.

Mavis
Owner of the Blue Anchor Café.

Joe Wilson
Friend of Lenny, Flo and Hetty.

Simon Spencer
Manager of the Hop Pocket.

Beth Cole
Vicar at Steeple Martin.

Adam Sarjeant
Libby's son.

Reg Fisher
Farmer from Pucklefield.

Charles Bertram
Landlord of the Puckle Inn.

Nick Stapleton
CEO of Stapleton Holdings.

Ron Stewart
Retired pop star.

Maria Stewart
Ron's wife.

Graham
Manager of The Sloop Inn.

Barney
A dog.

Ricky Short
Barney's owner.

Grant Pointer
Ricky's stepfather.

Debbie Pointer
Ricky's mother.

Linda Davies
Ricky's grandmother.

Dan and Moira Henderson
Residents of Steeple Martin.

Jinny Mardle
Libby's next door neighbour.

Chapter One

'I must go – I'm going to see Michelle today,' said Libby to her friend Fran Wolfe.

'Michelle who?' asked Fran.

'Michelle Wells – you remember. Used to be a singer and dancer. I tried to persuade her to audition for panto ages ago, but she said she'd given up theatre, professional and amateur.'

'Oh – the hairdresser! Don't tell me you're having your hair done?'

'Why not? It could do with a bit of tidying up.'

As Libby's hair had been frequently described as a Brillo pad, or, more charitably, a small briar bush, this was undoubtedly true.

'Good for you! What brought this on?'

'Oh, you know. I felt a bit – well, frumpy.'

Fran laughed. 'You are *not* frumpy! Have you got a special occasion coming up?'

'We both have – Gerry and Colin's housewarming party.'

Gerry and Colin had recently moved from temporary accommodation in Libby's home village of Steeple Martin to a new house overlooking the golf course and sea in the nearby village of Heronsbourne.

'So we have. But that's weeks away. They never managed to have one in the flat, did they?'

'Not a proper one, no.'

'So you're having your hair done in honour of the occasion?'

'Not just that.' Libby sighed. 'I felt my whole look needed a boost.'

Fran put her head on one side. 'Give up the whole charity-shop-couture look?'

'Don't be rude. Just because I'm not tall and elegant like you.' Libby sniffed. 'Anyway, I'd better get going.' She stood up and looked around the gallery-cum-shop belonging to Fran's husband, Guy, an artist, and spotted one of her own efforts, painted from the front window of Fran's cottage. 'Not sold yet?'

'Season hasn't started.' Fran sounded amused. 'Guy'll be after you for more then.'

Libby's paintings were just what tourists wanted, Guy insisted. A genuine memento of the old-fashioned seaside resort of Nethergate.

'Hmm.' Libby made a face. 'Well, I'm off. Love to Guy. Are you coming over to Steeple Martin on Wednesday?'

Wednesdays were the nights of regular gatherings at Steeple Martin's pub for an exchange of news.

'Maybe,' said Fran. 'Not much has been happening, though, has it?'

'Suppose not. We'll be there, though.' Libby collected her basket and pulled her coat up round her neck. 'See you.'

Libby drove back up the road from Nethergate, past Steeple Martin and on towards Canterbury, where Michelle's Beauty Salon stood in isolation on the outskirts.

The usual cheerful buzz of conversation and hairdryers greeted her as she walked in. Michelle, wielding a dangerous pair of scissors, waved them over her head and pointed to a chair. A smiling apprentice came up, relieved her of her coat and swathed her in a black cape. Five minutes later, she was seated before a mirror and Michelle was pulling at strands of her wet hair and scowling.

'You ought to look after your hair, you know,' she said.

'I wash it and brush it,' said Libby. 'I can't keep coming to you to have it ponced up every five minutes.'

Michelle laughed. 'Same old Libby. What do we want – just a chop and dry?'

Libby sighed. 'Do what you like. It'll look better than it does now, whatever you do.'

'So.' Michelle tugged a comb through the rusty locks. 'What's been happening?'

The next ten minutes progressed as all hair appointments do, with an exchange of news and gossip, until Libby became aware of a change in the atmosphere. Sliding her eyes sideways in the mirror, she saw a tall, pale man standing behind Michelle.

'I want to talk to you,' he said.

All the other stylists and apprentices were fluttering behind him.

'I'm busy.' Michelle's voice was hard. She was still concentrating on Libby's hair, although the scissors had stopped.

'I said, I want to talk to you.' The man's voice was as hard as Michelle's. 'Now.'

'I'm busy. Go away.' Michelle turned to face him. 'Go away.' She looked round. 'Girls? With me.'

Libby watched, fascinated, as the girls and Michelle formed a wall behind the man, who found himself being ushered firmly through the reception area and out of the door, which was then locked behind him.

Looking harried, Michelle rushed back to Libby. 'Sorry about that,' she said. 'I'll explain in a minute. I'm just going to phone the police.'

Libby watched her go through to the staffroom. Chloe, Michelle's sister, came and perched on the shelf in front of Libby.

'Her stalker,' she said. 'Third time she's phoned the police.'

'Really?' Libby's eyes were horrified. 'And he's coming in here?'

Chloe grinned. 'Long story. She'll explain.'

Eventually, Michelle came back, armed with a large mug of black coffee.

'Sorry, Lib.' She sat down in the empty chair next to Libby's. 'That was Neil.'

'Chloe said it's a long story. If you don't want to—'

'No, I'll tell you. Give me a chance to calm down. Unless you're in a hurry?'

'Not at all,' said Libby.

'Couple of years ago,' began Michelle, settling herself more comfortably, 'an old client of mine, Joan, went downhill and couldn't get out and about as much as she used to. So I started going to give her a wash and blow-dry every week at home. And Neil turned up.' She made a face. 'Her son. And insisted on taking me out to lunch to say thank you.' She shrugged. 'That was all right, I suppose. After all, I was putting myself out a bit. Anyway, he seemed to think there was more to it than a thank-you lunch.'

'Oh, Lord,' said Libby.

Michelle nodded. 'So it started. Phone calls. Waiting outside for me. And outside my house. Then things through the letter box.'

'What sort of thing?' Libby asked.

'Porn.' Michelle's mouth went tight. 'And the phone calls got worse. So I reported him to the police. They helped me put a block on my phone, but he carried on with everything else. So I reported him again. They cautioned him and told him he'd have a court order if he carried on. That's why he came here today.' She leant back and sighed. 'And I hope that's the end of it.'

'What did Phil say?' asked Libby. 'Silly question, I suppose.'

Phil had been Michelle's partner for only a few months.

'I didn't tell him most of it.' Michelle shrugged. 'I didn't want even more trouble.' She sounded tired.

Libby regarded her thoughtfully. 'No. I can see that.' The little she knew of Phil didn't convince her that he would take such information quietly. 'You aren't actually living together, then?'

'Good job, too, under the circumstances.' Michelle gave another tired smile and stood up. 'Now let's get on with your hair.'

Both of them ignored the subject with determination for the remainder of Libby's time in the chair, only returning to it when Libby paid her bill.

'Let me know if there's anything you think I can do,' she said. 'About – you know.'

'With your connections to the police, you mean?' Michelle shook her head. 'No, I'll just let it lie now. Unless he starts again, I suppose.'

Unconvinced, Libby left and climbed into her car. As she drove away, she was almost sure she saw the tall figure of Neil lurking in a small group of trees at the end of a driveway. She won a short battle with herself and didn't immediately turn round and hare back to the salon to report, but decided to ring Michelle and tell her as soon as she reached home.

On Wednesday, Libby made one of her regular sorties to a big supermarket in Canterbury. On the way home, her mobile burbled at least three times, which meant there would be three messages to check, and as she walked into her cottage the little red light on her landline's answerphone was also trying to attract her attention. She sighed, tripped over Sidney the silver tabby and went straight into the kitchen to put her shopping away and make tea. While she waited for the kettle to boil, she checked the mobile and found that all three calls had been from Fran, and she discovered that, when she checked the landline, that had been, too. She sat down on the sofa in front of the empty fireplace and called Fran back.

'What's so urgent?' she asked.

'I didn't know where you were, and you weren't answering for such a long time,' said Fran, sounding uncharacteristically flustered.

'Supermarket shop,' said Libby. 'Drive to Canterbury, do the shopping, drive home again. At least an hour and a half, wouldn't you say?'

'Oh, all right, I'm sorry.' Fran took a deep breath. 'But you'll want to hear this.'

'I'm sure I will. What?'

'Ian just rang me.'

'Oh? Nice but not startling. What did he want?'

Detective Chief Inspector Ian Connell had been a friend of both women for some years.

'It's really odd.' Fran paused. 'It's a woman.'

Libby frowned at the phone. 'What's a woman?'

'A former girlfriend.'

'Of Ian's?' Libby's voice went up a notch. This was a surprise.

'It's all a bit complicated.' Fran heaved a sigh. 'This woman got in touch with Ian, apparently. He hadn't heard from her for years – he didn't actually say how long – and she wanted him to look into something.'

'Bit of a cheek, surely?'

'Well, yes. But although he didn't want anything to do with her, he thought it sounded as though there was something to look into. So he's asked us.'

'He's asked us? To look into it?' Now Libby was staggered.

'Yes. And if we think there *is* something . . . well, then he'll do something official about it.'

'So he's using us again?' said Libby after a moment's thought. 'But isn't he still in trouble over using us in the last investigation?'

'I think that's exactly why he didn't want to go diving in straight away.' Fran made a derisory noise. 'Coward. Look, we'll come up to the pub tonight and I can tell you all about it properly.'

'Supposing Ian comes in? He usually does.'

'Not until later. I'll try and get there for eightish. Are you eating with Patti and Anne?'

Their friends Patti and Anne usually had a meal in the Pink Geranium before joining the others in the pub.

'Not tonight,' said Libby. 'We'll try and be there about eight, too.'

She rang off, feeling both puzzled and intrigued. 'To be fair,' she told Sidney, who was sitting hopefully by her feet with that 'Are you ever going to feed me?' look, 'he's actually been asking us in almost from when we first knew him. There was the business of the body in the Alexandria, and then the body on the island.'

6

Although, she reflected, it's mainly to see if Fran can pick anything up from her 'moments'.

Fran's 'moments' were her occasional flashes of psychic intuition. She had actually once been employed by a large London firm of estate agents to check out expensive properties for equally expensive clients, but since moving to Kent, they had been useful in penetrating the depths of murder investigations. However, as time had gone on and Fran became more and more settled in her life in Nethergate, these flashes had more or less disappeared, although DCI Connell lived in hope.

This sounded different, though. It almost, Libby thought, as she made her way into the kitchen to make tea, seemed as though he was trying to palm off his old flame to avoid dealing with her.

'Hmm,' she said, and switched on the kettle.

Chapter Two

Ben Wilde, Libby's significant other, was not averse to arriving early at the pub. This despite the fact that he had been working all day on his own newly restored hostelry, the Hop Pocket.

'I've been sifting through applications for the manager's job all day,' he told her. 'Can't seem to find one that's right.'

'Have you met any of them yet?' asked Libby.

'No.' Ben sounded gloomy. 'None of them appeal. I keep wondering why they want a live-in job at their age.'

'Whatever age they are?' Libby was amused.

'Well, yes. If they're young – have they had the experience and how long will they stay, and if they're older, why haven't they got a nice home of their own.'

'You won't ever know unless you talk to them,' said Libby.

'I know.' Ben sighed. 'Come on. Let's go and find out what Fran has to say. Take my mind off it.'

Fran was already in the pub, along with her husband Guy, to Libby's surprise. He joined Ben at the bar to buy drinks, while Libby went to the big round table they always used and sat next to Fran.

'Come on, then,' she said. 'Tell me all.'

Fran grinned. 'I've calmed down a bit now,' she said. 'It just seems so odd.'

'It does indeed.' Libby pursed her lips. 'Fancy Ian having an ex.'

Fran laughed. 'Oh, Libby! He's a good-looking single man with a good job. He's bound to have had relationships. Just that we haven't known about them.'

'Not since he's moved here he hasn't,' said Libby reasonably. 'We'd know then. And Edward lives underneath him, so he'd know.'

Ian lived in the first-floor apartment of a beautifully converted small Georgian manor house not far from Steeple Martin, while their mutual friend, Edward Hall lived in the ground-floor flat.

'Anyway,' continued Fran as Ben and Guy returned to the table, 'apparently this woman—'

'Does she have a name?' asked Libby.

'Sylvia. Don't know her other name.'

'Right, Sylvia. Go on.'

'She rang Ian on his personal number to report someone missing. Wait for it!' Fran warned as Libby opened her mouth. 'This was a homeless person she'd befriended.'

'Homeless?' repeated Ben and Libby.

'Yes. Sylvia belongs to a wild-swimming group in Nethergate, and used to chat to this man when she went for her swims.'

'I didn't know there *was* a wild-swimming group in Nethergate,' said Libby.

'Neither did I,' said Fran. 'We've got two premises on Harbour Street overlooking the beach and neither Guy nor I have ever seen them.'

'Nethergate Swans, they're called,' said Guy. 'I looked them up online and they exist. They must use the beach beyond the Alexandria. Quieter there.'

'Sylvia said she hasn't seen him for a week or so and she was worried about him.'

'It seems reasonable that she'd be worried,' said Libby, 'but not to report it to a DCI.'

'That's why she was doing it privately,' said Fran, 'and there isn't a permanent police presence in the town since they closed the police station, so she couldn't talk to the friendly beat bobby, could she?'

'So that's what we are now, is it?' Libby frowned.

'I can understand it,' said Ben. 'You both like investigating things – he hasn't got the time to waste, so why not?'

'I can see that,' said Fran, 'but it sounded as though he really didn't want to have anything to do with her.'

'If she's an ex, perhaps she was a nuisance when they split up?' suggested Guy.

'That makes sense,' said Libby. 'But I still feel we're being used.'

All three of her companions laughed at this.

'Come on!' said Ben. 'He's been using you ever since you met!'

'I know,' Libby confessed. 'I was only saying that to Sidney this afternoon.'

This produced more amusement just as the door opened and revealed the Reverend Patti Pearson manoeuvring her friend Anne Douglas's wheelchair through the gap. Both Guy and Ben leapt up to help, while Anne whooped with laughter. Once they were all settled round the table and Patti and Anne had been supplied with drinks, Anne demanded to know what they had been laughing about. This, naturally, involved repeating Fran's story about Ian, Sylvia and the disappearing homeless man.

Anne looked serious. 'We've got a huge problem with homeless people in Canterbury,' she said. 'I didn't realise it was the same in Nethergate.'

'Nowhere near as bad,' said Patti, 'but it's a problem in most towns now.'

'We've not seen any on Harbour Street,' said Fran.

'Or anywhere else near the front,' added Guy.

'I wonder where exactly his pitch was?' said Libby.

'Well, wherever it was, he's not there now,' said Ben, 'so you'd better talk to this Sylvia, hadn't you?'

'Did Ian give you her number?' asked Patti.

'Oh, yes.' Fran made a face. 'I'll ring her in the morning.'

'If I can do anything to help,' offered Patti. 'I do have some experience . . .'

'Of course,' said Fran, smiling at her. 'So what's been happening with you since we saw you last?'

Recognising a determined effort to change the subject, they all began recounting recent experiences, including Ben's fruitless search for a manager for the Hop Pocket.

'I might know someone.' Tim, pub-owner extraordinaire, who had helped and advised Ben in his restoration, leant on the bar counter, looking interested. Everyone turned to look at him.

'Don't know why you didn't ask me,' he said. 'I know a couple of ex-managers who've lost their jobs.'

'Due to the breweries selling off the pubs!' said Libby with an air of enlightenment.

'Exactly.' Tim grinned, lifted the hatch and came to join them. Immediately, he and Ben went into a huddle.

'Well, that's cheered him up, anyway,' said Libby. 'Now, what were we saying?'

She was halfway through giving them an expurgated version of Michelle's stalker problems when a blast of cold air heralded the arrival of Edward and Ian.

'Don't get up,' said Ian. 'Anyone want another drink?'

'Don't say anything,' said Fran to the other women as Ian and Edward made for the bar.

But they didn't need to.

'So, have you recruited the others to help you with the problem of Sylvia?' Ian sat down, carefully adjusting his immaculately pressed trousers. He smiled round at the group. 'See Edward? Complete innocence.'

Libby laughed. 'Did you expect her not to share it?'

'Of course not.' He looked at Patti. 'What did you think?'

'I said to the others,' she said, looking uncomfortable, 'if there's anything I can do – I've had some experience with homeless people.'

'I thought you might. What we don't know, though, is if this actually was a homeless person.'

They all looked surprised. Ben rejoined the group as Tim went back to the bar to serve Edward.

'You mean,' said Libby slowly, 'you think Sylvia was lying?'

'Not necessarily,' said Ian.

'The homeless man could be lying!' Anne crowed triumphantly. 'He isn't what he says he is?'

Ian laughed. 'Could be! Think you can find out?' He looked round at them all. 'I'm relying on the combined talents of – what do you call yourselves? Libby's – what?'

'Loonies,' they choroused.

'And it wasn't our idea,' said Libby. 'It was Harry's.'

Edward arrived with more drinks. 'And I'm a member,' he said. 'What are we supposed to be doing?'

'Chasing up Ian's ex,' said Ben with a grin.

'I don't believe it,' said Edward.

'And I don't want to get involved,' said Ian, 'so our friends here are going to form a wall between me and the lady in question.'

'What do you know about this swimming club?' asked Fran. 'Guy and I had never heard of it.'

'And I would have thought I'd have noticed wild women swimming,' said Guy.

'The Nethergate Swans, apparently,' said Ian. 'And, from what Sylvia said, I think they swim from somewhere below the car park.'

'Car park?' Anne frowned.

'At the end of Cliff Terrace,' said Patti. 'We've parked there.'

'It's on what used to be called The Tops, the cliffs above the town. The rest of it's a new estate now,' said Guy.

'I wonder if that's where they come from? These Swans?' said Libby.

'And where Sylvia saw the homeless man,' said Ian. 'That's what I want to know.'

'Yes, yes, all right,' said Libby. 'But we do have our methods, Watson.'

'Can you come down to me tomorrow?' asked Fran. 'I think we'd better sort out a strategy.'

'We'll let you know,' Libby said to the others.

'What do you think about this Sylvia business?' Ben asked Libby on the way home.

'I don't know.' Libby stared vacantly ahead. 'Ian doesn't seem to be unduly worried, does he? Do you think he's just giving us something to keep us out of mischief?'

'Seems a bit excessive, if that's all it is,' said Ben, guiding her round the corner into Allhallow's Lane.

'You don't think he's laughing at us, do you?' Libby turned a worried face towards her best beloved.

'*Laughing* at you?' repeated Ben, looking astonished.

'You know – making fun of our – "*investigations*".' Libby's tone put the word in italics.

'Of course not. He's simply making use of your undoubted talents.' But Ben looked doubtful, nevertheless. He stopped at the door of Number 17. 'Come on. Nightcap and bed. And stop worrying about it.'

On Thursday morning, Libby presented herself at Coastguard Cottage on Harbour Street in Nethergate, and told Fran of her doubts about Ian's motives.

'I don't think he'd be that devious,' said Fran. 'Not after last time.'

'I suppose not,' said Libby, 'but I've come to the conclusion that we don't know Ian half as well as we thought we did.'

'Because he's been careful to keep his private life to himself,' said Fran. 'We still don't know where he lived before he moved to Grove House, or whether he had girlfriends or partners.'

'Well, he didn't when he was making a play for you,' Libby stated firmly. 'He's not that sort of bloke.'

'It was hardly a "play" for me,' protested Fran, going faintly pink.

'So perhaps it's simply that he doesn't want to get entangled with her again?' suggested Libby.

'Which is more or less what he said in the first place,' said Fran, 'so we need to talk to her and find out if that's what she wanted.'

'OK. Which one of us is going to phone?' asked Libby, settling back into the window seat.

The two friends stared at each other, then said together: 'I'll do it.'

'I'll do it,' said Fran, 'and put it on speaker phone so you can join in.' She picked up her phone from the hearth beside her armchair. 'You'd better come over here, or you won't be able to hear each other.'

Libby moved to the footstool beside Fran, while she found the number Ian had given her and pressed the link.

'Sylvia Cranthorne,' an uncertain-sounding voice announced.

'Sylvia, hello. My name's Fran Wolfe. Ian Connell asked me to call you about the man you reported missing.'

Silence.

'Hello? Sylvia?'

Fran raised her eyebrows at Libby.

'Er – yes. Hello.' They heard a nervous cough. 'Can I ask why he asked you?'

'We're what Ian calls his special investigators. Me and my partner, Libby Sarjeant.'

'Hello!' said Libby loudly. 'I'm Libby.'

Fran made shushing gestures.

'Oh.' There was another pause. 'I thought he was going to look into it himself.'

Libby and Fran nodded wisely at each other.

'I'm afraid he's a bit too busy at the moment,' said Fran, 'and until he and the police know a bit more of the circumstances, he can't afford to release anyone.'

'And that's where we come in,' said Libby cheerfully.

'I see.' More silence. 'Oh, well, I suppose it won't do any harm.'

Odd phrase, mouthed Libby. Fran nodded.

'What can you tell us about him and how you came to know him?' asked Libby.

'Ian?' came the startled reply.

'No, the homeless man,' said Fran, while Libby stifled her giggles.

'Oh . . . right. Look, it's a bit difficult talking on the phone. I don't suppose we could meet, could we?'

'Of course,' said Fran. Libby nodded vigorously. 'Where are you?'

'Do you know Nethergate?' asked Sylvia.

'Yes.'

'Do you know a pub called The Sloop?'

'Yes. Shall we see you there?'

'About twelve?' suggested Sylvia. 'There's parking there.'

'Yes, we know it,' said Libby. 'Shall we see you at one of the tables outside? It's a nice day.'

'All right.' They heard Sylvia take a deep breath. 'See you in about an hour.'

Chapter Three

Libby and Fran were already seated outside The Sloop, the pub at the end of Harbour Street overlooking the tiny harbour, when a woman appeared from the car park at the back.

'That her?' muttered Libby.

The woman came to a halt by their table.

'Fran?' she asked.

Fran stood up and held out her hand. 'Yes. And this is Libby.'

Sylvia shook hands with them both and sat down. About Fran's height, with shoulder-length, gently waving hair, she looked to be somewhat younger than the two friends.

'Can I get you a drink?' asked Libby.

Sylvia opted for a spritzer and Libby went inside to the bar.

'I know it's unconventional,' said Fran with a smile, 'but we often run errands of this sort for Ian.'

Sylvia nodded. 'I know. I looked you up after we'd spoken on the phone. You've been involved in several murder cases, haven't you?'

Fran sighed. 'Yes, I'm afraid so. We seem to have a bit of a reputation.'

'Well, at least I know you're genuine,' said Sylvia. 'Oh, I'm sorry, that sounded rude.'

'It's fine,' said Fran. 'Sensible to check us out.'

Libby reappeared. 'Drinks are coming,' she said. 'Come on, then, Sylvia. Tell us about this man.'

Fran frowned at her, but Sylvia laughed. 'All right. It's going to sound a bit odd, I expect, and quite possibly me making a mountain out of a molehill.'

'Ian obviously didn't think so,' said Libby, crossing her fingers, 'or he wouldn't have asked us to look into it.'

'Who is he?' asked Fran.

'That's just it – I don't know.' Sylvia frowned. 'I'll start at the beginning, shall I?'

'Always best,' said Libby, and earned herself another glare from Fran.

'I belong to this group of wild swimmers, you see,' began Sylvia.

'Nethergate Swans?' put in Fran.

'Yes. Do you know about us? We swim from the beach beyond The Alexandria – do you know that?'

'Oh, yes,' said Libby.

'I live here,' said Fran hurriedly, to forestall Libby going into a long explanation about their connection to The Alexandria.

'Oh!' Sylvia looked surprised. 'Well, every morning – or most mornings – this man, obviously homeless, was on Victoria Place. I got to talking to him. The other women told me not to, but he looked so sad . . .' She paused. 'He was quite well educated, you know, articulate, well spoken – it just didn't seem right, somehow.'

'It can happen to anybody,' said Fran.

'Did he have a sleeping bag or anything with him?' asked Libby.

'Yes. And a sort of duffle bag. They were both rather – ragged, I suppose you'd say.'

'Where was he sleeping?' asked Fran.

'I don't actually know. I assumed under the little veranda round The Alexandria. But the thing is, he seemed to want to get to know me, but he was scared.' She shook her head. 'I don't know what of, but he was always looking over his shoulder, and if anyone else came anywhere near he'd sort of – shy away.'

'I expect a lot of them are like that,' said Libby.

'Did you ever see him at any other time of the day?' asked Fran.

'No. And I looked. I went down there at all different times – I live on the little estate, you know?'

'The Tops?' said Libby.

'That's it. So the little path down from there is my easiest way into town. But even when I was coming back home at night I never saw him.'

'He must have been very well hidden,' said Fran, kicking Libby under the table. Libby scowled and shut her mouth.

'How long had you been – well, friends?' continued Fran.

'Oh, months! Since before Christmas, anyway.' Sylvia smiled reminiscently. 'I used to look forward to seeing him.'

'And when did he stop coming?' asked Libby.

'Two weeks ago.' Sylvia took a long sip of her spritzer. 'He just wasn't there any more. At first, I thought he'd be back in a day or so – he'd done it before. But he didn't. None of the other women were worried.'

'I bet they just shrugged and said that was what those people were like,' said Libby.

'More or less.' Sylvia sighed. 'But *I* was worried. So I called Ian.'

'Where there's one homeless person, there are usually others,' mused Fran. 'Have you looked for them?'

Sylvia looked surprised. 'I thought that was only in big towns.'

'Sadly, it's everywhere.' Fran smiled ruefully.

'We could make enquiries,' said Libby, nodding at Fran, who was surely thinking of Patti and her connections.

'Could you?' Sylvia now looked doubtful.

'Don't you want us to?' asked Fran.

'Well, yes . . . I suppose I hadn't thought it through.'

Libby regarded her thoughtfully. 'What exactly are you worried about? Do you think something's happened to him?'

'Yes,' said Sylvia thankfully. 'Because he seemed so scared, you see.'

'Did he never give you any idea why?' said Fran.

'I never liked to ask,' said Sylvia.

The three of them fell silent. Then Fran said, 'Can you give us a description?'

'I don't know. I suppose – well, he was quite tall, ordinary-looking. Pale. Not much hair.'

'Do you mean he was able to afford a haircut, or he was going bald?' asked Libby.

'I don't know.' Sylvia looked helpless. 'I'm not much use, am I?'

Ignoring this, Libby said: 'Did he ever give you a name?'

'Only a nickname. "You can call me Rab," was what he said.'

'Not much help,' said Fran with a smile.

'No.' Sylvia sighed. 'I feel a bit of a fraud now. I'm glad Ian didn't come himself.'

'Oh, I don't know,' said Libby. 'I think there's enough there to be concerned.'

'You do? Why?'

'The fact that he was so secretive,' said Fran hastily. 'Did he tell you how he happened to become homeless?'

'He said he'd lost his job and his home. That was all.'

'Did he tell you what his job had been?'

'No. As I said before, I didn't like to ask.'

'Well,' said Libby after a moment, 'we'll go away and have a think about it, and make a few enquiries. Can we always get hold of you on the number Ian gave us?'

'Most of the time, although I might not be able to answer if I'm on a visit.'

'A visit?' Libby and Fran repeated.

'I work for an estate agent. I might be showing a property.' Sylvia looked at her watch. 'Which is where I should be in fifteen minutes.' She stood up. 'Thank you both for coming, and I hope it wasn't a waste of time.'

Libby and Fran also rose and said goodbye.

'What do you think?' Libby asked as Sylvia disappeared towards the car park.

'Very suspicious,' said Fran, 'but not for the reasons Sylvia thinks.'

19

'First – she really was trying to get back with Ian,' said Libby.

'At least using it as an "in",' agreed Fran. 'But she is worried. Do you think she fancied him?'

'Who – Rab? Doesn't sound very fanciable.'

'No. And he never asked her for anything.'

'We don't know that,' said Libby. 'She might not have wanted to tell us.'

'And he was scared.' Fran eyed her empty glass thoughtfully. 'That sounded real.'

'And he was never there except in the mornings.' Libby nodded. 'Sounds as if he was actually trying to get to know her, doesn't it?'

'It does. And why?'

'Playing on her sympathy,' said Libby. 'There must be a reason.'

'When do we ask Patti?' Fran grinned across the table. 'We both thought that, didn't we?'

'We can phone her this afternoon,' said Libby, 'but first I vote we go and check out The Alexandria.'

The Alexandria was a restored Edwardian concert hall with which Fran and Libby had a close, if rather sad, connection. These days, it played host to various visiting artistes and, more often than not, a summer End of the Pier Show, put on by the Oast Theatre Company, which Libby, Ben and his cousin Peter ran.

They left The Sloop and walked down Harbour Street. Fran popped into Guy's little gallery to tell him where they were going, and they continued along to the square, where the venerable Swan Inn dreamed in the spring sunshine, and on to The Alexandria. The big double doors opened onto Victoria Place and round the outside of the building ran an iron-railed veranda. At the back was a small door, now enhanced by large doors into a scenery dock. It was under this veranda that Sylvia had assumed her homeless Rab had been sheltering.

'But,' said Libby, leaning over at a perilous angle, 'I can't see anywhere he might have been hiding. The sand's all built up underneath – look.'

Sure enough, the beach had blown or been washed right up against the walls of the building and, from what they could see, was entirely undisturbed.

'Which means,' said Fran, 'that Rab was coming here every morning purposely to see Sylvia.' She turned and looked at Libby. 'That really is odd, isn't it?'

'Just like a stalker,' said Libby, and stopped. 'Hey – you don't think—'

Fran sent her a wry look. 'No, I do *not* think it's the same person who was stalking Michelle.'

'It could be,' protested Libby. 'It's a similar description. Tall, pale . . .'

'Thousands of businessmen who spend their lives in offices are tall and pale,' said Fran, levering herself away from the railings. 'Besides, Rab disappeared two weeks ago and you saw Michelle's stalker this week.'

'He could have changed his victim,' grumbled Libby as she followed her friend back towards the square.

'I tell you what,' she added as they walked back to Coastguard Cottage. 'He could have been hiding out somewhere else.' She stopped as inspiration struck. 'What about that little caravan park?'

'What little caravan park?' asked Fran.

'You know – up on the cliffs beyond the harbour. Past the cliff path that leads from the St Aldeberge road.'

'Not sure I've ever noticed it,' said Fran.

'Oh, it's only tiny, but the caravans are locked up all winter. Ideal to break into, I'd have thought. Come on, let's go and look.'

Fran sighed. 'Fool's errand,' she said, but followed her excited friend back towards The Sloop. Libby led the way past the car park at the back and the cliff path and along the deserted walkway.

'Up there,' she said. 'I think there's another path that leads down.'

Sure enough, a little further along, they came across another, far better maintained path with a small sign pointing upwards to 'Island View'.

'Told you so,' said Libby, and began to ascend.

They puffed their way upwards, until, to their surprise, they came upon a tall chain-linked fence.

'Where's the entrance?' said Fran.

'I don't know.' Libby frowned. 'Our Rab couldn't have got through here, could he?' She began to make her way along the fence and suddenly stopped. 'Look!'

Over the fence, they could see half a dozen caravans. But in front of them lay a huge open space of cleared ground.

'They're expanding,' said Libby.

Chapter Four

'Doubt if he would've been able to get in there to hide, then,' said Fran.

'There might be access round the other side on the road,' said Libby, standing on tiptoe.

'Wouldn't have thought so.' Fran frowned. 'I haven't heard anything about this. Mind you, I didn't even know there was a caravan park here.'

Libby turned to look out over the sea towards the little lighthouse and the island in the middle of the bay. 'It's a lovely situation,' she said, 'but I'd have thought it wouldn't be popular with the locals.'

'No,' said Fran, still frowning. 'It's all wrong.'

Libby looked round quickly. 'What?' she said sharply.

'It doesn't fit, does it?' said Fran. 'A big, modern caravan park here in Nethergate.'

'Oh.' Libby subsided. 'I thought you'd had a "moment". No, it doesn't fit.' She turned back to the path. 'I wonder how they got planning permission?'

'No idea.' Fran followed down the path. 'I thought the whole area was under all sorts of protective legislation.'

'So did I.' Libby looked back over her shoulder. 'Tell you who'd know – Jane!'

Fran cast her eyes to the sky. 'Look,' she said. 'We came here to find out about Sylvia and her homeless man, not to look into caravan parks. Talk to Jane by all means, but not now. I'm going back to relieve Guy for lunch – he'll be starving.'

'Oh, all right. I'll pop in before I pick up the car.'

Fran stood still. 'You *won't*!' she said. 'Call her when you get home. You can't just drop in and expect her to be available.'

Libby looked guilty. 'OK,' she said. 'I'll do that.'

By the time Libby got back to Steeple Martin, she had worked out what to do. First, she'd heat some soup. Then she'd search online for the Island View caravan park, then, possibly, the Nethergate Swans, then she'd call Jane Baker, editor of the *Nethergate Mercury*.

She'd barely had time to dish up her soup when her phone rang.

'Guy knew about it,' said Fran.

'Eh? What?'

'The caravan park – Island View.'

'And he hadn't told you?'

'He didn't think I'd be interested in a caravan park.'

'But surely it's going to damage the environment!' said Libby. 'You'd be interested in that.'

'He hadn't taken much notice of it himself,' said Fran. 'But apparently there has been quite an argument about it. There's some question about the legality of it.'

'I knew it!' said Libby triumphantly. 'I'll call Jane.'

'And don't forget we're supposed to find out about Rab,' Fran warned. 'I'll call Patti about homeless people.'

Libby took a hasty mouthful of soup and scrolled through to Jane's number.

'Hello, Libby,' came a tired and resigned voice.

'What's the matter?' Libby pushed away her bowl of soup.

'Immy's got chickenpox,' said Jane.

'Oh, Lord!' Libby, having had three children herself, was immediately full of sympathy. 'Look, I don't want to disturb you – get back to her. Or back to bed, whichever is most urgent.'

'It's all right. She's asleep and I've told the bosses I'm taking time off.'

'Can your mum give you a break?' Jane's mother lived in the self-contained garden flat in Peel House, which belonged to Jane and her husband, Terry.

'She's scared of shingles,' said Jane. 'Same virus, apparently.'

'Oh, yes,' said Libby, remembering.

'Anyway, what can I do for you? There haven't been any murders that I can think of?'

'No.' Libby felt uncomfortable. 'I really do only call you for info, don't I? I'm sorry!'

'Oh, don't be daft,' said Jane. 'Come on, what is it?'

'That little caravan park—' began Libby.

'Island View? Oh, you've got onto that, have you? Now why, I wonder?'

'No particular reason,' said Libby, surprised. 'Fran and I went for a walk up that way this morning –' no need to explain why – 'and found that it looks as though it's being developed. We thought it was all protected around there.'

Jane sighed. 'It is. And it's quite a long story.'

'Oh.' Now Libby was doubtful. 'Well, don't worry about it now.'

'No, It's all right. Tell you what, I'll go and make myself a cup of tea and find all the stuff about it and call you back. Is that OK?'

'Great, thank you, Jane. It's only us being nosy, you know.'

'You being nosy, you mean,' said Jane with a laugh. 'Go on. I'll call you in about twenty minutes.'

Libby took the opportunity to reheat her soup in the microwave, then made some notes in the notebook she always found preferable to a screen. By the time this was finished, her phone was ringing.

'Right,' said Jane. 'Pin back your lugholes.'

Libby grinned to herself. Jane's London background was coming out.

'Once upon a time – back in the fifties, I think – someone

started a little caravan park up there on the cliff. The land belonged to a family who – again, I think – had a farm. The St Aldeberge Road bisected it, so the piece of land on the cliff was never used. They put a few of those tin boxes there and rented them out. Then, as far as I can make out, the old man died and the son took over. He updated the site – put more modern caravans there and added a small facilities block. And there it's been sitting ever since.'

'When was this?' asked Libby.

'Seventies?' said Jane. 'Mind you, I'm guessing. The vans have been updated one by one, so that most of them are modern, up-to-date statics.'

'So what happened next?' prompted Libby when Jane seemed to have come to a halt.

'The family sold up.' Jane sighed. 'The son died, and his wife didn't want the bother. The old farm had already gone, years ago, and she wanted to move to Spain, apparently. And the little cara-van park was on a site of special interest—'

Libby's eyes widened. 'An SSI?'

'Apparently. It's a chalk cliff and a hang-out for some moth or other. And a couple of particular plants. A native orchid or some-thing, and one the moth feeds on. Anyway, it's an SSI and it has some other protective designation. So no one thought anyone would buy it.'

'But someone did,' said Libby, 'and despite all those protections they're trying to build on it?'

'Exactly. It's some holiday company, and their lawyers unearthed this thing called a Certificate of Lawful Development. If you have a caravan site that has been in existence for so many years – possibly seven, I don't know – without causing any problems, you can go ahead and develop. And not just develop but bypass all existing regulations, like being able to build permanent dwellings.'

'*What?*' Libby was horrified. 'That's outrageous! And the coun-cil have allowed this to happen?'

'I told you it was complicated.' Jane laughed. 'This company have tried to block our access to the site and to the documentation, but luckily the protest group—'

'Oh, there's a protest group?'

'Of course there is. I'm surprised Fran doesn't know about it,' said Jane.

'Guy did, but hadn't mentioned it,' said Libby.

'I wonder why? He'd know it would be right up Fran's street, surely.'

'That's probably why,' said Libby shrewdly.

'Anyway, the protest group have kept us up to date – mainly to try and whip up support. There's a group over in Devon who managed to raise enough money to take their complaint to the High Court, where the development was squashed flat, so the Island View lot want to do the same.'

'It's bloody iniquitous,' said Libby. 'How old is this legislation? It must be as old as the hills.'

'Apparently it's "under review". The whole system is under threat if this is allowed to continue.'

'Hey!' said Libby, struck by a sudden thought. 'Is this what's allowed those completely unsuitable industrial buildings to be turned into accommodation?'

'I don't know, but in this case the application is for at least six permanent residential units when no homes were supposed to be built there, apart from some statics to let as holiday accommodation.'

'Wow.' Libby sat back in her chair. 'No wonder people are up in arms. Has the protest group got a website?'

'Yes. I'll send you the link. And if you're going to poke about into it, let me know if you find anything.'

'Much as I'd like to, I don't think we've got any reason to poke around. We were just interested when we found the actual site.'

'And why were you there?' asked Jane, sounding amused. 'What *were* you poking into?'

'Oh, just an idea of mine.' Libby paused, wondering how much to tell Jane. In the end, she shrugged and decided to go for it.

'So there you are,' she concluded. 'Just looking for a disappearing homeless person.'

'I haven't heard anything about this,' said Jane slowly. 'And you say Ian Connell asked you to look into it?'

'We think he just wanted to get this Sylvia person off his back. I don't think he was taking it seriously.'

'But you are?'

'We thought there were a couple of things . . .'

'Which were?'

'Oh, just stuff we thought didn't sit right.' Libby thought for a moment. 'We wondered if this Sylvia was – er – embroidering a bit.'

'Oh, right.' Jane sounded disappointed. 'But why did you go looking for this man, in that case?'

'Well, we also wondered what had been his motive in talking to Sylvia?'

'Old as time, dearie,' said Jane. 'OK, then, if there's anything in it, you'll tell me, won't you?'

'If there's anything to tell,' said Libby with a sigh.

When she'd finished talking to Jane, she rang Fran again.

'Did you talk to Patti?' she asked.

'No, she was out, so I left a message.'

'Didn't you try her mobile?'

'Look,' said Fran with a sigh, 'if Patti's out, it means she's on parish business, so she won't want to bothered with us, will she? She'll get back to me when she can. Did you speak to Jane?'

Libby repeated what Jane had told her. Fran was, predictably, horrified.

'How can that be legal?' she gasped. 'I don't believe it!'

'Horrific, isn't it? No wonder not many people know about it. I used to have such faith in our legal system.'

'At least the High Court smashed that one appeal, though. It's a start,' said Fran.

'Jane asked if we were going to look into it,' said Libby.

'I might, for my own satisfaction,' said Fran, 'but we've no reason to look into it otherwise.'

'That's what I said,' said Libby with a regretful sigh. 'I wonder
who the developer is?'

'Now stop it, Lib. What did she say about Homeless Rab?'

'She didn't know anything about him. But she asked us to tell
her if anything comes of it.'

'So, meanwhile, we wait until Patti can tell us anything about
homeless communities in Nethergate.'

'And we don't do anything else?' asked Libby.

'Nothing to do really, is there?' said Fran.

Libby gave up.

Chapter Five

Over the next two days, Libby looked up the SSI on which Island View was situated, and discovered the rare moth, Fisher's Estuarine, and its favourite food, Hog's Fennel, both of which were only to be found in the UK on the North Kent and Essex coasts. She felt fiercely protective of them both.

Patti did come back to Fran, but said her opposite number in the Nethergate church had very little to do with the homeless of the town, of whom there were very few, apparently. There was, it turned out, a small group of people who informally supplied hot meals and blankets to anyone who applied to them. Fran was given a phone number, which she called, but they had no knowledge of anyone answering the description of Rab, a fact she reported to Sylvia and subsequently to Ian.

'I had a feeling there was nothing in it,' he said. 'If anything does turn up, let me know, will you?'

'So that's that,' said Fran when Libby called. 'We're off the hook.'

It was Sunday lunchtime at the Manor in Steeple Martin, and Hetty Wilde's guests were seated round the big pine table in the kitchen as usual.

''Ere,' said Hetty's brother Lenny Fisher, turning to the newest guest, Joe Wilson. 'Did yer see about that body?'

Everyone stopped talking and looked at Lenny.

'Body? What body?' asked Libby, glass of wine halfway to her mouth.

'Where 'im and me went to see that what's-it's-name – base.' Lenny looked at Joe. 'What was it?'

'OB,' said Joe, looking smug. 'Operational Base. What about a body?'

'They found one. On the news, it was.' Lenny tuned back to his plate of roast beef. 'Thought you'd know, gal.'

This last was addressed to Libby. Immediately, the rest of the guests, including Lenny's partner Flo Carpenter, began talking at once.

'All right, all right,' she said, tapping her glass with her knife to restore order. 'What about it, Lenny?'

'That mate of yours on TV. Him.'

'Campbell McClean?' suggested Libby, he being a local TV reporter.

'That's 'im. He was at that place Joe and me went to look at with the club. In the woods over near Shott. They found a body there.'

'Did they know who it was?' asked Ben.

'Didn't say so.' Lenny seemed to have lost interest.

Joe Wilson, who had been introduced to the family circle by Libby only a couple of months before, had struck up an immediate friendship with Lenny, being roughly the same age. He, in turn, had introduced Lenny to what he called his 'Old Codgers Club', with whom they had already taken several trips of local interest – usually, as Flo complained, to pubs.

'What was this Operational Base, Joe?' Libby asked him.

'OBs was what was the hideouts for the resistance men,' said Joe. 'Don't you know about them?'

'Yes, you do,' said Ben. 'When you went down to the seaside to help that friend of Fran's.'

'Don't remind me!' groaned Libby. 'Yes, I remember. All part of the SOE, weren't they?'

'Special Operations Executive.' Edward, another regular visitor to the Manor, looked up and flashed his bright-white grin. 'Is it one of the bases on public show, Joe?'

'Not official, like,' said Lenny, coming back into the conversation, 'but one o' them that everyone knows about.'

'Want me to look into it, Lib?' Edward raised an eyebrow.

'Me? Good Lord, no!' said Libby hastily.

Flo cackled. 'You wait,' she said. 'She'll be ferretin' around with her mate Fran soon as look at yer.'

Hetty stood up and cleared her throat. 'Ready for rhubarb crumble?' she asked.

After lunch, Hetty retired to her sitting room, accompanied by Joe, Flo and Lenny, while Libby, Ben and Edward loaded the dishwasher, before making their way down the Manor drive towards the cottage belonging to Peter and Harry, who owned the Pink Geranium, the vegetarian café a few steps down the high street, where Harry was the *chef patron*. After Sunday lunch service, with which Peter often helped, the friends foregathered in the cottage to exchange gossip, or, as Libby called it, news.

When they arrived, Harry was, as usual, sprawled on one of the sofas, still in his chef's whites, while Peter was assembling bottles and glasses.

'Alcohol or tea?' he asked, brandishing a bottle temptingly under Libby's nose.

'What do you think?' she replied, sinking into her favourite shabby chintz-covered armchair.

'What news from the front, then?' asked Harry, waving a languid hand.

'Funny you should say that,' said Edward. 'Lenny and Joe were talking about an old World War Two hideout they visited.'

'Joe? He was there again?' Harry sat up, intrigued.

'He and Lenny have got friendly,' said Libby.

'If you ask me,' said Harry darkly, 'he's after your inheritance, Ben, me boy. Got his eye on Hetty.'

Ben laughed. 'I'm sure you're right, Hal. Good luck to him – my mum needs someone in her life to look after.'

Peter handed Libby her whisky. 'So what was this old bunker they visited, then?'

'Not so much the bunker,' said Ben, grinning at Libby, 'more the body that was found there.'

Harry closed his eyes and flopped back theatrically, hand to brow. 'No!'

'Nothing to do with us,' said Libby. 'Lenny saw it on the local news, apparently. Now we don't get proper local papers we don't see that sort of thing.'

'Daft, isn't it?' said Peter, sitting down next to Harry. 'We don't all follow the local news on social media. I only hear things by word of mouth these days.'

'I don't suppose—' began Libby.

'No!' came the chorus.

'I was only going to say perhaps it could be that man who Ian wanted us to look into?' Libby said, disgruntled.

'What man?' asked Harry.

'Oh, go on, tell them,' said Ben in a resigned fashion.

So Libby told them all about Ian, Sylvia and Homeless Rab.

'What on earth put that into your head?' Harry stared, open-mouthed. 'That really is bonkers.'

'Well, theoretically it's possible, I suppose,' said Peter. 'But you'll never know unless Sylvia can identify him.'

'And unless the police post a picture of the dead man, she never will,' said Edward.

'We could ask Ian,' said Libby.

'Don't get involved,' said Ben. 'No reason to.'

But on Monday morning, Libby was given another reason to get involved in something completely different. Just as she was settling herself in the conservatory to begin work on another small picture for Guy's gallery, she was surprised to receive a call from Michelle.

33

'I'm really sorry to bother you, Lib,' she said, 'but I don't know what to do.'

'How can I help?' asked Libby, wondering what on earth she *could* possibly do to help confident, self-sufficient Michelle.

'Well.' Libby heard her take a deep breath. 'You remember Neil?'

How could I forget? thought Libby. Aloud, she said, 'Of course. Have you had any more trouble?'

'Not exactly.' Michelle paused. 'I told you about his mum, Joan, didn't I?'

'Yes,' said Libby.

'She called me today. On my personal mobile.'

'I was going to say – you aren't open on Mondays, are you? Besides, it's May Day – it's a Bank Holiday.'

'No. So I was surprised.'

'Did she want an appointment?' asked Libby when Michelle seemed to have come to a full stop.

'No. She wanted to talk about Neil.'

'Oh, glory! I didn't realise she knew about the – er – stalking.'

'She didn't – doesn't. Oh, it's awful, Lib!'

'Um, yes, of course it is.'

'No – you don't understand!' Michelle burst out.

You bet I don't, thought Libby.

'She thought we – he – we . . .'

'Were in a relationship?' suggested Libby.

'Yes.' Michelle's breath came out in a whoosh. 'He told her we were going out.'

'Right.'

'And she wanted to know where he was.'

'Oh!' Libby was surprised. 'She thought you would know?'

'Yes. You see, she seemed to think we were – well, virtually living together.'

'Golly! So did you tell her you weren't?'

'Of course I did, but she didn't believe me. Got quite shirty with me.'

34

'When did she last see him?'

'Wednesday – the day he came here. I said she should report him missing. What do you think?'

'Quite right,' said Libby. 'You don't want to be involved.'

'No, I don't, but she said it was obvious I knew where he was so what was the point.'

'Oh, dear.'

'Exactly. So do you think I ought to report him?'

'No,' said Libby firmly. 'You're nothing to do with him. It would only lead to awkward questions.'

'I suppose you couldn't . . . ?'

'Don't be daft!' Libby laughed. 'How could I report someone missing I don't even know?'

'Could you go and talk to her?'

'She doesn't know who I am! She wouldn't take any notice of me.'

'What do I do then?'

Libby paused, on the verge of saying, 'Nothing.' After all, Sylvia had been in the same position, oddly, and she actually had reported it, although it had ended up with Fran and Libby looking into it, not the police.

'I suppose,' she said slowly, 'you could report it to the police, saying the man who's been stalking you has disappeared, according to his mother.'

'You just said I shouldn't.'

'You could say what's-'er-name is an elderly and vulnerable client and you're worried about her.'

'I could . . . Well, I am. I always liked her. And she is a bit fragile.'

'There you are, then. It's her you're worried about, not him.'

Michelle let out another breath. 'There you see – you did know what to do. I'll call them now and let you know what happens.'

Libby switched off the phone and stared at the stretched paper on her easel, before deciding that another cup of tea would be a good idea.

This was very odd, she told Sidney. Two supposedly missing men within a week. It was very hard not to try to make a connection, but for the life of her she couldn't see what it could be. One a homeless man, albeit a rather unlikely one, and the other a stalker who lived with his mother. And neither, according to Michelle and Sylvia, of the type to be a physical pushover. A call to Fran would seem to be indicated.

'It does seem odd – you're right,' said Fran after Libby, fortified with tea, had explained. 'But I can't see a connection. If we were trying to make a case for them turning out to be the same man, it wouldn't fit. Sylvia's Rab went missing – what? – nearly three weeks ago now and you saw Neil yourself less than a week ago.'

'But,' said Libby thoughtfully, 'Rab disappearing could be him going back to his mother. Perhaps he was only pretending to be homeless. We did sort of think that might be the case, didn't we?'

'We? I think it's nonsense. Just trying to make a hypothesis fit the facts.'

'It's what I do best,' said Libby gloomily. 'Oh, well. We don't tell Ian, then?'

'I'm not sure he'd thank us,' said Fran. 'Maybe, if he turns up to the pub on Wednesday, you could mention it in passing.'

Libby was just on her way back to the conservatory when the landline rang.

'It's me,' said Ben. 'You remember Tim said he might know someone who may be suitable for the Pocket?'

'Yes?'

'Well, he's organised for this bloke to come and see me today – in about half an hour, actually. We're meeting at the Pocket.'

'Oh, good,' said Libby, slightly mystified. 'And?'

'I just wondered . . . well, there's no tea or coffee over there at the moment, so . . .'

'I can't carry tea and coffee all that way! Ask Tim. Or just take this bloke over for a pint when you've finished the interview.'

'I don't suppose Harry—'

'It's Monday, Ben! He's not open.'

'Oh. So he isn't. Oh, well. The pub it is. I just thought it might be awkward with Tim there.'

'Tim recommended him – why would it?'

'I don't know.' Ben sounded ruffled. 'You wouldn't like to join us?'

'Are you sure?' Libby laughed. 'Show him the worst, you mean? Yes, I'll come down. I'll be there in about an hour.'

Well, she told herself, at least it'll be a distraction.

Chapter Six

When Libby arrived at the pub, it was to find Ben and another man sitting at the bar roaring with laughter with Tim.

'Half, Libby?' called Tim, spotting her.

'Yes, please, Tim.' Libby went up to the bar and Ben vacated his stool for her.

'Libby, this is Simon. Simon, my partner, Libby.'

Simon, stocky and mousy haired, stood up and offered a hand.

'Hello,' he said. 'I've heard about you.'

Libby groaned.

'It's all right, Lib.' Tim put her half of lager in front of her. 'Remember I took you over to The Dolphin at Dungate that time? Well, Simon was relief manager there a couple of times, and Daphne and Paddy – remember them? – told him all about our visit.'

'Well, it was a bit of a nine-days wonder, that murder being so close to home,' said Simon.

'Anyway,' Ben hurried on, obviously worried that the conversation would get out of hand now that murder had cropped up, 'Simon had lost his pub at that time—'

'The brewery was retrenching,' said Simon.

Libby nodded.

'And they kept Simon on as a sort of floating relief,' continued Ben, 'but he'd really like his own pub.'

'And do you both think the Hop Pocket is it?' Libby looked from one to the other.

Simon sent Ben an anxious glance. 'I hope so.'

'I think so,' said Ben with a grin, and lifted his glass. Simon, with a relieved sigh, lifted his own, then they both toasted Tim.

Libby sat back on her stool and grinned at the smug-looking landlord.

'You realise he's going to whip all your business,' she said.

Tim laughed. 'No, he won't. You remember the original plan? I can go ahead with my plans for expanding the dining and events side of the business, and the Pocket will cater for all the grumpy misplaced regulars.'

'Like that Dan who lives down the lane beside it,' said Libby. 'With his lovely dog.'

'Colley, yes,' said Ben. 'You don't mind dogs, do you, Simon?'

'They're all part of the pub culture, aren't they?' said Simon. 'And I happen to love dogs, anyway.'

'You'll do!' said Libby, holding out a hand for Simon to shake. 'Has Ben taken you over the pub?'

'I have,' said Ben. 'And Simon approved of the flat.'

'Oh, good,' said Libby. 'It'd be a bit of a bummer if you didn't.'

'Sandwiches?' offered Tim. 'And I'd better get back to my other customers – more than the usual Monday.'

'Bank holiday,' said Libby. 'Although it doesn't feel like it.'

'We should have proper celebrations,' said Tim. 'Like they do in the other places.'

'Hmm,' said Libby, remembering some of those celebrations with something less than pleasure.

Sandwiches were provided, over which Libby learnt that when Simon had lost his old pub he'd also lost his wife, who took up residence in the cottage they'd bought for their retirement.

'So I'm very lucky Ben's taking me on,' he said, casting another anxious glance at his new employer, as if not quite believing his luck.

'Well,' said Ben, sliding off his stool, 'we'd better go back and do all the paperwork, if you've finished.'

'When do you think you'll be able to open?' asked Libby, also preparing to go.

'As soon as the licence is sorted,' said Ben.

'I thought you'd done that?' said Libby.

'We have to get Simon registered as the licensee,' said Ben. 'Magistrates and stuff.'

'Ah.' Libby turned to wave at Tim. 'And then we'll have a grand party, won't we?'

Simon and Ben both grinned. 'We will,' they said together.

Feeling a lot more cheerful, Libby walked home down the high street, stopping to buy some salt-marsh lamb chops from Bob the butcher.

'What are you doing open on a bank holiday?' she asked him.

Bob shrugged. 'Everybody's open these days,' he said. 'Only close on Sundays now.'

'That's sad,' said Libby.

'Taken a fancy to Alice's lamb, then?' said Bob, wrapping the chops in greaseproof paper.

Alice Gedding farmed sheep on Heronsbourne Flats down on the coast, and was getting quite a reputation for her lamb.

'Certainly am,' said Libby.

'And your mate Edward's taken quite a fancy to Alice, I hear?' Bob winked, as he handed over the package.

'Really?' Libby was startled. 'How do you know?'

'He's the one who brings over any special orders for me. Stands to reason.'

'Special orders?'

'I don't keep everything in stock, do I? So if I want a couple of legs, or some lamb shanks or Barnsley Chops . . .'

'Barnsley Chops?' Libby's mouth was hanging open.

'Oh, what a lot you don't know! I've actually given you a couple,' said Bob, with a grin. 'Never mind. You ask him.'

Libby took her chops home and called Fran.

'Do you know what Barnsley Chops are?' she asked without preamble.

'Eh?' Fran sounded bewildered.

'Barnsley Chops. Bob mentioned them.'

'Aren't they those double-sided chops?' said Fran.

'What, like double-sided tape?'

'No!' Fran gave an exasperated sigh. 'Never mind. Why do you want to know?'

Libby explained about Bob, Edward and Alice Gedding.

'We thought there might be something, didn't we?' said Fran. 'When Ian first introduced them.'

'He might have told us,' complained Libby. 'I spent all Sunday afternoon with him.'

Fran laughed. 'So is that all you wanted to ask me?'

'No,' said Libby, and recounted the saga of Ben, Simon and the Hop Pocket.

'Oh, I am pleased,' said Fran. 'Ben's seemed rather down about it, recently.'

'He has been,' agreed Libby. 'And I can't be doing with him moping.'

'That's unkind,' said Fran.

'It's just I don't know what to say to comfort him.' Libby sighed. 'Anyway, it'll be better now.'

'So you've decided not to pursue the two missing men, then,' said Fran.

'We—ell,' said Libby.

'No,' said Fran. 'Don't.'

Libby and Ben were enjoying a pre-dinner drink and watching the local television news that evening, when Campbell McClean appeared in a woodland setting.

'Police have confirmed,' he began, 'that the body discovered in woodland near Shott at the weekend appears to be that of a homeless man reported missing last week.'

Libby and Ben exchanged shocked glances.

'Sylvia's Rab!' said Libby.

'The man had no identification, and the police are appealing for information,' Campbell continued.

Libby stopped listening, but kept an eye on the screen. 'Do you suppose they'll get a police artist to do an impression?' she said. 'They won't stand a hope otherwise.'

'Bound to,' said Ben. 'Oh, well, at least you don't have to bother.'

Libby scowled at the screen. 'Do you think they took Sylvia to see the body?'

'They couldn't have identified him unless they did,' said Ben.

'I wonder why she didn't phone me.'

'Probably didn't think she needed to,' said Ben.

'I might call her,' said Libby, reaching for her phone.

'Not now.' Ben sounded mildly exasperated. 'She's probably just got in from work.'

'Not if she's been to see the body today,' said Libby. 'All right, I'll call her after dinner.'

There was nothing more on the news, so Libby went into the kitchen to cook her chops. She'd done no more than take them out of the greaseproof paper when her phone rang. Ben brought it in to her.

'Fran,' he said.

'Did you see the news?' asked Fran, before Libby could say a word.

'Yes. See? I said it could be. Did Sylvia call you?'

'No – did she call you?'

'No. I said to Ben I thought that was odd. I'm going to call after dinner.'

'Perhaps she didn't want to talk to us. After all, she's solved her mystery now. He didn't show up because he was dead.'

'I suppose they are sure it's him?' said Libby. 'They will have taken her to see him, won't they?'

'Yes,' said Fran slowly, 'but why?'

42

'Eh?'

'Why did they suddenly connect Sylvia's missing homeless man with the body? Ian wasn't taking it seriously – that was why he asked us.'

'That's a point.' Libby frowned at the chops. 'I don't suppose we could ask Ian?'

'No, of course we can't. Maybe if he goes to the pub on Wednesday you could mention it.'

'You said that before. I'm still going to talk to Sylvia, though,' said Libby.

However, there was no reply when she tried to call Sylvia's number after dinner, not even voicemail.

'I'll try again tomorrow,' she said to Ben.

'Why, though? You did what Ian asked you, and it looks as if the matter's been resolved. No need,' he said, reiterating an oft-repeated mantra, 'to get involved.'

No, thought Libby. Of course there isn't.

'Didjer see they know who that dead bloke is?' said Lenny, accosting Libby in the eight-till-late on Tuesday morning.

'Not quite,' said Libby, drawing him away from the other customers in the shop, who were all looking amused.

'What djer mean, not quite? It said they had.' Lenny looked affronted.

'They know he was a homeless man who'd gone missing, but they don't know his name or anything about him,' explained Libby.

'Oh, ah.' Lenny nodded wisely. 'Joe said he come from Nethergate.'

'Did he?' Libby was surprised. 'How did he know that?'

Lenny shrugged. 'Dunno. He lives there, don't he?'

'Er, yes.' Libby resolved to speak to Joe. 'I must get on, Len. Give my love to Flo.'

But first, she reflected, she would try Sylvia again.

She called Fran when she got home.

'I can tell there's been a murder,' said Fran with a sigh.

'What do you mean? Another "moment"?' Libby sat down on the sofa with a thump.

'No. The fact that I've had you on the phone at least twice a day for the last week.'

'You started it,' said Libby grumpily. 'Ian spoke to you first.'

'Yes.' Fran sighed. 'And I wish he hadn't.'

'Well, anyway,' continued Libby, not to be diverted, and told Fran what Lenny had said.

'Perhaps there's been an update on the news since yesterday evening,' said Fran. 'Hold on. I'll look up the website.'

There was a pause while Libby fidgeted and drummed her fingers.

'Yes, here we go,' said Fran. 'It says the homeless man whose body was discovered in woodland near Shott was last seen in Nethergate. And again asks for anyone with information, etc., etc.'

'Oh, that explains it,' said Libby. 'I wonder why they didn't put that out in the original piece?'

'They like to keep as much back as they can,' said Fran. 'And then release any more titbits one by one. You know that.'

'Oh, yes, so they can check if people are telling the truth.' Libby stared thoughtfully out of the window. 'Shall I try Sylvia again?'

'Just to find out if they took her to see the body? We know they must have done, so what's the point?'

'To see if she's all right?' hazarded Libby.

'Oh, come off it, Lib! You're just being nosy.'

Libby made herself a sandwich for lunch and sat down at the table in the window with her computer. Persuaded into buying it a few years ago by her nearest and dearest, despite an inbuilt aversion to modern technology, she now wondered how she'd ever managed without it.

The information Fran had relayed was all she could find on the man she was now convinced was Sylvia's Rab, so, with a sigh, she tried Sylvia's number again.

'Hello?' Sylvia was abrupt.

'Oh, Sylvia! Hello, it's Libby Sarjeant—'

'Yes.' Now Sylvia was resigned. 'I'm surprised I haven't heard from you before.'

'I did try,' began Libby.

'Look, I don't want to talk about it.'

'No, I'm sure – I just wanted to ask if the police took you to see the – er – body.'

'Of course they did.' Sylvia was positively antagonistic. 'What did you say to Ian?'

'Nothing!' said Libby, surprised. 'Except what you told us. I thought that was what you wanted.'

Sylvia made a harrumphing sound. 'So he brushed me off.'

'He what? But if they took you—'

'Some constable got in touch and said they would take me. They did. Two officers in uniform. Nothing from Ian.'

Well, that proved one thing, thought Libby. Sylvia had wanted to get in touch with Ian.

'At least they took it seriously,' she said.

'You'd have thought he would have said thank you.'

'Yes, you would,' agreed Libby, wondering why he hadn't.

'So, if that's all . . .'

'No, well, actually,' said Libby hastily, a thought popping into her head. 'You're an estate agent, aren't you? What do you know about the Island View caravan park?'

There was a silence at the other end.

'Why?' said Sylvia eventually.

'We heard about the redevelopment plans,' said Libby. 'Sounds a bit – contentious.'

'I don't know much about it,' said Sylvia. 'Nothing to do with us.'

Libby didn't have the nerve to ask which agent Sylvia worked with after that, so with a more-or-less friendly exchange of good-byes they rang off.

But she does know, thought Libby. I wonder why she was so

45

cagey? Time to look into the Island View development plans, she decided.

First of all, she looked up the link to the protest group Jane had sent her. Among a lot of other information, she found a detailed plan of the proposed site, which was even worse than she'd imagined. There were still half a dozen static caravans for rental, but the rest of the site was taken up with permanent park homes, all in their own little gardens. She could see how appealing these must be, particularly for retirees, but these appeared to have no age restrictions, which meant at least some of them would be occupied by families. Libby had nothing against children – after all, she'd had three herself – but the site, to be built as it was on sloping land, reaching down almost to the car park behind the Blue Anchor café and The Sloop Inn, did not look suitable for families.

The protest group itemised the various protections applying to the area, all of which precluded development, and explained the loophole provided by the outdated certificate of legal development. They had obtained the services of a lawyer, but his services would prove expensive, as would any ensuing court costs. There was a petition, which Libby signed and shared on her limited social media accounts. She called Fran again.

'No, listen,' she said when Fran sounded exasperated. 'I just can't understand how it has got this far. The council must have known about it. Those various protections, the SSI and so on, should have ensured that it was thrown out immediately.'

'Obviously this certificate is enough to make sure it goes through,' said Fran. 'But, yes, I'll sign the petition, for all the good it will do.'

'That's very defeatist.'

'The development company will have their lawyers on the case and they have a lot more money than the protest group. And I'll guarantee there'll be people in the town who will see it as bringing in lots of lovely money to the area.'

'I suppose so,' said Libby gloomily. 'Mavis would do well out of it. The Blue Anchor's the only café near the beach.'

'But I expect the proposed site will have its own café, and probably a shop, too. Did you look?'

'Oh, gosh, no! I'll look.' Libby clicked back onto the plan and, sure enough, there at the top were some buildings labelled 'Facilities'. 'I'll see if they say anywhere what that means.'

'You do that. But remember, Lib, this is nothing to do with us.'

Libby was indignant. 'You don't want a huge development right behind your house, do you?'

'No, and I'll sign the petition, and go to meetings, if they have any, but that's really all I can do.'

Libby rang off, feeling helpless. Fran was right, of course, but if there was anything practical she could do, she vowed to do it. And the next place to look, of course, was the website of the development company itself.

Stapleton Holdings proved to own several static home parks. Most included entertainment, leisure and shopping blocks, which didn't bode well, although Libby couldn't see that the Island View site would be big enough to accommodate all these. Frustrated, she closed the computer and went to make more tea.

'Libby,' said Ben later, 'I know it's a disgrace, but you're only getting interested because you haven't got anything else to do.'

'There's still Michelle's missing stalker.' Libby avoided his eyes.

Ben sighed. 'And you can't do anything about that, either. Why don't you come to the Pocket tomorrow and help me prepare for the opening?'

'I thought you were all ready. And why isn't Simon helping?'

'He will be. He's in the process of moving at the moment.'

'What is there to do?' asked Libby, now distracted in spite of herself.

'Make sure we've got everything – glasses, coasters, bar towels, teacloths—'

'I thought you'd done all that,' said Libby. 'What about the new printed coasters?'

'There, see?' said Ben triumphantly. 'I'd forgotten about those. Can we get some done in time?'

The Hop Pocket was to have new coasters and bar towels printed with its own new logo, designed for them by Guy, which was also featured on the signage outside. The only thing Libby was disappointed about was the lack of a proper hanging pub sign, but this, apparently, was considered a health-and-safety hazard by the powers that be.

'All right if there was one already there, but not a new one,' explained Ben.

'Silly,' sniffed Libby.

The exercise of retrieving the research they had done previously on printing companies and firing off emails asking for quotes kept Libby occupied for most of Tuesday evening, to Ben's relief.

'And,' he said, handing her a nightcap after she closed the laptop, 'it must be time to start thinking about the theatre again. It's spring – what about the summer show at The Alexandria? And a spring production of our own – we've only got hirers booked in.'

The Oast Theatre, an oast house converted by Ben, a former architect, stood next to the Manor. It had gone from strength to strength since it first opened with a play written by Peter, the run unfortunately marred somewhat by murder.

'I'll get hold of The Alexandria in the morning,' said Libby, 'and I suppose I could think about a production of our own. Small scale, perhaps? A comedy?'

Thankful to have diverted his best beloved's thoughts in a safer direction, Ben settled down beside her on the sofa and prepared to discuss drama.

Wednesday turned out to be a perfect spring day. Libby began by getting in touch with The Alexandria to discuss whether they wanted an End of the Pier Show in summer, about which they were enthusiastic, then called a couple of the key players in the Oast House company to gather their thoughts on a late spring production, which would normally have been well underway by now. As the only dates free were in June, it turned into an early summer production. This accomplished, she set out for the Hop Pocket.

To her surprise, she found not only Ben, but Peter and Tim huddled round the bar.

'Just telling him what he needs, dear heart,' said Peter, grinning at her.

'Tim's advising me on some speciality beers,' said Ben. 'As long as he can keep his posh wines and spirits, he's happy to let me have some of the other craft beers.'

'Do the suppliers mind, though?' asked Libby, hoisting herself onto a bar stool.

Tim shrugged. 'They'll sell just as much, perhaps more. We – the Coach, I mean – have never been known as a cosy village local, have we?'

'You have to us,' said Libby.

'Yes, but Tim's got more and more into the restaurant and rooms side,' said Peter. 'The restaurant doesn't impact on us – the Pink Geranium, I mean – and the two pubs won't impact on each other. You went into that at the beginning, didn't you?' he said to Ben.

'We'll complement each other,' said Tim. 'Anyway, you're all set to go. When can Simon come in?'

'The weekend, he thinks. Give him a week to settle in and we can open the weekend after,' said Ben. 'I can hardly believe it's actually going to happen. Any news on the coasters, Lib?'

'Several quotes came in this morning, and I picked the one that promised the quickest delivery. They're a smallish company and seemed to have a more personal touch.'

'There you are, then,' said Peter. 'All set to go. And that should be enough to keep even madam's mind off murder.'

'But,' Libby grumbled to Harry, after Peter had escorted her

49

across the road to the Pink Geranium, 'I'm not actually *involved* with the Pocket, am I?'

'Well, dear old trout, that was your choice. I remember you saying you didn't want to be.' Harry put a glass of red wine on the table in front of her, unasked.

'No, all right, but I had other things to do at the time.' Libby took a healthy sip from her glass.

'OK,' said Harry. 'So what do you want to be doing now? That body of Lenny's at Shott? Your hairdresser's stalker?'

'And the caravan park at Nethergate,' said Libby.

'Caravan park?' Harry raised an eyebrow.

Libby explained.

'I don't think you can get involved with that,' said Harry. 'Nothing to do with you.'

'Ripping up the countryside should be something to do with everybody,' stated Libby.

'Yes, dear,' sighed Harry.

'Oh well,' said Libby, after a moment's thought, 'I suppose I should just butt out.'

'Not like you, dear heart,' said Peter, emerging from the kitchen to join them.

'You wait,' said Harry. 'She'll be badgering Ian tonight, I guarantee.'

'Hmph,' said Libby.

Later, reviewing the options Harry had set out for her, she decided the only legitimate enquiry she could make was to Michelle about her missing stalker.

'You're pathetic,' she told herself, scrolling through her list of contacts. 'Pathetic and nosy. Why can't you leave things alone? – Oh, Michelle!'

'Libby.' Michelle sounded tired. 'Have you heard anything?'

'I was calling to ask you the same thing,' said Libby. 'You reported it to the police, did you?'

50

'Exactly as you said.' Michelle sighed. 'They didn't seem to be that interested. They said they'd need to talk to his mum, and she did call me yesterday complaining about it.'

'Where does he work?' asked Libby. 'Did she try there?'

'No idea.' Michelle sounded surprised. 'I never thought to ask. But she must have done, surely?'

'You don't know where it is?'

'No. I assumed something clerical, if I thought about it at all.'

'Keep your eyes and ears open. Just in case.'

'You don't think he'll start again?' Now Michelle was horrified.

'I don't like the fact that he's gone quiet *and* disappeared from home,' said Libby. 'Especially as his mum thought he was living with you.'

Michelle gave a short laugh. 'I don't follow your logic, Lib, but if you say so.'

Neither do I, thought Libby. I just think it's odd.

'Would his mum tell you where he worked?' she asked aloud.

'I don't know, but I'm not calling to ask her.' Michelle sighed. 'I'll let you know if I hear anything.'

'Why,' said Libby aloud to Sidney as she ended the call, 'do people ask me for advice and then sound annoyed when I try to help?'

Sidney opened one eye, sighed and closed it again.

Ben was far too full of plans for the Hop Pocket when he came home that evening to listen, so the first time Libby was able to voice her complaints was at the pub when Patti and Anne came in.

'Just us?' said Anne, looking around curiously. 'Fran not coming?'

'Not tonight,' said Libby.

'What about Edward?'

'Don't know. Maybe if Ian's able to come . . .'

'What's up, Libby?' Patti smiled her thanks to Ben as he placed her drink in front of her.

'Does it show?' said Libby. 'If you must know, I'm fed up with being asked to help and then being choked off when I try.'

'Tell us all,' said Anne, shifting her wheelchair a little closer to Libby.

The saga had just got as far as Michelle's irritable response that afternoon when Edward, followed by a tired-looking Ian, walked in. Anne beamed at them and opened her mouth. Patti poked her in the ribs. Anne looked indignant.

'I wasn't going to say anything!' she said.

Ben went with Ian to the bar and Edward sat down next to Libby.

'I hear Lenny and Joe's body has been identified,' he said.

'Sort of,' said Libby. 'Has Ian said anything?'

'Not a thing. Hardly seen him this week.'

'Will he tell us, do you think?' asked Anne.

Edward made a face. 'Don't know!'

Ian came back to the table and sat down next to Edward. 'Go on,' he said to Libby. 'You're dying to ask.'

Libby raised her eyebrows. 'Who, me? Ask about what?'

There were muffled sounds of hilarity around the table.

Ian sighed, a sound full of resignation.

'Oh, all right,' Libby muttered. 'How did you know to take Sylvia to identify that body?'

'Intuition?' hazarded Ian.

'Must have been more than that,' said Edward with his broad white grin.

'All right,' said Ian with a shrug. 'Fran and Libby obviously thought there was something worth looking into, and I'd be mad to ignore their hunches.'

Libby preened.

'Don't get above yourself,' said Ian. 'We know no more than that.'

'No other clues?' asked Anne.

'A lot of superficial cuts and bruises, as though he'd been pulled through undergrowth. Which he probably had been, given where he was found.'

'Which was where, exactly?' asked Anne.

Ian gave her a mocking look. 'In the woods near Shott.'

'Near us, then,' said Edward.

'Not too far,' said Ian. 'And that's all I'm saying.'

'There's an old operations base near there, isn't there?' said Patti. The others looked at her in surprise.

'I thought of it just now,' she said, looking a trifle embarrassed. 'Because of where it is.'

'Where?' asked Libby.

'It's in the grounds of a house. I remember it because of the name – it's vaguely ecclesiastical: Rogation House.'

Chapter Seven

Patti was met with blank stares.

'Ecclesiastical?' said Ben. 'You mean – religious?'

'It's a church festival,' said Patti. 'Funnily enough, it falls quite soon. Coincides with Ascension Day.'

'Yes,' said Ian slowly. 'I remember now.'

'If the OB is in their grounds, your people must have questioned the owners?' said Anne, beaming at Ian.

'Of course,' said Ian.

'What did you remember?' asked Libby. 'That it was a church festival, or the house?'

'The house,' said Ian. 'Of course. All premises in the vicinity were questioned.'

'Funny name for a house,' said Ben.

'A lot of the Victorians named their houses after religious festivals,' said Edward. 'Ascension House, Christmas House – you know the sort of thing.'

Tim was leaning over the bar. 'Wasn't there some sort of folk thing going on connected with that place?'

'Folk thing?' said Anne. 'What – like Morris dancers, you mean?'

'Sort of,' said Tim, frowning. 'Your new manager Simon would know, Ben. He's into all that.'

'We must ask him,' said Libby.

'Not relevant to my inquiry, though, Libby,' said Ian with a smile. 'And, as I said, I can't say anything else.'

With an effort, the subject was changed, and Edward began asking about the new manager and the opening of the Hop Pocket.

'Who owns that house – do you know?' Libby asked Patti, leaving the men to talk.

'No idea,' said Patti. 'The name just struck me. Can't remember now how I heard about it.'

'But you knew about the OB, though.'

'I think I looked it up after I heard the name. The OB's marked on the map.'

'Hmm. Be nice to know what the "folk thing" was, wouldn't it?'

Patti frowned. 'Now, don't go delving into things.'

Libby grinned. 'Would I?'

'Yes!' said Anne and Patti together.

They were all getting ready to leave when Libby touched Ian's sleeve.

'Did you get a missing-person report in the last few days?' she asked tentatively.

'Apart from our homeless man?' Ian smiled at her.

'Well, yes. It was my hairdresser, you see.'

'Who's gone missing?'

'No, she told me, and said she would report it. Although . . .'

'Although what?' Ian turned his full attention towards her.

Libby explained.

'It hasn't come to my attention.' Ian cocked an eyebrow. 'And he was a stalker, you say? Had that been reported?'

'Oh, yes, and he'd had an official warning. I actually saw him.'

'I'll have a look.' Ian stood up. 'And now I must get off. Early start tomorrow.'

'Will he, do you think?' Libby said to Patti and Anne, as Ian and Edward left the pub.

'He usually does what he says he will,' said Anne confidently.

'He's very busy, though,' said Patti.

'And he's treading very carefully after he got into hot water over the last case,' said Libby.

Patti nodded, standing up and preparing to help Anne manoeuvre her wheelchair through the door. 'Did you ever find anything out about the homeless community in Nethergate? If there's an organisation dishing out food for them, they must be there.'

'After they said they didn't know our man, I sort of gave up,' said Libby. 'Do you think I ought to?'

'I just wondered,' said Patti.

'She'll worry about them now,' said Anne, nodding wisely at Libby.

Libby grinned. 'I'll look into it – like Ian!' she said.

On Thursday morning, Libby sat on the sofa, laptop on lap, trying to decide what to look into first. In view of Patti's concern, she decided that the homeless of Nethergate should come first, so she dug out the number of the contact Patti had passed on.

'Hello, is that Verity? It's Libby Sarjeant. I'm a friend of Patti Pearson's – remember she asked you about a homeless man a week or so back?'

'Er – yes,' said a slightly surprised voice. 'Can I help you?'

'Well, I hope so.' Libby paused. 'I know you couldn't help before, but I was wondering. There's obviously a homeless community in Nethergate, isn't there?'

'Yes, but only a small one.' The voice was hesitant.

'Can you tell me where they usually congregate? Only my friend Patti didn't seem to know.'

There was a short silence. When Verity spoke again, she sounded uncomfortable.

'No reason why she should, really. And they don't seem to have a specific place, unless you count the top of the town where we set up the kitchen. They gather there on Tuesdays and Saturdays when we're there.'

'Have you got to know any of them?'

'Why are you asking?' The voice was now definitely uncomfortable.

56

'Um – we – Patti – was concerned. She wondered if she could help in any way.' Libby crossed her fingers.

'Oh.' The voice softened slightly. 'Well, all help is welcome, but she's got my number if she wants to get in touch.'

'Yes, of course. So,' Libby hurried on, 'you're there Tuesdays and Saturdays. Would that be near the station?'

'Yes.'

'Right. I'll pass it on,' said Libby. 'Thanks for your help.' She ended the call quickly.

'That went well,' she said to Sidney. 'I should have thought it through.'

After making herself a consoling cup of tea, she opened the laptop and typed Rogation House into the search engine. This produced various sites with brief descriptions and photographs of a large Victorian Gothic mansion. She learnt that it was built by a cloth merchant and suspected smuggler in the 1850s, but not much else. There was no evidence that it had ever been opened to the public, nor of the current owner, although she did find several references to the wartime operational base, again, without much detail.

Without much hope, she typed in 'Rogation Parade' and to her surprise found many more references.

'And you'll never guess!' she reported to Fran on the phone. 'There actually were parades! All over the country. Blessing the harvest or something.'

'Not in April,' said Fran. 'The upcoming crops, perhaps. What did Patti actually say about it?'

'Nothing – just that it's a church festival held about now.'

'That must be what the "folk thing" was, then,' said Fran. 'A procession round the village like Plough Monday, or wassailing.'

'Like the solstice and May Day,' said Libby. 'Or that thing I saw in Cornwall – Manannán mac Lir. With Cranston Morris – do you remember?'

'Nothing on the homeless people, then?'

'Only where they dish out the food on Tuesdays and Saturdays. I suppose—'

'No, Libby, we couldn't. Not helpful, then?'

'No.' Libby frowned at the laptop. 'Almost the reverse, in fact. I wonder why?'

'Libby!' Fran's voice held a warning.

'I know, I know. By the way, I thought about going to ask Mavis what she knows about Island View. She must know.'

'Island View? Oh – the caravan park. Yes, she might. She's open now – do you want to go for lunch?'

'What – now?' Libby sat up straight.

Fran laughed. 'Yes, now! Or in an hour or so, anyway.'

'Great idea. I'll be down asap.'

'At least an hour, please, Libby. I need to prepare for the onslaught.'

The hedgerows were glowing with the pale green veil of early spring under a clear blue sky. Libby felt quite uplifted as she drove towards Nethergate. She pulled in at the top of the hill that led down to the seafront to take in the view across the bay. In the middle sat the rocky outcrop known as Dragon Island due to its faintly dragon-like shape, to her left lay the small red and white striped lighthouse on the headland, and to her right the matching headland thick with vegetation. And, below, the little town with its cobbled alleyways, tiny harbour and ancient pubs. If she had to move anywhere from Steeple Martin, she thought, it would be here.

She drove along Harbour Street and parked behind Mavis's Blue Anchor café and the Sloop Inn, before walking back to Coastguard Cottage.

'That was quick,' said Fran, opening the door.

'I left straight away. I know you said at least an hour, but it was such a nice day . . .' Libby followed into the sitting room, and went immediately to the window seat, where she joined Balzac, the black and white cat.

'Well, you sit there and admire the view while I go and change,' said Fran, indicating her jogging bottoms and tee shirt. 'I can't go out looking like this.'

Libby pulled a face at her own jeans and oversized jumper. 'I do,' she said unnecessarily. Fran grinned and disappeared up the stairs.

The beach was almost deserted this early in the season, except for a couple of dog walkers. Later on, in a few weeks' time, it would be full of young families, keen to experience an old-fashioned British seaside holiday. There were no loud amusement arcades, huge ice-cream parlours or brash bars here, which, Libby thought, made it all the more unlikely that Stapleton Holdings should be attempting to open their holiday park.

Fran came back looking her usual well-groomed self, despite being in what she herself would call casual clothes. 'Ready, then?' she said.

'Yes.' Libby scrambled to her feet. 'You are sure Mavis is open?'

'Yes, Lib. We've had sandwiches from her at least twice in the past week.'

They strolled along Harbour Street past several shuttered cottages.

'Holiday cottages?' said Libby.

'Airbnbs.' Fran sniffed. 'Can't say I'm keen.'

'You don't begrudge people coming on holiday, do you?'

'You don't like the idea of the holiday park,' Fran countered.

'Not quite the same,' said Libby. And, anxious to avoid an argument, pointed to the little harbour where two small tourist boats were moored. 'Oh, look, George and Bert have the *Dolphin* and the *Sparkler* out already.'

'Yes, they were both out at the weekend,' said Fran. 'Taking it in turns.'

'I wonder how they feel about Island View?'

'Probably all for it,' said Fran.

'People would be too rowdy for them, surely?'

'You're making assumptions.' Fran went up to one of the few tables already set out in front of the Blue Anchor.

'And you never do?' muttered Libby under her breath. Fran shot her a suspicious look.

Mavis appeared to take their order, it being too early in the season for one of her inevitably sullen young helpers. She plonked an old tin ashtray in front of Libby, despite the fact that she'd been told many times that Libby had given up.

'Seen you having one now and then,' said Mavis, narrowing her eyes.

'Yes, well.' Libby looked away.

They ordered their sandwiches, and discussed what they should say to Mavis while she was away making them up. Bert and George emerged from the Sloop to have a cigarette and waved.

'What do they think about the new caravan park?' asked Libby, nodding towards the two boatmen as Mavis reappeared.

Mavis shrugged. 'Dunno.'

'What about you?' said Fran. 'Must say we were surprised.'

'Bound to happen,' said Mavis, folding her arms across her flowered overall. 'Seaside town.'

'But that area's protected,' said Libby, taking a large bite of her tuna sandwich. 'And the area's not big enough for the extra traffic, surely?'

Mavis pulled up a chair. 'Course it's not. Ruin us all, it will. Might as well retire now.'

'No!' said Libby and Fran together.

'Can't do nothing else.' Mavis sighed. 'We all complained to the council, signed that petition and all that, but no one's taken no notice.'

'That's terrible,' said Fran.

'We heard there's some legal loophole that can be taken to appeal,' said Libby. 'Did you know about that?'

'No. Only thing I've heard about is the security blokes they brought in to get rid of those homeless what were up there.'

'Homeless?' Libby practically shouted.

'Yeah – didn't you know?' Mavis looked surprised. 'Got rid of 'em with dogs, they did. Nasty business.'

Chapter Eight

'Why didn't we know?' Libby turned angrily to Fran.

'Don't look at me – it's not my fault!' Fran held her hands up in front of her face.

'No – but *no one's* said anything! Not Ian, not Sylvia – not even that Verity from the charity. They all must have known!'

Mavis was watching this with the liveliest interest.

'Tell us what you know, Mavis,' said Fran.

'Only what everyone knows. How come you didn't?' Mavis squinted suspiciously at Fran.

'I don't know.' Fran looked rather ashamed.

Mavis sniffed. 'First we heard it about it –' she jerked a thumb in the direction of The Sloop, 'was when that fence went up. Didn't even see any diggers or that going along behind us.'

'Didn't you get a notice from the council or anything? To say planning permission had been applied for?' asked Libby.

'No.' Mavis turned back to Fran. 'Did you?'

'No.' Fran shook her head. 'I wonder how they got round that one?'

'Online, I bet,' said Libby, 'and only there if you went looking. So what happened next?'

'Then someone comes down one day and says they've got security guards up there with dogs.'

'Who told you?' asked Fran.

'One of my regulars. Nobody you'd know. Some of us went up to look.' Mavis pulled a face. 'Nasty, it were.'

'What were they doing?' asked Libby.

'Pulling these poor souls out of them old caravans. With the dogs. See, we knew about 'em. Me and next-door used to give 'em stuff we had left over.'

'Oh, Mavis, I wish I'd known!' said Fran, obviously distressed.

'But you didn't know the man they put on the news?' said Libby. 'The one they found in the woods?'

Mavis shook her head.

'I wonder where they went?' said Fran. 'The rest of the homeless?'

'And why wasn't more made of it in the press?' added Libby.

'Kept it quiet, didn't they? What with the protest and all.'

'When was it?' asked Fran suddenly.

'Oh . . .' Mavis thought. 'Last week? Just before May Day. Someone shoulda said something.'

'I will,' said Libby. 'I'm going to tell Jane.'

'That the girl from the *Mercury*? Yeah, you tell her. Shouldn't get away with it, them Staple folk.'

'Staple folk?' Fran frowned.

'Stapleton Holdings,' said Libby. 'No, Mavis, they shouldn't. I really can't understand why the police weren't involved.'

'Like I said. Kept it quiet, didn't they?' She nodded at Fran. 'You didn't know nothing, did you?'

'Incredible.' Libby was furious. 'I'm going to tell Ian, too.'

'Be careful, Lib,' warned Fran.

Mavis nodded. 'Yeah. They come round here, they did. Trying to buy us off.'

'What?' Libby and Fran were aghast.

'All very smooth. "Don't want no unpleasantness, do we?" the bloke said. We both turned him down.'

'Why didn't you report it?' Libby was beside herself.

'We knew what he meant.' Mavis nodded.

'A threat,' said Fran.

'Yeah.' Mavis stood up. 'So don't you go letting on I told you.'

'We've got to do something about this,' said Libby, watching Mavis's retreating back.

Fran nodded slowly. 'What, though?'

'I said – tell Ian and Jane.' Libby's lips clamped together in a tight line. 'How did this happen?'

'If Stapleton Holdings are into the business of intimidation, it could be dangerous.'

'I'll tell Ian privately,' said Libby. 'There's got to be a link to Rab's death.'

'Looks like it.' Fran sighed. 'I'd leave Jane until after you've spoken to Ian, though.'

'I suppose so.' Libby chewed her lip. 'I'll try Ian now.'

'Private number, don't forget,' reminded Fran.

Libby scrolled through her contacts. 'Text, do you think?' she asked.

'Of course.' Fran smiled.

The text Libby sent was brief and to the point.

Important info received re: homeless people and the caravan park in Nethergate.

'It doesn't sound very striking,' she said sadly. 'I hope he takes notice.'

They strolled along the walkway beneath the cliff and gazed upwards towards Island View. 'This is all sounding dodgier and dodgier,' said Libby.

Back in Steeple Martin, she was surprised to find Ben and Simon in the kitchen of Number 17 eating ham and salad and drinking beer.

'Simon brought the beer over for me to try. It's one of the craft beers,' explained Ben. 'Want one?'

'Not for me, thanks.' Libby grinned at Simon. 'Is this the first stage of moving in?'

He grinned back. 'You could say that. I wanted to check what I needed to bring over for the kitchen.'

'I thought you weren't going to do food?' said Libby, surprised.

'For my own kitchen,' said Simon. 'I've got to re-equip.'

'Ah.' Libby perched on the edge of the table. 'While you're here—'

'I've already asked him,' said Ben. 'Go on, Simon. She'll love this.'

'The Rogation business?' Simon sat back in his chair. 'I'm surprised you hadn't heard of it.'

'None of us had,' said Libby. 'Is it really that well known?'

'Maybe not, unless you're into that sort of thing, you know, like Wassailing and Plough Monday.'

'So I believe,' said Libby. 'So what happens?'

Simon frowned at his beer. 'As far as I know, it started way back in pre-medieval times when the church instituted the custom of parading around the parish blessing the land and praying for good crops that year. Later on, they used to beat the bounds – you know what that means?'

'Beating the boundaries of the parish,' said Ben.

'Yes, only before then they used to beat young boys. Sort of initiation ceremony.'

'Nasty,' said Libby.

'Yes, well, it degenerated a bit, like these customs always do. And it just became a rather rowdy parade. Some said the whole thing was taken over by witches in the seventeenth century.'

'Well, they would. Everything was blamed on the poor old witches.' Libby sniffed.

'After that I'm not sure how it developed, but it continued well into the last century. Led by some character known as Old Rogue, who wore some weird costume and mask. The person who built Rogation House was supposed to be that generation's Old Rogue.'

'Who was he?' asked Ben.

'I don't know. I expect you could find out if you really wanted to.'

'It said he was a wool merchant and smuggler when I looked online. How do you know all this?' asked Libby.

'I used to have the pub in Pucklefield, and my folks retired there.' Simon smiled reminiscently. 'Rogue Days were always a bit special – all the men of the villages used to gather and dance – not Morris exactly, but a bit like it. And they had a mocked up Old Rogue with his dog, the Tolley Hound. Only that was a wooden model, like a hobby horse. And guest Morris sides came and danced, too.'

'So it's still going on?' said Libby, surprised.

'Yes, but in a very subdued way. The Puckle Inn was sold by the brewery, and the youngsters these days don't seem to have the time for it.' Simon sighed.

'And Rogation Days were when?' asked Ben.

'In the week running up to Ascension Day. Let's see.' He frowned. 'That would be – what – a couple of weeks' time?'

'It sounds fun,' said Libby.

'Oh, it was, in the old days. Mind you –' Simon leant forward – 'apparently, the serious stuff was kept hidden.'

'Serious stuff?' repeated Libby and Ben.

Simon laughed. 'The old stories were that there were underground parades led by a real Old Rogue, where all the old rituals were carried out. People even said they saw the Tolley Hound.'

'What is it?' asked Ben. 'Something like the Barghest? Or Black Shuck?'

'I think so.' Simon nodded. 'There's a Black Dog story everywhere in England, isn't there? We had a portrait of him in the pub.'

'Why Tolley Hound, though?' mused Libby.

'Because he helped collect tolls – or tithes – on behalf of his master.' Simon shrugged. 'Everyone local knew the stories. After all, the Old Rogue and Rogue Days were simply a jolly for the villages.'

'Just like May Day and the solstice,' said Libby.

'It's a bit gruesome,' said Ben, amused.

'I wonder if we could find a legend for Steeple Martin?' Libby slid off the table and went to put the kettle on. 'You could make a lot of it in the Pocket. Perhaps we ought to start a Morris side.'

'Oh, here we go.' Ben shook his head.

'She's right, though.' Simon grinned at Libby. 'Perhaps we could have a special Halloween parade, or something?'

'Yes!' Libby clapped her hands. 'We could make something up!'

'Don't encourage her,' said Ben with a sigh.

It was after Ben and Simon had gone back to the Hop Pocket that Libby had another thought and called Fran to talk it through. She began by telling Fran the story of the Old Rogue and the Tolley Hound.

'And I thought maybe that had something to do with Rab's body?'

'Oh, for goodness' sake, Libby! He said that *used* to happen. Not that it still did. Besides, the Rogue days, or whatever they were, aren't for a few weeks yet, are they? Stop trying to make things fit. Have you heard from Ian yet?'

'No. But I might mention it to him when he rings.'

'I wouldn't,' said Fran. 'He'll laugh at you.'

Discouraged, Libby ended the call, then opened her computer to see where Pucklefold was. It appeared to be a dot on the map, somewhere above Shott, on the edge of the ancient woodland that she had already ascertained surrounded Rogation House.

'I wish I knew who owned it now,' she said to Sidney, who had come to help her.

And then her phone rang.

'You said you had something to tell me.' Ian sounded anything but friendly.

'Er – yes.'

'Well, you do or you don't. Presumably you didn't phone for nothing.'

Libby bristled.

'I deliberately used your personal number so you could ignore it if you wished.'

'I haven't ignored it. What is it?'

'I wanted to know if you were aware of the removal of homeless people – with dogs – from the site of the proposed caravan site.'

There was a silence. 'Caravan site.' Ian repeated the words slowly.

'The one that shouldn't be allowed at all.'

'Yes. We are aware of that.'

'But not the homeless people.'

Ian cleared his throat. 'We checked there when we made an initial search for the missing man.'

'You didn't tell us.'

'It was as a result of you reporting back to us.'

'And you found nothing.'

'And the site manager allowed us to search the vans. We found nothing.'

'Because those that had been there had been removed by security guards with dogs.'

There was another short silence. 'How do you know?'

Libby sighed. 'The people who told us were threatened not to say anything.'

'*What?*'

'I'm sorry . . .' began Libby nervously.

'No, you're not. You'd better tell me the whole thing. But not over the phone.' Ian cleared his throat again. 'May I call round on my way home? It'll be about six.'

Libby sighed. 'Of course. Would you like to join us for dinner?'

'Um . . .' Ian was obviously struggling with himself. 'Could I take you and Ben to dinner? At the pub?'

Libby mentally consigned her proposed chilli back to the fridge.

'Yes, please. Shall we meet you there?'

'I'd prefer to talk to you in private first.'

'OK. We'll see you about six.'

Libby sent Ben a text to tell him about the change in plans, then called Fran to tell her of the surprising development.

'He actually *didn't know*!' said Libby excitedly.

'Are you sure?' said Fran doubtfully.

'Oh, yes. That's why he's coming to take us to dinner.'

'Hmm. Don't mention Mavis.'

'I expect he'll guess. So what else did we say we'd mention to him?'

'Heavens! I can't remember. Your Michelle's stalker?'

'Oh, yes! And the Old Rogue business.' Libby paused.

'That's got nothing to do with anything!' said Fran, sounding, as she often did, somewhat exasperated.

'Well, I'm going to mention it, anyway. Then it'll be off my conscience.'

'Good luck,' said Fran.

Chapter Nine

'It's all circumstantial, though,' said Ian later. 'No, thanks, Ben, I'm driving.'

Ben handed Libby a glass of wine. 'You could stay at Hetty's,' he suggested.

'Don't tempt me,' said Ian with a smile. 'I'm already playing hookey.'

'What are you supposed to be doing?' asked Libby.

'Directing operations from my desk. DS Trent is leading the inquiry.'

'Into Rab?'

'The homeless man, yes.'

'There was something else,' said Libby slowly.

Ben and Ian exchanged looks.

'Have you heard of the Old Rogue?' asked Libby, her eyes fixed on her glass.

'I've met many,' said Ian.

'This one's a sort of folk tale.' Libby risked a look at Ian's frowning face. 'Can I tell you about it?'

Ian sighed. 'I will have that drink, Ben, and I'll just give Hetty a ring.'

Drinks supplied and Hetty rung, Libby resumed her story.

'So,' she concluded, 'I just wondered if it could have anything to do with the body . . .'

'And what evidence have you that this whole thing is still going on?'

'Well . . . none, actually.'

'Just hearsay?'

'Er – yes.'

Ian looked at Ben. 'What do you think?'

Ben shook his head. 'Hardly feasible. And the Rogation Days, when all this was supposed to have taken place, haven't even happened yet this year. We talked a bit about it after you'd gone, Lib.' Ben pulled a face. 'There were some rather – unpleasant aspects to it. But all of that happened years ago and, as he said to you, Lib, it was mainly regarded as a fairy tale.'

'Illegal?' Ian raised his eyebrows.

'I would think so.' Ben shot a quick look at Libby.

Libby was looking disgruntled.

'Look, Lib.' Ian turned to face her. 'Remember we've been here before, with Cranston Morris and the Green Man murder. I doubt it could happen again. But, despite the fact that it's highly unlikely, I will have another look at the pathologist's report.' He frowned. 'Some of the injuries . . . well, they were what convinced us it was murder. No,' he said, noting Libby's excited expression, 'I'm not telling you any more than that. Now – is that all?'

'There was Michelle's missing stalker . . .'

'Yes, I did see the report, but it's being dealt with by another team. I can't interfere.'

'Oh.' Libby's face fell. 'Well, I did try.'

'You certainly did.' Ian finished his drink. 'Come on – I told Tim we'd be there by seven.'

Libby stood up and stretched. 'Forensics. You've never really talked to us about forensics.'

Ian looked amused. 'Should I have?'

'I just wondered. Where your pathologists were based. That sort of thing.'

Ian and Ben laughed.

'Planning a bit of undercover sleuthing?' asked Ben, throwing Libby's latest cape round her shoulders.

'No – I just wondered. You see so many of them on TV.'

'Ours don't go around solving crimes,' said Ian. 'Not exactly. We have one specialist who works out of a lab in Canterbury who we rely on a lot.'

'Not exactly like *Silent Witness*, then?' said Ben.

'Quite,' said Ian with a grin.

'So,' said Tim, placing menus on the bar along with the drinks, 'Simon told you what you wanted to know about all the folksy goings-on?'

'Yes, thanks,' said Libby, darting an uncomfortable glance at Ian.

'What Libby wanted to know, anyway,' said Ian, smiling at her.

Tim grinned. 'All grist to the mill, though, eh?'

Ben hastily shepherded them to the small table by the fireplace. 'Tell us more about the forensics, then, Ian,' he said.

'Are you being diplomatic, Ben?' Ian laughed.

'Possibly,' said Ben, with a wry grin.

'I'd like to know,' said Libby. 'I've always sort of taken it for granted, but there's a lot to it, isn't there?'

'Of course. We couldn't do our job without it. The victims on the Dunton Estate, for instance. Essential in that case.'

'So it's the SOCOs is it?'

'Scenes of Crime Officers, yes. Civilian members of the police force. And the pathologist, of course.'

'He or she's appointed by the Home Office, is that right?' said Ben.

'Yes. A local doctor usually comes along first, but often the pathologist will come out to look at the victims in situ. Especially if there's a doubt as to whether the site is the actual scene of the crime.'

'So then it isn't the scene of the crime?' said Libby.

'Oh, yes it is! There can be multiple scenes of crime – site of discovery, site of crime, sites of transport – all equally important.'

'So in the case of Rab the homeless man, the OB in the woods at Shott would be a site, but might not be the place where he was killed, so you'd have to find that – and how he was transported?' Libby leant forward, her elbows on the table.

'Yes.' Ian grinned at Ben. 'Now she'll want to meet the pathologist.'

Libby felt the warmth begin to rise up her neck. 'Aren't I allowed to?'

Ian threw up his hands. 'I give up. If I introduce you to Franklyn, will you promise not to expect answers to all your questions and not to badger him?'

'Franklyn? Is that his name?'

'Franklyn Taylor-Blake. And, to satisfy you a little further, I'm going to order a sweep of the caravan park by our CSIs.'

'Is that SOCOs?' asked Ben.

'Crime Scene Investigators, yes. So, Libby, will that do?'

Libby, smiling delightedly, nodded vigorously.

'You've made her day,' said Ben.

'He's made my *week*,' said Libby.

Over the next hour, they enjoyed one of Tim's Chef's Specials, courtesy of new chef Brendan, and finished up with one of Libby's favourites, Eton Mess, followed by Irish coffee, which she hadn't had since she was at drama school.

'Look, it's even in those special little glasses!' She beamed.

'With the handles that are too small to hold,' said Ben.

Ian, who had opted for straightforward black coffee, laughed at them. 'Is this Tim trying out his new dining experience on us?'

Ben nodded. 'He's going to do more of this when the Pocket opens.'

'I hope he's not going to close this bar,' said Libby. 'I'd still like to meet here on Wednesdays.'

'Traitor,' said Ben.

Tim leant over the bar. 'No – the big bar at the back will become the dining room and the lounge –' he jerked his thumb over his shoulder to the other side of the bar – 'will be the bar for the diners. What did you think of Brendan's efforts?'

'Very good.'

'Excellent.'

'Delicious.'

'Good.' Tim beamed and disappeared.

Libby's phone buzzed in her basket.

'Go on, answer it,' said Ben.

'Libby?' Michelle's voice shook.

'Michelle?' Libby jerked to attention. 'What's up?'

'He's been here.'

'Who – Neil? What did he say?'

'He didn't.' Michelle was struggling to speak. 'He came while I was out. How did he get *in*, Lib?' Her voice rose almost to a shriek. Ian and Ben both turned to look.

'Have you reported it?' Libby asked.

'N-no. They don't take me seriously.' Now Michelle was crying.

'Hang on.' Libby turned to Ian. 'Her stalker's been in her flat while she was out.'

Ian briefly closed his eyes, sighed and held out his hand.

'Michelle?' he asked gently. 'DCI Connell here. Tell me what happened.'

He listened, frowning, for a few moments, then got up and moved away from the table.

'Oh, dear,' said Libby, her eyes following him. 'That looks ominous.'

Ian continued listening, then speaking, before ending the call and returning to the table. He handed the phone back to Libby.

'I've told her to report it to whoever she spoke to before, and I'll get on to them, too.' He sighed and shook his head. 'We keep trying to get better at dealing with this sort of thing, but it doesn't seem to penetrate, sometimes.'

'You'd think with the deaths that have resulted,' said Ben, 'they'd take it seriously.'

'Yes, but, in fairness, some of the reports are – shall we say – less than urgent.'

'Eh?' Libby's eyebrows rose.

Ian smiled. 'When someone says they've told their tormentor they don't want to see them any more, and ask us to stop them doing so? We do have to wait and see if said tormentor is actually going to ask again.'

'Oh.' Libby nodded.

'But this sounds serious.' Ian shook his head again.

'He'd actually been inside her flat?'

'It appears so.' Ian was frowning.

'Bloody hell,' said Ben. 'How did he get in?'

'No idea.' Ian's lips tightened. 'I shall be having words.'

'I hope that doesn't make it worse for Michelle,' said Libby.

'It won't. Now, can we talk about something else?'

Friday morning was overcast and drizzly. Libby stared out of the window at Allhallow's Lane, clutching her third mug of tea and reflecting on her failure to draw any more useful information from Ian the previous evening. Despite her best efforts, he would be drawn neither on Sylvia, nor the mysterious Rab. All he would say was that investigations were ongoing. He did, however, promise that he would let her know about developments at the caravan site. Sighing, Libby put down her mug and picked up her phone.

'Well, what did you expect?' said Fran reasonably when the situation had been explained to her. 'At least he's interceded with Michelle and her stalker.'

'And I'm sure he *will* look into everything,' said Libby, 'but I don't think he was convinced by anything we'd found out.'

'Look, he came over to see you about it all, and you can hardly blame him for not wanting to talk about Sylvia. If he'd been in the habit of letting us into his love life, maybe, but he hasn't.'

'I know.' Libby sighed heavily, then brightened. 'But he did say he'd introduce me to their pathologist.'

'Did he? Goodness! Why?'

'I was just asking about forensics and stuff. I don't think I realised that SOCOs were civilians, did you?'

'I think I knew that,' said Fran, 'but I suppose we've never had much to do with that side of things, have we?'

'No, thank goodness.' Libby shuddered. 'Finding that body backstage at the beer festival was enough for me.'

'Which makes me wonder why you're always so keen to get involved with murder investigations,' said Fran.

Libby laughed. 'Daft, isn't it? Especially as it makes me unpopular in certain quarters.' She picked up her mug. 'So, what shall I do today? Any ideas?'

'A painting for Guy? Plan the production calendar for the theatre? Email potential performers for the show for the Alexandria?'

'Or phone Michelle and see what's happening with her,' said Libby. 'And, yes, I'll get round to all your suggestions.'

'You'd better,' said Fran. 'We're into May already!'

Libby rang off and took her mug back into the kitchen, before finding Michelle's number.

'Oh, Libby,' Michelle sounded harried. 'Your Inspector Connell certainly got things moving!'

'Really?' Libby sat down at the table. 'What's he done?'

'I've had those CSI people here already. All white suits and everything! They're still in my bedroom.'

'Goodness! Has anybody been to question you?'

'Oh, yes – an Inspector Mackintosh. Do you know her?'

'No. Was she nice?'

'Efficient,' said Michelle. 'I got the feeling she was a bit cross that she'd been told what to do.'

'That'd figure,' said Libby. 'I expect Ian will be seen as an interfering so-and-so.'

'Well, good for him,' said Michelle, now sounding stronger and less worried. 'At least something's being done. Oh – and they were going to talk to his mum, too. Now she'll hate me.'

'Can't be helped,' said Libby. 'Are you OK on your own? Do you want me to come over?'

'No, I'm fine. As soon as they've finished here, I'm going into the salon. Chloe's been trying to cover my appointments, but it's Friday, and we're always extra busy on a Friday.'

'OK.' Libby stood up. 'Well, you know where I am if you need me.'

'Yes, and thank you so much for sorting out your Inspector Connell for me.'

'He's a Chief Inspector, actually, and no problem. Have a good weekend.'

Libby went back into the kitchen and switched on the kettle, before deciding that a fourth cup of tea was probably a bad idea. Sighing, she opened the door to the conservatory and glared at the painting on the easel.

And the phone rang.

Chapter Ten

'I've been doing some digging,' came Jane Baker's voice. 'Proper investigative journalism stuff.'

'Really?' Libby closed the conservatory door and went back into the sitting room. 'What into?'

'Stapleton Holdings.' Jane sounded triumphant. 'And guess where their head office is?'

'Er – Nethergate?' hazarded Libby.

'No! Canterbury!'

'So they're local? That means they must have known all about the caravan site before they started all this. Or does it?'

'They'd make sure they knew all about any site they went for, wherever it was,' said Jane, 'but, yes, they probably had personal knowledge of it. Someone in the organisation might have spotted it and realised its potential.'

'Although I don't see what difference that makes to the situation,' Libby said thoughtfully.

'If I could find out if that was the case, it would make a brilliant story.' Jane sounded enthusiastic. 'I can see the headline: "Local man betrays town!" What do you think?'

'Isn't that a bit strong?' said Libby hesitantly.

'Well, maybe it could do with a bit of refining,' agreed Jane, 'but the idea's sound. Now I've just got to find out who it was.'

'You don't even know if there was a – a – a mole!' Libby finished triumphantly.

'A case for Sarjeant and Wolfe?'

'Oh, don't be daft!' Libby laughed. 'How on earth would we look into that?'

Jane sighed gustily. 'I don't know. But we must be able to find out somehow.'

'We?' repeated Libby with a grin.

'I bet you'll try to find out something about it,' said Jane, sounding hopeful.

'Did you find out who the head honcho is? CEO, or managing director or whatever?'

'I didn't check,' said Jane, sounding surprised. 'I don't think it actually said anything about owners. Why don't you have a look?'

'I did search online, but only when I was trying to find out who'd bought the site. I'll have another look.' Libby looked at her watch. 'I'll do it now, before lunchtime. Ben's new manager's moving in today, and I said I'd go over to see if there's anything I can do.'

'Manager? Manager of what?'

'His pub! You know about the Hop Pocket.'

'Oh, yes! It's finally opening, is it? Can I do a story on it? I wanted to do one when he was first looking into it, I seem to remember.'

'I'm sure he and his new manager would love it,' said Libby. 'I'll mention it and get him to ring you.'

'OK – and if you find out anything more about Stapleton Holdings . . .'

'I'll let you know.' Libby ended the call and scrolled down to Ben's number.

'Jane Baker would like to do a piece on the opening of the Hop Pocket,' she told him. 'She did ask when the whole thing first came up, but we were a bit occupied then.'

'We were, weren't we?' Libby could hear the smile in Ben's voice. 'Give me her number and I'll call her. We could do with the publicity.'

'Seems ages ago now, doesn't it?' Libby paused. 'Ben – do you remember Colin had that company called Hardcastle Holdings?'

'Yes?' Ben sounded puzzled. 'Why?'

'And it was simply a – what do they call it – an accommodation address?'

'Not quite – it was solicitors who dealt with anything they could and forwarded everything else to Colin. Why?'

'Is that what all holding companies are?'

'I don't think so. Again – why?'

'Jane's found out that the owners of that caravan site, Stapleton Holdings, are based in Canterbury.'

There was a short silence. Then: 'And?'

'Well, perhaps they aren't the *real* owners, if you know what I mean.'

'Libby!' Ben let out an exasperated snort. 'Please don't go trying to investigate this. It's none of your business.'

Libby opened her mouth and shut it again. 'OK,' she said. 'Sorry.'

But the first thing she did after ending the call was look up 'Holding Companies' on the laptop.

While she heated up soup for her lunch, she rang Colin Hardcastle.

'Why was your company called Hardcastle Holdings?' she asked after the pleasantries had been observed.

'Eh? What do you mean?' Colin was obviously taken aback.

'I looked up holding companies, and they look much bigger – and sort of more corporate.' Libby stirred her soup.

'Oh, I see!' Colin laughed. 'Or they're just a title, covering a multitude of – er – holdings.'

'Such as?' Libby decanted her soup one handed.

'I had several small businesses – small-scale property stuff, you know. So I just lumped it all together under "holdings" rather than "Hardcastle Limited" or something like that. Because I wasn't actually a limited company anyway.'

'What are you now?'

'Hardcastle and Hall.' Colin was obviously grinning. 'Has a ring to it, don't you think?'

'But what do you actually *do*?'

'Find properties in Spain for prospective buyers. Recommendation only. Why? Do you want one?'

'No, thanks – I'm not a bloated plutocrat. Just curious.' Libby sat down at the kitchen table. 'So a holding company could be just about anything?'

'I suppose so. Why? Is there a holding company you're looking into?'

'Sort of. Look, it doesn't matter. Ben's told me to leave it alone, so . . .'

Colin laughed. 'Fat chance! Come on, tell Uncle Col. Would you like me to look into it for you?'

Libby relaxed. 'Well, it's like this,' she began.

Colin didn't express quite as much outrage as everyone else had at the illegal desecration of Nethergate.

'You have to remember,' he said when Libby had finished explaining, 'that Gerry and I now live in a house that was also looked upon as a bit of a desecration.'

'Oh, but nothing like this,' said Libby.

'No.' Colin was obviously thinking. 'Would you let me look into it? It's an area I'm familiar with, after all. As in legal area, not Nethergate.'

'I'd love you to,' said Libby. 'Not that there's anything we can do about it, but . . .'

'Libby – is this linked to a murder, by any chance?' said Colin sharply.

Libby felt the colour creeping up her neck. 'Er . . .'

'It is, isn't it? Come on – tell me all. Now I'm not living in Steeple Martin I'm not up to speed.'

Libby sighed and gave in with good grace.

'So you think this homeless person was one of those removed by the park owner's heavy mob?' Colin spoke slowly.

'Maybe. It just seemed a coincidence.' Libby swallowed the last mouthful of her lukewarm soup. 'It seems a bit daft now.'

'And your friend Jane wants a story out of it?'

'Well, she thought, being local, perhaps . . .'

'If it's a fully fledged holding company, the local aspect can be ignored,' said Colin briskly. 'If it's simply a grandiose name like mine was, maybe. But you said the company had sites all over the country?'

'Yes, as far as I could see: Yorkshire, Norfolk, Suffolk, Essex and now Kent.'

'Hmm. All east coast,' said Colin. 'Just one site in each county?'

'I don't know – I think so. Does it make a difference?'

'To the size of the company, yes.' Colin paused. 'I'll have a look and see what I can find. I don't like the idea of using this legal loophole.'

'Neither do I,' said Libby. 'And there's a proper protest group – hang on, I'll send you the link.'

'Thanks,' said Colin. 'This'll keep me out of trouble while Gerry's off finding castles in Spain.'

'Is that where he is?' asked Libby, surprised.

'No – he's in the study upstairs. Wonderful what you can do on the internet.'

Libby rang off and remembered where she'd heard about holding companies before. Funnily enough, it had been during the very case Ian had mentioned last night, that of Cranston Morris and the Green Man. That had been Frensham Holdings, a company with three divisions – supplies, media and marketing. Perhaps Stapleton Holdings was the same, with one division being land grabs.

She cleared up her kitchen and collected her cape and basket. Time to go to see how things were doing at the Hop Pocket, she decided.

As she walked down the high street, Bob the butcher darted out of his shop.

'Did you enjoy your Barnsley chops?' He beamed at her.

'Yes, thank you,' said Libby, rather startled. 'And did you get the message about the show at The Alexandria?'

'Oh, yes.' Bob folded his arms and leant back against the wall. 'But what we all want to know is what about the panto?'

'Panto?' Libby stared.

'Yes – you know, it's behind you and all that.' Bob leered at her. 'No getting out of it this year, young lady.'

'Really?' said Libby weakly.

'We want to go back to normal, please, and so do the audiences. And it's May already.'

'You're the second person to say that to me,' said Libby. 'You really want me back, then?'

'Come off it, Lib. It was you who decided you needed a break, not us.'

Libby forbore to remind him that they'd all agreed with her.

'All right,' she said. 'Which one shall we do?'

'Oh, let's go back to dear old Cinders. Tom enjoys being one of the Uglies.'

Tom was the Oast Theatre's resident pantomime Dame, as Bob and his friend Baz were the perennial comedy double act.

'We need another Ugly,' said Libby. 'I shall think about it.'

'Your Ben would make a great Ugly.' Bob winked. 'There, think on that.'

Libby resumed her way along the high street, crossed over and turned down Cuckoo Lane, which she found was partially blocked by a large white van. Ben appeared from its depths, carrying a sizeable box.

'Have you come to help?' he called. 'Simon's upstairs – go and ask.'

'I'll follow you,' said Libby, realising that she could well be in the way.

Once inside, the realisation was confirmed. The small bar area was packed with boxes and furniture.

'I'll leave you to it,' she said. 'I'll be in the way.'

Ben rested his box on an upturned chair. 'You could be right,' he said. 'And Simon's offered to take us to dinner tonight at the caff. Could you go over and ask Harry if he can fit us in? It is Friday, after all.'

'OK. Do you want anything sent over? Beer?'

'We're in a pub, Lib,' said Ben with a grin. 'We have supplies.'

Libby wandered back to the high street feeling useless. Harry saw her from the window of the Pink Geranium and waved.

'You having another personal crisis, petal?' he asked, opening the door.

Libby raised her eyebrows. 'No! Well . . . yes.'

Harry ushered her inside and pushed her into the sofa placed in the left-hand window. 'Wine?' he said, and without waiting for a reply disappeared to fetch a bottle.

'Tell all,' he said, sitting down beside her and opening the bottle. 'Been warned off investigating, have we?'

Libby shrugged out of her cape and sighed. 'You could say that. Oh – and can you fit Simon, Ben and me in tonight? Simon's treat.'

'Just.' Harry grinned at her. 'Come on – tell Uncle Harry.'

Harry had been the willing recipient of Libby's innermost thoughts and woes for years, and had frequently been able to offer advice and even sympathy.

'OK, petal,' he said, when she had rambled her way to a halt. 'Lots of stuff to get your teeth into there, but nothing that really concerns you – is that the problem?'

'S'pose so.' Libby made a face.

'You talked to Ian's innamorato, so tick that one off.' Harry held up one finger. 'You told your hairdresser mate what to do, and even put Ian onto it, so tick that one off.' Two fingers. 'The caravan-park business is a public argument, so really nothing to do with you – tick.' Three fingers. 'What's left? The body of the homeless man – also nothing to do with you.' He held up four fingers. 'So don't you think, for once, you could *really* leave it all alone?'

Chapter Eleven

Libby stared at her glass.

'There's plenty to interest you right here,' said Harry. 'Summer production at the theatre, show at The Alexandria, the Hop Pocket—'

'That's nothing to do with me,' said Libby sharply.

'Your choice, don't forget,' Harry reminded her, as he had done before.

Libby sighed. 'I know. And Bob accosted me just now. Apparently, they want me to go back to panto.'

'Who's they?' asked Harry. 'And you always intended to, didn't you?'

'The Oast Company,' said Libby, picking up her glass. 'And, yes, I suppose so. Bob wants to do *Cinders* again.'

'Well, you haven't done it for a few years. Will you rewrite the script?'

'I expect so.' Libby brightened. 'Bring it up to date.'

'Not too up to date,' said Harry with a grin. 'Your audiences like traditional.'

'I know. And I'd better put the word out, too, or I won't have a cast. I shall need another Ugly.'

'Ugly? Oh – as in Sister.' Harry patted her hand and took a hearty swig from his wine. 'There, see? Lots to do.'

Libby didn't reply. Instead, she stared at the table in front of her in a slightly unfocused way.

'What?' Harry dug her in the ribs. 'Snap out of it.'

Libby slowly turned her head. 'I was just thinking,' she said.

'Yes, I could tell.' Harry shook his head. 'Never bodes well.'

'No, listen.' Libby sat up straight. 'How did Michelle know it was her stalker who'd broken into her house?'

'Eh?' Harry frowned at her. 'What are you talking about now?'

'Michelle said her stalker – Neil – had been in her house. How did she know? It could have been a straightforward burglary.'

'Perhaps he left a little message somewhere. Bathroom mirror? That's what they do on the telly. A warning message written in lipstick.'

'She didn't say anything about that.' Libby picked up her wine glass. 'I wonder if she's been making too much of this all along?'

'But you saw him, didn't you?' Harry was now looking confused.

'Yes, but that doesn't prove anything.' Libby shook her head. 'I could have just got suckered in. You know, with my famous nosiness. Fran said I keep trying to make things fit.'

'Um . . .' said Harry warily.

'Oh, it's all right.' Libby gave him a tired smile. 'I know what I'm like, and you're absolutely right, there's nothing for me to look into. Oh, I'm sure Neil the stalker did do the things Michelle said he did, but I'm really not sure about this break-in. And Michelle has been known to be a bit of a drama queen.'

Harry's eyebrows shot up and Libby giggled. 'I know – like me. Well, I shall try to confine my theatrics to the theatre in future.' She drained her glass.

'Pardon me for saying, but that'll be the day,' said Harry. 'Top up?'

Libby walked home trying to remember what she did on a day-to-day basis before she got involved in murder investigations. True, there were gaps between them, but they were usually filled with catching up on everything that had been neglected during said investigation. An involuntary laugh escaped her. How many times had she done this? Particularly over the last couple of years. When her nearest and dearest, or simply circumstances, had caused her to stop and think about her life. She thought about the theatre. Yes, that took a lot of time and effort, but it wasn't a proper job. She also handled the letting of the holiday properties belonging to Ben's family – the Hoppers' Huts and Steeple Farm – but that wasn't a proper job, either. The only things she was actually paid for were the paintings Guy sold through his gallery and shop, and they barely brought in enough to keep Sidney in cat food. But, she thought, as she turned the corner by the vicarage into Allhallow's Lane, when would she find the time to do anything else?

'Libby!'

A beaming face appeared at the vicarage gate.

'Beth!' Libby stopped and beamed back. Steeple Martin's vicar stepped through her gate between the tall beech hedges, tawny hair escaping its plait, as usual. 'How are you?'

'Fine, thank you. How are *you*? Haven't seen you for ages.'

'I've told you, you and John should come to the pub on a Wednesday.'

'We forget,' said Beth. 'You know, busy, busy. I hear Ben's almost ready to open his pub – will you be going there instead?'

'No – we'll still be going to the Coach. Besides, Ben's pub is theoretically only an ale house, and shouldn't be selling wine.'

'Shouldn't?'

Libby grinned. 'But there will be a limited selection available.'

'Oh, good. So what have you been doing? Solved any good murders lately?'

Libby made a face. 'No. I'm going to rewrite the script for *Cinderella* instead.'

Beth peered at her shrewdly. 'Problem?'

'Course not!' said Libby brightly.

Beth continued to look at her from narrowed eyes. 'Hmm,' she said. 'Well, it'll be nice to have you back at the helm for panto, anyway, if that's what the *Cinderella*'s for.'

'Oh, yes,' said Libby. 'And we're doing another End of the Pier

Show for the Alexandria in Nethergate, so I shall be far too busy for murders.'

'Never stopped you before,' said Beth. 'Well, must get on.' She made a face. 'I've got a funeral visit to do.'

'Oh, dear. Anyone I know?'

'Shirley Wright? Lives – or lived – in Lendle Lane.'

Libby shook her head. 'No. Natural causes I hope?'

Beth laughed. 'Oh, yes. Nothing for you there.'

Libby continued on to Number 17, where she was welcomed by a starving Sidney.

'No,' she told him, 'it is not supper time. Go away.'

She went through to the kitchen and switched on the kettle, wondering if it was too soon for tea on top of half a bottle of red wine. Wandering back to hang up her cape, she noticed the red light of the answerphone winking at her.

'Libby, it's Michelle. Can you ring me back when you've got a moment?'

Libby raised her eyebrows, picked up the phone and took it back into the kitchen with her.

'Michelle? It's Libby. You called me?'

Libby could hear the noise of the salon behind Michelle's distracted 'Oh, Libby!', then the muffled sound of her apology to her client. Then the background noise was shut off.

'Libby, listen. I think I made a mistake.' Michelle's voice came in a rush.

'It wasn't Neil who broke into your flat?' Libby poured boiling water into her mug.

'Oh, you know! Did they tell you?'

'Nobody's told me anything,' said Libby. 'It was an educated guess.'

'Oh.' Michelle deflated. 'How – why did you think that?'

'You didn't say anything about a message being left, or anything like that,' said Libby. 'No message on the bathroom mirror in lipstick?'

Michelle gave a shaky giggle. 'No, nothing. I – I just sort of assumed. And nothing was missing . . .'

'So why did you call me?'

'I – er . . .' Michelle paused. 'I wanted to apologise. Especially to the inspector.'

'Ah.' If truth be told, so did she.

'I feel so silly.' Michelle sighed.

'So who told you it wasn't Neil?' Libby stirred milk into her tea and carried the mug into the sitting room.

'One of the crime-scene people. She didn't exactly say it wasn't – I suppose she couldn't – but she said there were no typical signs. She looked at me as though I was a moron.'

'And Ian was the one who told them they had to look into it.' Libby was conscious of a sinking feeling somewhere in her abdomen. 'And I asked him to do it. No wonder he gets fed up with me.'

'It's my fault for over-reacting,' said Michelle. 'I'm sorry, Libby.'

Libby sat staring at the empty grate, hands wrapped round her mug. Michelle's phone call had just about put the tin lid on it, she thought. That's what comes of meddling. Now she felt both guilty and silly and horribly embarrassed into the bargain.

'I'm not sure I can face going out for dinner,' said Libby when Ben arrived home later that afternoon.

'What?' He stopped dead in the sitting-room doorway.

Libby hadn't thought it through. 'I – er . . .' she said.

Ben let out a breath and sat down heavily by the table in the window.

'OK,' he said. 'What's all this in aid of? What's happened now?'

'Um . . .' said Libby.

'Yes? Who's had a go at you?' Ben's eyes narrowed.

'No one, actually,' said Libby. 'Well, me, I suppose.'

'You've had a go at yourself?' Ben's eyebrows rose.

Libby made an exasperated noise and shifted in her seat. 'I just realised. After Michelle rang.'

89

Ben looked at his watch. 'The sun's probably over the yard arm by now. Let's have a drink and you can tell me all about it from the beginning.'

So Ben got the drinks and Libby told him all about it.

'A tale of woe, in fact,' said Ben when she'd finished. 'But really, love, it isn't that bad. And you didn't meddle in Michelle's problems – she asked you to help. Which you did. If it's anybody's fault, it's her own. As for the rest, Ian himself asked you to look into the homeless man, and finding out who he is – or was – is his problem, and the caravan park business? Well, that's of concern to everyone, particularly those who live in Nethergate. So why are you suddenly worrying about it?'

'I should have a job,' muttered Libby into her glass.

'Oh, not that again!' Ben stood up, hauled Libby to her feet and kissed her. 'We've all told you before – you have several jobs. You just don't get paid for them. Now, start thinking about that *Cinders* script and what you're going to put in the End of the Pier Show.'

Libby watched him leave the room and heard his hurrying footsteps on the stairs. He was right, of course he was. She was being pathetic. She sighed, sat down again and turned on the television for the local news.

Simon was already in the Pink Geranium by the time Ben and Libby arrived, a glass of beer in front of him, and Libby's son Adam, wearing his long Victorian apron, standing attentively by his side.

'Adam lives in the flat upstairs,' Libby explained as she and Ben sat down, 'and works here part time. Somebody did say he was becoming quite handy in the kitchen.' She beamed at her son, who looked embarrassed.

'I actually work with a garden designer,' he said quickly, and Simon looked interested.

'But let's not get into that right now,' said Ben. 'Can we have a drink, please, Ad?'

'Bottle of red and a beer?' replied Adam with a grin. 'Coming up.'

'Are you all moved in, now?' Libby asked, when Adam had gone.

'Yes, at least everything's in – it just isn't sorted out yet. Just got to take the van back tomorrow.' Simon leaned back as far as his chair allowed. 'Hard work, moving!'

'Is all the paperwork finished?' Libby asked.

Ben nodded. 'Simon didn't actually need a personal licence, as I hold one as the owner, and the Pocket has a premises licence, but he is renewing his. Always better to cover all eventualities.'

'So that's it, then,' said Libby. 'You can open when you want?'

'We think we're going to have what they call these days a "Soft Opening" next week,' said Simon, 'and then a big one in a couple of weeks.' He grinned at Libby. 'Actually, we did think of combining it with the Rogue Days.'

'But you said they'd stopped,' said Libby. 'And that's at Pucklefield, not here.'

'Ah, but you said wouldn't it be good to have something like that here,' said Ben. 'So Simon gave a couple of old mates a ring.'

'And, believe it or not, it *is* still going on,' said Simon. 'The Puckle Inn is now a freehouse and the new owner decided to revive the tradition a couple of years ago. I don't know why I hadn't heard.'

'So we thought we'd send you off to do a bit of research. We might be able to persuade some of the people who join in to come over and help us,' said Ben as Adam arrived with their drinks. 'What do you think?'

Chapter Twelve

Libby stared at her best beloved.

'You're *encouraging* me to go ferreting?'

Ben laughed. 'It's for our benefit. And we aren't asking you to look into murders – just the tradition of Rogation Days.'

'What about the Old Rogue and his dog?' asked Libby, taking a restorative gulp of red wine.

'They're part of the tradition,' said Simon. 'We'd have to nominate someone, of course.'

'I know!' said Libby. 'Your mate with the lovely Labrador, Ben!'

'Dan Henderson.' Ben nodded. 'I mentioned him to Simon, as he's likely to become one of the regulars. And he's a big bloke.'

'And his wife Moira is into a lot of folk stuff,' said Libby. 'I bet she'd be all for it.'

'That is one aspect that we might have to change,' warned Simon. 'The tradition is that it's basically all men. Wouldn't go down well these days.'

'There are a lot of women's Morris sides these days – and mixed sides. Let me see what I can ferret out,' said Libby. 'When can I go?'

Both men burst out laughing.

'What's the joke?' Harry appeared with menus, eyebrows raised. 'I mean, I know the old trout's amusing, but . . .'

Ben explained, and meals were ordered. 'I'll join you later,' said Harry. 'Enjoy.'

Later, when Harry had joined them with a new bottle of red

wine, Libby told him what had been the subject of the unseemly mirth.

'So you're going to be allowed to go nosing around?' he said. 'See? I told you not to worry.'

'Actually, I've been thinking,' said Libby.

'And eating at the same time? There's clever,' said Harry, and ducked as Libby aimed a slap at him.

'Seriously – Simon, would you have time to come with me to Pucklefield?' asked Libby. 'It might break the ice better.'

'I was going to suggest it,' said Ben. 'What about it, Simon?'

'Can we make it Monday?' asked Simon. 'I'd love to come with you, Libby. I haven't been over there since my father died.'

'Lovely.' Libby sighed with satisfaction. 'And if we go at lunch-time, we can maybe have a sandwich in the pub?'

On Saturday morning, Libby decided to make another trip to a supermarket in Canterbury, although choosing a different one this time. It always made her feel guilty for abandoning, however temporarily, the Steeple Martin shops, but there were some things that simply couldn't be bought there.

Inevitably, the supermarket in question had changed its layout, and while Libby was navigating up and down the aisles peering hopelessly at the shelves, she heard her name called.

'Trixie!' Libby beamed at the woman in front of her.

'I thought it was you.' The woman called Trixie made a face. 'Would have been terribly embarrassing if it wasn't. How are you? I hear great things about your theatre in – where is it? One of the Steeples?'

'Steeple Martin,' agreed Libby. 'And what about the dear old Playhouse? Are you still a member of the company?'

The Playhouse was the theatre in Libby's former home town, the other side of Canterbury, and where, in fact, she'd first met Peter and Harry.

'Oh, yes,' sighed Trixie. 'One of the diehards, that's me.'

'And still,' said Libby, suddenly remembering, 'doing all the May Day stuff with the Green Man and everything?'

'Yes, I still dance.' Trixie put her head on one side. 'Why do you ask?'

Libby cleared her throat and looked sideways at the aubergines. 'I just wondered . . .'

Trixie laughed. 'Not thinking of getting into it yourself, are you?'

'Actually . . .' said Libby.

'Yes?'

'Have you ever heard of the Rogue Days at Pucklefield?'

Trixie stared. 'Of course! We'll be over there in a couple of weeks' time.'

Libby found herself vaguely surprised. 'So it's quite well known, then?'

'In our circles, yes,' said Trixie. 'They dance at the Rochester May Day celebrations, and ours. And in turn we go to them. And we all dance at Steeple Mount on the Solstice.'

'No problems with women, then?'

'Not these days. The Pucklefield lot did hang on to the men-only rule longer than most of us, but they had to give in when the ladies' Morris sides started to outweigh the men.' Trixie narrowed her eyes at Libby. 'I know you were always nosy, Libby, but what do you want to know for?' Then she smiled knowingly. 'Is it for one of these murders you keep getting involved in?' She laughed. 'Good job you didn't do that when you were still with us at the Playhouse!'

Libby sighed. 'I don't actually cause them, you know.'

Trixie chuckled. 'Shame! I could think of a couple – anyway. Tell me. Is it for a murder?'

'No, simply that we're re-opening an old pub in my village, and we thought we'd like to celebrate the Rogation Days there. A friend's taking me over to Pucklefield on Monday.'

'Oh, great! If it doesn't clash, our side could come and dance, if you'd like us to.' Trixie looked eager.

'Give me your phone number, then, Trix, and I'll give you a ring when we've got it sorted.'

Libby continued down the vegetable aisle feeling pleased with herself, Trixie's number stored safely in her phone. Whatever else happened, the Hop Pocket's Rogue Days celebration looked as though it might go ahead, and, just to add to her sense of wellbeing, tonight, it appeared from a text from Ben, they'd been invited to Nethergate for dinner with Fran and Guy, so she didn't even have to cook. Result.

Inevitably, over dinner – a delicious Thai yellow curry – conversation turned to recent events. In particular, the proposed extension to Island View caravan site.

'Guy's got involved now,' said Fran, topping up her wine glass.

'Involved? How?' Libby retrieved the bottle from Fran.

Guy looked uncharacteristically bashful. 'Oh – I – er – offered my services.'

'What?'

'Services?'

Libby and Ben spoke together.

'I just thought it might help if I added my name.' Guy looked down at his plate.

'Of course! You're properly famous!' said Libby.

'Not really,' protested Guy.

'But you're well known in artistic circles,' said Fran.

'The only worry I've got,' said Guy, 'is that if these people push the affordable housing banner, they'll say I'm being nimbyish.'

'But they're going for the permanent park homes – they aren't affordable,' said Libby.

'Oh, I know,' said Guy. 'Believe me, now I've started, I can't seem to keep away from it. I've been looking into every aspect.'

'What about the company who own it now? Stapleton Holdings? Colin says it might not be a proper holding company, but just a title.'

95

'As far as I can see, that's just what it is,' said Guy. 'But I'll let you know as soon as I know more. And –' he made a face, 'I can't seem to get anyone to talk about the removal of the homeless people.'

'The police know about that now,' said Fran, 'or at least Ian does.'

'Which means that people like Mavis will be even more afraid of retaliation,' said Libby.

'What could the company do, though?' asked Fran. 'If they tried to do something to the building, or to The Sloop, there would be one heck of an investigation.'

'Let's hope it doesn't come to that,' said Guy. 'I'm in touch with the site in Devon that went to the High Court, so we've got a template to work from.'

After dinner, they decided to go to The Sloop for a drink and see if the regulars there were talking about the development, but when Guy asked the barman diffidently what the feeling was, he got a surprise.

'All talking about that chap they found over at Shott, they are,' said the barman. Seems he were one of the homeless they turned out of the old vans.'

Four faces stared at him.

'People knew him, then?' asked Libby eventually.

'Not to say *knew*,' equivocated the barman. 'We all knew they was up there.' He looked a trifle embarrassed. 'Mavis and my boss and me, we used to take leftovers up there, see.'

'Yes, Mavis told us,' said Libby, smiling at him. 'It was kind of you.'

The barman shrugged. 'Anyway, stands to reason he was one o' them, don't it?'

'So what are people saying?' asked Ben. 'Shocked, I suppose?'

'A lot of feeling against them developers,' said the barman.

'I should have been aware of this,' said Guy.

The barman raised an eyebrow.

'He's involved with the people trying to get it stopped,' said Fran.

'Ah.' The barman nodded. 'Trouble is, folk don't want to stand up and be counted, see? Scared of what might happen.'

'Mavis said you'd been threatened,' said Libby.

The barman looked quickly over his shoulder and leant forward. 'Don't do to speak too loud,' he said.

'So what do people think happened to the man they found over at Shott?' asked Fran.

The barman shrugged again. 'Had a bit of a go at one o' the heavies, maybe?'

'And the heavy went too far?' suggested Ben.

'Could be.' The barman gave the counter a swift wipe with a tea towel. 'Nasty busines. Don't want that sort o' thing in Nethergate. Always been a quiet place.' He moved down the bar to serve another customer.

The four friends went over to a table near a window.

'That could be what happened, you know,' said Libby. The other three nodded.

'It does seem most likely,' agreed Fran.

'Now the police know about the homeless being chucked out, do you think that's the line they're working on?' Libby asked.

'Makes sense,' said Guy. 'All the more reason to get the whole project stopped.'

'If we could prove that the developer – or his heavies – had murdered the body –' Libby paused at the sight of three amused faces looking at her. 'Well, you know what I mean, if we could prove that, it would definitely stop the project, wouldn't it?'

'It would, but it's not your job,' said Ben. 'Leave it to the police.'

'I agree,' said Fran. 'Just leave it alone.'

Libby huffed in frustration.

Libby and Ben had opted to stay overnight with Fran and Guy, and left to drive back to Steeple Martin after breakfast.

'Do you remember Gemma Baverstock and the Cranston Morris?' Libby asked suddenly.

'Not something you forget easily,' said Ben, frowning at the road ahead.

They passed the sign announcing 'You are leaving Nethergate, Seaside Heritage Town, twinned with Bayeau St Pierre'.

'I don't know why I didn't think of it,' said Libby. 'When Trixie was talking about her side yesterday, I should have.'

Ben flicked her a sideways glance. 'And?'

'Well, the Rogue people are more-or-less Morris.'

'So?' Ben asked after a pause.

'So we can have a Rogation celebration at the Hop Pocket and ask all the local Morris sides to come and dance. We could even have a parade through the village.' Libby turned excitedly towards Ben. 'And perhaps we could get up a Mummers' play, as well!'

Ben looked horrified. 'Libby! All I want is a nice quiet village pub!'

Libby glared at him. 'You were the one who suggested I go ferreting at Pucklefield – *and* you agreed Dan Henderson would make a good Old Rogue.'

'Yes, but I didn't want a three-ring circus.' Ben sighed. 'I should never have suggested it, should I?'

Chapter Thirteen

On Monday morning, Libby wandered slowly through the village towards the Hop Pocket on her way to meet Simon, who had volunteered to drive to Pucklefield. The lilac tree in the vicarage garden scented the air as she turned the corner into the high street and on the other side of the road she could see roses in the garden of Ivy Cottage. She waved cheerily to Bob standing in the open doorway of his shop.

'I've started rewriting *Cinders!*' she called as she paused before crossing the road.

Bob gave her a thumbs-up sign and beamed.

That was better, she thought. I'm no longer beating myself up, and I've got a project. Despite Ben's misgivings about turning Rogue Days into a fully fledged festival, the idea of a parade really appealed. And at Christmas, she thought, a Mummers' play could be a vehicle for publicising the pantomime.

Ben greeted her from his vantage point on a ladder outside the Hop Pocket as she turned into Cuckoo Lane. 'You're looking cheerful.'

'I'm feeling cheerful.' Libby stopped at the foot of the ladder and looked up at him. 'What are you doing up there?'

'Fixing the pub sign.' He moved sideways. 'There, see?'

Libby nodded approval at the sign. 'Looks like a proper pub now.'

Simon appeared at her elbow. 'Ready to go?'

'When you are,' said Libby. 'I'm looking forward to it.'

'I'll just go and fetch the car.' Simon went off down the un-named lane that led behind the Pocket and along the back of the old Garden Hotel and the newly restored Bat and Trap pitch.

Ben descended the ladder and kissed Libby's cheek. 'Don't go committing us to too much,' he said.

'I'll try not to.' Libby grinned at him.

'So you obviously know a bit about Morris and all the old traditions?' said Simon, as he drove them towards Pucklefield.

'Ben didn't tell you, then?' Libby turned to look at him.

'Not really. He was willing to listen to me talking about Rogue Days and the traditions in Pucklefield, but he didn't actually contribute much.'

'No, well – he doesn't always approve of me getting mixed up in murder cases.'

'And I gather you've done it more than once? I vaguely knew about the one when Tim took you over to Dungate.'

'Yes, The Dolphin. Nice pub.'

'What other murders have there been, then?' Simon sent her an amused glance. 'One that involved Morris, obviously.'

Libby sighed. 'Yes. Someone was stabbed inside the Green Man.'

'The Green Man? Where's that?'

'No – it's not a pub, it's a thing. A great big wire cage covered in greenery with a man inside it. Comes out on May Day.'

'Oh, yes! I've seen them, but we didn't have them at Pucklefield. But how awful! Did you solve it?'

'Not exactly. The police did, but I was in at the end.' Libby gave a delicate shudder.

'Well, what were the other traditions they had, leaving aside the Green Man?' asked Simon.

'The Oak King and the Holly King,' said Libby. 'And they fought over the Goddess.'

'Ah, so they incorporated the Goddess cult.' Simon nodded. 'Puckle Morris didn't, but they had a Hop Princess. Pucklefield's surrounded by hop gardens. I don't know whether they do now. But part of the Rogue Days celebrations was the Blessing of the Bines.'

'And that was part of the old celebrations, too? When they used to beat the bounds?'

'Yes. As I said before, it became much sanitised.'

'Except that you thought the old stuff still went on in secret,' said Libby.

'Not me, but people did.' Simon turned left off the road to Itching.

'Don't we go to Shott?' said Libby, surprised. 'I thought that was where Rogation House was?'

'It's between Shott and Pucklefield, and Pucklefield is down here.' Simon waved a hand towards what looked like an orchard. 'Apple country round here, as well as hops. Puckle Morris used to do the wassailing, too.'

'And Plough Monday?' asked Libby. 'Busy boys, then.'

'Oh, yes – but it was fun. I don't know if they still do them all.'

'They do Rochester Sweeps – my friend told me,' said Libby, mentioning the famous Kent May Day festival.

'I must say, I always enjoyed our Rogue Days.' Simon looked thoughtful. 'I wouldn't mind helping to set up a Steeple Martin side.' He shot Libby another look. 'You'd like to, wouldn't you?'

'Mmm.' Libby looked out of her window. 'I've never danced. Would you have a mixed side?'

'Oh, I think so.' Libby turned and saw that he was smiling. 'Don't you?'

Before them the countryside was opening and flattening out, and, just ahead, a church spire pointed up from a cluster of houses.

'Pucklefield,' announced Simon.

'Oh, it's lovely!' Libby leant forward. 'And is that the sea over there?'

'Yes – we've cut across, almost parallel with the Wantsum.'

The Wantsum was the old channel that had once cut off the Isle of Thanet from the rest of Kent.

Within seconds, Simon was guiding the car into the small car park behind the white-painted Puckle Inn.

Libby got out and stared around. 'Nice,' she said.

'I liked it, once upon a time,' said Simon. 'Very quiet, of course. Not as busy as Steeple Martin. Do you want to go straight in, or have a look round the village first?'

'Oh, look round, if that's all right with you.' Libby sighed with pleasure. 'It's like a picture-book village.'

'And that's the problem,' said Simon, leading the way into what appeared to be the main village street. 'The residents like it like that and don't want anything as common as an eight-till-late like yours messing up their village. They veto anything that looks as though it might attract real people.' He grinned at her. 'That's why the brewery sold it. Why I left, as a matter of fact.'

'Pity.' Libby shook her head. 'What the hell did they make of the Morris and Rogue Days? That's a bit messy, if you like!'

'Most of them went away for the week,' said Simon. 'I expect they still do.'

It took them all of ten minutes to cover the whole village, and Simon led them back to the Puckle Inn.

'The real locals, of course, loved it,' Simon went on, 'but a lot of them have been priced out now. None of their kids could afford to live here – and why would they want to, to be fair? No shops, no facilities, no school. That closed years ago.'

'No post office or bank, either,' said Libby, with a nod, 'so the elderly have no banking or pension facilities.'

'Exactly.' Simon opened the door into the pub. 'Such a terrible shame.'

A large man with a very red face turned from the bar.

'Si!' he bellowed, and came forward to enfold Simon in a hug. 'This the new missus?'

Libby laughed and Simon looked embarrassed.

'No,' he said, 'this is Libby – my boss. Libby, this is Reg Fisher.'

Libby held out her hand, which was promptly crushed in an

enormous paw. 'I'm not really his boss,' she said. 'Simon is going to manage a pub owned by my partner.'

Reg beamed at her. 'Said something like that. And going to start the old Rogue Days over there, he said?'

'That's why we're here,' said Simon. 'Pint, Reg? Libby – what can I get you?'

'Half of lager, please.' Libby turned back to Reg. 'You still live round here, then?'

'Family farm,' said Reg with a shrug. 'Tell you the truth –' he lowered his voice – 'we don't drink here most of the time. The old regulars, I mean.'

'Not surprised,' said Simon, staring at a price list behind the bar. 'Is there anyone serving?'

A small man with a floral waistcoat stretched across an ample frontage appeared at the end of the bar, rubbing his hands and oozing gentility.

'Ah! You would be Mr Spencer and – ah – Mrs Spencer?' he said, gliding to a halt before them.

'Mrs Sarjeant,' corrected Libby, the smile vanishing from her face.

'My boss,' said Simon again.

'Ah.' Mine host looked from one to the other as though not knowing who to address his blandishments to first. 'Charles Bertram,' he announced holding out a well-manicured hand.

Simon took it briefly. Libby didn't.

'Very nice of you to see us, Mr Bertram,' Simon said. 'Could we order a drink?'

'Oh – ah – yes.' Bertram looked flustered. 'Maria! Service, please!'

A young woman in an apron stuck her head through a doorway. 'Yessir!' she yelped.

'So, Mr – ah – Spencer.' Bertram ushered the little party to one of the many empty tables. 'I don't know how much I can help you. I have very little to do with the – ah – *celebrations*.'

'But I thought it was you who revived them when you bought the freehold from the brewery?' said Libby.

Reg rumbled a laugh beside her. 'Pressure group,' he said. 'Mr Bertram was keen to attract the old regulars – so we suggested it.' He looked up at Bertram from under his bushy eyebrows, a sly grin stretching his face.

Simon and Libby understood at once.

'So we should be talking to you, Reg?' With something like relief, Simon turned away from Bertram, who, with equal relief, nodded and retreated. Maria took his place with a tray.

'Thanks, girl,' said Reg, distributing glasses. 'Have one with us?'

Maria looked nervously over her shoulder. 'Not now, Mr Fisher, ta.' She scurried off from whence she had come.

'Bloody hell!' said Libby. 'Where did he come from?'

Reg emitted a bellow of laughter. 'You said it, girl! Not exactly a natural, is he?' He lowered his voice. 'Would you believe a gents' club in London?'

'No!' said Simon and Libby together.

'He was a steward?' said Libby.

'Not *a* steward, girl. *The* steward, the boss. Thought he'd come to a nice quiet village for his retirement.'

'Well, to be fair, it is a nice quiet village, Reg,' said Simon.

'Too quiet,' said Reg, wrinkling his nose.

'That's what I was telling Libby,' said Simon.

'Well, we get our way on Rogue Days,' said Reg, 'and even Boxing Day now.'

'How come?' asked Libby.

'He heard we were going round other villages dancing and doing the mummers' play, and asked us very nicely if we could do it here.' Reg beamed. 'So, o' course we said yes! Free beer at the end of the evening – great stuff.'

'So tell me what you do for Rogue Days,' said Libby. 'Simon's told me about the history, but what do you actually do now?'

'Well, now.' Reg settled his big elbows on the table. 'The dancers all line up at a word from the Squire—'

'He's the leader of the Morris side,' put in Libby.

Reg looked at her with approval. 'He is. I am, actually. And then after we've lined up, Old Rogue comes out of the pub with the Tolley Hound.'

'And who's the Rogue these days?' asked Simon.

'Old Jimmy Bottomley,' said Reg. 'Remember him?'

'Too old to dance, eh?' grinned Simon.

'And the dog?' asked Libby.

'Ah, now, Tolley's like our version of the Hobby,' said Reg.

'Oh! That's a better idea than having a real dog,' said Libby, remembering the wooden clacking heads of various Hobby Horses throughout the country – usually held above an all-enveloping costume and employed mainly in harassing the audience and chasing young women. 'And then what happens?'

'Well, we has a little dance,' continued Reg, 'then the Old Rogue leads us through the village. We stop at the church, even though it's not used any more, but sometimes one of the vicars from roundabout will come over and bless us. After that we go round the outside of the village, as far as we can, and beat the bounds. Then back here for a bit more dancing.'

'And do you go anywhere else to dance?'

'Morris side do, but not Old Rogue,' said Reg.

'You used to dance at a couple of the farms,' said Simon. 'And the big house.'

Reg let out a gusty sigh. 'Farms have been sold. And big house is a bit too far for a lot of 'em to walk – or dance. Shame, as that's where Old Rogue came from.'

'Is that Rogation House?' Libby was suddenly alert.

Reg beamed at her again. 'That's it, girl! You know it?'

'We know *of* it,' said Libby cautiously.

Reg nodded. 'Course it's got famous now. Old Stapleton's place.'

Chapter Fourteen

'*Stapleton?*' Libby's voice came out as a squeak, and Reg and Simon looked startled.

'That's him,' said Reg, frowning. 'You know him, then?'

'Not exactly.' Libby sighed, leant back in her seat and took a healthy swig of her lager. 'We know his – er – company.'

Simon was looking puzzled. 'We do?'

'No – not you, Simon. I meant Fran and me.' Libby turned to Reg. 'Stapleton Holdings – is that him?'

'That's right. Got a couple of caravan sites they have.'

'Caravan sites!' said Simon, with an air of enlightenment. 'The one you've been talking about?'

'Island View, yes,' said Libby grimly. 'Well! Who would have believed it?'

Reg was looking confused. 'Believed what?'

'Let me buy another drink and I'll explain,' said Libby, and got up to look for Maria.

When they were settled with fresh drinks, albeit a strictly non-alcoholic lemonade for Simon, Libby told them both the whole story of Island View.

'Up to his old tricks, then,' said Reg, nodding wisely.

'Old tricks?' repeated Simon.

'Bit of a reputation for sailing too close to the wind,' said Reg, tapping the side of his nose. 'Got staff up at the house who don't pay no tax, if you know what I mean.'

Libby's eyes were round. 'Not – illegals?'

Reg nodded again. 'So 'tis said. Poor souls.'

'Why doesn't he get caught? If he's a well-known businessman?'

'Knows which palms to grease, I expect,' said Simon. 'Why didn't I know anything about this? He was here when I was.'

'He used to keep himself to himself in those days,' said Reg. 'Till he could spread himself, as it were. Buys up everything he can lay his hands on now. And makes sure he can. Not that we've actually seen him for a year or so. Just feel his influence.'

'That sounds ominous,' said Libby.

'Tried it with me,' said Reg. 'But I wasn't having any.'

'What did he do?' asked Simon.

Reg shrugged. 'Dogs sent in with the sheep, fields damaged during the night – you know. Couldn't prove it was down to him, but everyone knew it was.'

They were silent for a moment, each contemplating the iniquities of Stapleton Esquire.

'So.' Reg sat up straight and fixed Libby with a beady eye. 'Reckon this body's something to do with Stapleton?'

'I wouldn't have thought so,' said Libby. 'You don't leave things like that on your own doorstep, do you?'

'It's not widely known that the OB is on Stapleton's land, though, is it?' said Simon. 'Maybe he thought it was a risk worth taking?'

'Wouldn't do something like that himself,' said Reg.

'No – he's got heavies,' said Libby. 'The people who turfed the homeless out of Island View.' She frowned. 'I could bear to know what happened to them, you know.'

'He wouldn't want 'em talking, would he?' agreed Reg. 'Heavies got 'em out, then bumped 'em off?'

'Wholesale murder? I doubt it,' said Libby. 'Where does he keep his illegal workers? More likely he shoved the homeless in there.'

'And just one of them died, so he was left outside the OB?' suggested Simon.

'Makes sense.' Reg leant as far back in his seat as possible and grimaced. 'Not made for real people, these chairs.'

'Will you tell your friend the policeman?' asked Simon.

'What?' Reg sat forward again.

Libby smiled. 'It was through a friend of ours we found out about the caravan park. We told another friend, who happens to be a policeman, about the removal of the homeless people from there, too.'

'He the one in charge of the body?' Reg squinted at her.

'Yes. Detective Chief Inspector Connell, Ian to his friends.'

'Who found the body?' asked Simon.

'I don't know!' said Libby, surprised.

'Wasn't a local,' said Reg, shaking his head. 'Walker perhaps? They get people going to see the OB – not that there's much to see. Just a hole in the ground.'

'Yes, some friends of mine went to see it with a club they belong to,' said Libby. 'They've taken all the electronics out, haven't they?'

'Yeah – and the bunks.' Reg nodded. 'Wouldn't have fancied camping out down there, meself.'

'No.' Simon pulled a face, then, leaning in and lowering his voice, said, 'Did you ever hear of it being used for the nasty goings-on with the Old Rogue, Reg?'

Reg's eyes swivelled sideways. 'We-ell,' he said.

'So you did,' said Libby. 'Just rumour, though?'

'Always plenty o' rumour,' said Reg, and buried his face in his pint. Simon and Libby looked at each other and raised their eyebrows.

'OK, so if we want to celebrate Rogue Days over at Steeple Martin,' said Libby, with a crashing change of subject, 'do we need Old Rogue?'

Reg and Simon regarded her with amusement.

'Loses the point a bit otherwise,' said Simon.

'Just be Morris sides dancing about the place,' said Reg. 'It needs to be blessing the crops – praying for a good harvest, sort of thing.'

'Like wassailing and the orchards,' said Simon.

'We could go to Ben's hop garden,' said Libby. 'So you think we need an Old Rogue as a sort of figurehead? And a Tolley Hound to keep people in line?'

'That's the idea,' said Reg, beam once more in place. 'And we'll come and dance with you.'

'That would be lovely,' said Libby. 'My friend Trixie said her side will come, too. That's White Horse Morris. You know them?'

'Aye. They dance over here with us.'

'Yes, she said they did.' Libby leant back satisfied. 'So which days do you dance? So we don't clash?'

'Tuesday, usually. You know Rogation Days are Monday, Tuesday and Wednesday before Ascension Day?'

'Yes. We thought we'd like to dance on Wednesday,' said Libby. 'I did, anyway. And our vicar will turn out, I'm sure.'

'Will you come and dance with us?' asked Reg. 'More than welcome.'

'Depends on how we get on recruiting members,' said Libby with a grin. 'So, any tips on dress? I don't fancy white shirt and trousers, somehow.'

Reg stood up and led them to a long, framed photograph on the back wall of the bar near the toilets. 'Likes to keep it as far out of sight as he can, old Bertram,' he said. 'This was taken a year or so before he bought the pub. See, this is us, Puckle Morris, in the middle. That's your mate's side, White Horse, that there's Cranston. All a bit different, see?'

'What about blackface?' asked Simon. 'Not used any more?'

'That was for disguise,' said Reg. 'Plough boys on Plough Monday, that sort of thing. Lots of sides used to do it, though. That's where you get "Guiser" from.'

'He's often like Old Rogue, isn't he?' asked Libby.

'That sort of thing,' said Reg. 'Unless there's a long history, most sides make up their own story these days. Get on to the Morris Ring or the federation. They'll put you right.'

Twenty minutes later, Reg saw them out of the Puckle Inn.

'Only does food weekends these days,' he said. 'No more "let's pop in the Puckle for a pint" at lunchtime.'

'Miserable,' said Simon.

'Oh, we tried.' Reg shrugged. 'Might just as well have stayed closed for all the good it's done us. Good luck with yours.'

'Well?' asked Simon as he drove them back towards Shott. 'Useful?'

'Oh, yes,' said Libby, gazing out at the May-dressed hedgerows. 'In more ways than one.'

'Ben'll kill me.' Simon looked sideways with a grin. 'We managed to raise more questions about your – what do we call them? – investigations?'

'You're learning,' said Libby.

'Other pub?' suggested Simon when he'd parked at the back of the Hop Pocket. 'We haven't had lunch.'

'I'll call Ben,' said Libby. 'We might have to ask for Tim's help in recruiting Morris men.'

'And women,' said Simon with a grin. 'Are you going to dance?'

'No, I'm not!' Libby was definite. 'There's already a faction in the village who object to me being involved in everything. I don't want to give them more ammunition.'

'Fair enough.' Simon took her elbow and hurried her across the high street.

'Ben?' said Libby into her phone. 'Simon and I are back – there was no food at the Puckle, so we're going to the pub – Yes – OK. See you there.' She tucked the phone away as Simon opened the door of the Coach and Horses. 'Will I ever get used to going to the Pocket?' she sighed.

'Eventually!' Simon grinned as he went up to the bar to attract Tim's attention.

When Ben joined them, they filled him in on the information Reg had given them. Tim leant over the counter and listened.

'Strikes me as a terrible waste,' he said when they explained about the Puckle and the bonhomous Mr Bertram. 'I know it's a quiet little village, but still.'

'Complete waste,' agreed Libby. 'Anyway, their dancers are going to come over and join in our Rogue Days celebration, so we've just got to recruit a side of our own.'

'I reckon we share them, Ben.' Tim cocked his head on one side. 'What d'you think?'

'Good idea. Shall we put up a couple of posters in here?' Ben paid for the drinks.

'And in the shops,' said Libby. 'They'll all take one.'

'What about this "soft" opening?' asked Tim. 'This week?'

'Friday?' Ben asked Simon. 'Will you be ready?'

Simon nodded. 'Will we advertise that with posters, too?'

'No.' Libby shook her head decisively. 'That would confuse everybody. Word of mouth will do for that. We just tell all our friends to spread the word.'

'And I'll bring a gang across from here,' said Tim.

'Really?' The other three looked at him in surprise.

'Why not? Mainly meals on a Friday. And Brendan hardly needs supervision.' Tim winked. 'Be nice to get away, to be honest with you.' He gave the counter a swipe with a tea towel. 'Now. Sandwiches? Soup?'

While they waited for their sandwiches, Libby called Guy and asked if he could do a recruitment poster for the Morris side featuring the new Hop Pocket logo.

'And the Coach logo,' said Ben.

Libby put her phone on speaker mode. 'Did you hear that, Guy?'

'Yes, but has the Coach got a logo?'

Ben reached for a menu while Simon looked up the website. 'No,' they said together.

'Right – I'll do a tart with a cart, then,' said Guy.

'A *what*?' said three voices.

111

Guy laughed. 'You'll see. I'll email it to all of you when it's done, OK?'

'So you found out about the owner of the caravan park, too, while you were at it,' said Ben after Libby had ended the call.

'Yes, but we weren't looking for it,' said Simon hastily.

'Well, no, I can see that it was rather a coincidence.' Ben smiled at Libby. 'And useful, no doubt.'

'Honestly, Ben, I was gobsmacked,' said Libby.

'She was,' agreed Simon.

Ben laughed. 'It's all right, Simon! You don't have to protect her. I can see it was a complete surprise. Are you going to tell Ian, Lib?'

'I expect he knows who the owner is – or whoever's SIO does. But it's interesting that this Stapleton already has a bad reputation, isn't it?'

'But not for murder,' said Ben. 'Or do you think he's added that to the list, now?'

'Reg thought he wouldn't get his hands that dirty,' said Simon.

'It's academic, anyway,' said Libby. 'We aren't involved.'

'I thought you wanted to get involved with the Island View protest?' said Ben. 'After all, Guy is.'

'If there's anything we can do, yes,' said Libby, 'but apart from signing petitions and perhaps going to meetings, I can't see that there will be.'

'But you'd want to find out about any illegal goings on,' said Ben. 'You always do.'

Libby shrugged. 'We'll see,' she said.

Chapter Fifteen

Guy's design for a poster arrived on Libby's phone before the sandwiches had been consumed, and she was able to show Tim.

'That's Guy's idea of a logo for you,' she said. 'He calls it the "Tart with a cart".'

The logo was a stylised silhouette of a crinolined lady climbing into a carriage. Tim was delighted.

'Would he do me one for the outside?' he asked. 'A proper pub sign?'

'You can get the people who did ours to do it,' said Ben.

Libby sent the poster to Tim's email address and he printed off half a dozen copies.

'You can drop them off on your way home,' Ben said to Libby. 'I'm going up to the hop garden. Better make sure it's all shipshape up there if we're going to bless it.'

On the way home, Libby gave copies of the poster to Bob the butcher, Nella in the farm shop and Ali in the eight-till-late, and, with sudden inspiration, rang the vicarage doorbell.

'Oh, you're in!' she said when Beth opened the door.

Beth laughed. 'If you didn't expect me to be, why did you ring the bell? Coming in?'

'I won't now – I'm a bit behind today,' said Libby. 'I would have put this through the letter box if you'd been out.' She handed over a poster.

'Wow!' said Beth. 'Rogation Days? Now, I've heard about

113

them doing this over at Pucklefield. Is that where you got the idea?'

'Sort of,' said Libby. 'They're coming over to dance with us, but we want our own side. And we wondered – if we're going to do it properly and bless the crops – would you be involved? Or would it be unseemly?'

'What a lovely word – unseemly!' Beth grinned. 'No, I'd love to. Shall I put this up somewhere? In the narthex, perhaps? Or no – I know! On the parish noticeboard at the bottom of Maltby Close.'

'Oh, yes, please, Beth! Great idea.'

'And I bet my John will want to join up.' Beth nodded slowly. 'He's always had a soft spot for a bit of Morris.'

Feeling encouraged, Libby trotted the rest of the way up Allhallow's Lane to Number 17, where she moved the big enamel kettle onto the Rayburn hotplate and rang Fran.

'So what do you want to do?' asked Fran when Libby had ground to a halt. 'Investigate this Stapleton person? I bet the police are doing that already. Once they knew about the removal of the homeless people, they're bound to have looked at the owner of the site.'

'It's the coincidence of the body being found on his land that's bothering,' said Libby.

'Well, the police will be looking at that, too,' said Fran. 'You just get on with organising your Rogue Day. I'm looking forward to that.'

'Are you?' Libby was surprised.

'Of course. And we'll come up for Ben's soft opening, too – is that this week?'

'Yes, we've just decided – Friday. And we're having a recruiting drive for Steeple Martin Morris, too. Well, you'll know about that. Guy's just done the poster for us.'

'Has he? I'm not in the shop today.'

'Yes – and they're going up all over the village. Even Beth's got one for the parish noticeboard.'

'So you've got plenty to do,' said Fran. 'And I'll see you on Friday. Let me know if there's anything I can do.'

By this time the big kettle was letting out irritated puffs of steam, so Libby put a teabag into a mug and poured on boiling water. She cast a guilty look at the big Brown Betty teapot, now sitting forlornly on a shelf next to the redundant tea caddy, and took her tea into the sitting room.

Ben arrived an hour later to find her asleep with Sidney draped across her chest.

'I'll make more tea, shall I?' he asked, having woken her, prince-like, with a kiss.

'Oh, yes, sorry.' Libby struggled to an upright position, seriously upsetting Sidney. 'How were the gardens?'

'Well, thank you,' called Ben from the kitchen. 'All bines duly twiddled.'

Hop bines, as the vines were known, began to grow and scramble up the supports in spring. They would then be manually 'twiddled' to the top of the strings, where they would continue to grow until harvested in September.

'We've already got some recruits for the Morris,' he said five minutes later, handing Libby a fresh mug. 'And one of the lads who works in the brewery knew all about the Pucklefield Old Rogue, too.'

'Really? How? Did he live there?'

'Yes – his mum and dad still do. Anyway, he's joining up.'

'So, all coming together, then,' said Libby.

'And without a murder in sight,' said Ben.

'Except for Homeless Rab,' said Libby.

Ben sighed.

On Wednesday, Libby held an End of the Pier meeting at the theatre, and used the occasion to drum up support for the Rogue Days and the new Morris side. Ben weighed in with an exhortation to attend the soft opening of the Hop Pocket on Friday, and Peter made a plea for more help in the backstage departments. The early summer production had been cast and was to be directed by one of the longstanding members of the company, so Libby felt that everything was as much in hand as it could be.

She, Ben and Peter locked up the theatre and walked down the drive to join Patti and Anne in the pub.

'And we must remember to start calling it by its name,' she said, 'to differentiate it from the Pocket.'

'That'll be difficult,' said Peter. 'Everyone's so used to it being simply "the pub".'

Libby was slightly surprised to find Ian and Edward ensconced at the big round table with Patti and Anne.

'I didn't realise you were rehearsing something,' said Ian, standing up. 'What is it this time?'

'End of the Pier Show again,' said Libby. 'I thought I'd mentioned it.'

Edward went to the bar with Ben, and Ian pulled out a chair for Libby next to Anne's wheelchair.

'A little piece of news for you,' he said.

'Oh?' Libby said warily. 'Is it good news or bad news?'

'I don't know quite how you'd categorise it,' said Ian, looking amused. 'We've got a name for the homeless body.'

'Sylvia's Rab? Really?'

'The body at Rogation House?' said Anne breathlessly. 'Wow!'

'Not actually at the house,' said Ian, 'but, yes, that body.'

'Well, go on, then!' said Libby. 'What's his name?'

Ian raised an eyebrow. 'Neil Barton. Ring any bells?'

'Neil –' Libby's mouth dropped open. '*Neil?* Michelle's stalker?'

'The very same.' Ian grinned at the three shocked faces in front of him.

'How did you find out?' Libby absent-mindedly took the glass Edward was holding out to her.

'Your friend Michelle persuaded her client Mrs Barton—'

'Oh – Joan. Yes,' said Libby.

'She persuaded her to report him missing officially. And she was shown the post-mortem photograph, as her description matched our John Doe in the morgue.'

'Oh, poor woman,' said Patti. 'Was that his wife?'

'His mother.' Libby pulled down the corners of her mouth. 'I don't know that that isn't worse.'

'I remember you talking about your friend's stalker and the missing homeless man,' said Anne. 'Does this mean they're the same person?'

'Yes,' said Libby, 'and when we first heard about them both, I kept trying to make them one person, but Fran said I was just trying to make things fit, and it couldn't possibly be the case. Because the timings didn't fit – but obviously they do.' She turned to Ian. 'So he just stopped being Sylvia's Rab and carried on being Michelle's stalker?'

'Looks like it,' said Ian. 'It also looks as though I'm now SIO. We're in the process of unravelling Mr Barton's life to see why he was posing as homeless and cosying up to Sylvia Cranthorne.'

Ben and Peter, who had arrived at the table to hear the last part of this conversation, looked at each other and groaned. Ian turned to look at them and laughed.

'I'm sorry! I'll try and keep her out of it, I promise.'

'Fat chance,' said Ben, and sighed.

'You've got a legitimate reason for searching the old Island View caravans now, though, haven't you?' said Libby, ignoring Ben.

'It's already been done once, after you told me about the removal of the homeless people, and they were as clean as a whistle,' said Ian. 'It's now going to be done again. Oh – and the certificate of legal use is being investigated, too. I gather Guy's been looking into that, as well.'

'So Stapleton Holdings had better look out!' said Libby. 'Oh!' She paused, her glass halfway to her lips. 'Stapleton. I was going to tell you.'

Ian closed his eyes. 'Oh, God,' he said. 'Sorry, Patti.'

Patti gave a rueful smile and Anne snorted with laughter.

Peter, Ben and Edward squeezed in round the table. 'Go on, then, Libby,' said Edward, looking interested. 'What about Stapleton?'

'Don't encourage her,' said Ben, laughing in spite of himself.

Ian glared. 'All right,' he said. 'Go on. What about Stapleton Holdings.'

'Fran says you'll already know. Or someone will,' said Libby nervously.

Ian sent a minatory glance round the table. 'Don't any of you repeat any of this, understand?'

'Yessir!' said Ben, saluting, and Ian gave him an even dirtier look.

After taking a fortifying gulp of Tim's best lager, Libby proceeded to repeat what she and Simon had learnt about Mr Stapleton and his holdings. Ian began to look interested.

'Well,' he said when she'd finished, 'I expect a lot of this is known already; I've only just come on the scene, but we'll certainly be looking into it all a great deal more thoroughly. And trying to find out where – and if – he's really holding trafficked workers.'

'I've noticed statements about modern slavery on a lot of company websites lately,' said Peter.

'So have I,' said Edward.

'Hot topic,' said Ian, 'and one I would have thought someone like Stapleton would have steered clear of.'

'It's so awful,' said Patti, obviously distressed. Anne reached over and took her hand.

'It is.' Libby nodded. 'And I wish there was something we could do about it.'

'Wipe it out wherever we find it,' said Ian.

'As long as those you find don't suffer,' said Patti.

Ian looked at her thoughtfully. 'I wish I could tell you they wouldn't.'

Peter tapped on his glass with a fingernail. 'Come to order, please,' he said. 'Let's talk about something more cheerful. Like the opening of the Hop Pocket.'

The atmosphere changed perceptibly.

'I'm looking forward to it,' said Edward. 'Will you be able to come, Ian?'

The opening was thoroughly discussed, moving on, inevitably, to the new Rogue Days celebration and the recruitment drive for the Morris side.

'We've already got a list of volunteers,' said Ben. 'Tim's been doing sterling work in here.'

'As long as you don't expect me to dance,' said Ian, and stood up. 'I must go. I've got an early start in the morning. Do you mind, Edward?'

'You're driving, boss,' said Edward with a grin. 'Won't hurt me to have an early night, especially as I've no doubt I shall be late on Friday.'

'That's a point,' said Ian. 'Do you think Hetty would let us hire two of the rooms at the Manor on Friday, Ben?'

'Of course she would,' said Ben. 'I'll tell her in the morning.'

'You'll come on Friday, then,' said Libby to Ian. 'Will you be able to?'

'Even if I'm late, I'll come,' said Ian. 'Oh, and will you want policing for the celebrations for your Rogue Day? If so . . .'

'No, we're only dancing round farmland, except for the little bit of the high street between here and the Pocket,' said Ben.

'Will I be able to come on Friday?' asked Anne diffidently when Ian and Edward had gone. 'Patti might not be able to, but I'd like to.'

'Of course!' said Libby. 'The chair will go through the doorway, won't it, Ben?'

'Easily,' said Ben. 'I'll have to have a look at the ladies' loos, though.'

'If there's a handle of sorts, I should be all right,' said Anne.

'I shall look into it first thing,' said Libby.

Chapter Sixteen

However, the first thing Libby did the following morning was, in fact, call Michelle.

'Did you know?' she asked. 'Has Joan called you?'

Michelle was making sounds suggestive of a landed fish. 'No!' she gasped.

'Well, just be prepared. The police might want to talk to you.'

'All – er – all right.' There was a pause. 'So it definitely wasn't him who broke into my house, was it?'

'Certainly wasn't,' said Libby. 'Now, I must go. I'll let you know if I hear anything.'

The next call was to Simon regarding the ladies' loos.

'All sorted,' he said. 'I'd already got grab handles as part of elf and safety.'

Finally, Libby called Fran.

'So you were right, after all,' said Fran. 'It was one and the same person.'

'Feels a bit spooky, actually,' said Libby. 'Like life imitating art.'

'Life imitating Libby,' corrected Fran. 'But at least it shows your detective instincts are intact.'

'Mmm . . . Begs the question – who broke into Michelle's house – flat – whatever?'

'Random burglar,' said Fran. 'Who else could it be? Surely, whoever murdered Stalker Neil would have no reason to? Nothing was taken, was it? And there were no cryptic messages anywhere.'

'No.' Libby frowned at Sidney, who had jumped onto the table, intent on joining in the conversation. 'What about Joan?'

'Joan?'

'Stalker Neil's mum.'

'As Michelle's burglar? I thought she was frail and elderly?'

'Well, Michelle said she was, because that was why she started doing her hair at home.'

'Hardly likely to have broken in, then. You're grasping at straws again, Lib.'

'I suppose so.' Libby let out a gusty sigh. 'I would like to talk to her, though.'

'Why, for heaven's sake? The police are going to look into every aspect of Neil's life, so there's nothing left for you to find out.'

Libby idly stroked Sidney's head. 'What about Sylvia?' she asked.

'I'm sure she'll be questioned again,' said Fran, 'and I wouldn't have thought knowing who he really is and not just his alias will add much to her evidence.'

'We need to know where he worked,' said Libby after a pause.

'*Libby!*' Fran exploded. 'Have you heard a word I've said?'

'Oh, yes.' Libby blinked and sat up straighter in her chair. 'Sorry. It's habit.'

'Being nosy? Yes, it is. And I know I've got my fair share, but really – the police are going to be looking into everything, now. Even those poor homeless people, because although the whole Island View situation doesn't appear to have anything to do with Stalker Neil, he was pretending to be one of them.'

'All right, sorry.' Libby drew her laptop towards her. 'By the way, speaking of homeless people, do you remember the name of Sir Andrew's homeless charity? The one we did the concert for?'

Sir Andrew McColl was a theatrical knight who had become acquainted with Libby and her friends through Harry, when he had unexpectedly inherited some property from an old friend.

'No, I don't – why?' Fran sounded suspicious.

'In case the Island View people are found,' said Libby innocently. 'They'll need help.'

'If the police do find them, I'm sure they'll help,' said Fran. 'What's the real reason?'

'That *was* the real reason,' said Libby. 'It just occurred to me.'

Fran sighed. 'If you say so. Oh, and Guy said to tell you the police have asked him to stop any action he or the protest group might be taking about the certificate of lawful development. Apparently, everyone thinks it might be illegal, despite what the council says.'

'I suppose the police have the power to stop it. And now they know that Stapleton Holdings are the owners of the site, and Neil's body was found on Stapleton's land—'

'And you've given them a possible link to the homeless . . .'

'You're right. They'll look into it all,' said Libby. 'Except why Neil was pretending to be homeless and chatting up Sylvia.'

'Hmmm.' Fran was silent for a moment. 'I suppose you could be right, there.'

'I could?'

'I wonder how deeply they'll go into that aspect of the murder.'

'Well, it was the start of the whole thing,' said Libby. 'They should.'

'Look, I must go,' said Fran after another pause. 'Guy's off to some exhibition or other, so I'm in charge of the shop. Let me know if there are any developments.'

'See?' said Libby to Sidney, after she'd ended the call. 'She is interested, really.'

She made herself the fourth cup of tea of the morning and sat down with the laptop.

'Estate agents,' she muttered. 'Nethergate estate agents.'

There were several. Eventually, by going to all the websites, she found what she was looking for. Brooke and Company, on

Nethergate High Street, had a discreet little banner advertising 'Luxury Park Homes, coming soon'.

'Bingo!' she said out loud, and rang the company's number.

'Could I speak to Sylvia Cranthorne?' she said confidently when a bright female voice answered.

'Who's speaking, please?'

'Mrs Sarjeant,' said Libby, put on the spot.

'Just putting you through,' said the incurious voice.

There was a wait long enough to make Libby think Sylvia wasn't going to answer, then:

'Is that Libby?'

'Yes, Sylvia – I took a chance that Brooke's was your company.'

Sylvia sighed. 'And you were right. How did you guess?'

'I looked for a company advertising park homes,' said Libby, feeling rather proud of herself. 'Which you won't be selling after all now, will you?'

'How do you know?' said Sylvia sharply.

'The site's been put on hold by the police, hasn't it?' Libby smiled smugly at the laptop.

'Er – I – I –' Sylvia took a deep breath. 'I don't actually know.'

'Well, it will be, even if you haven't heard. Now that the police are investigating.'

'What exactly are they investigating?' asked Sylvia cautiously. 'Do you know?'

'You know Rab's been identified, don't you?' said Libby.

'No! Who is he?'

'And as he was pretending to be homeless,' Libby went on, ignoring the question, 'the police want to know about the homeless people who the owners turned off the site. And, of course, about the owners and the legality of the development.'

'But it's a holding company! And they've got permission to develop.' Sylvia was now sounding extremely agitated.

'But there's some doubt about their certificate of lawful

123

development,' said Libby. 'And how much do you actually know about Stapleton Holdings?'

'Um,' said Sylvia.

'Exactly. And was your Rab trying to find out about it all, by any chance?' Libby crossed her fingers.

More silence.

'Oh, well, I'll take that as a yes, then,' said Libby eventually. 'Why didn't you tell the police?'

'I – I didn't think it was important,' said Sylvia in a small voice. 'Will you tell them now?'

'I think you should,' said Libby virtuously.

'Couldn't you tell Ian? He'll listen to you – you said so yourself.'

'I'll try,' said Libby, 'but I expect he – or someone – will want to speak to you in person.'

Sylvia sighed. 'All right. Will you let me know?'

'If I can,' said Libby. 'Speak to you soon.'

Almost as soon as she had ended the call, her phone rang again.

'Libby!' Michelle sounded shaky. 'Joan just called me.'

Oh, dear, thought Libby. 'What did she say?' she asked aloud.

'She's still blaming me!' wailed Michelle.

'Eh? She can't possibly think you killed him!'

'No – she's not making much sense, actually. She just kept saying if he hadn't got mixed up with me it wouldn't have happened.'

'He lived with her, you said?'

'Yes – I told you!'

'I know, I know. So she relied on him.'

'Yes – for everything. He was like her husband.'

'Eww,' said Libby.

'No, not like that – he did all the jobs around the house, put the bins out – you know. She used to say she didn't know what she'd do without him.' Michelle sniffed. 'I felt so sorry for her.'

124

So do I, thought Libby. 'Has she got friends?'

'I don't really know. She used to talk about the club, but I don't know what club.'

'How did she talk about it? I mean, did she say "I'm going to the club tonight", or "I'm going to the club for lunch" or anything like that?'

'That sort of thing, yes. I know they had a Christmas party.' Michelle sighed. 'It was often club things she had her hair done for. Vintage something? I wish I'd taken more notice.'

'It really isn't your fault,' said Libby. 'Do you think she'd talk to me?'

'You said you wouldn't before.' Michelle was accusing.

'The situation has changed somewhat,' said Libby. 'Can you give me her phone number?'

'I'll text it,' said Michelle. 'Can you stop her calling me?'

'I don't know,' said Libby. 'I'll see what happens. By the way, where does she live?'

'Just outside Canterbury on the way to Harbledown. It's rather nice, actually – a little close of sort of executive houses. I'll send you the address as well.'

'Well, that was illuminating,' Libby told Sidney, and sat back to think.

Neil Barton was turning into a very interesting character. The stay and support of his elderly mother, the creepy stalker of Michelle and the undercover 'homeless' investigator of Sylvia Cranthorne. A man of many parts.

And I really need to find out which one is the real Neil Barton, thought Libby.

Vetoing the idea of a fifth cup of tea, she called Fran again.

'Yes, I know you're in the shop, but can you talk – or listen – just for a minute? Right.' And Libby explained, as concisely as she could, what she had learnt in the last half hour.

'What made you think Neil was pumping Sylvia for information?' asked Fran when Libby had finished.

'Just what I said earlier – pretending to be homeless and chatting her up. He must have known Brooke and Co. were the selling agents. He targeted her, didn't he?'

'Looks like it. But, as I said, the police will be looking into that angle.'

'But she wanted me to tell Ian. And Michelle wants me to talk to Neil's mum.'

'You said she gave you the address. Where is it?'

'Near Harbledown. Michelle said it was a small estate of executive houses, which doesn't fit, somehow.'

'Maybe Joan had a good job before she retired, or Neil's dad left her well provided for. And Neil was obviously working, so there was still an income.'

'Yes.' Libby squinted through the window at the pale grey sky. 'It's just all so odd. I mean – who would have thought it? Two suspicious men turn up at the same time, in different circumstances and turn out to be the same person.'

'Well, you obviously thought it,' said Fran. 'You were trying to link the two right from the start.'

'It's still odd,' said Libby. 'So do you think I ought to go and see this Mrs Barton?'

'You can't turn up out of the blue. I suppose you could try ringing her, but what would you say, for heaven's sake?'

'No idea. She'd probably think I was a journalist and chuck me out. I might go and have a look at her house, though.'

'What on earth for?' Fran's voice rose in surprise.

'Oh, I don't know. Sheer nosiness, I suppose. And should I tell Ian what Sylvia said?'

'I honestly don't think it's worth it, Lib. As I keep saying, they'll have found out about it all by now, I expect.'

'It looks as if he was suspicious of the development, though, doesn't it? Perhaps he was an industrial spy?'

Fran laughed. 'Perhaps he was. Going undercover as a homeless person and a stalker. Sounds like a bad TV drama.'

'Oh, you can mock,' said Libby with a sigh. 'All right, I won't do anything.'

'Except work on the End of the Pier Show,' said Fran.

'That doesn't start until the end of July,' said Libby. 'I'll just get on with another couple of little pictures for Guy, then, shall I?'

'And help with the Rogue Days celebration,' said Fran. 'Go on, get on with it.'

Chapter Seventeen

Friday, and the day the Hop Pocket was to open. By the time Libby woke up, Ben had long gone, and a mug of cold tea stood on her bedside table. In the kitchen she found a note.

'Gone to the brewery and then on to the Pocket. We won't open until this evening at seven. Don't cook.'

'Right,' said Libby. 'What do we eat, then?' She shook her head, switched on the electric kettle and opened a packet of cat food for Sidney. She had just poured boiling water into a mug when the rattle of the letter box signified a mail delivery, rare in these days of internet communication. She wandered through the sitting room to the tiny hall where she was astonished to find what looked like a pile of greeting cards, most of which were addressed to the Hop Pocket, or occasionally to Ben.

She retrieved her mug and rang Ben's mobile.

'You've got a lot of cards,' she said.

'Cards?'

'Good luck cards, I assume. I didn't realise people sent them these days.'

'From suppliers, I guess,' said Ben.

'Then why did they come here?'

'Oh! Don't know. Open one and see.'

'No fear! They're addressed to you or the Pocket. I'll bring them round when I'm dressed.'

An hour later, breakfasted, showered and dressed, Libby set off.

'Hey, Lib!' Bob the butcher waved from the doorway of his shop. 'See you tonight!'

'Tonight?' Libby looked blank.

'The Pocket, idjit.' Bob grinned and retreated.

To Libby's surprise, Ali and Ahmed also rushed out into the street and called out good wishes, Nella did the same from the farm shop, and Beth, in full vicarly regalia (which probably meant a funeral, thought Libby), waved from Maltby Close. 'See you later!' she called.

'Everybody seems to know about tonight,' Libby said, arriving at the Hop Pocket in a flurry of cape and scarves. 'Even Beth said she's coming.'

Ben, up a ladder pinning bunting over the bar counter, grinned down at her. 'Good marketing campaign,' he said. 'Word of mouth.' He descended the ladder. 'Where are these cards, then?'

Libby handed them over, and Simon came to help open them.

'Look – here's one from Sir Andrew.' Ben stood it on the counter. 'And this one's from Max Tobin – Andrew must have told him.'

Max had brought his troupe of danseurs to the Oast Theatre to premiere a new ballet a few years previously.

'This is from the Glover's Men,' said Simon. 'Who are they?'

'Another company that performed at the theatre,' said Ben. 'Someone's been doing a good job of promoting us!'

'This is from Abby and Coolidge,' said Libby. 'That's Dame Amanda Knight and her husband, Simon.'

'Who also performed at the theatre, I assume?' Simon shook his head. 'You do move in posh circles, don't you?'

'They aren't, really,' said Libby. 'They're just all theatricals of one sort or another. Don't worry – we won't bring them in here.'

'Why not?' Ben bristled slightly.

'Whoops, sorry!' Libby made a face.

'Hmm,' said Ben, not mollified.

'So, Simon – have you got some volunteers for the Morris side?' asked Libby hastily.

129

'Oh, yes, plenty,' said Simon, giving her a wink. 'And they'll all be here tonight.'

'What are we doing about rehearsing, then?'

'We were lucky there,' said Ben. 'You remember I mentioned the lad at the brewery?'

Libby nodded, standing the rest of the good luck cards on the bar counter.

'Well, he got in touch with a friend of his who still dances when he can with White Horse Morris, but lives here, and he's delighted to have a local side, so we've rather arbitrarily appointed him leader—'

'Squire,' said Libby.

'Yes, Squire. And young Albie's going to be – what was it, Si?'

'Bagman,' supplied Simon. 'That's—'

'Treasurer,' said Libby.

'And the Squire's also going to be the "Foreman",' said Simon, 'as he's going to teach the dancers.'

'What's his name?' Libby asked.

'Duncan Cruikshank,' said Ben. 'It's all happened so quickly.' He leant over and gave Libby a kiss. 'Well done you for thinking of it.'

'Even though you weren't sure at first?' Libby gave him a friendly buffet on the arm.

'Even so.' Ben laughed. 'We haven't got a name, though.'

'Not Steeple Martin Morris?' said Libby, raising her eyebrows.

'I don't see why not,' said Simon. 'Or do you have to get permission from someone to use the name?'

'We didn't when we named our Steeple Martin Bitter,' said Ben. 'But when Duncan and Albie have finalised their side, we'll ask them.'

'Have any women volunteered?' asked Libby.

'Dan's missus – Moira,' said Ben. 'And he's going to be Old Rogue.'

'Is someone going to be the Tolley Hound?'

'No,' said Simon, 'because we'd have to find someone to make the head, and we haven't got that much time, so Dan's going to bring his dog.'

'That's what I said!' Libby was delighted.

'Colley's going to have a decorated collar, apparently,' said Ben.

'And why haven't you told me any of this before?' asked Libby.

'There hasn't been much time,' said Ben. 'And you've been occupied.'

'I just don't believe it's all happened – what? Since Monday?' Libby shook her head. 'I suppose I'd better get hold of Cranthorne and White Horse – oh, and Pucklefield.'

'All done,' said Simon, with a grin. 'Once Albie mentioned it to Duncan, there was no holding him. He knows everyone on the circuit, it seems.'

'Blimey,' said Libby mildly. 'And they'll all be here tonight?'

'So we're told,' said Simon. 'Duncan wants to do a sort of official speech, he says, and Tim said he'll be here for that. That's why it'll be at nine, to give him time to get organised over the road first.'

'I think it's incredibly nice of him to be so supportive,' said Libby.

'He's told you several times, he can increase his rooms and dining trade – and young Brendan's already getting a reputation. He'll be fine.' Ben peered up at his bunting. 'Should I hang the cards up there, do you think?'

Libby left them to it, assured that Harry was going to deliver dinner at 6.30 for the three of them so she had nothing to do for the rest of the day. She stood at the corner of Cuckoo Lane and thought.

'Whatcher doin', gal?' Flo appeared at her elbow. 'Lost a pound and found a ha'penny?'

Libby looked up and grinned. 'Hello, Flo. I was just wondering what to do. Ben and Simon are getting the Pocket ready for tonight and I'm at a loose end. Are you coming?'

'To the Pocket? Yeah, we'll come down with Hetty. That Joe's comin' over, too.'

'Oh.' Libby was struck with a thought. 'You know Lenny and Joe went to see that OB place where the body was found?'

'Yeah. Set you off, that did.'

'Well – did they have to get permission from the land owner?'

'Search me,' said Flo, looking surprised. 'Went with that club of theirs. Why don't you come back with me and ask Len?'

'Good idea.' Libby tucked her arm through Flo's and set off towards Maltby Close.

Lenny obligingly turned off the television when Flo ushered Libby into the small, cluttered living room.

'What I wanted to ask you, Len,' said Libby, 'was did you have to ask permission to go and see that OB?'

'No idea. We went with the club.' Lenny looked as surprised as Flo had.

'Ah, yes, the club. What exactly is it?'

'Whatdjer mean – what is it? 'S a club.' Now Lenny was bewildered.

'Where do you meet?'

'We goes on trips.' Lenny shrugged. 'Joe just took me along with 'im.'

'Oh, right.' Libby gave up. 'Well, I expect I'll see you tonight, won't I?'

'Not 'arf! Lookin' forward to it, ain't we, Flo?'

Libby wandered aimlessly home, not knowing quite what to do next. What she *should* do, of course, was start a new painting for Guy. It was already May, and by June the holiday season would have started – at least for families with pre-school children and the somewhat older holidaymakers, who rather liked her pictures. But, as usual, inspiration seemed to have deserted her. So, as so frequently happened, a little internet research seemed called for.

Typing 'WW2 Operational Base, Shott, Kent' into the search engine brought up a plethora of results, not all of which appeared helpful. However, eventually, she found a reference, which did confirm that the base was indeed on private land, but gave no further details. Frustrated, she sat back and glared at the screen.

The landline rang.

'Colin!' Libby said thankfully. 'I'm so glad you called.'

'Really? Why?'

'I was bored.'

'Oh, thanks! Just the plaything of an idle hour, am I?'

Libby laughed. 'No, it's just that I haven't got anything to do, and Ben's all tied up with the opening of the Hop Pocket tonight. You are coming over, aren't you?'

'Wouldn't miss it,' said Colin. 'We're still fighting over who's going to drive!'

'How about staying at the Manor? Hetty's got plenty of room.'

'Would she mind?'

'Of course not! Shall I give her a ring?'

'No – give me the number and I'll do it. Now – do you want to hear what I've found out? Not that it's much.'

'Yes, please,' said Libby.

'Stapleton Holdings is a somewhat grandiose name, as I said it might be,' Colin began. 'It is actually one company with a couple of different arms. They own a few holiday sites with posh websites, although they aren't very posh at all.'

'I thought they owned quite a few,' said Libby.

'Well, that's the odd thing. There are only four that are active. Their other sites are undeveloped, yet they have, as I said, posh websites. What happens when someone tries to book I've no idea.'

'Hmm,' said Libby. 'What else?'

'There's a small haulage business – half a dozen five-tonne vans, but I couldn't find out what they were transporting – and a cleaning and maintenance arm. Neither of those seem to be trying to attract custom, so I assume they are there simply to service the holiday parks. Obviously, I couldn't poke about into their finances like the police could, but from what I could see they look solvent.'

'What about Stapleton himself?

'He's on the letterhead as N. Stapleton, CEO. And their offices are in Canterbury, just off the ring road, as far as I could make out. On the west side, anyway.'

'West?' Libby frowned, trying to visualise a map of Canterbury.

'Yes, the way you'd go out to join up with the A2 to London. Past Harbledown and the turning to Rough Common.'

'Oh!' Harbledown again. 'Could you tell how big the company is? In terms of employees?'

'No, sorry. I said it's not much. I didn't go to Companies House – you could get more info there, but it isn't always filed correctly. I was trying to find out the dirt!'

Libby laughed. 'And there wasn't any?'

'Not that I could find. Nothing came up in internet searches – no nasty little stories in the media or anything like that. Suspiciously clean, in fact.'

'Oh,' said Libby again. 'I'm probably just trying to make things fit, as usual.'

'You usually do,' said Colin. 'Make them fit, I mean.'

'Sometimes.' Libby sighed. 'Thing is, we've learnt that he's by no means as pure as the driven snow.'

'I know – you said.'

'Yes, but even more. It's rumoured that he has illegal migrant workers at his big house in the country, and he tried to use intimidation tactics to gain more land – although why he needs more land I've got no idea. He's got enough already.'

'I'd stay well clear of him, then,' said Colin. 'Sounds as if he might have a long reach.'

Ending the call, Libby checked the time. It was still too early for lunch, but possibly about the right time for a visit to an old friend.

Chapter Eighteen

It occurred to Libby, as she drove towards Itching, that perhaps she shouldn't turn up on the old friend's doorstep unannounced. However, she could say she was just passing, although that was a trifle unlikely, as Perseverance Row didn't lead anywhere.

'I could be visiting Cass and Mike,' she said out loud. 'And just decided to pop in on the off chance.' Saying it out loud didn't make it sound any more likely.

Libby's cousin Cassandra lived with Mike Farthing of Farthing's Nursery, just down Rogue's Lane, off the Shott village green. Perhaps it would make more sense to visit them rather than Sandra Farrow in Perseverance Row. They were also rather more likely to be in.

Cassandra saw Libby's car draw up on the forecourt and came out to meet her.

'This is a nice surprise!' she said, enfolding her cousin in a hug. 'To what do we owe the pleasure?'

'I bet I know.' Mike had appeared behind Cassandra and dropped a kiss on Libby's cheek. 'You're investigating that body that was found up in the old woods, aren't you?'

'Um – not exactly,' mumbled Libby as she was led into the office-cum-shop of the nursery.

Cassandra raised an eyebrow, fixing her with the icy stare that had cowed generations of schoolchildren. 'So what is it *exactly*?' she asked.

'Stop being a headmistress,' said Mike with a grin. 'Coffee, Lib?'

Libby grinned back at him. 'Yes, please. And you were nearly right.'

'About the body?' said Cassandra.

'Except that I'm not investigating the body. I just wanted to know if you knew anything about the man who owns the land. Stapleton, isn't it?' Libby settled down on one of the stools provided for visitors.

'Nick Stapleton, yes.' Mike looked surprised. 'We've done some work for him in the past.'

'Oh? What, landscaping? Providing plants?'

'Bit of both.' Mike handed over a mug of coffee. 'He'd seen Lewis's garden on TV and wanted a parterre like the one he's got. Your Adam did that.'

'Well, Mog did the design,' said Libby. Adam's day job was working as assistant to garden designer Mog, and they both worked for Lewis Osbourne-Walker whose restoration of his house, Creekmarsh, and its garden had featured on his regular television show.

'I know that. Anyway,' said Mike, settling down on his own stool behind the counter, 'he asked if I could do something similar. In the end, I just drew him the design and provided the plants. He said he could provide the labour himself.'

'So you didn't do any work on the ground, as it were?'

'No.' Mike shrugged. 'I wasn't too bothered – it would have taken a hell of a lot of time, and he doesn't strike me as someone who would be easy to work for. He's also got very long pockets.'

'He's mean?' asked Cassandra. 'But he's got pots!'

'That's how he got the pots, I expect,' said Libby. 'Well, that's confirmed what I suspected.'

'Suspected? What do you mean?' Cassandra was in headmistress mode again.

'We think he's employing illegal migrant workers at the house, and probably on the land,' said Libby.

'Who's we? You and Fran?'

'And some of the locals in Pucklefield.'

'I didn't know you knew people over there,' said Mike.

'Yes, and a couple of their Morris side will be coming over to our opening tonight.' Libby beamed at them both. 'Are you coming?'

'Oh, the Hop Pocket!' said Mike. 'Yes, we'll pop over for a bit.'

'Morris side?' Cassandra's brows were up.

'Yes – it's all happened rather quickly,' said Libby, and went on to explain about Old Rogue and the Morris sides.

'I've heard of Old Rogue,' said Mike slowly, leaning his elbows on the counter. 'Wasn't a very savoury character, by all accounts. And the Tolley Hound was more like a Barghest than anything else.'

'Yes, I know, but that was back in the eighteen hundreds, as far as I can make out,' said Libby.

'Somebody told me some of the old practices had been carried on – or revived, anyway,' said Mike. 'Don't know how accurate that was.'

'When was that?' said Libby. 'Someone else told us that.'

'Oh, ages ago,' said Mike. 'Can't see it happening these days. And that was when the Old Rogue was the owner of Rogation House originally, wasn't it? Can't see Nick Stapleton involved in that sort of thing.'

'I was actually wondering,' said Libby diffidently, 'if you could get into the woods. I'd like to see the OB. Some friends of ours went to see it a few weeks ago, before the body was found.'

'I didn't know you were interested in World War Two history,' said Cassandra, narrowing her eyes.

'Oh, yes.' Libby opened her own eyes very wide, the picture of innocence. 'I must tell you all about the time Fran and I found one down on the south coast.'

'I think you can go into the woods,' said Mike. 'There's no fencing this side, anyway.'

'How would you get there, then? Along Perseverance Row? Or along the road past The Poacher?'

'Past The Poacher would be best,' said Mike, 'but you be careful. Remember what happened when you went poking about down there before.'

'That was different,' said Libby, waving a dismissive hand.

'You're not thinking of going today, are you?' said Cassandra. 'Surely you've got things to do at home?'

'Well, no. Ben and Simon, the new manager, have got everything in hand, and Harry's doing an early dinner for us, so I haven't got anything to do.'

'So you decided to go ferreting again,' said Cassandra, and sighed. 'Well, please don't get into any more trouble.'

'It's all right. I'm not going today. I might pop in on Ron and Maria while I'm over here, though.' Libby stood up.

'You going to quiz them about Stapleton?' Mike grinned. 'I wouldn't bother. Ron tried to get some money out of him for some homeless charity a year or so back and got a flea in his ear for his trouble. You can imagine what he'd say.'

Ron 'Screwball' Stewart had been lead singer and guitarist with the prog rock band 'Jonah Fludde' and lived with his wife Maria further down Rogue's Lane towards Bishop's Bottom. He was not known for the moderation of his language.

'So what's all this about illegal workers?' asked Cassandra. 'Like those gangs you found out about before?'

Libby and Fran had become inadvertently involved with the exposure of an illegal migrant smuggling ring some years previously.

'I don't know,' admitted Libby, 'but it sounds like it.'

'Well, I doubt if Ron would know anything about that,' said Mike.

'He might be interested, though,' said Libby. 'If he's involved with a homeless charity – would that be the one Sir Andrew's involved with? The one we did the charity concert for?'

'Probably,' said Cassandra. 'He and Andrew got on very well, as I remember.'

'But I can't see that he'd want to get involved if there's going to be an investigation,' said Mike. 'I assume the police will be involved?'

'I suppose so,' said Libby vaguely. The other two regarded her suspiciously. 'I won't hold you up any longer,' she continued hastily, moving towards the door. 'Thanks for the coffee.'

'We'll see you tonight,' said Mike. 'Look forward to it.'

Cassandra gave her a hug. 'Just don't go poking around.'

Libby drove back to the green and parked in The Poacher's car park.

'Hello, stranger!' The landlord grinned across the bar counter.

'Hello, Sid.' Libby grinned back. 'I was just over at Cass and Mike's and thought I'd pop in.'

'Coffee?' Sid Best waved his hand at a new state-of-the-art coffee maker.

'No, thanks. Mike gave me some.' Libby hoisted herself onto a bar stool. 'Did you know Ben's opening the Hop Pocket tonight? Don't suppose you can come, can you?'

'Then you suppose wrong! I got cover in specially. Getting a lift with Sandra and Alan.'

'They're coming, too?' Libby was delighted. 'Blimey! We'll never get everyone in.'

'And I hear,' said Sid, tapping his nose, 'that you might be having a little guest turn?'

'Really?' Libby was surprised. 'More than I know, then.'

'Oh, bugger!' Sid looked mortified. 'I've spoilt it now, haven't I?'

'No, because I still don't know what you're talking about,' said Libby. 'Anyway, while I'm here, I wanted to know what you knew about Rogation House?'

It was Sid's turn to look surprised. 'Stapleton's place? Why d'you want to know?'

'Oh, you know . . . that body.'

'The one found in the OB? But that's not near the house.'

139

'But it's on his land, isn't it? And was it actually found *inside* the OB?'

'In the doorway, I think,' said Sid. 'Don't suppose anyone would want to go inside.' He winked.

'Oh? Why?'

'Supposed to be a witch's hangout, isn't it.'

Oh, not again, thought Libby. 'Really?' she said aloud. 'But I thought it was dug out during the war.'

Sid shook his head. 'It was there already. Found witch bottles all round the entrance, they did. Put 'em back after the war.'

'Oh, yes – they're supposed to keep places safe from witches, aren't they? Like burying shoes under doorsteps.'

'And dead cats in the walls,' said Sid. 'Anyway, they say it's still in use.' He nodded wisely. 'Devil worship now, though.'

'Heavens!' said Libby, eyes wide. 'I never knew any of this! Does it link up with the Old Rogue legend?'

'I suppose someone might have tried to make a connection,' said Sid, 'but the Old Rogue only started in the Victorian era, when that bloke built Rogation House and fancied himself – I don't know – a wizard or something.'

'Yes, I think I knew that, although I heard the legend went back further than that.' Libby frowned. 'And the Victorian Rogue started beating the bounds, only he was beating boys – is that right?'

Sid leant his elbows on the bar. 'And worse. For fertility of the crops – and the hops, I think.'

'You know a lot about it,' said Libby. 'I'm glad I asked.'

Sid shrugged. 'Always been interested in folk legends. And we always have the Pucklefield Morris dance here on all the festival days, you know, Samhain, Imbolc, Beltaine and Lughnasa.' He cocked an eyebrow at her. 'Take it you know about them?'

'Oh, yes.' Libby sighed. 'So the OB predates the war. And did the original, nineteenth-century Old Rogue use it?'

'No one knows for sure, but if he was going in for all the nasty stuff I would have thought so, wouldn't you?'

'Yes.' Libby nodded slowly. Then she slid off her stool. 'I'd better get off. Ben'll probably have found me something to do by now.'

'See you later, then,' said Sid. 'Let me know if you need anything else.'

Libby drove away from the Poacher thinking hard. It looked more and more as if there were two Old Rogues celebrating Rogation Days in the area, and only one of them was for public consumption. Could Nick Stapleton really be conducting the old rituals – even if they were less than two hundred years old – or had she made that up herself, simply because the body had been found on his land? If she was honest, that could well be the case, and, after all, it had little bearing on the potentially dodgy development of the Island View site in Nethergate.

'Honestly,' she said to herself. 'Your imagination will be the death of you.'

Chapter Nineteen

By eight thirty that evening, it was obvious that the Hop Pocket's 'soft' opening was a success. Libby had been surprised by the amount of Steeple Martin locals who had turned up, and even more so by the rather more far-flung friends who had made the journey. Even Sir Andrew had arrived, hard on the heels of the other Andrew, Professor Andrew Wylie from Nethergate. Sid from The Poacher, along with Sandra and Alan Farrow, and George, from the Red Lion in Heronsbourne, had both forsaken their own pubs to support the new one. Tim had, as promised, brought a little coterie over from the Coach and Horses, and Reg had brought a couple of his Pucklefield Morris side over. Another surprise was the appearance of Ron and Maria Stewart with Cassandra and Mike.

'You didn't tell me they were coming!' Libby hissed in Cassandra's ear.

'Nice surprise?' Cassandra murmured back. 'Thought you'd be pleased, seeing that you were keen to see them earlier.'

Libby gave her cousin A Look.

But there was one more surprise. Tim climbed onto a chair and made the universal call for attention by tapping on his glass.

'Ladies and gentlemen,' he began. 'We're here to wish Ben and Simon all the very best with the re-opening of the Hop Pocket.' He paused for the spontaneous burst of applause. 'And, just as a little surprise, we have a little set from our famous chum, Ron – or you may know him as "Screwball" –' pause for laughter – 'Stewart.'

The applause rang out and Libby caught Ben's surprised and delighted expression. Ron, who'd managed to clear a space for himself in a corner, hoisted his guitar into position and began.

'Surprise!' said a voice behind Libby.

'Maria!' Libby folded Ron's wife in a hug. 'A lovely surprise!'

'And no one let the cat out of the bag?' asked Maria.

'Well,' said Libby, remembering Sid's words earlier, 'Sid nearly did, but I didn't know what he was talking about.'

'And Cass tells me you were asking about Nick Stapleton.' Maria's eyes were fixed on her husband. 'Not a popular name in our house.'

'No, Cass said. Something about a homeless charity?' Libby whispered. 'Tell me later. We ought to be listening.'

Maria grinned. 'Of course we should.'

Libby edged through the crowd towards the bar and ducked under the hatch. Ben put his arm round her.

'A success!' she said, and kissed him on the cheek.

'So's Simon.' Ben nodded towards his manager, who was leaning on the bar between two of the locals, both of whom cradled pints of Ben's Steeple Bitter. Libby sighed with relief. It was all going to be all right.

After Ron's surprise set, there was another surprise, when Harry, Peter and Adam arrived bearing trays of Harry's special 'vegbites'.

'You were here earlier, weren't you?' said Libby to Peter. 'I didn't see you go.'

'Oh, we were so organised, petal,' chirruped Harry over his shoulder. 'Only took early bookings for tonight, and Pete slipped out under cover of all the applause for our Screwball.' He gave her a nudge. 'Didn't know about that one, either, did we?'

'Certainly didn't,' said Libby happily. 'Aren't people nice!'

'Can I just announce,' called Ben from the bar, 'you won't get nice little nibbles any other night. You want to eat you go to the Coach or the Pink Geranium, who provided these lovely vegbites. Enjoy.'

Libby found herself next to Ron and Maria, and thanked Ron for his set.

'Pleasure. Got used to Steeple Martin now, haven't we?'

'Good. We're not as quiet as Bishop's Bottom, though,' said Libby.

'No.' Ron eyed her speculatively. 'And what are you going after nasty Nick Stapleton for?'

'Not exactly going after.' Libby looked down into her glass. 'Just – er – interested.'

'Murder,' said Maria. 'That's it, isn't it?'

'Well . . .' said Libby.

'I went to see him, you know,' said Ron, settling his back against a wall. 'I got a bit involved in Andrew's charity after that concert – you know.'

Libby nodded.

'So we were trying to get a bit of a shelter going down here in Nethergate.'

'Really?' Libby was surprised. 'No one's told us about that!'

'Never came off, did it? We just couldn't raise quite enough money. I thought Stapleton could afford it – he'd just bought Island View at that time. This was before the planning issues, and I thought – well, he's interested in promoting the town; it would be an obvious step, wouldn't it?' Ron shook his head. 'He more or less laughed in my face. Called them a blight on society.' He took a breath. 'I was escorted from the premises.'

'Where was this? Rogation House or his office in Canterbury?'

'Rogation House. I thought, as a neighbour . . .' He shook his head again. 'So he got a couple of goons to show me out. No – that's not right. There were goons there, all right, but it was the poor bloody minions who had to do it. And I'll tell you something. If they were in this country legally, I'm a bloody Dutchman.'

Libby gaped at him.

Maria nodded. 'I know. Ron reckons he's part of a people-smuggling ring. Brings in illegals to exploit.'

'Someone else told me he thought he was employing illegal

migrants.' She nodded over to the other end of the bar, where Reg and Dan Henderson were deep in conversation.

'He's a farmer, isn't he?' said Ron. 'Yes, I thought so.' He took a healthy gulp of beer. 'If I could have been sure, I would have reported him, but there was nothing to prove it. I reckon his minder was a crook, though.'

'Blimey!' said Libby. 'So you think he's a thorough going villain?'

'I reckon so!' Ron grinned at her. 'We're doing a fundraiser for the Island View protest group – did you know? Nail our colours to the mast. Your mate Guy's idea.'

'I didn't know!' Libby gasped. 'Nobody tells me anything!'

'Only just decided,' said Ron. 'This evening, in fact. He buttonholed me just after we arrived.'

Libby looked round to see if she could see Fran. She couldn't.

'That's great news,' she said. 'I shall be there – er – where?'

'Well, that's the thing.' Ron looked at Maria, then back at Libby. 'Guy's idea is that we try to get The Alexandria. What do you think?'

Libby stared at him. 'So it isn't confirmed. In fact, you don't even know if you can do it.'

'We thought – Guy and me – that if you and Fran put in a word for us—'

'I've told them what I think.' Fran appeared from behind Libby. 'I said we'd put in that word, but—'

'Yes, but . . .' Libby shook her head. 'I don't know who we'll be able to get in touch with tomorrow, being a Saturday. Still –' she smiled at Maria and Ron – 'we'll do our best.'

As Ron's attention was claimed by Sid from The Poacher, Libby drew Fran aside.

'You didn't tell me about that.'

'I hardly had time, did I? Guy made a beeline for Ron almost as soon as we arrived, and by the time I caught up you were busy with everybody else.' Fran shook her head and laughed. 'I always

145

knew my husband had an impetuous streak. Good job he hadn't broadcast his idea to the world. Still, it's a good idea.'

'Yes, it is, if we can get The Alexandria. And thankfully Ron didn't specify a day, did he?' Libby looked into her glass and found it empty. 'Come on, let's get another drink.'

'Ron said he'd fit in whenever we could get the venue,' said Fran, following Libby to the bar through the crowd.

'Good.' Libby leant over the bar to catch the attention of Simon or Ben. Simon finished serving a customer and hurried over.

'Great though this is,' he said, 'I hope it isn't *quite* this busy on a regular basis! What can I get you?'

Libby told him and turned back to Fran. 'Did you have a chance to talk to Ron apart from about the fundraiser?'

'No – why?'

'I've been ferreting again,' said Libby, making a face. 'Shall we take our drinks outside? Then I can tell you.'

Outside, they wandered down the little footpath that led to the Bat and Trap pitch and Libby told Fran everything she'd learnt that day.

'Why didn't you ring me this afternoon?' asked Fran. 'You usually do.'

'I ended up going to the Manor to help Hetty get the rooms ready. She's got quite a few guests tonight.'

'Speaking of which, I don't see Ian or Edward,' said Fran. 'I was sure Edward would be here, at least.'

'I'm sure he will. I've got a feeling he may have been going to pick up Anne, as she wasn't sure if Patti could make it.'

'He's not bringing Alice, then?' Fran quirked an eyebrow.

'No – he hasn't introduced her formally over here yet. I expect it's difficult – she's got kids, hasn't she?'

They turned and retraced their steps.

In fact, only ten minutes later, Ian, Edward and Anne pushed their way into the pub, Anne hooting with laughter as usual at the crowd's efforts to make room for her wheelchair.

'You made it,' Libby said to Ian.

'Just,' he said. 'A success, then?'

'Certainly is! Everyone we've ever known is here, I think. Even Hetty's turned out.'

'With Joe Wilson, I see,' said Ian, who could see over the heads of the rabble to where Hetty, Flo, Lenny and Joe sat in state at the end of the bar.

'Yes.' Libby smiled at Anne. 'If we could get through the crush, I'd take you over to introduce you. You've never met Ben's mum, have you?'

A little while later Duncan Cruikshank was introduced to the crowd by Ben as the new 'Squire' of the Steeple Martin Morris, who in turn, introduced young Albie as the 'Bagman', and invited anyone who was interested in joining the side to talk to either one or both of them. As far as Libby could see, there was a lot of interest, and Dan Henderson was introduced as the Old Rogue and a meeting set up – in the Pocket, of course – for Sunday evening.

After that, there was no further opportunity for private conversation with anyone, until, towards midnight, Simon having had the forethought to ask for an extension to the opening hours, they got rid of the last customers. Fran, Guy, Colin and Gerry, Edward and Ian had all volunteered to help with the considerable clearing up – Edward once he had walked Anne home to New Barton Lane.

'We wondered if Edward would bring Alice with him tonight,' said Fran innocently to Ian, dumping several glasses on the bar.

'Did you?' said Ian, smiling slightly.

Libby sighed from her place in front of the sink.

'Leave the man alone,' said Ben. 'And now tell me how you think it went tonight?'

'It was brilliant,' said Libby, 'but we might need to do something about the outside area. There's nowhere to sit. We could have a couple of benches along the side towards the Bat and Trap pitch.'

147

'And one actually on Cuckoo Lane,' said Simon. 'There were plenty of smokers out there tonight.'

Ben grinned and raised his eyebrows at Libby. 'And who's we, Tonto? I thought you weren't going to have anything to do with the Pocket?'

Libby bridled and everyone laughed. 'I got all the coasters and beer mats ordered, didn't I?' She flapped a tea towel at Ben.

Edward appeared at the doorway from Cuckoo Lane. 'Anything left for me to do?' he asked. Ian handed him a broom. 'And you'll be interested in this, Lib. Anne was telling me she was looking up your Old Rogue at her library the other day.' Anne worked for the library in Canterbury and could always be relied upon for research into whatever Libby and Fran happened to be looking into.

'For the Morris side?' asked Simon.

'Not so much,' said Edward, 'more to find out about Old Rogue himself. And it turns out he was a pretty nasty character.'

'Oh, no!' said Ian. 'What did you have to say that for?'

Chapter Twenty

'Actually,' said Libby, 'Sid Best from The Poacher was telling me the same thing, but that was probably only hearsay.'

'I expect it is,' said Edward, shooting Ian an apologetic glance. 'But you can ask Anne yourself.'

'We will,' said Fran diplomatically, 'and now, what does everyone think about Guy's idea for an Island View Protest Group fundraiser with Ron?'

'What's that about?' asked Gerry, who was polishing glasses behind the bar. 'Is that the caravan park you were telling me about, Col?'

'That's the one,' said Colin, 'and by the look on Ian's face, we don't want to talk about it right now. Fundraiser sounds good, Guy. When's that happening?'

Fran and Guy were staying with Ben and Libby. They walked home together through the silent high street.

'Thank you for not plaguing Ian tonight,' said Ben. 'I thought when Edward told us what Anne had said—'

'That's why I butted in,' said Fran. 'We can always give Anne a ring.'

'Besides,' said Libby, 'Sid had already told me quite a lot about the legend – and the OB itself.'

'What about it?' asked Ben.

'Apparently – and you'll love this – it used to be known as a witches' haunt. They found witch bottles there when they dug it out in the war.'

Ben and Guy exchanged looks.

'Could we save further explanations for another time, please?' said Guy. 'I'd rather talk about this evening.'

'Thanks, Guy.' Ben gave him a grin. 'So would I.'

Libby laughed. 'Well, tell us what the locals thought about it. After all, they're the important people from now on in.'

'They seemed to like it,' said Ben, 'and Simon's going to be a popular landlord. Dan said he can see himself popping in every day.'

'I wonder what Moira will have to say about that,' said Libby.

'And you'd better not do it,' Fran said to Ben, 'or Simon will think you don't trust him.'

'No chance,' said Ben. 'I shall be glad to leave it all to him.'

On Saturday morning, Ben persuaded Guy to leave Sophie in charge of the gallery for a little longer and go for a tour round the now fully functional brewery. Libby made more tea for herself and coffee for Fran, which they took into the sitting room.

'Now tell me what you've decided about this Stapleton character,' said Fran. 'He's a villain who acquires sites by apparently dodgy means and also traffics – what, Eastern Europeans? – to help him do it?'

'Something like that,' said Libby, 'and, talking about acquiring sites, hadn't we better try and get hold of someone about The Alexandria?'

Fran sighed and took out her phone. 'I suppose so. Do we settle for any day?'

'Ron didn't seem to mind, so yes.' Libby sat back and watched while Fran made the call. Ten minutes later it was all settled.

'Last week in June,' said Fran. 'Did you get that? They were delighted on all counts. They've got nothing much in until after that, apparently, and they aren't keen on the Island View development, either.'

'What about publicity?' asked Libby.

'They've got a new marketing company, she said, so if we – or Ron – can send through any publicity material, they'll get on to it straight away.'

'It wouldn't hurt to get on to Jane,' said Libby, 'and she could perhaps do a proper interview.'

'And one of us will have Campbell McClean from *Kent and Coast* on the phone or the doorstep, I bet,' said Fran.

'You could put him on to Guy as it was his idea.' Libby reached for her own phone. 'I'd better call Ron.'

Ron, too, was delighted, and promised to drive some publicity material over to Nethergate that very day.

'Once I've found out where it needs to go,' Libby said to Fran, ending the call.

'I've got that,' said Fran. 'The marketing company is actually based in Nethergate, so it can go direct.'

'Excellent,' said Libby. 'All in all, a good morning's work.'

Later in the morning, after Fran and Guy had gone back to Nethergate, Ben and Libby decided to go and see Simon for a lunchtime drink.

'I want to see if any of the locals have turned up yet,' said Ben, flinging Libby's cape round her shoulders.

He needn't have worried. When they arrived, there were already at least a dozen customers in the bar, and they were followed in by several more.

'We might have to think about casual staff,' said Simon. 'I'll know by the end of the weekend.'

Libby's phone rang in her pocket. Leaving Simon and Ben deep in staffing discussions, she answered.

'Libby,' said Fran. 'Mavis has found a dog.'

'Eh?' said Libby.

'She called me almost as soon as I walked through the door – she must have been watching for me.'

'To tell you she'd found a dog?'

'Yes. Well, actually, it was her and the manager of The Sloop.' Fran let out a sigh. 'They knew the dog, you see. It belonged to one of the homeless people. They used to save scraps for him, Mavis said.'

'Oh, poor thing! And he got left behind when his master was turfed out?'

'That's what they think must have happened. She said they've been looking after him since just after she talked to us about it, but they're getting worried about him. He stays outside all day sitting with his nose on his paws just watching.'

'For his master.' Libby nodded to herself. 'So what did Mavis think you could do?'

'She wanted to find out if we knew any more about the situation because they're thinking they'll have to take him to the rehoming centre.'

'I'm surprised they haven't done that already,' said Libby.

'I think they were hoping the boy might come back for him,' said Fran.

'He still might, if the removal wasn't permanent,' Libby said with foreboding.

'Oh, don't say that.' Fran sighed again. 'Anyway, I'm going down to see him, and I said I'd meet Ron and Maria at The Sloop for a drink after they've dropped off the publicity material. I thought you might want to come, too.'

Libby looked across at Ben, now happily behind the bar counter helping Simon. 'Yes, I'd love to,' she said.

'I told Ben I'd have lunch down here,' she said when she met Fran outside the Blue Anchor. 'Where's the dog?' She waved through the window to where Mavis was working behind the counter.

'Over here,' said Fran. 'Graham's tied him to a table leg so he can't run away.'

Graham, the young manager of The Sloop, looked up and

smiled at Libby. 'Come to meet Barney, have you?' He indicated something underneath the table.

Libby bent down and a pair of sad brown eyes looked up at her. She felt the constriction in her throat as she held out a hand for the long nose to sniff and, clearing her throat, stood up.

'I could kill that man,' she said.

Graham looked startled. 'What man?'

'I think she means Stapleton,' said Fran.

'Ah.' Graham looked down at the dog. 'If it was him, yes.'

'Who cleared the homeless from the site? Of course it was – he owns it,' said Libby viciously. She lowered herself cautiously to the ground and began, tentatively, to stroke Barney's head. After a moment, he shuffled himself a little nearer.

'When you rescued Jeff-dog, you had a home for him,' Fran warned. 'This time you haven't. We've both got cats, and Hetty couldn't cope with another dog.'

'Why is Libby sitting on the ground?' said a new voice.

'Ron!' said Fran.

'Can't get up at the moment,' said Libby with a grin. 'I'm comforting a dog.'

Maria crouched down beside her. 'Oh, he's beautiful!' she said. 'Where did he come from?'

'Sit down and I'll tell you,' said Fran. 'Can we have some drinks, Graham?'

By the time the story had been told, Barney had his head on Libby's lap.

'I'd get up now, Lib,' said Ron. 'Or poor Barney's going to get too attached, then when you go he'll suffer another loss.'

'Oh, hell,' said Libby. 'Why didn't you stop me, Fran?' Her voice cracked.

'Come on.' Maria held out a hand to help her up. 'Gradual detachment, that's the secret.'

Libby struggled to her feet and pulled out a chair. Barney didn't move.

'What can we do?' asked Maria.

'He ought to go to the dog sanctuary,' said Fran.

'But suppose his owner does come back?' said Maria.

'Then one of us would take him over there,' said Ron.

'One of us?' Libby smiled at him.

'You could ring me,' said Ron gruffly.

Graham brought the drinks.

'He can stay here for another day or two, and I can feed him. Then, perhaps Monday, we'll have another think. But I hate having to leave him outside at night. He won't come in – he's still watching.'

Everyone at the table was silent.

'To be honest,' said Graham, 'I'm doubtful that his owner will come back. I don't like to think what might have happened to him and his mates.' He rubbed a hand over his normally cheerful face. Everyone nodded.

'Bloody Stapleton!' exploded Ron.

'Course,' said Libby, 'if we didn't have a seriously skewed system in this country we would have fewer homeless people—'

'Let's leave politics out of it for now, Lib,' said Fran with a grin.

'Did you want lunch, by the way?' asked Graham. 'Only the kitchen's going to close in a minute.'

'No, we'll have Mavis's sandwiches, thanks,' said Libby.

'You can eat them here,' said Graham with a smile. 'If you don't want to leave Barney.'

As a trial separation, Libby went across to the Blue Anchor to place an order for sandwiches, while Ron, Maria and Fran discussed the upcoming concert at The Alexandria. When she returned, she sat a little further away and tried to ignore both the dog and her own feelings.

When Ron and Maria got up to go, Graham came out to say goodbye.

'And let us know what you decide to do,' said Ron, bending down to give Barney a last pat.

'I think Barney might have a home if his master doesn't come back,' said Libby, watching the Stewarts disappear round the back of the Blue Anchor to the car park.

'Have they got pets?' asked Graham.

'I've never met any, so I don't think so. And they live in Bishop's Bottom, with a big garden that backs onto open country so it's an ideal place.'

'Well, let's hope it all turns out all right,' said Graham, clearing plates and glasses. 'Just wish that bloody Stapleton had never bought the site.'

'It wouldn't have surprised me,' said Libby, watching him go, 'if *that bloody Stapleton* had been murdered, not Neil.'

'He does seem to have engendered a lot of ill feeling,' said Fran.

'You mean he's made a lot of people angry,' said Libby.

'Same thing, isn't it?' said Fran, surprised.

'Just posher,' said Libby. 'And, actually, the anger has only emerged because of this situation, when everything has begun to come out.'

Fran nodded. 'Come on, let's say goodbye to Mavis.'

'I'll just say goodbye to Graham,' said Libby. 'You know, I've never known his name before? All the years we've been coming here . . .'

When they walked the short distance to the Blue Anchor, Libby resisted a last glance at Barney, knowing it would set off the bout of tears that hadn't been far away for the last hour.

'I'd have him in here,' Mavis said as she came outside with them to see them off, 'but I don't think he'd settle. Let me know what happens – I'm so bloody mad now I don't care about his flamin' threats!'

'And that's another one on the suspect list,' said Fran with a grin.

'We'll be queuing up if he ever shows his face,' said Libby. 'I'd better get back and drag Ben out of the Pocket.'

'It's his new toy,' said Fran. 'He'll get tired of it soon.'

155

'And then what? Over the last couple of years, we've had the hop garden restored, the brewery set up and now the pub reopened. He'll have to find something else to keep him occupied.'

'Not to mention Steeple Farm and the Hoppers' Huts being renovated,' said Fran.

'And all the bedrooms in the Manor refurbished.' Libby nodded and sighed. 'Oh, well.'

It was just after six o'clock on Sunday morning when Libby was woken by the landline phone ringing beside her bed.

'Mmm?' she grunted into the mouthpiece.

'Libby!' Fran practically screeched in her ear. 'Barney's owner's back!'

Chapter Twenty-one

'Wha–aa?' said Libby, sitting bolt upright and startling Ben.

'In the night! Barney started barking like mad – we could hear him from here – he woke us all up!'

'And then what?' Libby swung her feet out of bed and felt for her slippers.

'Guy went out in his dressing gown and went over to The Sloop. We'd seen all the lights were on from the window. And there was Graham outside with this boy – honestly, Lib, he can't be more than eighteen – who was on the floor with Barney. And then Mavis arrived, so I went over, too.'

'Oh, Fran.' Libby's eyes had filled. 'I don't believe it! After what we were saying yesterday, it's almost as if we conjured him up.'

'More things in heaven and earth, Horatio?' suggested Fran. 'I wouldn't be surprised.'

'I wish you'd had one of your moments when we met Barney,' said Libby. 'I'd have felt better then.'

'Well, I think you'd better come over this morning and hear the whole story. I'd say we'd have lunch at The Sloop, but you've got to go to Hetty's, haven't you?'

'Hmm,' said Libby. 'I'll see . . .'

Ending the call, she filled and switched on the electric kettle. Under the circumstances, she was sure Hetty wouldn't mind her missing lunch for once – or perhaps she could run down to

157

Nethergate early and be back in time? The kettle boiled and she filled two mugs. Time to ask Ben.

Who, she discovered, had gone back to sleep, but woke again when she climbed in beside him.

'I've got something to ask you,' she said.

When she'd finished her explanation, Ben was fully awake.

'I can understand you wanting to go,' he said, 'but what's it going to achieve? Or are you going to tell Ian and suggest he comes, too?'

'I think I'll wait until we hear what the boy says,' said Libby.

'Are you sure he's still there?'

'Fran seems sure.' Libby frowned. 'Anyway, what about Hetty and lunch?'

Ben sighed. 'I'll say you're on a dog-rescuing mission. That'll get you off the hook.'

Libby called Fran and said she'd be with her in an hour. 'And where are the boy and Barney right now?'

'Mavis made him sleep in her spare room,' said Fran. 'Even Barney. I think she'd like to adopt them.'

'Good. Ben thought they might have run away.'

It was so early when Libby arrived in Harbour Street that she was able to find a parking space right outside Coastguard Cottage.

'No one will be up yet,' said Guy. 'I am because I've got to open the shop, but everyone had a disturbed night.'

'I bet Mavis didn't go back to bed. I didn't,' said Fran.

'Have you phoned Ron yet?' Libby asked.

'No, you do it. You know them both better than I do,' said Fran. 'Then we'll wander over and see if Mavis is up. I saw the cleaners go into The Sloop, so I expect Graham's up, too.'

By the time Libby had explained the situation to Ron it was almost nine thirty. He said he and Maria would be with them within the hour, and not to make any decisions without him.

'He's really taken this to heart, hasn't he?' she said to Fran as they walked down to the Blue Anchor.

'Stapleton must really have upset him when he turned him down,' said Fran, 'although I think he and Maria were very touched about the plight of Barney and his owner.'

'Yes, and, as I said, I think Mavis might have a fight on her hands if she wants to adopt!' Libby grinned as Mavis came out of the Blue Anchor to greet them.

'Boy's still asleep,' she said. 'Coffee? Come inside, then.'

'Shall I tell Graham we're going to have a case conference?' asked Fran.

'A what?' Mavis grunted. 'Nah. I'll call him when the boy gets up.'

'Has he said any more?' asked Fran. She turned to Libby. 'All he said last night was he had to get back for Barney.'

Mavis shook her head. 'Just thank you. And asked if I was sure about the dog coming inside.' Mavis snorted. 'As if!'

Mavis had just brought their coffee when Graham came through the door.

'Brought a couple of things,' he said, putting a carrier bag down on the table. 'Might be a bit big, but I don't suppose that matters.'

Mavis peered into the bag. 'Trousers?'

'Joggers,' said Graham. 'Couple of pairs of underpants, tee shirt, hoodie, socks. Shoes were a bit too difficult.'

'That's really nice of you, Graham,' said Fran.

'And we can always buy him some shoes,' said Libby.

'I'll go up and see if he's awake,' said Mavis, and disappeared to the back of the café with the carrier bag.

'What's going to happen now?' asked Graham. 'Do you think he'll want to stay?'

'No idea. He might be scared to stay round here in case the goons who took him away came back.' Libby scowled. 'I just hope he can give us something we can use in evidence.'

'To do what, though?' asked Fran.

'To get Stapleton convicted, of course,' said Libby. 'And get this bloody development stopped.'

'What about the body?' Graham hitched himself onto the edge of the table. 'Reckon he's got anything to do with that?'

'Well, it was on his land,' said Fran. 'But unless he's still carrying on the undercover Old Rogue business, I can't see it.'

'Old Rogue?' Graham looked puzzled.

By the time Libby and Fran had filled Graham in on the story of the Old Rogue, past and present, Mavis had appeared downstairs with Barney, who padded over to greet Libby, looking much more cheerful.

'Left him in the bath,' Mavis explained. 'Thought he'd been given the Crown Jewels by the look on his face.'

'I wonder when he last had a bath,' mused Libby. 'Doesn't bear thinking about.'

'Clothes he took off ain't too bad,' said Mavis. 'I'll stick 'em through the washer.'

It was another ten minutes before their guest made a self-conscious entrance wearing his borrowed finery. Barney let out a bark of greeting and ran to meet him.

'Come and sit down, boy,' said Mavis. 'Want a cuppa?'

The boy sidled into a chair and nodded, looking quickly and furtively at Graham, Libby and Fran.

Libby opened her mouth and Fran sent her a warning look. She subsided.

'Barney's pleased to see you, then?' said Graham.

The boy nodded, with a small smile.

'Did Mavis let him sleep on the bed with you?' said Fran. 'I bet she did.'

The boy nodded again, the smile staying in place as he looked down at his dog, who placed a trusting paw on his knee.

'The clothes don't fit too bad?' said Graham, waving a careless hand at the jogging bottoms.

'Had to roll 'em up.' The boy's voice sounded cracked, as though he wasn't used to using it. 'Thanks.'

160

'Pleasure.' Graham grinned at him, and was rewarded with a wider smile.

Mavis appeared with a large mug of tea and a sugar bowl. 'Now, boy. Breakfast? Egg and bacon do you?'

The boy's eyes widened. 'Yes, please!' he croaked.

'Why don't we take Barney for a run on the beach while we're waiting?' suggested Graham. 'He needs the exercise, even if you don't.' He stood, picked up Barney's makeshift string lead and waited for the boy to join him. Fran and Libby watched them go out of the shop and along to the steps down to the beach.

'Barney won't run away, will he?' said Libby.

'He didn't even try to when he was here waiting for his master, did he? He won't let him out of his sight now.'

'And it's mutual, isn't it?' Libby's eyes were filling again.

'Go on with you, you daft bat!' Fran nudged her in the ribs. 'It's a happy ending!'

'Happy for now,' said Libby with a sigh.

Graham, Barney and the boy returned well before Mavis arrived with the breakfast, Graham raising his eyes at the women knowingly. 'Reckon he's hungry,' he said. 'Or just doesn't want to go far from safety,' he added in an undertone.

'We've got to find out what happened,' said Libby.

'But we've got to let him tell it in his own time,' said Fran.

'No – we don't want to give him the third degree,' said Graham.

'It's very nice of you, Graham.' Libby waved a hand. 'You know – all this. Looking after Barney and the boy.'

Graham's cheerful pink face turned an even deeper pink, and he put a hand up to ruffle his fair hair. 'Well, you know. Could've been me, couldn't it? I wasn't happy at home, but I got a job as a barman and the landlord and his wife looked after me. I was lucky.' He nodded towards the boy, now sitting at the table and smiling up at Mavis as she placed plates in front of him. 'See, now, that might just be what's happening here. I reckon old Mavis is a mother figure.'

'You could be right.' Libby smiled, too.

Her phone warbled in her basket.

'Mum says look after the dog,' said Ben.

Libby laughed. 'She doesn't mind?'

'Of course she doesn't. Said would you go up and see her when you get back. I think she wants to know the whole story.'

'OK. I'll call you when I leave.' Libby ended the call. 'That was my partner, Ben,' she said to Graham. 'I was supposed to be at his mother's for lunch.' She looked at Fran. 'I suppose we're eating here now, aren't we?'

'Traditional roast?' suggested Graham. 'Won't be as good as your Ben's mum's, but still.' He winked. 'I'll go and add you to the sheet. Three of you?'

'Yes, please,' said Fran. 'Although Guy's might be a takeaway.'

'And we might need two more,' said Libby, nodding towards two figures approaching from the car park. 'Here's Ron and Maria.'

Ron looked as though he would make straight for Mavis and the boy, but hesitated when Maria pulled on his arm and Fran and Libby both appeared beside him.

'Let him settle,' said Fran.

'But—' began Ron.

'They're right, Ron,' said Maria. 'Don't frighten him.'

Ron sighed theatrically and sat down next to Fran's chair.

'Will you be staying for lunch?' Graham asked innocently.

'We are,' said Libby.

'Yes,' said Maria decisively. 'Save me cooking.'

Graham stood up and went back into The Sloop.

'He's really nice, isn't he?' said Libby. 'Don't know why we haven't got to know him before.'

'We have, a bit,' said Fran, 'but we tend to go to the pubs in Steeple Martin more than we do here.'

'Shall I get you a drink?' Libby asked Maria.

Ron stood up again. 'I'll go. Anyone want a refill?'

By the time they were all settled back at the table and Graham had rejoined them, saying his staff could cope without him for a bit longer, it looked as if Mavis was persuading the boy to come over and talk to them. Libby had an idea.

'Hello, Barney!' she called. 'Come and say hello.' She went round the table and held out her hand. As she'd hoped, Barney recognised her voice and started towards her, only to be held back by his makeshift lead.

'Come on, then, boy,' said Mavis. 'Let's go and talk to them, shall we?'

Slowly, the boy stood and began to walk forward. Barney gave a cheerful bark and bounded towards Libby, almost pulling his master off his feet. This relieved the tension, and everyone laughed.

'Now then,' said Mavis, when the extended company had settled round the table. 'What's your name, boy?'

'Can't keep calling you "boy",' said Libby.

'Rich – Ricky.' The boy kept his eyes on Barney.

'OK, Rich-Ricky,' said Ron. 'Can you tell us what happened to you when they took you away from here?'

Ricky lifted anxious eyes. 'I can't,' he said.

Chapter Twenty-two

After a long pause, Mavis nodded. "Fraid o' that,' she said, sitting back and crossing her arms.

'Ricky.' Fran leant forward. 'You're safe now. You're with us – and you already know Mavis –' she gestured towards Mavis – 'and Graham. Just tell us what happened when they made you leave the caravans. And who were they?'

Ricky lowered his eyes again. 'They said not to say anything.'

'Did they say what would happen if you did?' asked Maria.

Ricky shook his head.

'Just made it sound as though they'd be after you again.' Ron nodded.

Ricky looked at him. 'I was scared for Barney.'

'Of course you were,' said Libby. 'But you're back here, with Barney, and, believe me, we aren't going to let anything happen to you. So tell us – what happened to all the others?'

Mavis got up and fetched the mug Ricky had been using. 'Want another cuppa, love?' she asked.

Ricky nodded and seemed to relax.

'They came in early,' he began. 'I don't know what time. I was with Sparky and Al, and they just dragged us out. They had dogs. I told Barney to run.'

'And apart from you, Al and Sparky, who else was there?' asked Fran.

'Don't know their names, but there were four others in the

other vans.' Ricky shuddered. 'They got us in this big truck and drove us away.'

'Did they say anything?' Ron was leaning forward.

'Not really. We didn't see them again till they let us out.'

'And do you know where that was?' asked Maria.

Ricky shrugged. 'Slip road somewhere off a motorway. M2, I think. But I don't think they were supposed to let us go there. They were arguing.'

'And was that when they threatened you?' asked Libby.

Ricky nodded. Mavis came back with a fresh mug of tea.

'So how did you manage to get back here?' Graham was frowning. 'Difficult to hitch on a motorway.'

'We all managed to get into a sort of shopping place,' said Ricky, folding his hands round his mug. 'Found somewhere to sleep when we couldn't get lifts. But none of the others wanted to come back here. I got a lift yesterday on a lorry. He dropped me up the top of the town.'

Everyone sat back and looked at each other.

'And what about Rab?' asked Libby. 'Tall bloke – pale. Was he with you?'

Ricky looked bewildered. 'Don't know a Rab,' he said. 'Weren't any tall blokes, really.'

'So where do you think the others are now?' asked Ron.

'They were all making for Maidstone,' said Ricky.

'Good,' said Ron. 'They can get help there.'

'And you never saw any of the men who took you away before?' Fran had obviously been thinking.

Ricky shook his head.

'So you don't know if they really came from the owner of the site?'

Ricky shook his head again and rubbed his arm. 'They didn't give us the chance to ask,' he said, not adding, to his credit, 'you idiot'.

'No.' Fran was frowning at the table.

'Perhaps they didn't come from – you know, him?' hazarded Libby.

'Oh, I'm sure they did,' said Fran. 'I was just wondering . . .'

Graham looked at Ricky, then at Ron. 'Should we tell the police?'

Ricky shot up from his seat. 'No police!' he shouted.

'All right, boy, all right.' Mavis patted him on the shoulder. 'Shall we go back over there, then? You can have another little nap, eh?'

Ricky sent a wary and accusing glance at Graham and nodded.

They all watched him follow Mavis back to the Blue Anchor, Barney trotting happily at his side.

'Sorry.' Graham rubbed his face in what Libby realised was an automatic gesture. 'Wrong thing to say – but shouldn't we?'

Ron looked at Libby. 'Down to you two, I think.'

Libby nodded.

'Oh, yes,' Graham said with an air of enlightenment. 'I forgot you've got connections with the police, haven't you?'

'Yes, I think we ought to tell Ian – off the record, perhaps,' said Fran.

'If they come to talk to him now, he'll run away again,' said Maria.

The other four nodded their agreement.

'Could we take him home with us?' asked Ron.

'I think he's bonded with Mavis,' said Libby. 'We don't want to uproot him yet.'

'There's no garden for the dog, though,' said Ron.

'And it's a bit too close for comfort as far as Stapleton's concerned,' said Fran.

'And Mavis is too busy to keep an eye on him all the time,' agreed Libby. 'Shame, though.'

'Don't do anything for a couple of days,' said Graham. 'I can make sure I go with him when he takes Barney for a walk.'

'Do we really think Stapleton – or his men – would go after him?' said Maria. 'What about the others they took?'

'They don't know where they are,' said Libby. 'Stapleton or his goons could find out about Ricky easily.'

'But,' said Ron thoughtfully, 'until we turned up, Ricky didn't know anything about Stapleton. He doesn't even now, really, does he?'

'And don't let's mention the name in front of him,' said Maria.

'But if he's seen here,' began Graham.

'Where you and Mavis were threatened,' added Libby.

'They could put two and two together,' finished Fran.

They all fell quiet. Then Graham stood up.

'I must get back,' he said. 'When do you want your lunch?'

'When it's most convenient for your kitchen,' said Maria. 'Shall we come inside?'

'I'll call you when it's ready,' said Graham. 'About half an hour?'

'I'm going to wander down and have a look at your Alexandria,' said Ron. 'Coming?'

The three women shook their heads.

'So who's this Rab you mentioned?' asked Maria when Ron had strolled off along Harbour Street.

'Ah,' said Libby. 'I forgot you didn't know about Rab.'

She and Fran explained.

'And I think, now,' finished up Libby, 'we'd definitely better talk to his mum.'

'If she's been phoning your friend and accusing her of knowing where he is, I can't see her knowing anything useful,' said Maria.

'Well, she isn't now, because she knows he's dead,' said Fran.

'But she's still accusing Michelle,' said Libby. 'You're right, though, Maria. It doesn't sound as though she'd know anything.'

'Pity,' said Maria. 'Would have been useful background.'

'Club,' said Fran suddenly. 'Michelle said she went to a club. That would be for – er – retirees, wouldn't it?'

'I suppose so,' said Libby. 'Why?'

'Joe and Lenny belong to a club like that, don't they?'

'But it's in Nethergate, and this woman lives the other side of Canterbury.'

'It could be a different branch,' said Fran.

'Bit of a long shot,' said Maria. 'And surely the police will have asked her all those sorts of questions?'

'Yes,' sighed Libby. 'And they always get there before we do.'

Mavis rejoined them as they were finishing their traditional Sunday roast dinners.

'Left 'em watching telly,' she informed them. 'So what are we going to do about them?'

'How old is he?' asked Libby. 'If he's over eighteen, he can choose what to do himself. If he's still a minor, the state might step in.'

'We really need to know what he was running from in the first place,' said Fran. 'He's not old enough to fall into the "lost job, home, family" category.'

'Could be drugs,' suggested Ron, 'although he doesn't look like it.'

'Family, then,' said Libby.

'Fallen out with new step?' queried Maria. 'Parent remarried?'

'Could be,' said Fran. 'So where do we go from here?'

'Talk to Ian,' said Libby, 'strictly off the record, but not actually about Ricky. Just about what he's told us.'

Ron looked dubious. 'But will he take it seriously? He'd probably need to talk to Ricky himself.'

'But there's no concrete evidence of anything, whether he talks to Ricky or not,' said Maria. 'In fact, all you really want the police to do is investigate this Stapleton person, and Ricky doesn't seem to know of him. He didn't know who owned the site, or even, reading between the lines, whether the men who took him off the site had any right to do it.'

'You're right,' said Libby. Ron patted his wife's shoulder proudly.

Graham emerged from the pub and hurried over to join them.

'Sorry,' he said, 'did you want anything else? Coffee?'

'What are you sorry for?' asked Ron, surprised. 'What have you done?'

'Oh, nothing!' Graham's cheeks turned pink. 'I've left you alone too long, that's all. I got held up behind the bar.'

'That's all right,' said Libby. 'I don't want anything else, thanks – I'm full!'

Ron and Maria ordered coffee, and Mavis said she'd get her own if she wanted it. When Graham returned with the coffee, he sat down with a sigh.

'You forget how busy Sunday lunchtimes can be in the season,' he said. 'And the news was on.'

'And?' prompted Fran as they all watched Graham expectantly.

'Oh, it was just another local murder,' he said. 'They all started talking about it.'

'*What?*' said Libby.

'Another one?' said Ron.

'Where?' said Fran.

'I don't know – Canterbury, I think they said.' Graham looked bewildered. 'Nothing to do with us here, though. It was a woman.'

'Not identified?' asked Maria.

'I don't think so.' Now Graham looked slightly put out. 'I wasn't really paying attention – I was busy.'

'Yes, yes, of course,' soothed Fran. 'Sorry, Graham, we've all been thinking too much about murders.'

'Oh, that's all right.' Graham looked at Mavis. 'Decided what to do about the boy, then?'

'He can stay with me,' said Mavis, looking belligerent.

'That's great, Mavis,' said Libby. 'We don't think anyone else need be involved, Graham, certainly not if Ricky's over eighteen. But we want to find out why he ran away in the first place.'

'In case he runs away again.' Graham nodded wisely. 'Shall I talk to him?'

'You?' said Ron.

'Well, why not?' Graham bridled.

'You're nearer his age than any of us,' said Libby. 'Might be a good idea.'

Mavis nodded slowly. 'I'll bring him over a bit later.'

'And we'll go,' said Libby. 'Don't want to crowd him.'

'We'll go, too,' said Maria. 'Won't we, Ron?'

'But I wanted—' began Ron, scowling.

'We'll let you know.' Graham grinned at the other man. 'Don't worry.'

As Libby and Fran walked slowly back down Harbour Street to Coastguard Cottage, Libby's phone rang. She managed to fish it out of her pocket before it went to voicemail.

'Jane!' Libby raised her eyebrows at Fran. 'What can we do for you?'

'What do you know about this woman who's been murdered?' said Jane.

'Eh? What woman?'

'In Canterbury. Came through on the wire.'

'Oh, yes, we heard. Why should we know anything about it?'

'Because she was the mother of the body they found in the woods!'

Chapter Twenty-three

'What?' said Fran, taking in Libby's stunned expression.

Libby switched the phone to speaker.

'Do you mean our body? The one I talked to you about? *His* mother?'

'Well of course *that* body!' Jane sounded irritated. 'Didn't you know?'

'Of course not! When was it – I mean she – found?'

'Didn't say. What I got was "Police have revealed that the woman found dead in her home in Canterbury was the mother of the man found dead two weeks ago in the woods near Shott." No idea when she was found.' Jane sighed. 'I was sure you would know.'

'Sorry – no. If we find anything out, I'll let you know. Will you do the same?'

'You're more likely to find out than I am,' said Jane. 'See you.'

'Well!' said Libby, putting her phone back in her pocket.

'Well indeed.' Fran resumed her walk towards home. 'You can't go and see her now.'

'No, but it looks as though she knew something, doesn't it? Why didn't I go and see her when Michelle told me about her?'

'You had no reason to.' Fran opened the door of Coastguard Cottage. 'Do you want tea before you go home?'

'Trying to get rid of me?' Libby threw off her cape and sat down on the window seat. 'Yes, please.'

Fran grinned and went through to the kitchen.

Libby gazed out of the window at the familiar view and thought. Balzac joined her and butted her chin with his head.

Fran came back. 'Letting it draw,' she said, sitting down in the chair by the fireplace. 'So what are you going to do?'

'Nothing we can do,' said Libby. 'Too late now. And I don't suppose Ian will tell us anything.'

'He might question Michelle,' said Fran. 'To see if Joan said anything to her that might give a clue.'

'He might.' Libby nodded. 'But surely Michelle would have told either the police – or me – if she had.'

'You know what they say on the TV – anything, however insignificant. I'll get the tea.'

'I'll phone Michelle,' said Libby when Fran came back with the tea. 'Or do you think I'd better wait until tomorrow?'

'Wait,' said Fran. 'It's not as if you can offer any help, is it?'

'Hmmm.' Libby resumed her contemplation of the view out to sea. After a moment, she turned back to Fran. 'Could we have a recap, do you think? Would you mind? Even if it's only for my own satisfaction. I know I – we – can't do anything, but I'd like to make sense of it all.'

Fran gave her a wry smile. 'Can't do anything? OK – I'll buy it. Where do you want to start?'

'With what we now know, I suppose,' said Libby.

'And not what we've surmised?' Fran cocked her head on one side. 'That'll make a change.'

Libby scowled at her. 'Sarky. Right. We now know that Neil Barton lived with his mother, Joan, in a nice house near Harbledown, outside Canterbury. We also know that he was posing as a homeless person and cultivating Sylvia Cranthorne, an estate agent working for Brooke and Company, who are, or will be, marketing the residential park homes at Island View.'

'We also know,' put in Fran, 'that the permission for the development of Island View is potentially illegal, if the Certificate of Lawful Development is not genuine.'

'We don't actually *know* that,' said Libby. 'It's an assumption. What we *do* know is that a person called Nick Stapleton has bought the Island View site and had half a dozen homeless people evicted from the site.'

'That's also an assumption,' said Fran. 'Young Ricky didn't know who the men were who evicted him.'

'It's a reasonable assumption, though, as Stapleton owns the site.'

'Another assumption is that Stapleton knew, or found out, that Neil was sniffing round,' Fran went on.

'And that he had Neil killed – simply because Neil's body turned up on his land,' finished Libby.

'But they were all assumptions, and you said we were looking at the facts we actually know,' said Fran. 'All we know is that Neil's body was found on Stapleton's land.'

'All right, all right.' Libby was testy. 'Another perfectly reasonable assumption is that Joan Barton knew something about her son that led to him being killed.'

'Do we,' said Fran, after another moment's thought, 'think that Stapleton and Neil knew each other?'

'Or,' said Libby, 'simply that they knew *of* each other?'

'I'm inclined to think,' said Fran, 'that Neil knew of Stapleton and all his works.'

'And was trying to find out about it all and expose him!' Libby almost bounced with enthusiasm.

'And Stapleton found out,' agreed Fran.

'Yes!' Libby beamed at her friend.

'But,' mused Fran, 'would that be enough to kill Neil? An illegal development?'

'And where does that leave his mum?' Libby's face fell. 'That scenario doesn't leave any room for her.'

They fell silent, sipping their tea.

'So are we going to assume that Neil's murder was nothing to do with Island View or Stapleton?' asked Libby eventually.

'Unless the mother's murder is nothing to do with Neil,' said Fran.

'Nah,' said Libby. 'I don't believe in coincidences.'

'In that case . . .' Fran frowned. 'I don't know.'

'Mum has to have been killed because she knew something about Neil's murder,' said Libby.

'Or guessed,' said Fran. 'She didn't appear to know he'd been murdered before she identified him. She thought he'd run off with Michelle.'

'So,' said Libby slowly, 'when she found out he'd been murdered, she guessed whodunnit.'

'So either she knew of a connection with Stapleton or whoever it was who killed him.' Fran shook her head. 'Which is exactly where the police are, I should think.'

'Further on than that, I reckon,' said Libby. 'They'll have gone through Joan's life and times with the proverbial fine-toothed comb.'

'Of course, we haven't even looked at the other suspect for Neil's murder,' said Fran.

'What other suspect?' Libby looked surprised. 'There isn't one – at least, not that we know of.'

'Sorry, Lib.' Fran made a face. 'What about Michelle?'

'Wha–?' Libby's mouth fell open. 'You can't mean that!'

'If not Michelle, what about her partner?'

'Phil?' Libby looked thoughtful. 'That's a possibility. I don't know him, really, but he is a bit – well, a bit . . .'

'A bit what? Likely to lose his temper? A bit rough? What?'

'Both of those,' admitted Libby. 'And I suppose Joan would be an obvious victim under those circumstances.'

'Yes, because she knew the connection between Neil and Michelle. After all, she introduced them.' Fran stood up. 'More tea?'

Libby looked at her watch. 'No, I think I'd better be going. Hetty wanted me to call in and tell her about Barney.'

'And you'll have to catch up with the Sunday gathering at Pete and Harry's,' said Fran with a grin.

'If I have time,' said Libby.

'We had an early lunch, so I expect you have.'

'Right.' Libby collected her cape and bag. 'Keep thinking.'

'I will.' Fran gave her a friendly push towards the door. 'Go on. Get a move on.'

In fact, Ben was still sitting with his mother, Flo, Lenny and Joe at the big kitchen table when Libby arrived. She gave them an abbreviated version of Ricky and Barney's story, before Hetty shooed them both off even before they'd loaded the dishwasher.

'Plenty of us to help,' said Hetty. 'Reckon you've got a lot more than that to talk about.'

'How did your mother get to be so wise?' asked Libby as she and Ben walked down the Manor drive towards the high street.

'A lifetime's experience,' said Ben. 'Remember what she lived through when she was young.'

Libby sighed. 'Don't like to think about it.'

'Tell me what else happened this morning, then. Or do you want to wait until we get to Pete and Harry's?'

'Wait, I think,' said Libby. 'I want opinions. And just for my own satisfaction, because there's absolutely nothing I can do about any of it.'

Peter opened the door of the cottage and waved them in. Harry, as usual, sprawled on the sofa still in his chef's whites.

'The old trout is pregnant with news,' he observed. 'This is ominous.'

Libby collapsed into her favourite armchair and made a face at him.

'She says she wants opinions,' said Ben.

'That's easy,' said Harry. 'Don't do it, that's my opinion.'

'Seriously,' said Libby. 'I just want to tell you a story.'

'As long as it hasn't got Old Rogues and ghost dogs in it,' said Peter, handing her a glass of red wine, unasked.

'No, it hasn't. Anyway, we had enough of that on Friday.' Libby settled back and began her story.

By the time she had finished, her listeners were all looking serious, and Peter had an arm round Harry, on whom Ricky's story had obviously had an effect.

'Poor little bugger,' he said now, clearing his throat.

'He's been rescued, Hal,' said Peter. 'Like you were.'

'And I think he'll have a choice of homes,' said Libby. 'Both Mavis and Ron Stewart want to take him in.'

'But he isn't what you want an opinion on, is it?' said Ben. 'You want to know who killed Neil and why?'

'And who killed his mum.' Harry sat up straight and took a healthy sip of wine. 'So what are you going to do about it?'

'Nothing we can do,' said Libby, looking surprised. 'I just wanted to know what you all thought. Is Stapleton behind the murder? Or is it Michelle and her partner?'

Ben and Peter looked at Harry.

'I don't know,' he said. 'But Stapleton's behind everything else. Evicting those poor sods – and young Ricky and his dog –' he paused – 'and you said illegal immigrants? Trafficked, poor buggers. You need to get him just for that.'

'I expect the police will, if it all turns out to be true,' said Libby.

'There can't be any doubt about who was behind the eviction,' said Ben.

'More like a kidnapping,' said Peter.

'He could argue that he was within his rights as he owns the site,' said Libby.

Harry made a growling sound and finished his wine.

'Where did the boy come from originally?' asked Peter, topping up Harry's glass.

'We don't know, but we want to find out,' said Libby. 'It wasn't the right time to ask today – he was still very wary.'

'Could I talk to him?' asked Harry. 'After all, I've been there. He might talk to me.'

'I think Graham at The Sloop had the same idea,' said Libby, 'but yes – if you're off tomorrow, we could go down and see him.'

'I thought you told her not to do it?' Ben said with a grin.

'And remember what happened last time you went out for a Monday walk together,' said Peter.

'We didn't do any harm,' protested Harry. 'And we won't this time, will we, petal?'

'Of course not,' agreed Libby. 'After all, the police won't have anything to do with Ricky, so we won't be treading on any toes.'

'As long as he's over eighteen,' warned Ben.

'Oh, I'm sure he is,' said Harry blithely. 'He can say he is, anyway.'

Peter and Ben shook their heads and exchanged resigned glances. 'Bad as each other,' said Peter.

On Monday morning, Libby was just about to leave to pick up Harry when the phone rang.

'Ian!' Libby felt a distinct disturbance somewhere around her solar plexus. 'What's the matter?'

'Nothing, but I wondered why you hadn't called me.' Ian sounded as though he was smiling.

'Why?'

'I can't believe you haven't heard that our victim's mother has been murdered.'

'Oh. Yes, we did hear.' Now Libby was puzzled. 'But why should we have rung you?'

'Because you wanted to know all about it?' Ian laughed. 'Oh, come on, Lib! That's what you usually do, isn't it?'

'But there's nothing Fran or I can do about it, and we aren't involved, are we? Or only on the periphery, anyway.'

'And you weren't going to tell me about the boy and his dog?'

Libby could have kicked herself. 'Oh, bother. Yes, I was, actually, only the news about Neil's mother put it out of my head. How do you know?'

'Would you believe Ron Stewart rang me? He seemed surprised you hadn't been in touch.'

'Yes, well, I did say I would tell you. Why did he call, anyway?'

'He's got a bee in his bonnet about Nick Stapleton.' Ian sighed. 'As have many people.'

'So's Harry,' said Libby. 'We're going down to see the boy this morning.'

'Don't interfere, Libby.' Ian's voice changed.

'We aren't.' Libby was indignant. 'Ricky's over eighteen. You can't touch him. And Harry's got rather a fellow feeling for him. We thought he might open up to Harry – tell him where he came from.'

'Well, all right.' Ian was grudging. 'But no poking about in anything else.'

'No, sir,' said Libby. 'And are you going to tell me about Neil's mum?'

Ian sighed again. 'I suppose so. Her neighbour noticed her paper was still sticking out of her letter box and let herself in. What will we do when no one has paper deliveries any more? No more convenient doorstep signs of trouble.'

'And what had happened to her?'

'Blunt force trauma. No signs of a break-in and, as far as we can see, nothing taken, although there were some drawers left open.'

'Someone looking for something to connect her to Neil's murder?' suggested Libby.

'One might think so.' Ian sounded amused. 'And that's all I'm telling you. And now off you go and talk to young Ricky. We'll leave him alone, but if you get anything that might be of the slightest interest to us, let me know. Please.'

'Well,' said Libby to Sidney as she gathered up her car keys. 'Looks as though we're involved, after all.'

Chapter Twenty-four

Harry was uncharacteristically quiet on the drive to Nethergate. May had turned grey, and the sharp spring green of the hedgerows was muted, the colour leached from the white and pale pink of the blossom. Libby shifted uncomfortably in her seat and sneaked a look at the stern profile next to her.

'Eyes on the road, petal.' A small smile lifted Harry's mouth. 'What are you nervous about?'

'How Ricky will react, I suppose,' said Libby. 'You've been very quiet.'

'I've been wondering what Ricky will say, too, but also what and how much you report to our favourite DCI.'

'I needn't report anything,' said Libby. 'I can just say he didn't say much.'

'Get real, chuck.' Harry turned sideways in his seat. 'You can hardly say that. No, what I was thinking about was what he ran away from. Would Ian – or the force – be duty bound to tell his parents, or school, or whoever it was reported him missing in the first place.'

'If he's over eighteen, they can't do anything about it,' said Libby.

'You've been saying that, but suppose he isn't over eighteen? The people he ran away from might be able to prove he isn't.' Harry tapped her leg. 'See what I mean?'

Libby frowned. 'They might force him to go back, you mean?'

'And he'd simply run away again.' Harry turned back to face the road. 'Nice view that.'

They had reached the crest of the hill overlooking Nethergate, with its picture-postcard roofs tumbling down the hill towards the half-moon bay.

'I was only thinking that the other day,' said Libby. 'If ever I left Steeple Martin, I'd like to live here.'

'You'll never leave, you silly old trout. You'd miss us all too much.' Harry gave her a complacent smile and crossed his arms. Libby sighed and couldn't help smiling.

Harbour Street had cars parked nose to tail along its length, so Libby parked behind the Blue Anchor. As they walked round to the front, they saw Fran coming to meet them.

'Does Ricky know we're coming?' asked Harry.

'I left it up to Mavis whether she told him or not. She said he was fine this morning.' Libby peered through the window of the café. 'Look, there they are.'

Ricky turned to face them as Harry opened the door, a wary expression on his face.

'Coffee?' asked Mavis.

'Could I have tea?' asked Libby as the other two accepted. 'Hello, Ricky. How did you sleep?'

'Great, thanks.' Ricky gave her a half smile, and Barney stood up to greet her, tail wagging furiously.

'This is our friend Harry,' said Fran, pulling out a chair.

'Hi, Ricky.' Harry held out a hand. Ricky tentatively took it, and Libby saw that, in an instant, a bond was formed. Mavis paused in pouring boiling water into a mug and Fran's hand stilled while pushing her hair away from her face.

'Fancy a walk?' said Harry. 'Barney could do with a bit of a run, couldn't he?' He bent down, holding a hand out, palm down, for Barney to sniff, which he obligingly did, following up with a friendly lick.

'Yeah, thanks.' Ricky stood up and picked up Barney's lead,

which Libby noticed was a new red one, to match his new red collar. 'Graham brought them over this morning,' the boy explained.

'Been very good, that Graham,' said Mavis, arriving at the table with a tray. 'Put yours in one o' those cardboard efforts,' she told Harry, who gave her a daring kiss on the cheek. Mavis blushed.

The three women watched as man, boy and dog left the café, seemingly in perfect harmony.

'Do you think—' began Libby, turning to Fran.

'Harry recognised—' agreed Fran.

'What?' said Mavis. 'Think he knows young Ricky?'

'No.' Libby shook her head. 'We think . . . um . . .' She looked at Fran for help.

'We think Ricky might be gay, like Harry,' Fran explained.

''Ere!' said Mavis, looking horrified. 'He's not going to—'

'No!' said Fran and Libby together.

'I think Harry realised Ricky's gay – it forms a bond, you see,' said Libby. 'And it's probably why Ricky ran away from home – or school, or whatever it was.'

Mavis nodded slowly. 'Makes sense. Think the boy'll tell Harry?'

'I think so,' said Fran. 'Harry was in the same boat, you see, when he was young.'

'Ah.' Mavis turned to peer out of the window, from where the now small figures of Harry and Ricky could be seen almost level with The Alexandria. She turned back to Fran and Libby. 'Drink your coffee before it gets cold,' she grunted, before stomping off back to the kitchen.

'What shall we do now?' Libby asked, sitting down at the little Formica-topped table. 'Apart from drink our coffee?'

'How about going to see if anything's happened at Island View?' suggested Fran.

'We'd better drink our coffee first,' said Libby. 'We didn't get ours in one of those cardboard efforts like Harry.'

'And yours,' said Fran with a grin, 'isn't even coffee.'

181

Coffee and tea duly finished, Fran called through to Mavis that they were going out to look at Island View.

'Notices up all over it,' said Mavis, popping her head out of the kitchen. 'Watch yourselves.'

Sure enough, when they reached the high chain-link fence, they found large warning notices attached to it, informing the public that the site was patrolled by security guards.

'What there isn't,' said Libby, peering through the fence, 'is anything saying what the site is going to be, or where to apply for further information.'

'Perhaps we should look round the other side,' said Fran. 'You said before you thought there would be access from the road.'

'Bound to be,' agreed Libby. 'That would be the main way in.'

'But,' said Fran slowly, 'Stapleton – or whoever – will now know that the police are looking at the site, so they may have scaled back their operations. Laying low for a bit, perhaps.'

Libby nodded. 'Ian did say they were going to send SOCOs in to search the vans, didn't he?'

'He will have to have got a search warrant for that,' said Fran. 'Do we know if he did?'

'No.' Libby let out a frustrated sigh. 'We don't even know if he's spoken to Stapleton yet.'

'True.' Fran frowned. 'Somebody will have, surely, because of Neil's body being found on his land. He did say that, didn't he?'

'Yes, but just that everybody round about had been spoken to. It probably wasn't Ian, and at that stage they didn't know it was Neil, and we didn't know anything about Island View, either.'

'Well, we and the police know now,' said Fran, 'so they are probably making inquiries.'

They walked slowly back to the Blue Anchor.

'Harry and Ricky are coming back,' said Libby.

'So's Barney,' said Fran as the dog came bounding back up the steps from the beach and made straight for Libby.

'Ooof!' said Libby, trying to fend off damp, sandy paws.

'Barney! Here!' yelled Ricky, running in pursuit. 'Sorry, Libby.' He dragged the dog off and fastened the lead onto his collar. Harry was laughing.

Mavis appeared, looking surprised.

'Let's sit out here,' said Harry, swinging one of the white-painted iron chairs away from its table. 'Barney'll need a bit of a wash before he goes inside.'

Libby and Fran sat down while Ricky tried to calm his excited dog. Mavis stood in her doorway, frowning, just as Graham emerged from the doorway of The Sloop. Libby looked round the assembled company and wondered who was going to speak first, and, come to that, what they were going to speak about. Harry grinned at her.

'So, young Ricky, what are we going to do with you?' he said, giving the boy a playful buffet on the arm.

Ricky gave him a bashful smile. 'I don't know,' he said. 'As long as you don't send me back home.'

Everyone stared, first at Ricky, then at Harry.

'No one can do that, Rick, not now you've turned eighteen. Oh, yes,' Harry said to the others, 'just last week. So he can live where he likes.'

Ricky shrugged. 'If I had any money.'

Mavis cleared her throat. 'Anyone want more coffee?' she asked.

Fran, Harry and Ricky all said yes, and Libby opted for more tea.

'I'll come and help you,' said Ricky. 'Stay, Barney.'

When he and Mavis had disappeared into the café, Libby turned to Harry.

'So?' she said.

'What I thought,' said Harry. 'Mum widowed, married a homophobic bastard second time around. He didn't say much, but I can imagine.' The corners of Harry's mouth turned down. 'And Barney was the last straw. Bastard said he had to live outside or be put down. And wasn't going to let Ricky's mum support him through uni.'

183

'Bloody hell!' said Graham.

'And the woman didn't stand up to him?' Libby gasped.

'Had he got a place?' asked Fran.

'From what the boy said, Mum was infatuated, and yes. He had a place at Medway to do cultural studies and media with journalism.'

'He could still take that up,' said Fran.

'No funding,' said Harry. 'He didn't say much, as I said, but I can guess. He just walked. I asked if he'd tried to get a job, but he said he couldn't without somewhere to live.'

'We could give him somewhere to live,' said Graham.

'Does he know what he wants to do?' asked Libby. 'Does he want to go to uni?'

'I think so, but he's one confused youngster at the moment.' Harry looked towards the café, from where Ricky was emerging carrying a tray. 'Ask him.'

'What do you want to do, Ricky?' asked Libby, when they were all settled with their drinks of choice. 'Do you want to go to uni?'

Ricky looked at his feet. 'Can't, can I?' he growled.

'Suppose we could find out about funding?' suggested Fran. 'Ask Edward?' she said to Libby and Harry.

Ricky looked up. 'How?' he said.

'If we find you somewhere to live,' said Harry, 'and you get yourself a job for the time being—'

'Here,' said Mavis. 'Haven't hired for the season yet.'

'Brilliant!' said Libby.

'Great idea!' said Graham.

'What about that?' Harry said to Ricky.

'Work here?' Ricky looked at Mavis. 'For you? Would I live here, too?'

'I had a thought about that,' said Fran.

All eyes turned towards her.

'Well, Sophie's not living in the flat at the moment, is she?' She looked at Ricky and pointed across to Harbour Street. 'We've got a flat above a shop over there, Ricky. Would you mind living on your own?'

Ricky's face was a study in puzzled hope.

'Blimey!' said Graham. 'Wish we could solve all the world's problems as easily as that!'

Chapter Twenty-five

'It's not a long-term solution,' said Fran. 'Just until Ricky sorts himself out.'

'What do you think, Rick?' Harry leant forward, elbows on knees.

Ricky's face turned red, and he stared down at Barney. 'Er . . .' he said. Barney stood and placed his long nose on Ricky's knee.

'That means yes,' said Libby.

Ricky looked at Mavis. 'Can I really?' His voice came out as a croak.

Mavis cleared her throat. 'Course. Have to work hard, mind.'

Ricky's face lit in the widest smile Libby had ever seen, and he turned to Fran. 'Could I really stay in your flat?'

Fran nodded, smiling.

'Hope Guy doesn't mind,' said Harry, stretching out his legs and beaming round the table.

Fran stood up. 'I'll pop over and tell – *ask* – him,' she said.

Ricky looked back at Mavis. 'What would I have to do?' he asked.

'Come on, then.' Mavis stood up. 'Let's go and see.'

'What about Barney?' Ricky hesitated.

'Leave him with us for now,' said Harry, and they watched Ricky go happily into the café with his new employer.

'Different boy, isn't he?' said Graham. He leant over and put out a hand. 'I'm Graham, by the way.'

Harry shook it, laughing. 'Sorry! Hi, Graham, I'm Harry. Ricky's a lucky boy, isn't he?'

'If Mavis and Graham hadn't found Barney, it would have been a different story,' said Libby with a sigh. 'So did he say anything about the goons who kidnapped him?'

'No.' Harry shook his head. 'I honestly don't think he knows much. He fell in with a couple of the other homeless, who took him to the caravan site not long after he first ran away.'

'Yes – just when was that?' asked Graham. 'Not long, surely?'

'Only a few weeks, as far as I can make out,' said Harry. 'He wouldn't say exactly where he'd come from, but I don't reckon it can be far away. We'd better ask Ian to check on missing persons, Lib.'

'I just hope the stepfather doesn't come after him if they find out where he is,' said Libby.

'If he was as awful as Ricky said he was, I should think he'd be glad to be rid of him,' said Graham.

'But the mother might,' said Libby.

'Sufficient unto the day, petal. Young Rick's fallen on his grubby little feet – let's just be grateful for that.' Harry looked at Graham. 'Even though the old trout can't have a drink because she's driving, I think I might.'

Graham laughed. 'Do you let him talk about you like that?' he asked Libby.

'He's my best friend next to Fran,' Libby told him. 'He's also the *chef patron* at the Pink Geranium restaurant in Steeple Martin.'

'Oh!' Graham stood up. 'I'm honoured. Drinks on the house, then.'

After Graham had left to fetch Harry's beer and Libby's spritzer, which she had insisted wouldn't put her over the limit, she sat back in her chair and regarded her best friend thoughtfully.

'Did he actually admit he was gay, or did you bully him into it?'

'I just let him know I knew. Then the rest tumbled out. He's been worried that if all these nice people who had rescued him, as

187

he put it, found out he was gay, they'd throw him out. That bloody man did a great job on the poor sod.'

'But you were able to reassure him?' said Libby. 'It beggars belief that there are still people like that out there.'

'Oh, come on, Lib. Racism, sexism and homophobia are still rife. Endemic in some institutions. Luckily for our Edward, not in universities, it seems.'

'That reminds me,' said Libby, 'should we ask Edward about any funding schemes there might be for Ricky?'

'We can ask,' said Harry doubtfully, 'but I very much doubt if there are.'

'Here comes Fran.' Libby waved.

'And here comes Graham with the drinks,' said Harry. 'He'll have to go back for another one now.'

'So what did Guy say?' asked Libby, when Fran had been served with her drink and Graham had gone back to supervise his bar staff.

'As long as it isn't permanent, and will he keep it clean?' Fran laughed.

'Such a shame he couldn't tell us anything about Stapleton or the heavies.' Libby frowned into her spritzer.

'Perhaps he'll remember more bits and pieces as he relaxes a bit,' said Harry. 'Now, drink up, chuck. I need to get back to the treadmill.'

'But it's Monday!' said Fran.

'Ordering and restocking,' said Harry. 'And I'd quite like to spend a bit of quality time with my husband, if you don't mind!'

Leaving Mavis, Graham and Fran to sort Ricky's life out for him, and promising to be on hand if needed, Libby drove Harry back to Steeple Martin.

'Lunch?' he asked as he got out of the car. 'I can throw an experimental leftovers soup together for Pete and me, and there'll be plenty for you.'

'OK. I'll just go and put the car away.' Libby pulled away just in time to see Ben emerge from Cuckoo Lane. She stopped and let the window down.

'Have you been interfering at the Pocket again?' she called.

Ben grinned and crossed the road. 'Just seeing how the weekend went,' he replied. 'We are going to have to get in extra help.'

'Pity young Ricky will be down in Nethergate, then,' said Libby. 'Or you could have roped him in.'

'What?' Ben frowned.

'I'm going to have soup with Pete and Harry once I've parked the car,' said Libby. 'Go in and wait for me.'

When she got back ten minutes later, Harry had filled Peter and Ben in on the morning's dispositions, opened a bottle of red wine and retired to the kitchen to concoct the soup.

'Been playing Good Samaritan, then, have we?' said Peter, with a grin.

'It's Mavis and Fran who are going to be doing most of it,' said Libby, sinking into a chair. 'I expect we'll have to buy some clothes or something.'

'And talk to Edward about uni funding,' said Ben.

'Yes.' Libby sighed. 'All a bit overwhelming.'

'At least it keeps you away from murder,' said Peter, then narrowed his eyes. 'Or does it?'

'Ricky can't contribute anything to that,' said Libby. 'Speaking of which, I'd better tell Ian that nothing of any use came up this morning.'

'He knew you were going, then?' said Ben.

'Oh, yes.' Libby fished out her phone. 'He asked me to keep my ears open. I don't think they're getting anywhere with the investigation.'

'And now they've got this second murder,' said Peter, and shook his head. 'And you can't do anything about it.'

'No.' Libby sent him a fulminating glare.

'I suppose,' said Ben, 'the theory that Stapleton killed your homeless person—'

'Neil,' put in Libby.

'Neil, is a bit too obvious. Did Ricky say Neil was with them at the caravan site?'

'No, that's the odd thing.' Libby paused, her finger hovering over her phone. 'He didn't seem to know him at all. At least, not from our description.'

Harry arrived with a tray of soup bowls and a cottage loaf. 'Grubs up,' he said.

'So,' said Ben, after they'd all been served, 'if he wasn't turned off the caravan site with Ricky and the others, the only reason for suspecting Stapleton is that Neil was found on his land.'

'Which means,' said Harry, 'that the whole "illegal caravan site" thing is a red herring.'

'I suppose so,' said Libby gloomily. 'And it looked so promising.'

'But we know about it now, which is a good thing,' said Ben, 'and if the police can find anything about the migrant workers, that will be good, too.'

'What about the mother?' asked Peter. 'Do you know anything about her?'

'Only what Michelle's told me,' said Libby.

'OK – recap,' said Peter. 'Michelle is your hairdresser friend who this Neil person was stalking. And the dead woman is the stalker's mother – is that right?'

Libby nodded and took a mouthful of soup. 'Ow – hot.'

'Come from a hot place, as I keep telling you,' said Harry. 'Blow on it.'

'So another logical suspect for Neil's murder would be Michelle,' said Peter. 'As we were saying yesterday.'

'Or her partner,' agreed Libby. 'And if it was either one of them, again, as we said, his mum would know of the connection and therefore might be a threat.'

'No – hang on,' said Harry, pausing with his spoon halfway to his mouth. 'That doesn't add up, because the police already knew of the connection.'

They all looked at each other.

'There must be something in Neil's life that made him a target,' said Ben.

'And Joan – his mum – knew about it,' said Libby. 'Well, we'd sort of got that far already. And so have the police, I should imagine.'

'So all you've got to do is find out what nasty little secret Neil had in his life,' said Peter. 'Apart from stalking innocent women, that is.'

'Or what he knew,' said Harry. 'He could have found something out by accident.'

'And told his mum?' queried Libby. 'Would he?'

'He must have been close to his mum,' said Ben. 'He was still living with her, and he must have been – what – forties?'

'There are a lot of people in their thirties and forties still living with their parents these days,' said Libby darkly.

'Because if they didn't,' said Harry, 'they'd be homeless. Circle of life.'

The other three looked at him in surprise. Peter reached across and patted him on the arm.

'Well, there we are, then,' said Ben. 'Find out what Neil knew.'

'It *could* have been something about Stapleton,' said Libby, unwilling to give up her favourite villain.

'I'll tell you who you ought to ask,' said Harry, wiping his bowl out with a hunk of cottage loaf. 'That what's-her-name woman – Ian's ex. She started all this, after all.'

'Sylvia?' Libby paused with her hand on her wine glass, an arrested expression on her face. 'You think he might have said something to her?'

'I don't know, do I?' said Harry. 'Did she tell you what they talked about?'

'No.' Libby frowned. 'She said he told her he'd lost his job and his home – that was about all. And that was lies, wasn't it?'

'And you still don't know where he worked?' Peter raised an eyebrow.

'I was going to ask Joan about that,' said Libby. 'If I went to see her.' She looked sideways at Ben. 'If, I said.'

Ben shook his head at her.

'So where he worked could be the clue to the whole business,' said Peter.

'But how could where he worked have got him killed?' asked Libby.

'Unless he had some connection with the police or social services or something,' said Harry.

'Or the county planning office,' suggested Ben.

'But *murder*?' said Libby. 'That's a bit drastic.'

'Ask what's-her-name,' said Harry, standing up. 'I told you.'

Ben went back to his office at the Manor and Libby went home. Finally remembering, she sent Ian a message and put the big kettle onto the Rayburn hotplate. Then she sat down at the kitchen table and rang Fran.

'We've decided to let him stay with Mavis for a bit while he settles down,' said Fran. 'He seemed a bit worried about going to the flat.'

'Well, he's never lived on his own, has he? Apart from when he ran away,' said Libby. 'And he does seem to have bonded with Mavis. What I was going to say was – should we get him some clothes?'

'I was thinking that,' said Fran. 'How about we take him to Canterbury on a shopping trip?'

'Good idea,' said Libby. 'Now – about Neil's murder.'

Fran groaned.

Chapter Twenty-six

'No, listen,' Libby went on. 'Harry said why don't we ask Sylvia if he said anything to her during their morning meet ups. You know – about where he worked or anything. The boys thought that might be why he was killed.'

'What – because of where he worked?'

'Yes, that's what I said,' Libby agreed, 'but he might have given her a clue of some kind.'

'I don't think so,' said Fran slowly. 'After all, he was playing a part, wasn't he? The poor homeless man. He wouldn't have told her the truth about anything.'

'Oh, yes! We didn't think of that,' said Libby, much struck.

'But it wouldn't hurt to ask,' said Fran. 'He might have let something slip.'

'Except that she hasn't really wanted to talk to us since that first time.' Libby, tapped the table thoughtfully.

'And she knows a lot more about the Island View development than she lets on, didn't you think?' Fran asked. 'So perhaps we ought to talk to her anyway.'

'But I thought we'd decided that Neil's death didn't have anything to do with Island View,' said Libby.

'But there's the homeless connection,' said Fran. 'Even if he wasn't living with them, he was pretending to be part of the homeless community.'

'Hmm.' Libby was doubtful. 'Anyway, you don't think he

would have let anything slip to Sylvia, so it isn't worth talking to her.'

'Nooo . . .'

'What?' Libby sat up straight. 'What have you thought?'

'I just wondered,' said Fran, 'if *Sylvia* had let something slip to *him*.'

'Ohhh.' Libby let out a long breath. 'Something he wasn't supposed to know?' She thought for a moment. 'But about what? About Brooke and Company selling the site?'

'You said she told you he was trying to pump her for information,' said Fran. 'And that would be why. Because she worked for the estate agent who was selling the homes.'

'So he was trying to find out about the site, the homes, probably the certificate of lawful development and possibly – Stapleton himself,' finished Libby triumphantly. 'So there we are – back at Stapleton.'

'I thought you were trying to find an alternative suspect,' said Fran, amused.

'Trouble is, it always comes back to Stapleton,' sighed Libby.

'And the police will have worked that out,' said Fran. 'I bet they've already questioned him.'

'Bother,' said Libby. 'You're right.'

'Oh – and I had another thought,' said Fran. 'You know Sylvia said she hadn't seen Rab, as she called him, for a couple of weeks? Well, we now know that he was alive and kicking, because you saw him at Michelle's. So how do we know Sylvia hadn't really seen him?'

Libby frowned. 'I suppose we don't. And, come to think of it, we don't know when he died, apart from the fact that it had to be after I saw him that Monday. But what difference does it make, anyway?'

Fran sighed. 'I don't know. I'm as bad as you are. Why can't we leave it alone?'

'Because it's a puzzle,' replied Libby, 'and neither of us can resist a puzzle. And now I'd better free up the phone in case Ian's trying to ring. I left him a text.'

'He'd use the landline,' said Fran, 'but I've got to go, anyway. Let me know if you hear anything.'

'And you let me know when we're going on Ricky's clothes trip.' Libby ended the call. The big kettle was issuing irritated puffs of steam on the Rayburn, so she made her mug of tea and took it into the sitting room.

Was Sylvia Cranthorne that duplicitous? And, if so, why? She could hardly be regarded as a murder suspect – after all, she had reported Neil – or Rab – missing. And was he trying to pump her for information, or was it the other way round? But if she was trying to obtain information from him, what was it? If she thought he was what he said, a homeless person, what information could he have had, and about what? It didn't make any sense.

Sidney had just jumped up beside her, preparatory to inserting himself onto her lap when the landline rang.

'OK, Lib, what have you got for me?' Ian sounded quite light-hearted.

'Nothing much,' admitted Libby, going back to the sofa to dislodge Sidney. She reported everything that had happened that morning and finished up by telling him about the proposed shopping trip.

'In that case,' said Ian, 'while you're in Canterbury, you can bring him into the station for a chat.'

'But he doesn't know anything!'

'He's the only one of those displaced people we can lay hands on, isn't he? Therefore, a person of interest.'

'That makes him sound like a suspect,' Libby grumbled. 'Oh, and while you're there, have you actually questioned Nick Stapleton yet?'

'What about?'

'Oh, *Ian*!'

Ian laughed. 'As we thought Neil Barton was a homeless person from Nethergate, and we found out – thank you – that homeless people had been removed from a site owned by Stapleton, of course he was questioned. And, yes, he's a nasty piece of work, and we now have the relevant department inquiring into the work force he seems to have assembled at his estate.'

'And are they illegal migrants?' asked Libby.

'I couldn't possibly say.' Ian sounded amused. 'And before you ask, yes, I was hoping your young lad might have some information that would help our inquiries.'

'And what about Neil's mother?' Libby waited for the reprimand. It came.

'Libby, you know I can't tell you anything about that. It's not even my case.'

'But they must be linked!' protested Libby. 'Why isn't it your case?'

'Libby.' Ian had stopped being light-hearted and approachable. 'Leave it. Thank you for your help with Ricky Short—'

'Ricky Short? You know his name?'

There was a faint hissing noise in Libby's ear, indicative of annoyance. 'Ricky Short was reported missing by his mother five weeks ago. He is an adult, therefore we have to have his permission to inform her of his whereabouts.'

'Right. Thank you.' Libby took a breath. 'I'll let you know when we bring him into Canterbury, shall I?'

'Please.' Ian's tone softened. 'And I expect I'll see you on Wednesday. Are we still meeting in the Coach?'

'Well,' Libby said to Sidney after she'd ended the call, 'that didn't go as well as I'd hoped.'

But at least, she thought, she now knew that Nick Stapleton had been questioned. And, for what it was worth, she knew Ricky's surname. But it didn't sound as though Stapleton was a murder suspect. In which case – who was?

Cui bono?' said Ben when Libby put the question to him over dinner. 'That's what the TV detectives always want to know.'

'Well,' said Libby, twirling spaghetti on her fork, 'apart from the standard answer of "the murderer", I don't see that it gets us anywhere.'

'But that's just it,' said Ben. 'It's the person who benefits who turns out to be the murderer.'

'I know that.' Libby grinned at him. 'But because we don't know anything about Neil's life, we can't tell who benefits.'

'What do you know about his mum – Joan, was it?'

'Only what Michelle told me.' Libby thought for a moment. 'Actually, come to think of it, there is something . . .'

'Oh? What?' asked Ben warily.

'She belonged to some sort of club, Michelle said. She had her hair done when she was going to a meeting.'

'Club? What – like the WI?'

'I suppose so – but more for older ladies,' Libby said. 'Old bats, Harry might say.'

'Like Joe and Lenny's old codgers' club?' said Ben.

'Of course!' Libby blew him a tomatoey kiss. 'I'll ask Len.'

'He won't know,' said Ben. 'Joe might. But I don't see how.'

'If it's a proper organisation, like the WI or something, he might.'

'If it's a proper organisation, you don't need to ask Joe,' said Ben. 'It'll be online. But if you find it, what good will it do?'

'I could maybe talk to the members, see if any of them were particular friends of Joan's.'

Ben looked doubtful. 'I don't think Ian would like it.'

'No.' Libby put her spoon and fork neatly together on her empty plate. 'Have you finished?'

With a sigh, Ben shooed her away from the table. Libby dropped a kiss on his head and went to fetch her laptop.

'Well,' she said, after ten minutes of concentrated searching, 'there isn't even a Women's Institute in Harbledown.' She sat back and looked at Ben, who had just finished loading the dishwasher. 'Now what?'

197

'Didn't you say she lived *near* Harbledown? Perhaps you ought to find out exactly where.' Ben gently closed her laptop. 'Come on – it's relax-in-front-of-the-TV time.'

Libby gave in gracefully.

The following morning, she phoned Michelle at the salon.

'Where exactly did you say Joan lived?' she asked without preamble.

'Why?' Michelle was sharp. 'She's dead.'

'I know that. I wanted to find out about that club you said she went to.'

'Oh.' Michelle deflated. 'I can't think why. I know they had the odd meal in a pub – that's about all.'

'And it was *near* Harbledown, not exactly *in*.'

'Yes – Foxhole Close. I thought I sent you the address?'

'No – you said you were going to, but you didn't. I'll look it up.'

'But why do you want to know?' asked Michelle. 'It can't matter now. They're both dead.'

'And somebody killed them, Michelle. Don't you want to know who? Or why?'

Michelle sighed. 'As long as they don't think it was me. Or Phil.'

'Do you think they might?' Libby's metaphorical ears pricked up.

'Oh, they've questioned us both. I suppose if you can prove it was someone else they'd leave us alone.'

Libby forbore to ask if Michelle had any sneaking suspicion of Phil. 'Right, then,' she said. 'I'll get on with it.'

Foxhole Close, when she finally located it via a homes-for-sale site, turned out to be deeper into the countryside than Harbledown itself, built on land that had obviously belonged to the large hop farm next to it. Further along the little lane was a thatched and whitewashed pub, The Fox and Hounds, after which Foxhole Close had obviously been named. Its website extolled the virtue of its beers, wines, food and gardens. She called Fran.

'No, I do not fancy a lunchtime drink in the country. I'm on shop duty today.' Fran sounded irritated.

'Sorry,' said Libby. 'Well, do we know when we're going to take Ricky for his shopping trip, then?'

'Tomorrow,' said Fran. 'Is that all right with you?'

'Yes,' said Libby, 'but I need to tell you what Ian said.'

She reported both Ian's and Michelle's conversations, finishing up with her reason for wanting to go for a lunchtime drink.

'I just thought this Fox and Hounds pub might be where Joan's club held their meetings, and I might find a couple of her friends.'

'Unless there's someone who can introduce you, you don't stand a chance,' said Fran.

'We've done it before. We didn't know Sid at The Poacher when we first went in there.'

'That was different,' Fran said testily.

'All right, all right.' Libby gave a silent sigh. 'So what time tomorrow are we going shopping?'

'We'll pick you up about half past ten,' said Fran. 'See you then.'

Meanwhile, Libby thought, returning the landline phone to its cradle, she would drive over to Harbledown herself. Just to see what it was like.

Chapter Twenty-seven

It wasn't until she had searched Harbledown thoroughly – not difficult, it wasn't large – that she stopped at a pub and asked.

'Ah!' said the friendly barman. 'You want Upper Harbledown,
back across the A2. Fox and Hounds is on one of the lanes past the
green.'

Crossing the A2 involved going back towards Canterbury and
then out again, and when she reached Upper Harbledown she was
beginning to get thoroughly fed up, so took the first likely turning
she saw and hoped for the best. Happily, it turned out to be the
right decision.

The hop farm, represented by two enormous oast houses, both
converted into living accommodation, seemed also to form part of
Foxhole Close, which proved to be a small close of individual
detached houses. Libby stopped the car just outside the entrance
and saw blue-and-white police tape fluttering around the doorway
of one of them. Nothing to be learned there, then. She drove on
and almost missed it.

The Fox and Hounds stood less than a hundred yards from
Foxhole Close, its densely planted hanging baskets swaying
softly in the almost non-existent breeze. What had obviously
once been a carriage entrance to the left of the front door pointed
to a car park, and Libby, with trepidation, drove through. She
wasn't feeling anywhere near as sure of herself as she had been,
but she was hungry. And, she told herself, even if she found out

nothing about Joan Barton and her club, she could at least have lunch.

The pub, dark and chilly inside, was almost empty, apart from two couples, sitting as far apart as possible. The large fireplace was also empty, and at first Libby could see no one behind the counter. However, as she approached, a small dark-haired girl materialised at the far end.

'Yes?' she said.

'Do you do lunches?' asked Libby, looking vainly for a menu, or even a chalkboard.

'No.' The girl sighed. 'Don't do nothing much, these days.'

Taken aback by this obviously defeatist attitude, Libby stood still, nonplussed.

'Oh,' she said, rallying. 'I thought this was where a friend of mine used to come for – for meetings. Her club.'

The girl turned away. 'Not any more,' she said.

'You mean the Golden Oldies?' piped up a voice from one of the occupied tables.

'I suppose so – I – um – I never knew the name.' Libby turned and saw a woman of about her own age smiling at her.

'They used to meet here,' said the woman, 'but when they converted the old oast houses, they made a sort of community centre there for the residents, so they meet there now. I was going to join, but now they're not in the pub, well . . .'

'Yes, I see what you mean,' said Libby, not knowing quite what she did mean by that, but having to say something. 'That would be what is now Foxhole Close, I take it?'

'That's right,' said her new friend. 'Very expensive those properties. Whole place was bought up a few years ago.'

'After The Plough closed,' muttered her companion. 'Bloody shame.'

'Don't mind him,' said the woman. 'Some property developers moved into the village. Spoilt it, some said.' She sighed. 'And this pub's going the same way. Won't be here much longer.'

'Oh, what a shame,' said Libby, this time meaning it. 'It must have been lovely here.'

'It was.' The woman sent a fulminating look towards the girl behind the bar, who was diligently ignoring them. 'But if you want food, The Coach and Horses in Harbledown is good. The other side of the A2.'

'Yes, I know it,' said Libby. 'Oh, well, I'll try there. Thanks for your help.'

She went back to the car, and paused, surveying the pretty old building. It was a shame to see so many pubs, the heart of their communities, closing. Still, she thought, at least she knew now that this was where Joan Barton had attended her club. Or, rather, where the club had been. Now in one of the large oast houses she had passed on her way here. Oast houses that, apparently, had been bought up and converted by a property developer.

'Hmm,' she said to herself.

She got into the car and drove slowly back up the lane, slowing to a crawl past Foxhole Close. There was nothing to indicate anything other than upmarket homes from the outside, and rather nice ones, at that, thought Libby. Surely, the fact that a property developer had been involved was a coincidence . . . After all, it would have to have been a property developer who had converted the oast houses and built the homes, wouldn't it? And there were other property developers working in Kent. Apart from Nick Stapleton.

Deciding that there was now no point in eating out, Libby decided to go home, and drove back towards Canterbury, where she coursed her way around the ring road, throwing the police station a grumpy glare as she passed.

Libby was just heating up soup in the microwave for her belated lunch when her phone rang.

'Guess what!' Ben sounded quite excited.

'What?' Libby opened the microwave.

'We've just had a call from The Glover's Men! It came through here because they rang the theatre.'

'Good heavens! What did they want?' Libby paused in the act of taking the bowl to the table.

'To know if we happened to have a gap in our schedule around midsummer.'

'*No!*' Now Libby almost dropped her bowl. 'They aren't! Are they?'

'Yes, you've guessed! A production of *Midsummer Night's Dream* – on the booth stage again!' Ben was almost bubbling with excitement.

'And you said it wouldn't play well on a booth stage,' said Libby, sitting down at the kitchen table. 'How come, anyway? Bit short notice.'

'Their original venue had to cancel. No idea why. Anyway, I checked, and we can do it!'

The Glover's Men were an off-shoot of National Shakespeare, an all-male troupe who took their inspiration from The Lord Chamberlain's Men, and performed, as their predecessors had done, on a booth stage, a sort of tent they erected on existing theatre stages. Their previous production at the Oast Theatre had been *Twelfth Night*, and had been unfortunately dogged by murder and scandal.

'I'm surprised that they want to come back,' said Libby, 'but I'm glad they do. You're sure we can fit them in?'

'Oh, yes,' said Ben. 'And I thought it would be a nice distraction for you.'

'Oh, yes?' Libby burned her mouth on an unwise mouthful of soup. 'From what, pray?'

Ben sighed. 'You know perfectly well. Anyway, pleased? Can I call Pete?'

Libby laughed. 'Of course. And tell your mum. She'll have her rooms full again.'

Libby finished her soup uninterrupted. Ben was right, of course. It was a great and welcome distraction, and should serve to keep her mind off murder and mayhem of all kinds. Except, naturally, it wouldn't. She got up, put her bowl in the dishwasher and retired to the sitting room, where Sidney deigned to move along the sofa to allow her to sit down. She scrolled through the contacts list on her phone until she found Joe's number.

'Hello, love.' Joe sounded surprised. 'What can I do for you?'

'This is a long shot, Joe,' began Libby apologetically, 'but you know your club?'

'Our Old Codgers Club?' Joe was amused. 'I should do! Why?'

'Well, is it official? I mean, is it part of a national organisation? Or is it just a group of locals who get together?'

'We-ell,' said Joe slowly, 'it *is* a group of locals who get together, but we've sort of got together with some other groups, too.'

'I don't suppose one of them was called the Golden Oldies, was it?' Libby almost held her breath. Joe laughed.

'We're all Golden Oldies, Libby, girl! But I don't think there's one that actually call themselves that.'

Libby deflated. 'Oh.'

'What was it you wanted to find out?' asked Joe. 'Where is this group?'

'Out Harbledown way,' said Libby. 'You know that body found in the OB? His mum belonged to a club of some sort over there.'

'Ah, yes. Now, she was murdered, too, wasn't she?' said Joe. 'So that's why you want to know?'

'Actually, I'm not sure why I want to know,' sighed Libby. 'I just thought I might find out a bit more about Neil – that's the body – if I could talk to her friends.'

'And I expect the police have already done that, don't you?' said Joe. 'But, as it happens, I do know a bit about the group over there.'

'You do?' Libby perked up.

'I don't suppose it'll do you any good, though. Tell you what – I'm coming over to Steeple Martin tomorrow. Going to the Coach for a bit of dinner with Flo and Lenny – and young Het, of course. And you'll be in the Coach, too, won't you? As it's Wednesday.'

'Yes,' agreed Libby. 'But can't you tell me now?'

'Not much to tell, really. It all started off with the WI.' Joe made a harrumphing sound. 'And, far as I know, some of the girls –' Libby stifled a laugh – 'they started going to the pub after. What was it called? The Fox, was it?'

'Fox and Hounds,' Libby told him.

'That's it. And some of the husbands joined in, and it sort of grew out of that. Don't know as they had a proper name. Anyway –' Joe sounded as though he was getting himself comfortable – 'then when they opened this community centre, they all moved over there. I heard the pub's on its last legs. Shame.'

'It is. I've been there,' said Libby. 'And it's such a pretty place, too. But the village is tiny, and I don't suppose there's much custom. Well, thank you, Joe. You're right, I don't think it helps. I can hardly go barging in and start asking questions, can I? I wouldn't know how to get into this community centre, anyway.'

'Bet you could, knowing you.' Joe laughed again. 'You could find another group to join, but that wouldn't get you into the Golden Oldies, would it?'

'Oh, they have other groups there, do they?'

'Yeah, keep fit, art classes, all that stuff. Now, what's it called.' Libby imagined Joe frowning at his big television. 'Something to do with hops. You look it up, girl. Tell me tomorrow what you find out.'

Libby ended the call with a smile. He was good value, was Joe.

'Right,' she said to Sidney. 'I'll look it up, as he said. So –' she retrieved the laptop from the table in the window – 'something to do with hops.'

In fact, typing 'Foxhole Close Community Centre' into the search engine brought it up straight away. There it was, the Hop House Community Centre, Foxhole Close, Shittenden.

'Shittenden?' Libby said out loud. She typed that into the search engine, and discovered that there was actually a village, or a hamlet, called Shittenden, running approximately from Foxhole Close, past the Fox and Hounds and on to a collection of cottages, after which the lane carried on in a meandering fashion towards Chartham Hatch.

'Well, well,' she muttered to herself, and went back to click on the link for the Hop House Community Centre, which turned out to have a very professionally done website, on which she found a list of the activities on offer, which ranged from art classes to yoga, including, along the way, creative cooking, creative writing and wildlife watching. Scrolling down, she found a section extolling the virtues of the 'Oast Room', predictably round, and housing a bar. This was available for hire to local groups, it proudly announced, and gave a list of those currently enjoying its amenities, including, to Libby's delight, the Vintage Drinkers.

Chapter Twenty-eight

'Did you know your mum was going out to dinner tomorrow?' Libby asked Ben that evening as they enjoyed a pre-prandial drink in front of the local television news.

'No?' Ben's eyebrows shot up. '*Out?* To dinner?'

'At the Coach, with Joe, Flo and Lenny,' said Libby, grinning at his surprise.

'But she only went out on Friday,' said Ben.

'Is there a limit to the amount of times she goes out?' asked Libby. 'And she goes to the meetings of all her friends in Carpenter's Hall, doesn't she? Oh, and that reminds me—'

'That's different,' broke in Ben. 'That's during the day.'

'Oh, Ben! I thought you were an enlightened male of the species. We women can go out when we want, you know.'

Ben looked a little shamefaced. 'I'm sorry. I'm just not used to her going out.'

'And enjoying herself,' added Libby. 'Are you sure it's not Joe you're worried about? It would be normal to be jealous, after all.'

Ben looked down into his glass. 'Maybe it is a bit of that,' he admitted. 'But I like Joe. And as I said to Hal, Mum needs someone to look after.'

'Well, they haven't actually announced that they're an item,' said Libby, 'so let's not count our chickens.'

Ben smiled at her. 'You're very good for me, you know, Lib. Now, what were you going to say? Something reminded you?'

'Yes – old people's clubs. I think I've found the one Neil the Stalker's mum belonged to.'

'You have?' Ben looked blank.

'I wanted to see if I could find it to perhaps talk to her friends. See if they knew anything about Neil. Or why she was murdered.'

'Libby! You can't go barging in like that!' Ben sat up straight with a jerk, spilling some of his whisky.

Sighing, Libby admitted, 'Fran said that, too.'

Ben mopped at the spilt whisky with a tissue. 'Well, you'd better tell me all about it,' he said, setting the glass down on the hearth and turning off the television.

'I must say,' he said when she had finished, 'I like the idea of the Vintage Drinkers. I suppose that's what we are, too.'

'We're not that old!' said Libby indignantly. 'I'm not, anyway.'

Ben regarded her with amusement. 'Doesn't look as though you'd be eligible to join, then.'

'No.' Libby finished her drink. 'Come on, dinner'll be ready. And tomorrow Fran and I are taking Ricky to buy new clothes. Did I tell you?'

Libby was waiting at the window when Fran's little Smart car drew up outside the next morning. Ricky leapt out of the passenger door and grinned widely as she came out to meet them.

'No Barney?' said Libby, as Ricky climbed into the cramped space behind the seats.

'We didn't think he'd appreciate being tied up outside a lot of shops,' said Fran, 'so he's stayed with Mavis. Graham's going to take him for a walk.'

'He's happy, then, is he?' Libby craned round to see Ricky.

'Yes.' He nodded vigorously. 'He's getting very spoilt. All the customers give him treats.'

'Mavis and Graham's customers,' added Fran. 'Word seems to have got about.'

'Oh.' Libby made a face at Fran, who gave an infinitesimal nod.

By the time they reached Canterbury and parked in the multi-storey car park, Ricky had filled Libby in on everything he'd done since she saw him on Sunday, which included building a sandcastle with two visiting children who had fallen in love with Barney.

'He's very good with children,' said Ricky seriously.

'Where would you like to go to look for clothes?' Fran asked him when they arrived outside Marks and Spencer. 'Here?'

Ricky made a face. 'My mother always brought me here. And Debenhams.' He looked wistful. 'I quite liked Debenhams.'

'Oh, of course! It's not there any more, is it?' said Libby. 'Shall we just walk down the high street until we find somewhere you'd like to have a browse in?'

'We could try in here,' suggested Ricky, looking up at the big store to their left. 'I always wanted to go in here.'

Fran and Libby exchanged smiles and let Ricky lead them into the store. Cheap, cheerful and fashionable, it provided everything Ricky needed at far less cost than either of the women expected.

'I don't suppose it will last,' said Fran doubtfully, fingering the thin fabric of a hooded sweatshirt as they left the store.

'I don't suppose Ricky cares,' said Libby. 'Are we stopping for lunch?'

Hearing this, Ricky turned. 'Do you mind if we don't?' he said. 'I think I ought to get back to Barney. And –' he looked rather nervously over his shoulder – 'I don't want to bump into anybody.'

Libby stood still, head on one side. 'Like who?'

Ricky looked at the floor.

'The goons who took you from the caravans aren't likely to see you here,' said Fran.

'And the owner of the site wouldn't recognise you,' added Libby. 'Anyway, what could they do to you?'

'People you used to know?' asked Fran gently. 'Did you live in Canterbury?'

'Near,' muttered Ricky.

'Your mum?' asked Libby, suddenly enlightened.

'Not my mum.' Ricky turned and began to walk towards the car park entrance. The women followed.

'His stepfather, then,' whispered Libby. 'The one who caused all the trouble.'

But Ricky could not be persuaded to say any more on the way home, although he regained his good spirits, and insisted on coming into Number 17 Allhallow's Lane when they dropped Libby off to meet Sidney.

'We'll see you tonight,' said Fran as she restarted the car.

Libby's eyes widened. 'You will?'

'Yes,' said Fran with the suspicion of a wink. 'Both of us.'

Libby contained her soul in patience throughout the afternoon, deciding that Fran would probably be put out if she tried to ring. She warned Ben that their friends were joining them, and although he asked why they weren't coming for dinner, he made no other comment.

Patti and Anne were already in the pub when Libby and Ben arrived, and Peter was at the bar.

'Pete not needed tonight?' asked Libby, sitting down at the big round table next to Anne's wheelchair.

'No, Harry's quite quiet. Your Adam's there, and Donna was there earlier, too,' said Anne. 'So, come on, tell us what's been happening.'

Libby repeated the events of the past week, pausing only to thank Peter for her beer. Patti already knew about Ricky and Barney, as Fran had called her over the weekend.

'But it seems that Ricky, and the rest of the homeless Stapleton evicted, were only a red herring,' said Patti, at length. 'Seeing that Rab – or Neil, or whoever he was – wasn't really homeless after all.'

'So was he trying to find things out from that woman, or was she trying to find things out from him?' asked Anne.

'That's what I was wondering,' said Libby.

'And his mother,' said Patti. 'You think she knew why he was murdered?'

'I can't think of another reason for her to be murdered so soon after him.' Libby shook her head. 'But Ben and Fran don't think I should try and infiltrate this Vintage Drinkers club to ask questions.'

'No, you shouldn't.' Patti frowned at her.

'Do you think the property developer behind Foxhole Thingummy is the same person?' asked Anne. 'The Island View one?'

'Everything seems to come back to him,' said Libby. 'Although I can't see that even if he was behind it, it would have anything to do with the case.'

'Be interesting to find out, though,' said Anne.

'What would?' said Peter, coming in on the end of the conversation.

Anne explained.

'Easy enough to find out,' said Peter, taking out his phone.

'Don't encourage her,' said Ben plaintively.

'Too late.' Peter looked up triumphantly and proffered his phone.

And, sure enough, in a short explanatory statement, the centre declared itself as having applied for charitable status, after having been developed by Stapleton Holdings, along with Foxhole Close and Mews.

'I suppose the Mews is what they call the flats in the oast houses,' said Libby, sitting back and sighing. 'So there he is again. I told you – everything leads back to bloody Stapleton.'

'And, as you just said, what does that have to do with Island View or the murder?' said Patti.

The door opened and Fran preceded Guy into the bar.

'Did I hear the word murder?' said Guy.

'Of course you did,' said Peter. 'It's Wednesday and we're in the pub. Naturally we're talking about murder.'

Ben went with Guy to fetch drinks and Fran pulled out a chair next to Libby.

'What did he say?' Libby was impatient.

'What did who say?' Fran raised her eyebrows.

Libby tutted. 'Ricky, of course.'

Fran laughed. 'I'm surprised you didn't ring me as soon as you thought I'd be home.'

'I – er – well.' Libby went a little pink. 'I nearly did.'

Anne pushed her chair a little nearer the table. 'Oh, come on, Fran. Tell us.'

'Well,' said Fran, addressing Patti and Anne, 'you know we took Ricky shopping and he admitted he used to live near Canterbury, which was where his mum took him shopping?'

Patti nodded. 'Yes?' said Anne.

Fran looked at Libby. 'We were right. The stepfather works in Canterbury.'

'So it was him Ricky didn't want to see?' Libby frowned. 'Something I don't understand, though, is why he wasn't bothered about seeing any of his schoolmates. If he lived near Canterbury, surely that's where he went to school, and all the local school kids from miles around congregate there after school and at weekends. Or was he bothered about them, too?'

'I think I know that, too,' said Fran. 'Oh, thank you, Ben.' She smiled up at him as he placed a glass of wine in front of her. 'Am I not driving this evening, then?' She looked at Guy, raising interrogative eyebrows again.

'We're staying over with our charming friends,' said Guy. 'And I brought our toothbrushes just in case we were invited.'

'Devious, these men, aren't they?' Libby grinned at Ben and Guy, now ranged either side of Peter. 'Now, carry on. Ricky and his schoolfriends. You were saying?'

'Ricky didn't go to school in Canterbury.' Fran grinned at the surprised expressions on the faces around her. 'I'd better tell you the story.'

'Yes, you had,' said Libby, settling back in her chair.

'Well, it turns out that Ricky and his mum lived on the outskirts of Tunbridge Wells, and Ricky went to – wait for it—'

'Tunbridge Wells Grammar!' guessed Libby.

'Indeed he did.' Fran nodded and took a sip of wine. 'And then his mum met this man. Ricky never liked him, but obviously couldn't say much to his mum, but it wasn't until they married and moved to the stepfather's house that he showed his true colours.'

'I dread to think,' muttered Patti.

'Ricky had been taken in by a schoolfriend's family during the week so that he could continue at the school, which wouldn't be long term, as he was due to leave this summer. But then he came home after a couple of weeks to find that Barney had been chained up outside for the whole week. Ricky's mum had been feeding him, and managed to stop the stepfather from having him put down.' Fran took another sip of wine, looking increasingly unhappy. 'So then there was an almighty row, which is when Ricky was told he wouldn't be going to uni and he had to get rid of the dog.' She shrugged. 'So Ricky walked.'

Chapter Twenty-nine

Her listeners stared at her in silence.

'Poor little sod,' said Guy at last.

'Where is the stepfather's house?' asked Peter.

'You'll never believe this,' said Fran. 'Steeple Cross.'

Libby groaned. 'You're right – I don't believe it.'

'Isn't that where they do that Moroccan food?' asked Ben. 'Near Dark House?'

'That's the one,' said Libby. 'So he didn't run far, did he?'

'He got onto the main road and took the first lift that was offered,' said Fran. 'And he thought there was less chance of him being found if he didn't go to Canterbury, because he wasn't sure how he'd get from there to London.'

'Is that where he was making for?' asked Anne. 'I suppose they all do, don't they?'

'Ian said his mum reported him missing five weeks ago,' said Libby, thoughtfully. 'What about A levels? If he'd got a place at uni?'

'I asked him that,' said Fran. 'He took them early, apparently, which is why he wasn't worried about walking out of school. He'd only carried on going to get away from the stepfather.'

'Bright boy, then,' said Guy. 'I suppose he'd have to be to get into the school in the first place.'

'What's the stepfather's name?' asked Patti.

'And where does he work?' added Anne. 'I mean, what does he do?'

'I don't know the answer to either of those questions,' said Fran. 'He clammed up and shot out of the car as soon as I pulled up behind the Blue Anchor.'

'Why did his mum take him shopping in Canterbury if they lived in Tunbridge Wells?' asked Ben.

'I don't know.' Fran shook her head.

'Must have been a while ago, too,' said Libby, 'if they went to Debenhams. It's been closed for ages.'

'Well, I think it's best we leave well alone,' said Guy. 'Ricky seems happy enough living with Mavis for now, and as far as I can see he has nothing whatsoever to do with your murders.'

Everyone looked at him in surprise. It wasn't often Guy expressed an opinion in a discussion about murder.

'Well said, Guy,' said Peter, standing up. 'Anybody ready for another drink?'

Even Libby was unwilling to continue the conversation after that, so it was that when Ian arrived half an hour later he walked into an animated discussion about the new Morris side and the following week's Rogation celebration.

'Edward not coming?' Libby asked him when he sat down at the table.

'I haven't been home,' said Ian, and indeed, thought Libby, he looked exhausted. 'I thought he might be here.'

'You know you can always stay at the Manor,' said Ben. 'If you don't want to drive home, that is.'

'Yes, we can ask Hetty,' said Libby. 'She's in the dining room.'

'Really?' Fran looked astonished. 'Here?'

'Yes, with Joe and Flo and Lenny,' said Libby, standing up. 'And I've just remembered I was supposed to tell Joe something.' She sent a quick look at Ian and left the table.

She found Hetty's party relaxing with brandies at the far end of Tim's dining room. They all greeted her cheerily.

'I won't disturb you, but I found that community centre, Joe,' she said. 'You were right – it's called the Hop House Centre.'

'Knew it was something to do with hops,' nodded Joe. 'Did it help?'

'Not sure.' Libby grinned round the table. 'Enjoy your brandy – and, oh, Hetty! Can Ian stay tonight? He looks exhausted.'

'Course he can. Bed's made up, and he's got his own key,' said Hetty gruffly.

'Thanks, Het.' Libby beamed at her and returned to her own party.

'Hetty says you can stay and you've got your own key,' she told Ian. 'I didn't know that.'

'I told you,' said Ben, 'she treats him more like a son than me.'

Ian gave them a half-hearted smile. 'So why didn't you bring your young man in to see me today?' he said to Libby, whose hand flew to her mouth.

'We forgot,' said Fran. 'Sorry.'

Ian sighed.

'We do know a bit more about what happened to him, though,' said Libby tentatively. 'I don't know if it helps.'

'Well?' Ian looked at Fran. 'Are you going to tell me?'

Fran launched once more into Ricky's story.

'I've just thought!' said Libby when Fran reached the conclusion. 'You know what his stepfather's name is – his mum reported him missing, didn't she?'

Ian looked amused. 'And that matters why?'

'Um . . .' Libby looked at Fran. 'I'm not sure.'

'What is it, Ian?' asked Patti.

'Pointer,' said Ian. 'Grant Pointer. And don't go nosing into Mr Pointer's affairs. It would be a bit like poking an angry donkey.'

'That's an unfair comparison,' said Libby. 'I like donkeys.'

Ian shook his head and finished his whisky in one gulp. 'I'd better go and pay my respects to my hostess.'

'Leave it, Lib,' said Ben as Ian disappeared into the dining room. 'He's tired and he doesn't need you pestering him.'

Libby had just opened her mouth to reply when the door opened

216

again, and Harry walked in, bowed and with a flourish ushered in Edward and Alice Gedding.

After a flurry of greetings, when Alice was introduced to Patti, Anne and Peter, whom she hadn't met, Alice turned to Libby.

'Did you like the Barnsley chops?' she asked. 'Your butcher told me you'd bought some.'

'They were lovely,' said Libby. 'But how come you were eating at Harry's? I didn't think a sheep farmer would be happy eating vegetarian.'

'Good food's good food, whatever type it is,' said Alice with a smile. 'So have we walked into a meeting of your murder committee?'

Peter, Ben and Guy groaned.

'Better not ask!' said Edward, grinning and placing a glass of red wine in front of Alice.

It wasn't until Libby and Fran were walking back to Allhallow's Lane behind Ben and Guy that Libby had a chance to tell Fran what she'd been thinking.

'Don't you think we should look into Grant Pointer?' she asked quietly.

'Why?' Fran looked at her sharply.

'Even Patti wanted to know,' said Libby.

'She just asked what his name was.' Fran pursed her lips.

'I think he's a person of interest,' said Libby.

'You heard what Ian said. He's obviously met him and thinks he'd be a bad man to cross.'

'He's a bad man all right,' observed Libby.

'Interesting, though,' said Fran as they turned the corner at the vicarage. 'Ian made very little comment on Ricky's story.'

'And he didn't ask any questions.' Libby was frowning.

'Just goes to show – the police know a lot more than they let on,' said Fran.

Ben let them into Number 17 and offered nightcaps, which Guy and Libby accepted. Fran asked for tea.

'It'll keep you awake,' said Libby, going to put the kettle on. Fran followed her into the kitchen.

'I was thinking,' she said. 'Perhaps we could take Ricky to meet his mum – on neutral territory, of course.'

'Would Ricky want to?' asked Libby.

'He seems very fond of his mum.' Fran shook her head. 'That's why I can't understand why she didn't stand up for him more.'

'It's always difficult when a parent has a new partner,' said Libby. 'You and I know that well enough.'

'Yours took Ben in their stride,' said Fran. 'It's mine who were the problem.'

'But then again,' said Libby, pouring water into a mug, 'Ours were all adults and had left home. Ricky was still at school.'

'Anyway, shall I suggest it?' Fran took the mug, and fetched milk from the fridge. 'Meeting his mum?'

Libby looked at her friend suspiciously. 'Is this a sneaky way to find out about stepdad Grant? After you warned me off?'

Fran smiled a little guiltily. 'Might be.' She prodded her teabag before fishing it out. 'As you said, he could be a person of interest.'

'Well, you two,' said Ben when they returned to the sitting room, 'what do you think about Edward and Alice, then? Don't tell me you haven't got an opinion.'

'It's lovely,' said Fran. 'But we don't want to pry. Do we, Lib?'

Libby opened and shut her mouth. 'Of course not,' she said. 'All we have to do now is find someone for Ian.'

The cry of protest could, no doubt, have been heard at the Manor.

There was no chance for further conversation before Guy and Fran left in the morning, although Ian called Fran and asked her to bring Ricky in to see him, preferably that morning.

'I'll follow you home,' said Libby, 'then we can both take him. I'll drive this time.'

By the time they reached Nethergate, Fran had called Mavis and asked her permission to steal Ricky away again.

'It's official police business,' said Libby. 'No permission needed.'

'I was being polite,' said Fran with an admonitory frown.

'You get a proper back seat to sit in this time,' Libby said when Fran ushered Ricky into the Silver Bullet. Fran caught her eye and pulled a face.

'Nothing to be worried about.' Libby turned the car and drove back along Harbour Street. 'Our friend Ian's quite nice, for a policeman.'

'Very encouraging,' muttered Fran.

Libby shut up.

'Did you ask?' she ventured when they reached the outskirts of Canterbury. 'You know, about . . .?'

'Haven't had a chance, have I?' Fran frowned. 'I got home and went straight to the Blue Anchor. You were with me.'

'Ah.' Libby shut up again.

At the police station, Fran and Libby were left sitting in the reception area while Ricky was taken upstairs to see Ian.

'Well?' said Libby quietly when they were alone. 'Are we going to suggest it?'

'What — seeing his mother?' Fran shook her head. 'Not today, I think, do you? Not after hauling him off to the police station. He'll want to get back to Barney.'

'His comfort blanket,' said Libby.

Fran looked at her and smiled. 'Exactly.'

But when Ian brought Ricky back to them, after a surprisingly short time, he had other ideas.

'Ricky,' Ian said, placing a kind but implacable hand on the boy's shoulder, 'thinks it would be a good idea if he saw his mother.'

Libby didn't miss Ricky's wince, though he kept his eyes on the floor.

'Really?' Fran sounded a mite disbelieving. 'Ricky?'

'It wasn't Mum's fault,' he mumbled.

'We thought,' Ian went on, 'you could take him to meet her.'

'On neutral territory,' said Libby, with a glance at Fran.

'Precisely,' said Ian. 'I thought perhaps St Aldeburgh?'

'The church?' Libby's eyes widened.

'The village,' said Fran. 'Or Felling. The Tea Square, maybe.'

The Tea Square was a café in the small town of Felling, some miles from both Nethergate and Steeple Martin, and even further from Steeple Cross.

'Good idea,' said Ian. 'What about it, Ricky?'

'How're you going to let her know? He'll find out.' Ricky set his jaw and glared at Ian, who, for once, looked helpless.

'Leave it to us,' said Fran briskly. 'We'll let you know, Ian.' She stood up. 'Come on, Ricky. Let's go home.'

Ian and Libby, equally surprised, followed Fran and Ricky outside.

'Let me know if she doesn't,' Ian murmured to Libby.

'Now,' said Fran, once they were safely back on the road to Nethergate. 'Are you sure you really want to see your mum, Ricky?'

In the driver's mirror, Libby saw Ricky's face darken. 'Yes,' he croaked eventually.

'Where does she go regularly?' asked Fran, swivelling in her seat to look at him. 'Is there a shop she always goes to? A friend she often calls in on?'

'Not in Steeple Cross.' Ricky cleared his throat. 'My nan, though . . .'

'Your nan?' said Libby. 'Where does she live?'

'Near a place called Tenterden,' said Ricky. 'Do you know it?'

'I do,' said Libby, when Fran shook her head. 'The other side of Ashford. And does your stepdad visit with your mum?'

'No.' Ricky shook his head vigorously. 'They don't get on.'

'Why didn't you stay with Nan while you were at school?' asked Libby. 'It's not too far to Tunbridge Wells from there.'

'Nan lives in a flat in a special village,' Ricky explained. 'There isn't room.'

'Sheltered accommodation?' suggested Fran.

'I think that's it. Could I meet Mum there?' Ricky looked hopeful.

'If you ring your nan and suggest it, you have to make her promise not to tell anyone else,' said Libby.

'Can't you ring her?' asked Ricky.

'She doesn't know us,' said Fran. 'She probably wouldn't believe us.'

'All right,' said Ricky. 'Shall I do it now?'

'Why don't you wait until we get back to the Blue Anchor?' suggested Libby. 'Then you can do it in private.'

Mavis insisted on bringing them tea while they waited for Ricky to make his call, and was still listening to the explanation of their plan when he reappeared from inside the café, accompanied by Barney.

'She says,' he said, waving his phone about, 'she's coming over this way today, and why don't we all go and meet her.'

'Where's she going?' asked Fran.

'Near Canterbury,' said Ricky. 'A place called – what, Nan?' He paused. 'Oh, yes. A place called Shittenden.'

Chapter Thirty

After a moment of stunned silence, Libby cleared her throat. 'Could I have a word with Nan?'

'Libby wants a word, Nan,' said Ricky, and handed over his phone.

'Hello, Mrs – oh. Sorry, I don't know your name.' Libby shook her head at herself.

A comfortable laugh issued from the phone. 'It's Davies, love, but call me Linda. I can't tell you how relieved –' There was a rather strangulated pause.

'Yes, I know, Mrs – Linda. I can't imagine what you and Ricky's mother have been through. But he's safe, I can assure you. And so's his dog.'

'Yes, he said.' Mrs Davies sounded a bit more in control. 'So what was it you wanted?'

'Ricky just wanted to see his mum,' said Libby, 'and we thought it ought to be on neutral ground, so to speak. He said you were going to Shittenden . . .'

'No, that won't do if he wants to see Debbie.' Libby didn't want to go there, either, but she wondered why Linda didn't. 'And not where he's staying now, either. Where do you live, dear?'

'Steeple Martin.' Libby pulled a face at Fran and shrugged. 'Would that be all right?'

'Nice village,' said Linda. 'How about I take Debbie there for lunch tomorrow. Would that suit?'

'That would be great,' said Libby. 'Shall I check with Ricky?'

'He'll be fine. I'll just take your number, in case –' She paused. 'In case Debbie can't come.'

'All right.' Libby let out a breath. 'Do you like vegetarian food? Only we have a restaurant in the village and Ricky's already met the owner.'

'That sounds lovely, dear. And I can't thank you enough.' Linda's voice went wobbly again.

'Oh, I've hardly done anything,' said Libby hastily. 'It's the people here in Nethergate who've been so good.'

She gave Linda Davies her mobile number and handed the phone back to Ricky.

'Now, why did she say Shittenden would not be suitable for a meeting with Ricky's mum?' Libby asked Fran.

'And why was she going there in the first place?' said Fran. 'It's hardly a popular destination, is it?'

'And there's nothing there,' said Libby. 'Only the pub, and that looks as though it's on its last legs. Such a shame – it's so pretty.'

'Perhaps Tim could find another displaced landlord,' said Fran. 'I do hate to see all these pubs closing down.'

'I know.' Libby nodded sadly. 'If the Fox and Hounds had a decent landlord, they could run a community shop in there, or even a sub-post office. That's been done before, hasn't it? But if the barmaid was anything to go by, I don't think the place stands a chance.'

'Anyway, that's beside the point,' said Fran. 'What we need to know is why Ricky's nan is going to Shittenden. What's her name, by the way?'

'Linda Davies, and his mum's name is Debbie,' Libby told her. 'What are you thinking?'

'It's just such a coincidence,' said Fran. 'I mean we'd never heard of Shittenden until you went poking around, had we? And suddenly, not only our second murder victim lives there, but the development where she lives has been built by your main suspect.

And then Ricky's nan turns out to have a connection there, too. You couldn't make it up.'

'You know,' said Libby, settling back in her chair, 'it's all looking a little bit contrived. I keep saying everything comes back to Stapleton, but it's as if everything's been *arranged* that way. Know what I mean?'

Fran frowned. 'But how could it be?'

'Well, let's go back to the beginning.' Libby held up one finger. 'Rab – or Neil – was found in the OB on Stapleton's land.'

'Which we didn't know belonged to him back then,' said Fran.

'But before then, Sylvia had reported him missing. I wish Ian had let me talk to his pathologist – what was his name? Franklyn, that's it.'

'Why? And Ian wouldn't let you do that, anyway.'

'I'd just like to know what injuries the body had sustained, that's all.'

'Ugh!' said Fran. 'That's gruesome.'

'Yes, but I wanted to know if there was a link to the Old Rogue,' said Libby.

'Oh, we're back at him, are we? I thought the Old Rogue and all his works had been discounted.'

'I'm wondering now if we weren't set on the Old Rogue trail as a misdirection,' said Libby.

'Eh? How do you make that out?' Fran's eyes were wide in surprise. 'You found out about that through Tim at the Coach, and Simon. You're not thinking Simon's a plant now, are you?'

'No, of course not.' Libby was scowling down at her feet.

'Well, stop thinking about it now,' said Fran. 'Ricky's coming back.'

Ricky was all smiles as he came back to them, Barney bouncing at his feet.

'Is it all right, Libby?' he asked. 'Nan says we'll meet at a restaurant – is that Harry's place?'

'Certainly is,' said Libby. 'Fran, will you bring Ricky? Or shall I come and get him?'

'Of course I'll bring him,' said Fran. 'I think we'd better give him driving lessons if he's going to be going out and about so much.'

Ricky immediately looked crestfallen. 'Oh, I'm sorry!' he said. 'I didn't mean – could I get the train?'

'Don't be silly!' Fran laughed. 'I was joking. And it's hardly been your idea, has it? All this driving around.'

'No, I suppose not.' Ricky still looked subdued.

'Oh, cheer up, Ricky!' said Libby. 'You're going to see your nan and your mum tomorrow. That's exciting, isn't it?'

Ricky was silent. Then, leaning down to stroke Barney's ears, he mumbled: 'Suppose he won't let her come?'

Fran and Libby exchanged glances.

'Your stepfather?' said Libby. 'But your mum won't tell him where she's going, will she?'

'Surely she'll just say she's going out to lunch with your nan. And he won't want to go, then, will he?' added Fran.

'No.' Ricky looked up, his grin almost impish. 'Nan's too much for him.'

'I like Nan already,' said Libby.

They left soon after that, Ricky going cheerfully to the kitchen, where Mavis was teaching him to create sandwich fillings while Barney lay peacefully in the doorway of the café, ready to greet lunchtime customers.

'I was thinking,' said Fran, as they stopped by Libby's car. 'It was you who brought up the whole Old Rogue business in the first place, so it was hardly designed as a misdirection.'

'It was Simon who told us about him,' protested Libby.

'But it was you asking about folk traditions, wasn't it?'

'Because Tim mentioned it – or was it?' Libby frowned. 'Anyway, you're right. And I tried to get Ian to look into it.'

'And make out that Stapleton was the modern-day Old Rogue. See – all your fault.' Fran grinned at her friend.

'He is a bad lot, though,' said Libby defensively. 'Even Ian admitted that. And they're looking into the migrant workers.'

'But the only thing *really* linking him to Neil's death is the removal of the homeless people from Island View.'

'So he isn't the villain, then?' said Libby.

'You said yourself he's a bad lot, so, yes, he's a villain, just not necessarily a murderer.'

'And not the Old Rogue, either?'

'Not unless you uncover a hidden cult,' said Fran. 'Which, I suppose, we've done before.'

'I don't see how I could do that,' said Libby. 'We have no access to Mr Stapleton.'

'Or the Old Rogue, except for the Rogation celebrations next week.' Fran opened the car door. 'Go on, off you go. I've got to go and relieve Guy in the shop.'

Libby drove home almost without noticing where she was going. Looking back over the last few weeks, she had to admit she had been guilty of quite a few flights of fancy. All, she told herself, with a basis in reality. Finding out about the Old Rogue hadn't been in vain, though, as that had resulted in the formation of the new Steeple Martin Morris and the Rogation Days celebration. Amazing, she congratulated herself, how quickly that had all come together, although perhaps it was down to other people as much, or possibly, more than it was to her.

Anyway, tomorrow, they would see Ricky reunited with his mother and grandmother, although how that was going to work in the long run was anybody's guess. How would Ricky's mother react? She was obviously fairly newly married, so she was hardly likely to leave her husband in favour of her son. Libby shook her head and frowned. Debbie Pointer struck her as a bit of a wimp.

Ben and Libby went to the Hop Pocket for a drink that evening. They were gratified to find it comfortably full of locals, including

Dan and Moira Henderson, accompanied by Colley the dog, who got up politely to greet them.

Simon gave them a welcoming grin and indicated the young woman by his side.

'This is Gwennie,' he said. 'I put the word out that I needed help, and old Steve −' he nodded towards a group of drinkers huddled over a corner table − 'told his daughter. And here she is!' He sent Ben an anxious look. 'That's OK, isn't it, Ben? You did say . . .'

'Of course it is.' Ben leant over the bar and offered Gwennie a hand. 'Welcome, Gwennie.'

'And I'm Libby,' said Libby, following suit.

'Oh, I know who you are,' said Gwennie with an answering smile. 'And I love the pantos.'

'Oh, thank you.' Libby glanced at Ben. 'I think I'll be back with *Cinderella* this year.'

'See?' said Ben as they hoisted themselves onto a couple of bar stools. 'Plenty to keep you occupied without murder. We've got the play in a week or so, then the Glover's Men and the *Dream*, and then planning dear old Cinders.'

'I know.' Libby smiled at him. 'I'm very lucky, aren't I?' She took a sip of Simon's new lager and nodded appreciatively. 'But I'd still like to know who killed Neil and his mum.'

'I'm sure the police will get to the bottom of it,' said Ben.

'Hello, you two.' Dan Henderson came up to the bar, empty glasses in his hands. Gwennie moved forward to serve him. 'Slumming it with the locals, are you? Or just checking up on your investment?'

'Never!' said Ben. 'It's Simon's pigeon now. I'm staying well out of it.' He looked around the bar with satisfaction. 'Nice place to come for a drink, though, isn't it?'

'Certainly is. And it's the headquarters of Steeple Martin Morris now, too.' Dan took a sip of his fresh pint. 'Very handy for me.' Dan and Moira lived just down Cuckoo Lane from the Pocket.

'Oh – and Reg – you know Reg? – well, he was telling me yesterday that the police have been all over Pucklefield in the last few days.'

'Really? Did he say why?' asked Libby.

'Something about that bloke your friend Ron was talking about last Friday. No one seemed to like him.'

Ben groaned.

'Nick Stapleton?' suggested Libby.

'That's the one!' said Dan.

Chapter Thirty-one

'I must ring Reg,' said Libby.

'No, you mustn't,' said Ben. 'Leave it alone. Besides, you haven't got Reg's number.' He narrowed his eyes at her. 'Or have you?'

'Well, I have,' said Dan. 'Let me know if you want it.' He went back to his wife and dog.

'Look, Lib.' Ben took her hand with a sigh. 'You'll know as soon as everyone else does. If you call Reg, it just looks as if you're being nosy.'

Libby set her lips in a stubborn line. 'But I told Ian—' she began.

'No – if I remember, Ian told *you* the police were investigating reports of illegal migrant workers.'

Libby subsided.

They stayed for one more drink, then walked slowly home.

'Did you enjoy that?' Ben asked, flinging his arm round Libby's shoulders.

'Eh?' said Libby, startled. 'Enjoy what?'

'The drink in the Pocket.' Ben laughed. 'I should make that a shout line for the pub.'

'What, "Drink in the Pocket"?' Libby smiled. 'Has a ring to it. And, yes, I did enjoy it. It's going to be popular. Well, it already is.'

'And no – what did Alice call it? – ah, yes. No Murder Club.'

Libby gave him a look.

★

As soon as Ben left for the brewery the next morning, she called Fran and repeated what Dan had told them.

'Ben said I mustn't phone Reg at Pucklefield,' she finished up, 'but how else do I find out?'

'It'll probably be all over the news,' said Fran. 'And I very much doubt if you'll get any inside info from Ian.'

'No, I suppose not.' Libby stared out of the window. 'Anyway, I'd better make sure Ricky's mum and nan are definitely coming today before I do anything else.'

'I thought you'd already done that?'

'Ricky's nan confirmed yesterday, but she said she was worried that his mum might get cold feet.'

'She is a bit of a wimp, isn't she?' said Fran. 'Much as my own daughters annoy me, I'd stand up for them whoever was threatening them.'

'Are we sure stepdad *was* threatening Ricky?' said Libby. 'Or just preventing him doing what he wanted?'

'I'd call not funding him through uni and saying he'd have his dog put down threatening, wouldn't you?' Fran made a sound suspiciously like a snort. 'Make the phone call, then, and let me know if it's called off.'

But the meeting wasn't called off, and by one o'clock Libby, Fran and Ricky were sitting at the big table in the window of the Pink Geranium. Ricky was fidgeting in his chair.

'Barney stayed with Mavis, then, did he?' asked Libby in an attempt to make him relax.

'No, with Graham again. He likes taking him for walks.' Ricky smiled down into his cola.

'Ey-up,' Harry whispered from behind Libby. 'Incoming.'

She looked up in time to see a pleasant-looking woman with white hair opening the door, a small, plump woman hovering nervously behind her.

'Nan!' Ricky shot to his feet, setting his glass rocking dangerously.

In the flurry of greetings, it was clear to Libby that, though Ricky obviously loved his mother, he was far more comfortable with his grandmother. By the time they were all seated, with Ricky between his female relatives, she thought she could understand why.

Harry took drinks orders and left them with menus.

'Is it all vegetarian?' Debbie Pointer asked, almost the first thing she'd actually said. Her mother and son looked at her with resignation.

'Yes, dear,' said Linda. 'And very good it is, too.'

'And good for you,' piped up Ricky. His mother gave him a doubtful look.

'Now,' said Libby, before hostilities could break out, 'would you and Debbie like a bit of time to yourselves, Ricky? There's a nice little yard out the back. Harry won't mind if you go through the kitchen.'

Debbie stood up immediately.

'Will you ask him, please?' Ricky looked pleadingly at Libby, who smiled and went back towards the kitchen. After she'd ushered Ricky and his mother to the little white iron table in the yard, she returned to the others, collecting an opened bottle of red wine on the way.

'Phew!' she said to Linda, sitting down. 'Bit sticky?'

Linda eyed the red wine enviously. 'Wish I could, but I daren't. And yes, Libby, definitely sticky.'

'Didn't she want to see her son?' asked Fran, disbelief in her voice.

'Oh, yes, but she wanted to know why he couldn't go to her.' Linda shook her head. 'Honestly, I sometimes wonder if she really is my daughter.'

'She seems almost afraid of her husband, doesn't she?' said Libby hesitantly. 'I'm sorry if I'm speaking out of turn . . .'

231

'No, you're absolutely right.' Linda nodded. 'I was against the marriage from the start – soon as I met him – but what can you do? Ricky's dad had been dead for – what? Eight years? – and it was me who introduced them, in a way.'

'Really?' Fran and Libby both leant forward.

'Yes. I took her to a party.'

'Oh, well, it's hardly your fault, is it?' said Fran.

'It wasn't the sort of party for a young woman,' said Linda, although Debbie was hardly young, thought Libby. At least in her forties. 'But my friend had invited me, and it was a sort of public affair.'

'Oh?' encouraged Libby.

'Yes. It was a formal opening. Where my friend lives, they opened this community centre – quite a posh one. That's where I was going yesterday.'

Libby was conscious that she was holding her breath.

'Not the Hop House Centre?' said Fran.

'That's it!' said Linda with a broad smile. 'Do you know it?'

'Er – yes.' Libby took a large gulp of wine. 'I was only over at Shittenden the other day.'

'Well, I never!' Linda sat back in her chair looking mildly astonished.

'Yes, I – um – I went to the Fox and Hounds. I meant to have lunch there, but . . .'

As she had hoped, Linda filled the gap. 'Oh, I know. What a shame, eh? My friend and I often went there for lunch – lovely little pub.'

'From what I was told,' said Libby, feeling her way, 'it was the Hop House Centre that sounded the death knell for the pub.'

'Oh, it did, dear.' Linda shook her head. 'Not that we realised it at the time, of course. We thought the centre would be great for keep fit, art classes, that sort of thing. But then they opened up the bar, and – well, I don't like to cast aspersions, but –' she glowered round the table – 'as far as I can make out they offered *incentives* to groups to meet there.' She nodded knowingly.

'Money?' hazarded Libby.

'I think so. Mind, I won't be quoted.'

'No, of course not,' agreed Libby. 'But it was at the opening of the centre that you introduced Debbie to her husband?'

'Not actually introduced,' amended Linda. 'But he was there, and he came up to introduce himself.' She shrugged. 'I can't blame him – she was the youngest woman there, and believe it or not, she's actually quite attractive.'

Fran and Libby laughed.

At this moment, Ricky and his mother reappeared via the kitchen, annoyingly, as far as Libby was concerned, as she wanted to know more about Grant Pointer and his relation to the Hop House Centre, or to its guests. However, the two of them looked happier than when they'd gone out.

Harry came up to take their lunch orders, and gave Ricky a pat on the shoulder and a wink. Debbie sniffed. Linda, assessing the situation, gave Libby a beaming smile.

'So, tell us. Harry's a friend of yours? Both of you?'

Libby explained her place in the village, and that of Harry and Peter, while Fran told them how she had come to know them all. By the time they'd finished, even Debbie was looking interested.

'We haven't got much over in Steeple Cross,' she said. 'Just the pub.'

'But it does that wonderful Moroccan food,' said Libby. 'We've all been there for meals, and Harry's got quite friendly with the chef.'

'Oh, you know it?' Debbie frowned.

'Libby tends to know all the pubs in the area,' said Harry, arriving with cutlery. 'Her partner, Ben, even owns one.'

Libby scowled at him.

'That big one almost next door?' asked Linda.

'No, it's just down a little lane almost opposite here.' Harry pointed out of the window with a fork.

'And you all seem to know one another,' said Linda. 'I miss that.'

'Oh?' Fran leant towards her. 'I thought Ricky said you lived in – a – well, a complex,' she finished in some confusion.

Linda laughed. 'A retirement village,' she corrected. 'Not exactly sheltered accommodation, but not far off. But I don't know any of them. Not properly. I only moved there because I wanted to be nearer to Debbie and Ricky. Couldn't afford anything else.'

'We said you could come to us,' mumbled Debbie, gazing into her glass.

Ricky and Linda looked at her in disbelief, while Libby and Fran exchanged surreptitious smiles.

Harry brought their soup and baskets of bread. 'Proper stuff this time,' he said to Libby. 'Not leftovers.'

Debbie viewed her bowl with something like horror, and everyone else laughed.

'Harry makes soup for us with any leftover vegetables he has sometimes,' explained Libby. 'Not for the paying customers, though.' She looked up at Harry. 'Don't tease,' she said.

'Looks as though you've got plenty of places to eat here,' said Debbie, after a moment's silence while they all sampled the soup. 'The pub next door, here and your partner's pub.'

'Oh, our pub doesn't do food,' said Libby. 'That was part of the bargain. The landlord next door helped and advised, and Ben said he wouldn't do food. The pub next door is building up its reputation as a gastro pub.' She shook her head. 'I would have thought that pub over at Shittenden could have done the same, wouldn't you?' She looked at Linda. 'And there was another one I visited while we were researching local Morris customs. Would have been a terrific venue, but the landlord didn't seem popular.'

'Where was that?' asked Linda.

'The Puckle Inn, in Pucklefield,' said Libby. 'Do you know it?'

Debbie dropped her spoon. 'But that's . . .' she said, looking round wildly.

Ricky, who hadn't said a word since he came back from the yard, gave his mother a disgusted look. 'Mu-um!' he said.

'You know it, then?' asked Fran. 'Pretty place, isn't it?'

Libby frowned and opened her mouth to ask Fran how she knew, never having been there, but on encountering Fran's decidedly minatory glare, shut it again.

'Yes,' muttered Debbie, picking up her spoon again.

Linda, after casting her eyes heavenwards, picked up the baton. 'Yes, that Fox and Hounds over at Shittenden.' She nodded at Libby. 'Smashing little place. Can't say the community place – what do they call it again?'

'Hop House Centre,' supplied Libby.

'Yes, that place. Doesn't exactly have the same – oh, I don't know – feeling.'

'Ambience?' suggested Fran, with a twitch of her lips.

'That's it. Ambience.' Linda looked at her daughter. 'Does it, Deb?'

Debbie shrugged, keeping her eyes on her soup.

'You were going over there yesterday, you said.' Libby cast a swift glance at Ricky, who had finished his soup and was buttering a large piece of bread. That he was embarrassed was obvious.

'Yes. I told you my friend took me – us – to the opening of that place? Well, she'd moved to one of the houses there – Foxhole Close.'

Libby and Fran stopped even pretending to eat.

'She died, you see.' Linda put down her spoon, her eyes glazing over. 'They were having a little gathering for her last night as they can't have a funeral yet.'

'Oh – why?' Libby managed to ask.

'She was murdered.' Linda shrugged and pulled a tissue from a pocket. 'Terrible, isn't it?'

Chapter Thirty-two

'Joan Barton.' Fran leant over and put a gentle hand on Linda's arm.

'Yes!' Linda looked up, surprised. 'Did you know her?'

'I met her son,' said Libby, aware that her heart was thumping so hard and fast she was sure everyone else could hear it.

Linda looked at her. 'Neil,' she said. Libby nodded.

'So you knew Joan, too?' Fran said to Debbie.

'Oh, yes.' Debbie kept her eyes on her plate.

Linda made an obvious effort to pull herself together and gave a tremulous smile. 'As I said, Joan took us to the opening of the Hop House Community Centre. And introduced us to Debbie's husband.' She made a face at Libby. 'He was there representing the developer, wasn't he, love?'

Fran, much more in control than her friend, turned an interested face back to Debbie. 'That's Stapleton Holdings, isn't it?' she asked.

Debbie nodded, still keeping her eyes down.

Ricky grunted. 'Yes, it is,' he said. 'Runs around doing their dirty work, doesn't he, Mum?'

'*Ricky!*' Debbie and Linda said together, outraged.

Libby stood up. 'Debbie, you look as though you could do with a bit more peace and quiet,' she said. 'This has all been a bit much, hasn't it?'

Debbie, tears now coursing down her cheeks, nodded.

Harry appeared from the kitchen.

'Could she have a lie-down in the flat?' Libby whispered to him.

Ricky stood up and pulled his mother to her feet. 'I'll go with her,' he said gruffly.

'That was all a bit unexpected,' said Libby after Harry had shepherded Debbie and Ricky out through the kitchen again. 'So Grant Pointer is working for Nick Stapleton.'

Linda nodded. 'And he took a real shine to Debbie. Mind, he takes a real shine to anything in skirts.' She sighed. 'Why he decided to marry Debbie, I shall never know.'

'Bit of a womaniser, is he?' said Fran.

'Dreadful. It's not as if he got anything out of it. Debbie's got no money.' Linda sat back and gazed out of the window onto the high street. 'You know, I could be happy in a village like this.'

'And Pointer really was as awful to Ricky as Ricky said he was?' Libby ignored the change of subject.

'Oh, yes, dear. Mind, he didn't show it until they were married. All the time Debbie and Ricky still lived on their own, it was fine. It was when he moved them into his house. And I swear all the business with telling Rick he couldn't go to university was just being nasty for the sake of it. And the dog – well, he didn't want a nasty dog messing up the nice new house his boss had set him up in, did he?'

Fran and Libby shook their heads.

Harry came to ask if they would like anything else. Linda and Fran opted for coffee, and Libby asked for another glass of wine.

'It really does seem lovely, here,' said Linda wistfully. 'You don't know of anywhere for sale, do you?'

Libby's eyebrows shot up. 'Really?' she said.

'Oh, I'm so sick of living where I do now.' Linda sighed. 'I want friends, and somewhere Rick could come and stay like he used to. If his mum's going to stay married to that sh . . . *person*,' she amended.

'Does she know about his womanising?' asked Fran, nodding thanks to Harry as he placed a coffee cup in front of her.

'She doesn't say, but I'm pretty sure she does. He's been very – oh,

I don't know — *shifty*, if you know what I mean. Just this last few weeks. She's wanted to see me more than she did.' Linda stirred her coffee. 'And mark my words, she'll be back here in a minute, saying she's got to get home.'

'Already? It isn't dinner time,' said Libby.

'Oh, he rings her. Wants to know where she is all the time.'

'That's abusive behaviour,' said Fran. 'Why does she put up with it?'

Linda cocked her head and raised an eyebrow. 'Got my suspicions,' she said.

Sure enough, within five minutes, Debbie and Ricky came back to the table. Debbie looking more in control and Ricky, frustrated.

'I'd better be getting back, Mum,' she said, then turned to Fran and Libby. 'It was lovely to meet you, ladies, and thank you so much for all you've done for Ricky.'

Linda fumbled in her bag and pulled out a credit card.

'No, no!' said Libby and Fran together. 'This is on us,' said Libby.

Ricky escorted his mother and grandmother back to their car, and Harry stood watching from the doorway.

'That is one very fractured relationship,' he said. 'But Nan seems all right.'

'I think she is,' said Libby. 'And she thinks this would be a nice place to live.'

Harry turned back with a smile. 'And so it is. Where will you put her?'

Amid the laughter, Ricky came back and sat down.

'Well?' said Fran. 'How do you think it went?'

'I don't know.' He shook his head. 'She's so upset, but I don't think it's just with me.' He looked up hopefully. 'Do you think she's upset with him?'

'We don't know, Ricky,' said Fran. 'But at least you're in touch again. And your nan's on your side, isn't she?'

'Yeah.' Ricky gave her a smile. 'Nan's all right.'

*

Fran and Ricky left soon after that, and Harry and Libby waved them off before going to sit back at the table.

'It's just too much of a coincidence,' said Libby. 'His stepfather working for Stapleton.'

'But a red herring, petal. How can that have anything whatsoever to do with your murders?'

'Oh, I don't know. But you must admit it's strange.' Libby heaved a sigh. 'I mean – young Ricky runs away from his wicked stepfather only to end up on a site managed by the wicked stepfather's boss. Weird.'

'But hardly stage-managed by stepfather *or* boss,' said Harry.

'No.' Libby finished her glass of red wine. 'Can you keep the rest of this for me?'

'No.' Harry screwed the top back on the bottle. 'You can take it home with you and get quietly drunk in the kitchen.'

Libby, however, had no intention of getting quietly drunk. Deprived of private conversation with Fran at least until Ricky had been taken back to the Blue Anchor, she made her way up Manor Drive and round the back of the Oast Theatre to the brewery, standing at the edge of the hop garden, which was now beginning to look well established.

Inside, she spotted Albie, he who was now Steeple Martin Morris's Bagman, up a ladder at the side of one of the huge mash tuns. Hoping not to startle him into falling in, she edged round until she was within his eyeline.

'Hi, Albie,' she called. 'Seen Ben anywhere?'

Albie pushed his mask down. 'Hello, Libby.' He began to climb down. 'He's in the other barn with Duncan and the others.'

'The others?'

'They're rehearsing for next week. The Morris?' He took his mask off and slipped it into the pocket of his white coat.

'Oh, right. I'd better not disturb them, then.' She turned away, then looked back. 'Ben's not dancing, though, is he?'

Albie grinned. 'Nah. Just can't seem to stay away, though.'

Libby nodded ruefully and went back outside. After a moment's thought, she walked round the theatre and up to the big oak door of the Manor. Wondering if she would disturb Hetty in the middle of an afternoon doze, she paused in the hall, before a skitter of claws on floorboards announced the arrival of Jeff-dog.

'That you, gal?' called Hetty.

'Yes, Het,' Libby called back. 'Am I disturbing you?'

'Too late now,' said Hetty, emerging from her sitting room. 'Tea?'

'Yes, please.' Libby followed her hostess into the kitchen and automatically went to retrieve the milk from the big American-style fridge Ben had recently had installed.

'I met someone today who said she'd like to live in the village,' she began conversationally.

Hetty paused in the act of pouring boiling water into a teapot to warm it. 'Ben said you was meeting that young Ricky's mum and grandma.' She stared at Libby and waited.

'Yes.' Libby sat down at the table. 'His grandma. Nice woman. Lives in one of those retirement villages.'

Hetty made a dismissive sound and gesture. 'Can't be doing with 'em.'

'In some circumstances—' began Libby.

'Not ours,' said Hetty firmly, emptying the pot and spooning in tea leaves.

'No, well,' said Libby. 'This lady – Linda – lives in one. And she says she's not keen and she thought it looked nice here, with everyone knowing everyone else. That's how she put it, anyway.'

'What do you want me to do about it?' asked Hetty, pouring more water into the pot.

'Nothing!' Libby looked startled. 'I was just telling you.'

'Reckon she'd fit in with the old biddies, do yer?' Hetty and Flo had a small coterie of friends who met regularly in Carpenter's Hall in Maltby Close.

'Well, she would,' Libby said thoughtfully.

'Hardly know 'er,' said Hetty, putting the teapot on the table. 'Wait and see.'

'Yes, Het.' Libby smiled and helped herself to a biscuit, thoughtfully placed near her right hand. 'Young Albie at the brewery said Ben was over in the small barn with the Morris dancers.'

Hetty rolled her eyes. 'Got to have a project, my boy, hasn't he?'

'He doesn't need another one,' said Libby. 'He's running what's left of the estate, the hop garden, the brewery *and* now the Hop Pocket.'

Hetty allowed herself a small proud smile. 'Pass the milk, gal,' was all she said.

Libby was slightly surprised to receive a call from Fran on her mobile as she was walking back down the Manor drive.

'I was going to ring you when I got home,' she said.

'I was wondering why you hadn't rung already,' said Fran.

'I went to Hetty's for tea. What's up?'

She heard Fran heave a sigh. 'Ricky's not happy about his mum.'

'No, I gathered that. Did he say something else, then?'

'Yes. He didn't want to, but in the end it just burst out of him.' Fran paused. 'He thinks Pointer is hitting his mother.'

'Oh, bugger. Listen can I ring you back when I get home? This isn't a conversation to have in the street.'

'OK,' said Fran. 'I'm just not sure what we should do.'

'Nothing right now. I won't be five minutes.'

Libby almost ran home past the Pink Geranium and Bob the butcher's shop, rounding the vicarage corner too fast and nearly tripping over Beth.

'Sorry – can't stop,' she gasped and skidded to a halt outside Number 17. Once inside, she switched on the electric kettle, regardless of the fact that she had already had a large mug of tea with Hetty, and returned Fran's call.

'OK – start from the beginning,' she said.

'Well, you know Ricky asked us if we thought his mum was

upset with his stepfather? And he said to his mum that his step-father did Stapleton's dirty work?'

'Yes.'

'He thinks his mum knows what the stepdad does, and he's started hitting her to keep her quiet. He was trying to get her to admit it today, but she wouldn't.'

'Obviously,' commented Libby.

'Anyway, he wants to do something about it. He said he wasn't certain when he ran away, but he's sure he saw bruising on his mother's arms today.'

'And Nan said she had her suspicions, didn't she?' said Libby. 'And you said that him wanting to know where she was all the time was abusive behaviour. I'm surprised he let her report Ricky missing in the first place. The boy must have been a right nuisance to him.'

'So what do we do?' asked Fran. 'If anyone reports Pointer, he'll take it out on Debbie, and probably try and find Ricky, too.'

'We need evidence,' said Libby. 'Not just of abuse – but of criminal behaviour.'

'Abuse is criminal behaviour,' protested Fran.

'You know what I mean. Can't we link him in somehow with Stapleton's goings-on?'

'The police haven't even been able to do anything about Stapleton himself,' said Fran. 'Although I suppose they might be close with the migrant workers.'

'But they won't have him behind bars,' said Libby. 'So we need something else. I wish we could link Pointer to Neil's murder, somehow.'

'Well, he had met his mother,' Fran suggested.

'At a public event,' said Libby. 'I doubt if we could make that work.'

'How about,' said Fran slowly, 'if we ask Sylvia if she knows him?'

'Oh!' Libby sat down hard on a kitchen chair. 'And find out if he had anything to do with Island View? Now, that's a good idea!'

Chapter Thirty-three

'But,' said Ben when she told him about the idea later, 'the police already know there's something dodgy about Island View, so they'll be investigating Stapleton and all his works, won't they? And it's hardly likely that they'll put anybody, Stapleton or his lieutenants, behind bars for it.'

'Hmm.' Libby scowled at the pot of chilli she was stirring. 'So what do we do?'

'I don't think you should get involved,' said Ben. 'The best thing to do would be to persuade Ricky's mum to leave. But it doesn't look as though she'd do that.'

'No. She's too frightened. And he'd go after her. I'm surprised he hasn't tried to find Ricky already.'

Ben took a bowl of rice from the microwave. 'Stop worrying about it and let's eat,' he said.

But, naturally, Libby didn't stop worrying about it. Apart from her innate inclination to nose out the murderer or murderers of Neil Barton and his mother, she was highly indignant, not to say angry, on behalf of both Ricky Short and his mother, who appeared to have suffered at the hands of the frankly primitive Grant Pointer. So she rang Brooke and Company on Saturday morning and asked to speak to Sylvia Cranthorne.

'Hello, Sylvia,' she said brightly. 'It's me, Libby Sarjeant.'

243

'Did you give a false name?' asked Sylvia. 'I wouldn't have agreed to speak to you otherwise.'

'Well, yes, I did,' Libby confessed. 'But I wanted to ask you a question.'

'Look,' said Sylvia with a heavy sigh, 'I've told you, I don't know anything more about Island bloody View except that it's been taken off our books and, as far as I know, the whole development has been shelved.'

'Right,' said Libby. 'So you don't know anything about Stapleton Holdings or who works there?'

'No!' Sylvia's voice rose, almost to a shriek.

'You see,' Libby went on, unperturbed, 'we now know that your Rab was alive and kicking for a couple of weeks after you said you last saw him. So we wondered if there was anything he'd said to you that would indicate that he was leading a double life?'

Another gusty sigh echoed in Libby's ear. 'Oh, for goodness' sake,' said Sylvia. 'What has that got to do with Stapleton Holdings?'

'Well, you know that,' said Libby. 'You admitted that Rab was trying to find out about Island View from you.'

'Now I'm really confused. Yes, he was. But I didn't get anything else from him.'

'Did he get anything from you? Did you tell him about the site?'

'Just that it was going to be developed. Look, what is all this?'

Libby realised she was not going to get much else out of Sylvia Cranthorne, so she gambled on one last question.

'Oh, well, never mind,' she said. 'I suppose it was Grant Pointer who told you the site wasn't going to be developed, wasn't it?'

There was an infinitesimal pause. 'Gra– who?' Sylvia cleared her throat. 'Pointer? Who's he?'

Libby grinned to herself. 'Oh, it doesn't matter,' she said. 'Thanks for your help, Sylvia. Bye.'

Ending the call, she immediately called Fran.

'Sylvia knows Pointer,' she said, 'and I'm pretty sure there's more she isn't telling us.'

'Look, I'm serving, Lib,' said Fran, sounding flustered. 'It's Saturday, and we're almost into the season. I'll ring you back at lunchtime.'

Fran being unavailable, she thought of Harry. But Harry, too, would be busy. Saturday mornings were always busy at the Pink Geranium, the denizens of Steeple Martin being traditionally devoted to a decent cup of coffee after shopping for their locally produced meat and vegetables in the village. Libby often felt a twinge of middle-class guilt at her good fortune, having come from a very working-class family, but consoled herself that Hetty – and Flo Carpenter, come to that – came from the same background.

She wondered about driving down to St Aldeberge to see Patti, but she was almost certainly going to be officiating at a wedding or two, it being spring and the season for brides. So who could she talk to? Ben was up at the brewery again, and wasn't particularly sympathetic anyway, and Peter, love him though she did, always made her feel slightly inadequate. Feeling abandoned, she wandered out into the garden and peered up at the cherry tree.

'Is that you, Libby?' came a voice from the other side of the fence.

'Yes – Jinny? Are you all right?' Libby went over and pulled herself up on her toes to see into the next-door garden.

'Yes, I'm all right, dear.' Jinny Mardle peered out of her back door, soft white hair lifting slightly in the breeze. 'I've just got this hip, you see.'

'Hip?' Libby frowned. 'Look, I'll come to your front door. Won't be a moment.'

She darted through the cottage and out of the front door to find Mrs Mardle beaming from her own door.

'I didn't want to bother you, dear,' she said. 'But this hip's got worse, you see.' She waved a shiny black walking stick at Libby. 'And sometimes, even with this, it's a bit difficult . . .'

'What do you need, Jinny? And why on earth haven't you let me know before?' said Libby, following her neighbour inside.

245

'Just milk, dear.' Jinny smiled hopefully. 'Colin and Gerry are coming over for a bite to eat today – did they tell you? – and I don't like to send them straight out to the shop as soon as they arrive. I hate to ask, but when I heard you in the garden . . .'

'Don't be silly,' said Libby. 'I'm here most of the time. I can always go to the shops for you.'

'Oh, I get the deliveries most of the time these days,' said Jinny, 'although I feel a bit guilty not using the village shops. But the supermarket's so easy.'

'I was thinking that myself only this morning,' said Libby. Well, almost. 'I'll pop out and get your milk now. Anything else while I'm there?'

Pleased to have something to do, Libby shut her front door and set off for the eight-till-late. Passing the vicarage gate, she spotted Beth coming down the path.

'Not in such a rush today?' she asked.

'No, sorry about that.' Libby took in the full clerical garb. 'Wedding?' she asked.

'Yes, there are still some people who don't feel it's completely obsolete,' Beth said.

'Sorry.' Libby pulled a face. 'How are you? How's John?'

'We're fine, but listen. I'm glad I've seen you. I heard you were trying to help some homeless people?'

Libby raised her eyebrows. 'Well, not exactly. One homeless boy's more like it. Where did you hear that?'

'Very vaguely via Patti. What's it all about? Can we help?' Beth stopped before crossing the high street.

'We've sorted out our homeless boy,' said Libby, 'but if we come across any more, I'll let you know.'

'Right.' Beth gave her what used to be called an old-fashioned look. 'Don't just leave the church out of it. We're here to help.'

Libby carried on to the eight-till-late feeling guilty. She bought Mrs Mardle's milk, then had a sudden thought. Hoping Beth's wedding party hadn't already arrived, she rushed down Maltby Close to the church, which, thankfully, was still bride-less.

'What?' Beth looked surprised. She now wore her white surplice and was adjusting her stole. 'Do you need me after all?'

'Sort of. There's a woman we've just met, and we think –' Libby took a deep breath and leant heavily on a pew – 'that she's being abused by her husband.'

'This "we" is you and Fran, I take it?'

'And the woman's mother and son,' added Libby.

'What would you like me to do?'

'Tell me what to do,' said Libby. 'I'm stumped.'

'Can it wait? Say until this evening?' asked Beth. 'I've got three weddings this afternoon.'

'That's sort of ironic,' said Libby with a rueful smile. 'But yes, of course. Tell you what – come and have a drink at the Hop Pocket this evening. Would that be OK? You never made it to the opening, after all, did you?'

'John'll love that,' said Beth. 'See you later, then. Now, shoo. Or you'll get caught up in the first wedding – and you don't look much like a guest.'

Libby left the church more slowly and walked back down Maltby Close, exchanging waves with Flo on the way. She wasn't exactly sure what Beth could do for Debbie Pointer, but at least she could feel she was doing something.

Back at Mrs Mardle's cottage, she found Colin and Gerry already there, and was pressed to stay for a pre-lunch cup of tea. Jinny Mardle had looked after Colin when he was a boy growing up in Steeple Martin, and retained the status of a favourite grandmother.

'Colin was just telling me about those poor homeless people,' she said now, sitting down behind the tea tray Gerry had just carried in. 'And that caravan park. I remember that, years ago. Colin had forgotten, but I took him down to stay in one of those vans a couple of times. You loved that beach at Nethergate,' she said to Colin with a fond smile.

'Really?' Libby was wide-eyed with surprise.

'I remember now,' said Colin. 'It's not a very clear memory, and it could have been anywhere, but the things that stick in my memory are Punch and Judy on the beach, and fish and chips from a shop on what I now know is Harbour Street. And the caravan.' He smiled at Jinny Mardle. 'It was very old fashioned, but I loved it, didn't I?'

'You did, ducks.' Mrs Mardle nodded briskly. 'And it don't seem right that it should be made into one of these great holiday-camp type places. Not right at all.' She busied herself with the tea, looking militant.

'Well, yes, that's what we thought,' agreed Libby.

'No need to worry,' said Colin. 'I got in touch with our solicitor—'

'The one who deals with all our overseas purchases,' put in Gerry.

'Yes, him,' said Colin, 'and he had a poke about into the so-called certificate of lawful development. And it isn't legal. He informed the council, who made a great deal of noise about it, and the upshot is that the police have cordoned off the whole site.'

'Yes, we knew about that,' said Libby, 'but well done you. Will the police prosecute anybody?'

'We gather there's quite an investigation going on,' said Gerry, 'but as far as we can tell, nothing to do with your murders.'

Mrs Mardle shook her head. 'She will keep getting herself mixed up in these things,' she muttered.

'How did they expect to keep the whole thing quiet?' asked Libby, accepting a cup of dark-brown tea.

'If it hadn't been for your homeless people,' said Colin, 'I doubt it would have come to light.'

'They aren't *my* homeless people,' objected Libby. 'But it's a jolly good job it did come to light, however it happened.'

'According to Mavis, it was you who alerted the police. She and Graham at The Sloop were too scared to do anything.'

'How do you know that?' Libby stared at him.

'We don't live far from Nethergate, remember? And we go over to The Sloop for dinner at least once a week.'

'And Ron Stewart was talking about it at the opening of the Hop Pocket, wasn't he?' said Gerry. 'Although we were surprised when he said Stapleton had slung him out on his ear.'

'Really? Why?'

'To be fair,' said Colin, 'he did say Stapleton was surrounded by – what did he say? Goons?'

'And minions, yes,' said Libby. 'Meaning the illegal migrants, we thought. So why were you surprised?'

'Because Stapleton doesn't appear to be able to throw anybody anywhere.' Colin put down his cup. 'According to our sources, he's little more than a cipher. Alzheimer's, they think.'

Chapter Thirty-four

Libby watched all her theories crumble into dust.

'Alzheimer's?' she repeated in a whisper.

'Nasty.' Mrs Mardle shook her head. 'I do the crossword every day to keep my brain going, you know.'

All three of her listeners gave her a fond smile.

Gerry helped himself to a biscuit from the tray. 'It was our solicitor who found out, completely by accident. He had been trying to make an appointment with the Stapleton Holdings legal team – which turned out to be one female legal executive and her assistant – and ended up gatecrashing the building because he wasn't getting anywhere. And Mr Stapleton himself went crashing into the office, apparently.'

'Goodness!' said Libby, round eyed. 'What happened next?'

'His minder, at least, that was who Jonathan took him to be, hustled hm out.' Colin chuckled at Libby's expression. 'So not such a big bad wolf after all.'

'Bad enough,' said Gerry.

'Your solicitor – Jonathan, was it? – why is he doing all this? Just for love?' Libby put down her cup.

'He'd had a run-in with Stapleton Holdings himself over another plot of land they were trying to acquire,' explained Colin. 'So there we are. Stapleton's had his teeth pulled.'

'Why didn't you tell me this before?' asked Libby after a pause.

'We only found out yesterday,' said Gerry, 'and we thought we might see you today.'

'Oh, yes. Right.' Libby nodded. 'Oh, well. He probably hasn't murdered anyone then, except perhaps by mistake.'

'What, lashing out, you mean?' said Colin, his head on one side. 'Possible, I suppose.'

They all fell silent.

'Well, I think we ought to talk about something nice,' said Mrs Mardle briskly. 'Not all this nasty murder stuff.'

They all laughed.

Libby returned home after these surprising revelations, made herself a sandwich and waited for Fran to call. When she did, she sounded exhausted.

'It's been mad,' she said. 'I'm in the flat, because I couldn't be bothered to walk down the road home. So what was so urgent?'

Libby tried to pull her thoughts into some kind of order, and began at the beginning with her phone call to Sylvia.

'So there we are,' she concluded. 'And I'm wondering if she knew about Stapleton's trouble, and that was what she was trying to conceal. She definitely knew Grant Pointer – or at least his name – so perhaps he's been doing all the business and trying to keep the real state of affairs quiet.'

'I don't see why,' said Fran after a minute. 'Stapleton Holdings is a company, not a single person, so if one person is out of commission, it shouldn't matter. Except for things like signatures, I suppose.'

'And perhaps he did all the stuff about Island View when he wasn't quite compos mentis and they've been trying to hide the fact,' said Libby.

'Possible,' said Fran. 'Anyway, it doesn't seem to have anything to do with Pointer or Debbie. And I can't see what it has to do with Neil Barton and his mother, either.'

'He could have lashed out at Neil, perhaps?' suggested Libby.

251

'And then his faithful cohorts buried the body, or, rather, chucked it in the OB.'

'But what about his mother? She was found at her home.' Fran sighed down the phone. 'And where would he have lashed out at Neil, anyway? If he's kept under close guard?'

'We don't know that,' said Libby, 'and it could be that Neil was with the homeless people, even though Ricky didn't know him. Or,' she said, suddenly struck with inspiration, 'Neil went to see Stapleton to challenge him, and he struck out then.'

'Possible,' said Fran, 'but whatever the rights and wrongs, we're not going to get anywhere with it, and I'm sure the police will have found out about all of it anyway.'

After this dispiriting conversation, Libby gave up. She put a curry into the slow cooker, went into the garden with a book and settled down to read the afternoon away. At some time after four, Colin put his head over the fence to say goodbye.

'We're going to dinner with Dotty next door this evening, and they eat early,' he said, 'so we'd better get going. I'll give her your love, shall I?'

'Yes, do,' said Libby, who had fond memories of Colin and Gerry's next-door neighbour, Dotty Barlowe, an ex-Londoner like herself. 'And thanks for all the info,' she added. 'And thank your solicitor for me, too.'

Ben was delighted to hear that he was to spend an evening in the Hop Pocket.

'Only no interfering,' Libby warned him.

'Would I!' he protested with a sly grin.

Beth and her husband, John, followed them into the pub almost as soon as they arrived at the bar.

'We saw you go past,' said John. 'Hi, Simon.'

Libby looked surprised. 'Oh, you know Simon?'

John laughed. 'As an upstanding member of Steeple Martin Morris, of course I do – even if he hasn't been here long.'

'I told you John would be interested, if you remember,' said Beth.

'So you did,' said Libby. 'It's all happened so quickly – I haven't quite taken it in yet.'

Ben handed them all glasses and indicated a spare table near the door. 'You go and sit down,' he said. 'I've got something I need to talk to Simon about.'

'No—' began Libby.

'Interfering. I know.' Ben winked at John and they went back to the bar.

'What's all that about, do you think?' said Libby, watching them.

'No idea,' said Beth. 'But while we're on our own, tell me about this woman you've befriended.'

'Not exactly befriended,' said Libby. 'I'd better explain.'

'Well,' said Beth, when Libby and both their drinks were finished, 'I don't honestly think there's much anybody can do if she won't admit it's happening. Even if he were to really hurt her badly, if there were no witnesses and she refused to press charges, the police would be hamstrung.'

'That's what I thought,' said Libby sadly.

'I used to help out at a refuge near my last parish,' Beth said, her eyes far away. 'It should have been a place of hope, but it was one of the most depressing places I've ever been. You wouldn't believe how many women used to sneak out to meet their husbands, and often just left altogether and went back to them. It was the children I felt most sorry for.'

Libby nodded. 'What astonishes me in this case is how the man kept that side of himself under wraps until after they were married. And why? Why did he marry her? She hasn't got money. And her mother thinks he's a chronic womaniser.' She shook her head. 'It doesn't make sense. And if he's violent, after all, we haven't got proof, but if he is, do you think it would escalate to murder?'

'Well, of course, it might,' said Beth, 'but your victim's a man, isn't he? Doesn't fit.'

'Oh, no. So it doesn't.' Libby was dispirited.

'Don't you think,' said Beth consideringly, looking down into her empty glass, 'it would be a good idea to mention the situation informally to your friend the policeman even if it isn't murder?'

A man passing their table carrying two pint glasses cast a surprised glance at Beth.

'Evenin', vicar,' he said, and sat down at his own table.

'Now it'll be all round the village I'm helping you with murders,' said Beth, sighing.

'Not actually *with* murders,' said Libby, giggling.

Ben called over from the bar. 'Another drink, girls?'

'Girls!' snorted Beth.

'Yes, please,' said Libby. She turned back to Beth. 'So mention it casually to Ian – DCI Connell – and leave it to him. He has already warned me about poking my nose into Grant Pointer's business, so he won't be best pleased.'

'I wouldn't advise doing anything else,' said Beth. 'You could lay yourself open to prosecution.'

'I suppose so.' Libby sighed.

'Big sigh,' said John, sitting down next to his wife. 'Am I interrupting?'

'No,' said Beth, and gave his hand a squeeze.

'Good, because Ben and I have had an idea.'

'Oh, dear,' said Libby.

John looked at her doubtfully.

'No, it's all right,' said Libby. 'Go on – what is it?'

'Well, Beth, you know that old upright piano in the back room at the village hall?' John looked at his wife hopefully.

'Ye-es,' she said.

'We wondered if we could, perhaps, lend it to the Pocket?'

Libby thought he had much the same look as Barney did when he was gazing at his master, and stifled a laugh.

'I know where this is going,' she said.

Beth looked baffled. 'But what for?'

'Oh, come on, Beth!' Libby laughed out loud now. 'You've heard of the old pub pianos? And all the sing-songs round them?'

'But that's —' Beth looked from Libby to her husband. 'It's sort of folk tales, isn't it?'

'Not a bit of it,' said Ben, arriving with a tray of drinks. 'Still goes on, especially in some of the old London pubs.'

'And Newmarket, I believe,' said Libby.

Ben nodded enthusiastically. 'So what do you think?'

'Great idea, but who would play it?' asked Libby.

'Me, for a start,' said John, with a smug grin.

Beth cast her eyes upwards. 'First Morris, now pub piano. What next?'

'Anyone could play, like the pianos in the London stations,' said Ben.

'What about a music licence?' said Libby.

'Simon's going to look into that on Monday, but doesn't think there'll be a problem.' Ben smiled round the table.

'As long as the regulars don't mind,' said Libby, casting an eye round the bar.

'Well, we'll find out when we come in here after the Old Rogue parade next Wednesday,' said John. 'If we can get the piano here.'

'You can walk it round, surely?' said Beth. 'Along the back way.'

The path at the side of the Pocket led along past the refurbished Bat and Trap pitch and along the back of the high-street buildings to the churchyard.

'What about tuning?' asked Libby.

'We've got a regular tuner we use for the proper church hall piano.' Beth laughed. 'What he'll think about this one I hate to think!'

'So it's all set for next Wednesday, is it?' Libby asked. 'The parade and everything?'

'Oh, yes,' said Ben. 'Everyone's really enthusiastic.'

'What about Pucklefield? Are you going over there for their parade on Tuesday?'

'Yes, and I'm going, too, to bless their crops and hop gardens,' said Beth. 'I'm looking forward to it.'

'Can I come?' Libby turned to Ben.

'Of course. I assumed you would.' Ben raised his glass to her. 'Here's to Steeple Martin Morris and the Rogue Days parades.'

Chapter Thirty-five

Sunday again, and the usual suspects were gathering round Hetty's huge kitchen table. To Libby's surprise, Ian arrived just after she and Ben, looking tired, but not unduly stressed. Edward, already seated and occupied in opening bottles, looked surprised.

'Why didn't you say?' he said. 'We could have shared the journey.'

'I've got to go straight on,' said Ian, 'but thanks all the same.'

Libby, putting out glasses, cast Ian a curious glance. He caught her eye and smiled.

'No, Libby, it isn't to do with Neil and Joan Barton. Peripherally, maybe.'

'Oh?' said Libby hopefully.

'And I can't say any more than that.'

Libby narrowed her eyes at him. 'With Stapleton?'

Ian sighed. 'I told you, I can't say anything.'

'Leave 'im be, gal,' said Flo. 'Poor bugger.'

The rest of the table looked as if they were in agreement with Flo. Libby subsided.

'Tell us about this 'ere lad, then,' said Lenny. 'Got a dog, ain't 'e?'

Thankfully, Libby launched into Ricky's story, which took them through until they were all served with roast lamb and all the trimmings.

'And all this came from that woman reporting someone missing,' said Edward, tucking in. 'Amazing.'

'Except he wasn't missing,' said Libby, 'because I'd actually seen him that very week, although I didn't realise it at the time.'

'And it wasn't actually her reporting it,' said Ben. 'It was you and Fran finding out about the homeless people from Mavis, wasn't it?'

'Ye-es,' said Libby, 'but we wouldn't have been asking about Island View if it hadn't been for Sylvia.'

Ian was listening to this exchange with the liveliest interest.

'I think I might have to speak to Sylvia, after all,' he said.

'She'd love that,' said Libby with a grin.

'Her agency was going to be selling the properties on that site, weren't they?' said Edward.

'Yes. I'm assuming they knew all about the Certificate of Lawful Development,' said Libby.

'What's that?' asked Flo.

'Never mind, Flo,' said Ben, frowning at Libby. 'Not important.'

Libby and Edward exchanged guilty smiles.

When Ian took his leave after apple pie and custard, he motioned Libby into the hall.

'What have you heard?' he asked.

'Eh?' Libby was puzzled.

'You rather leapt on Stapleton when I said I had to go to work. I assumed you'd heard something.'

'Well.' Libby got her thoughts in order. 'Apparently Stapleton's got Alzheimer's. So I wondered if it really was him who was behind Island View – if it was illegal – and the migrant workers.' She smiled, winningly, she hoped, at Ian. He, in turn, scowled at her.

'Just don't interfere,' he said.

Libby watched him leave. 'Well,' she said to herself. 'Sounds like what Colin found out is true.' She sighed in frustration. That meant, as she had thought yesterday, Stapleton wasn't behind the murders. Bother.

But what about all his underhand tactics over at Pucklefield? And was all her investigation of Shittenden and the Hop House Centre for nothing? She went slowly back into the kitchen, where a discussion was underway about the projected route of the Rogation Day parade.

'Have you been told off?' Ben asked quietly.

'Sort of,' admitted Libby. 'But I think I got it all wrong, anyway.'

Fifteen minutes later, Libby, Ben and Edward walked down the drive to see Peter and Harry.

'We really ought to do something different, you know,' said Peter, as he opened the door. 'We've got far too predictable.'

'Oh, don't change things,' said Edward. 'I've only just got used to the Steeple Martin routine.'

'You're not always here,' said Harry, as usual still in his whites and sprawled on the sofa.

'Especially now Alice is on the scene,' said Libby.

Edward gave them all a rather self-satisfied smirk.

Peter supplied drinks and settled down next to Harry on the sofa.

'What's new, then?' he asked.

'And how's young Ricky?' asked Harry.

'Ricky's fine as far as I know,' said Libby. 'I haven't seen him since we had lunch with you.'

'And what about that woman Harry told you to talk to?' Peter lifted Harry's feet onto his lap.

'Sylvia? I think she knows more about the Island View development than she's letting on, but otherwise I don't know. Oh,' Libby remembered, 'Colin found out that the bloke behind the development, you know, Stapleton Holdings, has got Alzheimer's. So whatever's been going on, it isn't him.'

'Well, that's a turn-up for the books,' said Harry. 'I reckon it's young Rick's wicked stepdad.'

'What, the murders?' said Ben.

'All of it,' said Harry. 'Illegal migrants, dodgy development, murders, the lot. He sounds a right piece of work, that one.'

'I must admit, I did wonder,' said Libby. 'Everything I thought Stapleton had been behind could have been Grant Pointer instead.'

'And how will you find out?' asked Edward. 'Ian's not going to tell you.'

'I don't know.' Libby sighed. 'I suppose I ought not to try.'

'You could ask that Sylvia again,' said Harry. 'She's got to know something.'

'I have a feeling she's going to stop answering my calls,' said Libby. 'And, in a way, I don't blame her.'

Monday morning, and Libby decided to try to find out a bit more about Joan Barton. Linda hadn't talked much about her over lunch at the Pink Geranium, only to say that it had been she who had been instrumental in introducing Ricky's mother to Grant Pointer. Libby decided a call to Linda was indicated.

But Linda's phone went to voicemail and Libby was stumped.

'But I don't know what to do!' she wailed to Fran.

'Oh, for goodness' sake, Lib! I can't stop to talk now. I'm helping Guy restock the shop. It'll be proper summer season starting this weekend.'

'Do you want some help?' asked Libby hopefully.

'No!' Fran sounded unflatteringly definite. 'You could get on with a couple of little pictures for the gallery, though.'

'Oh. Yes, I could.' Libby sighed. 'So we're leaving the whole thing alone, are we?'

'Yes, we are. Guy's been told that Island View is officially not happening, so there's nothing to do there—'

'What about the fundraiser at The Alexandria?'

'They need funds to pay for the legal advice they've already had,' said Fran. 'Now, go away and do some painting. We'll see you Wednesday.'

Libby heaved a theatrical sigh and wandered into the conservatory. She stared guiltily at the paper stretched invitingly on the easel and then out into the garden. For a minute, she didn't know where the ringing was coming from, until she realised she'd left her phone in the kitchen.

'Hello?' she gasped, picking up.

'Oh, Libby, it's Sylvia.'

Sylvia? Libby almost dropped the phone.

'I thought you weren't going to pick up.' Sylvia sounded annoyed.

'No – ah – yes. I was – er – in another room.' Libby pulled herself together. 'What can I do for you?'

'I was wondering,' Sylvia began, and then stopped.

'Wondering what?'

'Well, you know you were asking about that caravan site?'

'Yes?' Libby felt her heartbeat speed up.

'You mentioned somebody called – um – Painter, was it?'

'Pointer, yes.'

'P-Pointer, yes, that's it. I wondered – who he was?'

You know perfectly well, thought Libby. What is all this?

'I thought you would know,' she said aloud. 'He does all of the business for Stapleton Holdings.'

'Oh.' Sylvia cleared her throat. 'No – I don't think so. And – we're not handling the caravan site any more, I told you.'

'Yes, and I assumed Grant Pointer would have told you about that.'

'Yes, you said.'

There was another long pause. She doesn't know what she's doing, thought Libby. And what precisely *is* she doing?

'What exactly do you want to know, Sylvia?' she asked eventually. 'You haven't been that helpful when I've asked *you* questions.'

'Well, no, but I didn't know anything, you see,' said Sylvia in a rush, 'and I wanted to know what had been going on, so I thought I ought to ask this Pointer person.'

'Right,' said Libby. 'Why?'

'Why?' repeated Sylvia. The silence was longer this time, and Libby wasn't going to help her out. Eventually, Libby heard an indrawn breath.

'It's just . . . well. I need to know if I've done something illegal.' Sylvia's voice trembled.

Ah! Now we're getting to it, thought Libby.

261

'Like what?' she said aloud.

'It's this legal-development thing.' Libby heard Sylvia moving and guessed she was getting out of earshot of someone. 'I didn't know anything about it at first. I was just asked to sell these new homes. I must say, they looked rather nice.'

'They are,' said Libby. 'I've stayed in one.'

'You have?' Sylvia's voice faltered.

'When Fran and I were asked to look into something down on the South Coast. Go on. Why do you think you were doing something illegal?'

'Well, if my bosses were in on it – I mean, if they knew the site was illegal – could I be prosecuted, too?'

Sylvia sounded really frightened, thought Libby.

'And I wondered,' the shaky voice went on, 'if this Pointer person knew about it, too.'

Libby frowned. Now, why had Sylvia asked that?

'Well, of course he did,' she said. 'He works for Nick Stapleton, doesn't he?'

'Yes – I mean,' Sylvia caught herself up, 'I suppose he does.'

After a minute, Libby lost patience. 'Look, Sylvia – what are you playing at? It's perfectly obvious that you know Grant Pointer, as, indeed, it's perfectly obvious that you knew what your homeless Rab was trying to do.'

'What?' Sylvia almost shrieked. 'What was he doing?'

'Oh, really.' Libby shook her head in disbelief. 'He was trying to find out about the legality of Island View, wasn't he? Why?'

Sylvia was sobbing now. 'I don't know! I didn't tell him anything.'

'So why were you asking me about Grant Pointer? You know who he is, and my guess is you knew perfectly well that he and your bosses had connived in the plan to develop the Island View site. And now you're worried you'll get caught up in the fall-out. Honestly, Sylvia! And while we're chatting so nicely, tell me why you reported Rab missing. And why did you want to tell Ian?'

Silence. Again.

Libby let out an exasperated sigh. 'Fine. I'll let Ian know what you've told me—'

'I haven't told you *anything*!' wailed Sylvia.

'Oh, yes, you have.' Libby laughed. 'And I'd look for another job, if I were you.'

She clicked off the phone and stood staring at it. Sylvia was scared out of her wits, that much was obvious, but of what? Or whom? The police? Grant Pointer? Not Nick Stapleton, if he really was out of action. Or was that a polite fiction? No – Colin had told her about that, and he had no reason to lie. It had also been apparent from Ian's attitude yesterday that what Colin had learnt was true. She sighed and scrolled to Ian's official number.

'DCI Connell's phone,' said a female voice.

'Oh,' said Libby, wrongfooted. 'Is he there? Could I speak to him, please?'

'I'm afraid he isn't available at the moment,' said the voice. 'Who's speaking, please?'

'My name's Libby Sarjeant. Don't worry. I'll try later.'

'Can I take a message?'

'No, it's fine, thank you. Thank you,' repeated Libby, and ended the call.

'Right,' she said to Sidney. 'I'm going down to Nethergate to drag the truth out of Sylvia Cranthorne.'

First, she called Ben, who turned out to be busy in the big barn with Duncan Cruikshank on Morris business, and told him where she was going.

'You're poking your nose in again, aren't you?' said Ben. 'Exactly what Ian told you not to do yesterday.'

'But this is new information!'

'No, it isn't. You already knew Sylvia had been economical with the truth. The fact that she knew Pointer is really not relevant.'

'But she's scared, Ben. And if she's scared of Pointer, the police need to know.'

'Then tell the police!' said Ben.

'I've tried. Ian's not available.'

'Then tell another of your police friends. Rachel – how about her?'

'I'll try,' said Libby, crossing her fingers.

One thing Libby hadn't counted on was the distinct lack of petrol in the tank of the Silver Bullet. Annoyed, she realised she would have to go to the petrol station on the Canterbury road before setting off for Nethergate.

She was grumpily tapping her foot while petrol flowed expensively into her tank when a friendly face appeared round the side of the petrol pump.

'Cheer up!' said Joe, proprietor of Cattlegreen Nurseries, a little further up the road. 'Haven't you got any murders to solve?'

'Oh, Joe! You made me jump.' Libby replaced the hose back into the pump and pushed her debit card into its greedy slot.

'Looking forward to Wednesday, are you?' Joe replaced his hose into the other side of the pump. 'Coming up to bless us, apparently, your Morris men. And the vicar, Owen tells me.'

Joe's son Owen sang in the church choir.

'Yes, it's all going well,' said Libby. 'And it's happened so quickly.'

'Good thing for the village,' said Joe. 'Community spirit and all that. Owen says some of the choir will be following the vicar, too.'

'Oh, that's lovely,' said Libby. 'We're going over to Pucklefield tomorrow to dance with them, too. Well, the Morris side are – I'm just a hanger on.'

'Nice pub over there,' said Joe. 'Used to pop into the Puckle sometimes when we got veg from one of the farms.' He shrugged. 'Before that bastard – sorry, Libby, but he is – took the farm over.'

'What bastard?' Libby held her breath.

'Pointer, his name was. Worked for someone else, of course, but he went in with a gang and more or less turned poor old Jimmy out.'

'How did he get away with that?' asked Libby, wondering where she'd heard the name Jimmy recently.

'Oh, I don't know.' Joe pointed over Libby's shoulder. 'You've got someone waiting for your pump.'

'Oh, right, thanks.' Libby paused with one foot inside her car. 'Will we see you on Wednesday?'

'Told you! You'll be blessing my crops!'

Libby drove away from the petrol station, wondering about Grant Pointer, who seemed to be taking over the role of major villain from Nick Stapleton. And Jimmy – now she remembered. Someone who was too old to dance – Reg had mentioned him when she and Simon went to Pucklefield. So who really was to blame in this catalogue of evil? Pointer or Stapleton?

She eschewed the usual car park behind the Blue Anchor when she arrived in Nethergate, and made for Cliff Terrace instead. She got out of the car and went to gaze out over the town while she called Fran.

'So how do you expect to talk to her?' Fran sounded cross. 'Drag her out of her office by main force?'

'Lunch?' suggested Libby. 'I suppose you wouldn't . . .'

'No, I wouldn't. And don't go bothering Jane, either.'

Libby sent a guilty look behind her at Peel House where, presumably, Jane Baker was beavering away on behalf of the *Nethergate Mercury*.

'All right,' she said. 'But I'm still going to try to see Sylvia. She's hiding something.'

She ended the call and began to walk along Cliff Terrace towards the high street. She'd just passed Peel House when she heard Jane's voice.

'Hoy! Libby!'

She turned to see Jane hurrying down the steps from her front door.

'I thought it was you!' Jane panted to a halt. 'Are you going to see Fran?'

'No, actually. I was . . . um.' Libby stopped, wondering how much to tell Jane.

'Is it about Island View?' Jane looked excited.

'Sort of. But that's been stopped now, hasn't it?'

'Yes – but that isn't the best bit.' Jane peered closely at Libby. 'You sure you haven't heard the news?'

'No – what news?'

'There's been another murder!'

Libby stared, open-mouthed.

'Well – say something!' said Jane.

'D-do you mean – a *connected* murder? Something to do with the others?' Libby's head was whirling.

'Yes! The man who organised the clearance of the homeless people. Pointer – that was his name: Grant Pointer.'

Chapter Thirty-six

Libby was gobsmacked. Pointer – dead?

'But—' she began.

'I was sure that was why you were here,' said Jane, looking disgruntled.

'No,' said Libby. 'How do you know? Oh – "the wire" I suppose.'

'Actually, it was the police control room.' Jane looked away. 'We – ah – monitor the calls. And it was here, so we – I mean, I – couldn't avoid it.'

'Where?'

'Where else? The caravan park.'

'Island View? But why?'

Jane shrugged. 'I don't know – but Stapleton Holdings still own it, even if they can't do what they wanted with it. And Pointer worked for them.'

'How do you know that?' asked Libby.

Jane looked surprised. 'It's no secret. I told you – he was the man who organised the clearance.'

'Right.' How had she missed that? wondered Libby. 'When was he found?'

'This morning. There's still a security patrol apparently.'

'Oh? Stapleton Holdings or police?'

'Stapleton Holdings. They don't want anyone breaking in there, do they?'

'It'll be police now it's a crime scene,' said Libby, and sighed. 'Oh, well. I'd better go down and see – oh, *bloody hell*!'

'What?' Jane stared at Libby's horrified face.

'Nothing.' Libby looked away, then turned back. 'Look, Jane, I can't tell you now. But I promise if I hear anything that's – well, repeatable – I'll tell you.' She tried a rather lopsided smile. 'See you.'

She was aware of Jane watching her as she ran back to her car, but no way was she going to reveal what had suddenly struck her. Ricky Short was Grant Pointer's stepson, he had a grudge against him and was currently living a stone's throw from where his body had been found.

She drove down the high street and into Harbour Street, where she came to a dead stop. The car park was cordoned off, only to be expected, she thought, but, worse, so were the Blue Anchor and The Sloop. And, predictably, Harbour Street itself was packed with cars. Knots of people gathered on both sides of the road.

She drove slowly down to the jetty and managed to turn round, wondering where she would be able to park. She began to drive back down Harbour Street when she saw Fran emerge from Guy's shop. She lowered the window.

'I thought I saw you,' said Fran. 'Have you heard?'

'I'd parked up on Cliff Terrace and Jane came rushing out to tell me that Pointer's body had been found.' Libby chewed her lip. 'And then I thought – Ricky.'

Fran nodded. 'So did the police.'

'Oh, no.' Libby dropped her head onto the steering wheel.

'Look, you can't stop here,' said Fran. 'Go down to The Alexandria. You can park round the side there. I'll call and let them know you're coming.'

Libby nodded, put the car in gear and set off again. She crossed the square into Victoria Place and edged round the side of the concert hall, just managing to avoid the 'No Parking' sign. She put her head through the main door, saw no one and left.

Fran was waiting for her outside Coastguard Cottage.

'I've put the kettle on,' she said, leading the way inside.

'How do you know about Ricky?' asked Libby, following into the kitchen.

'Mavis phoned me.' Fran shook her head as she poured boiling water into mugs. 'She was in a terrible state.'

'What happened?'

'Apparently, they'd seen the police arrive earlier, and wondered what was going on, and then two policemen arrived at the door and asked Ricky to go with them. They were quite polite, Mavis said.' Fran handed over a mug and pushed a bottle of milk across the table. 'Graham's got Barney, who started howling as soon as Ricky left.'

'I expect he thinks the same thing's happening all over again,' said Libby, her throat tightening at the thought.

Fran sat down at the table. 'I suppose it was inevitable that they would question him, and it doesn't sound as if he's under caution or anything.'

'Why couldn't they have questioned him in the Blue Anchor? Why did they have to take him in?' Libby thumped the table in frustration.

'*I* don't know,' said Fran. 'And don't go asking Ian, either.' She took a sip of tea. 'Did you get to see Sylvia?'

'No. No point now, though. My suspect's just been bumped off.'

'Very sensitive, I'm sure.' Fran quirked an eyebrow.

'Well, now we know Stapleton's not capable any more, I'd assumed Pointer was the one organising the migrant workers and everything. Jane just told me it was him who organised the clearance of the homeless at Island View.'

'He could still have been the one doing all that, probably carrying on from where Stapleton left off,' said Fran.

'And what? Someone didn't like what he was doing so killed him?' Fran shrugged. 'Something like that.'

'But in that case, what about Neil Barton and his mum?' Libby swallowed a mouthful of tea and spluttered. 'Hot.'

Fran smiled. 'What does Harry say? "Comes from a hot place."

As to Neil Barton – if he was trying to find out from Sylvia about Island View, perhaps he threatened Pointer.'

'And his mum?'

'She found out?' Fran frowned. 'Honestly, I haven't got any idea.'

Libby sat back in her chair and stretched out her legs. 'How would she have found out, though? There's got to be some connection.'

'How?' Fran shook her head. 'If Neil threatened Pointer, who then killed him, how would his mother know that?'

'Perhaps Neil told her,' suggested Libby.

'I wouldn't have thought it was the sort of thing you'd tell your elderly mother,' said Fran.

'We tell Hetty everything,' objected Libby.

'Hmm.' Fran leant forward. 'Perhaps there was a reason he told her. Perhaps – perhaps she knew Pointer.'

'Well, she did!' Libby sat up, enlightened. 'Pointer was at the opening of the Hop House Centre, and Neil's mum took Ricky's mum and grandma with her!'

'I didn't get the impression that they knew one another, though,' said Fran doubtfully.

'Do you remember we wondered how Joan Barton had afforded a house in an upmarket estate?' Libby was thoughtful.

'*You* wondered,' corrected Fran.

'OK, *I* wondered. And we – all right, I – wondered if Neil had such a good job he could afford it?'

'Yes, quite likely. He was a man in – what? – his forties? Just his sort of house. He could have brought his mother to live with him, not the other way round.'

'But Michelle was certain it was the other way around.' Libby frowned. 'And Stapleton built those houses.'

Fran raised her eyebrows. 'So now there's a connection between Joan Barton and Stapleton?'

'It sort of makes sense, doesn't it?' said Libby. 'Suppose Stapleton set Joan up in that house?'

'Oh, come on, Libby! You're doing it again – trying to make the facts fit the fantasy.' Fran shook her head at her friend. 'What possible reason could he have had to do that?'

'She was someone from his past? She had something over him?'

Fran laughed. 'So he killed her? But you said yourself – Stapleton's not capable of doing that these days.'

Libby sighed. 'No, you're right. Oh, well, I suppose I'd better go home, then.' She stood up. 'Will you let me know if you hear anything about Ricky?'

'Of course I will. I'll go over and see Mavis later if I'm allowed past the cordon.'

Libby walked slowly back to The Alexandria to pick up her car. Everything had changed, she thought. Four weeks ago, she had met Michelle's stalker, and then she and Fran had been asked to talk to Sylvia Cranthorne about a missing homeless person. These two men had turned out to be the same person, and things had got more and more convoluted ever since. And, she acknowledged as she started the car, Ian no longer wanted their help, and, in fact, had not shared anywhere near as much information as he usually did. She sighed, and turned into the high street.

She drove past Brooke and Co. and wondered if Sylvia was in there trying to sell houses, or if she was hiding out at home. And who was she frightened of? If it had been Grant Pointer, that threat was now removed, but maybe she didn't know that yet. Libby briefly contemplated calling to tell her, then rejected the idea. It was looking as though all her ideas had been wrong, and, apart from Ricky, she decided she had better have nothing more to do with any of it.

Ricky, though, was a different matter. She wondered if Linda and Debbie had been told of the morning's events, but decided it wasn't her place to tell them, and she would probably get into trouble if she did. Besides, Debbie was Pointer's wife, so she would surely have been told by now. Gritting her teeth, she made a determined effort to concentrate on the drive home and realised she was hungry.

The red light was winking on the answerphone when she arrived home.

'I had to get this number from directory enquiries.' Linda's voice was slightly muffled. 'I couldn't find your mobile. Can you give me a ring back? Debbie's in such a state.'

Linda had omitted to say exactly why Debbie was in a state, but Libby assumed she had been told about her husband, and possibly about her son being questioned. She went into the kitchen to forage for lunch, taking the phone with her.

'Oh, Libby! Thank you for calling.' Linda sounded less muffled, but more agitated. 'Have you heard about Grant?'

'Yes,' said Libby, tipping soup into a saucepan. 'And Ricky.'

'Ricky?' Linda screeched. 'What's happened to Ricky?'

'Calm down!' Libby shifted the phone to her other ear and stirred the soup. 'The police are questioning him. I thought Debbie would know.'

'Oh, my God!' There was a pause. 'They – they're questioning Debbie, too.'

'Oh, dear.' Libby sighed and rolled her eyes at Sidney. 'Well, I can't see that either of them could have had anything to do with the – ah – death. But Fran's going to call me as soon as they let Ricky go back to Mavis, so I'll call you then.'

'Don't you think . . .' Linda paused. 'I mean, now Grant – well, he's not there . . . couldn't Ricky go home?' she finished in a rush.

'I suppose he could, if he wants to,' said Libby, 'but it's up to him, isn't it? As I said, I'll let you know as soon as I hear anything.'

She had barely finished the call when her mobile rang.

'Are you at home?' asked Ben.

'Yes.' Libby sighed.

'Did you go to see Sylvia Cranthorne?'

'No. I saw Jane and Fran, though. Grant Pointer's been found dead at Island View.'

'Ah. Yes, I heard.' Ben paused. 'Do you know any more about it?'

272

'No, except that Ricky's been taken in for questioning. And his mother's being questioned, too. How did you hear about it?'

'Guy called me. I think he was worried about you and Fran getting more involved.'

'No chance,' said Libby. 'We've given up. Oh, and Ricky's grandma called. I'm not quite sure what she wanted, but I'm beginning to change my mind about her coming to live here.'

'Was she going to?'

'Didn't I tell you? I told Hetty. Grandma thought it seemed like a very friendly place, she said. Anyway, apart from Ricky, I don't want anything more to do with it. I'm just going to look forward to our Rogue Days.'

Despite a determined effort to start redrafting the *Cinderella* script however, Libby found herself unable to concentrate, and was relieved when Fran called later in the afternoon.

'They sent Ricky home in a police car,' she said. 'Well, back to Mavis, anyway.'

'Thank goodness. Has he told you what happened? Linda called me to see if I knew anything.' She paused. 'She wanted to know if Ricky would go home.'

'I don't know – I haven't spoken to him. Mavis called me, and said he wasn't very happy. He and Barney have gone for a walk on the beach. But I don't think he'd want to go home. Certainly not yet.'

'No.' Libby stared at her computer screen in thought. 'I think he probably sees his mum as a bit of a traitor. And something we didn't ask her about when we met her was the Puckle Inn.'

'Oh, yes! She knew it, didn't she? Or Pucklefield itself, anyway.'

'And I wonder why?' Libby thought for a moment. 'I'd like to have another chat with Debbie Pointer.'

Chapter Thirty-seven

A chat with Debbie Pointer being quite obviously out of the question under the present circumstances, Fran offered to go over and see Ricky, ostensibly to check that he was no worse after his session with the police.

'You can also ask him about Pointer's womanising. I bet he knows,' said Libby.

Ten minutes later, Ben arrived, full of plans for the following day, when they were to go to Pucklefield to help celebrate Rogation Days. Duncan Cruikshank, in fact, had gone so far as to hire a coach to take them all over there.

'A full-sized one,' enthused Ben, 'as there'll be so many of us. All the dancers, the vicar, several members of the choir and various hangers-on.'

'Like me,' said Libby.

'And me,' said Ben with a grin. 'Although I seem to be unofficial Quartermaster.'

'And what have you been supplying?' asked Libby, with narrowed eyes. 'Apart from beer, that is.'

'Well, space to rehearse in the barn,' said Ben, 'and I might have found a few white shirts and trousers.'

'You mean you bought them,' said Libby with a fond smile.

'Might have done,' said Ben. 'Is the kettle on?'

While she made tea, Libby told him about Fran's phone call.

'And Ricky had gone out on his own?' Ben frowned. 'Was that wise?'

Libby looked round at him, surprised. 'Wise? What do you mean?'

'Weren't you worried about Ricky's safety when he first appeared?' asked Ben. 'Because of what he might have seen?'

'Well, yes, but we didn't know the whole story then.'

'You don't now. If your chief villain, Stapleton, has now proved to be out of commission and next in line – what's-'is-name – is dead – well. Someone killed him, didn't they? Someone who knew what had been going on, whether Stepdad killed the homeless man and his mum or not.'

Libby's hand was arrested in the act of handing over a mug.

'And you think they might go after Ricky? They might think he saw someone? But when?'

'When they were all cleared off the caravan site, of course.'

'But Ricky said he didn't see anyone. And there was no one there who looked like Neil.'

'He *said* he didn't,' repeated Ben. 'But he doesn't really know what or who he saw, does he? Didn't he say the heavies wore masks?'

'I think he meant balaclavas,' said Libby. 'But you're right. He could be in danger.'

Ben handed her her own mug and led her through to the sitting room. 'It makes a horrible kind of sense,' he said, sitting down beside her on the sofa. 'Someone killed Neville—'

'Neil.'

'Neil, then, whether it was the same night that everyone was cleared from the site or not. It makes sense to think that he was killed because he knew about the site clearance and probably the fact that the site itself was illegal anyway.'

'And his mum?'

'She must have known or guessed – or found out – who did it, so she had to die, too. You'd worked that out already, and I'm sure the police have.'

'So perhaps they know who the killer is?' said Libby hopefully.

'If they do, let's hope they've arrested him,' said Ben, 'because they *don't* know that young Ricky's gone wandering off all over Nethergate on his own.'

'Should we tell Ian?' asked Libby.

'I should think he's a bit tied up at the moment,' said Ben, 'and we don't know if he's SIO on this latest murder.'

'We took Ricky to see him in Canterbury,' said Libby. 'And Fran told him what happened at the meeting with Ricky's mum.'

'But Stepdad wasn't dead, then,' said Ben.

'Oh, no!' Libby clapped her hand to her mouth, wide-eyed. 'You don't think it was Ricky's mum or grandma who killed him?'

'Well, the mum certainly had a motive from what you've said.'

'And they've taken her in for questioning,' said Libby, 'so she can't go after Ricky. Anyway, she wouldn't hurt her son, would she?'

Ben shrugged. 'Who knows? And if they've let Ricky out, they might have let her out.'

'Not if they think she's the killer.' Libby stood up. 'I'm going down there.'

Ben stood up, too, and gently removed the mug from her hand. 'I'll come too. And call Fran first, to see if Ricky's come back.'

Ben's big four-wheel drive was parked at the brewery, so they took Libby's little Silver Bullet. Ben drove while Libby spoke urgently to Fran on her mobile.

'He hasn't come back yet,' she said to Ben, pulling nervously at her seat belt. 'Fran's gone to ask Graham if he's seen him, and said she'll tell Guy.'

'Don't worry too much,' he said. 'It's broad daylight and there will be plenty of people around on the beach.'

'No one except Sylvia ever saw Neil when he was pretending to be homeless,' said Libby. 'And that was on the beach. Next to it, anyway.'

'Two things, there,' replied Ben, accelerating up the Nethergate road. 'It was winter, wasn't it? Or almost, and you aren't sure exactly when Sylvia saw him anyway.'

'Hmm.' Libby chewed her lip. 'And *she's* scared of something, or someone, too. I thought it was Pointer, but now he's dead . . . When she called this morning, I was determined to find out who it was. I wish I had now.'

'Could it be her boss?' asked Ben after a moment. 'The estate agent? I mean, it looks as if he was in league with Stapleton – or this Pointer – doesn't it? If they were selling the mobile homes? Although it doesn't seem a good reason for murder.'

'Yes!' Libby's insides did a thump of apprehension. 'Sylvia actually said –' She looked at Ben, horrified. 'Oh, God, that's it! She said if her bosses were in on the scheme, could she be prosecuted, too, and she wondered if Pointer was in it, as well. Oh, bloody hell! She'd guessed the whole thing, hadn't she?' Libby's voice was shaking.

'Then we'd better put an alert out for her, too,' said Ben grimly. 'I suppose you had better tell Ian, after all.'

Libby called Ian's official landline. The person who answered took the message, sounding extremely puzzled, but promised to pass it on.

'I don't think he knew what I was talking about,' she told Ben. 'And I must admit it sounded garbled even to me.'

'Well, let's hope that Ian understands it when he gets it,' said Ben. 'I'm not sure I understand it, either.'

They completed the drive to Nethergate in silence. Today, there was plenty of space to park along Harbour Street, and Libby was out of the car almost before Ben had put on the hand brake. Fran met her at the door of Coastguard Cottage.

'He's not back yet!' she said.

'Is anyone looking for him?' asked Libby.

'Graham's gone along the beach and Guy's gone after him.' Fran looked over towards the Blue Anchor. 'Mavis stayed there in case he comes back.'

'What about the caravan park?' asked Ben, arriving beside Libby.

'We'd have seen him go past,' said Fran. 'Besides, it's still a crime scene. The place is swarming with people in white suits.'

'We were a bit worried about Sylvia, too,' said Libby. 'She was definitely very scared of something, or somebody, when I spoke to her this morning.'

'Oh – she's all right!' said Fran, surprised. 'I saw her earlier.'

'Where?' asked Libby.

'How much earlier?' said Ben.

'I was in the shop,' said Fran. 'Just after I spoke to you, Lib, when I told you Ricky had gone for his walk. She went past on the square.'

'Which way was she going?' said Libby.

'I don't know – she came from the high street and I wasn't paying much attention.'

'The Alexandria?' suggested Libby. 'She said the Nethergate Swans used to swim just beyond there.'

'That was early in the morning and they wouldn't be swimming from there when The Alexandria is open,' said Ben. 'And it wasn't long ago Fran saw her, so she's probably safe. I think we should be looking for Ricky. Just in case.'

'The Tops,' said Libby. 'That's where Sylvia lives. And there's the car park up there.'

'Why would Ricky go there?' Fran asked.

'I don't know.' Libby stared down at the beach. 'Perhaps Graham and Guy have found him by now.'

'Do we go after them, or strike out somewhere else?' asked Ben just as Fran's phone trilled inside the house. She almost fell over her feet trying to reach it. When she came out, her eyes were wide with surprise.

'They can see him!' she said. 'Right at the other end of the bay. And –' she swallowed hard – 'he's with someone else.'

Ben and Libby exchanged looks. 'Come on, then,' said Libby.

'You stay here, Fran, just in case. We'll go along Victoria Place and drop down onto the beach. It'll be quicker.'

Ben nodded and set off at once, while Libby stayed to give Fran a quick hug before trotting after him.

Neither of them spoke until they were down on the beach beyond the Alexandria.

'There!' said Libby as they spotted two tiny figures huddled against the cliff face. 'And where's Barney?'

Ben pointed, and Libby saw Graham and Guy with a frantic Barney, a hundred or so yards in front of them.

'Oh, God,' muttered Libby, and set off at as much of a run as she could manage on the sand.

By the time they reached the two men, Libby was panting and had the worst stitch she'd had in years.

'We saw them,' Graham was explaining, 'and Ricky obviously saw us, because he let go of Barney.' He frowned. 'But I don't know what's going on over there. Fran told us you were coming, so we decided to wait. We don't know what might happen if we get too close.'

'Well, we'd better try,' gasped Libby. 'Go on, you go ahead, but not too fast.'

Slowly, the little procession moved forward, Barney straining at his lead.

'If there was a problem,' Guy muttered, as they grew closer, 'something would have happened by now.'

The other three murmured their agreement, then, as they got nearer, Libby noticed something.

'It isn't someone trying to harm Ricky!' she said, standing still. 'Look, he's got his arm round someone. He's protecting them!'

'Why did he let Barney go, then?' Graham looked puzzled.

'To let you know he was all right,' said Libby.

'I thought it was to stop the dog getting harmed,' said Guy.

Libby drew herself up, ignoring the pain in her side. 'Let's see,' she said, and marched off towards the cliff.

Now she could see Ricky properly, but he wasn't looking at her. His head was down, as if he listening to the other person. She turned back to the others with a look of surprise on her face.

'It's Sylvia!' she said, and hurried forward to the foot of the cliff.

'Hello, Libby.' Ricky looked up and gave her a tired smile. 'This is Sylvie.'

'Sylvia?' said Libby. 'I didn't know you knew Ricky. What's happened? Are you both all right?'

'I don't know Ricky.' Sylvia's voice was hoarse.

'I didn't know what to do,' said Ricky. 'She was so scared.'

'Yes, you seemed scared on the phone,' Libby said, trying to peer into Sylvia's face.

Sylvia gave a huge gulping sob.

'Could you take her now, please?' said Ricky, standing up as well as he could on the rocky ledge.

By this time, the three men had arrived, and all stepped forward to help Ricky down, while Libby held out a hand to Sylvia, who took it and almost collapsed on top of her. Ben and Guy came to disentangle them.

'Who was it, then, Sylvia?' asked Libby gently, handing over a crumpled tissue. 'Who did it? Who were you afraid of?'

'The police,' said Ricky, who was on his knees making a fuss of his dog. 'She thought they'd found out she killed my stepfather.'

Chapter Thirty-eight

'You called her Sylvie,' said Libby to Ricky when they all sat together in the Blue Anchor after two kindly officers in uniform had taken Sylvia away.

'That's what my stepdad called her,' said Ricky. 'I knew about her and all his other women. He never bothered to hide them from me, just from Mum.' He shook his head. 'How could she be so *stupid*?'

'How did you meet her today?' asked Fran. 'Was she on the beach?'

Ricky nodded. 'Right by The Alexandria.' His face took on an expression of awe. 'I've never seen anyone so angry!'

'I thought you said she was scared?' Graham was leaning forward, elbows on knees.

'She was. She was angry *because* she was scared.' Ricky frowned. 'Does that make sense?'

They all nodded.

Graham had provided drinks from The Sloop, and Mavis had brought out a large platter of sandwiches. Ben now took one and said: 'How about you tell us everything she said, Ricky? We all need to know.'

Ricky sighed and fed Barney a piece of ham sandwich. 'It wasn't very nice.' He looked down at the floor. 'She was going on about my stepdad, saying he'd made her lie, and he'd killed old Mrs Barton—'

'You knew Mrs Barton, then?' said Libby, cutting through the expressions of shock at this statement. 'Of course, she was friends with your nan, wasn't she?'

Ricky nodded. 'Sylvie said she'd killed Mrs Barton's son, Neil, by mistake –' more expressions of shock – 'because he found out she'd done something about the caravan park.' He looked up and nodded wisely. 'I expect he found out because he was old Mr Stapleton's son.'

This reduced the entire company to a shocked silence.

'Neil –' Libby began in a cracked voice. She cleared her throat. 'Neil Barton was Stapleton's *son*?'

Ricky looked surprised. 'Yes.'

'And Mrs Barton . . .' Fran shook her head.

'Was his mum,' said Ricky. 'I've known them all my life.'

'But when we asked you if you'd seen him at the caravan site, you said you hadn't,' said Libby.

'You didn't ask me that.' Ricky frowned at her.

'You asked about Rab,' Fran told Libby.

'And I said a tall, pale bloke,' said Libby. 'You said there weren't any.'

'Well, I didn't know you meant Neil,' protested Ricky indignantly. 'And, anyway, I didn't see him there. I only saw him with my stepdad a couple of times apart from when I saw him with Auntie Joan.'

'Auntie?' repeated Graham.

'Courtesy title, I expect,' said Fran. 'Did Sylvie tell you when she killed Neil, Ricky?'

Ricky shook his head. 'No. But she said my stepdad was going to tell the police that she'd been behind the caravan-site idea. And she said she hadn't, but she'd helped.'

'What was she doing at the caravan site last night? Or was it this morning?' asked Guy.

Ricky shrugged. 'She didn't say. She was just crying and asking me to protect her.' He lifted his eyes to Mavis. 'I didn't know what to do.'

Mavis stood up and put a motherly arm firmly round the boy's shoulders.

'You did the right thing,' she said gruffly. 'And now it's time you had a bit of a rest. Been a long day,' she added mildly.

As she ushered Ricky through to the back of the café, she turned to the others. 'You can stay and finish your drinks,' she said.

'Well,' said Libby when the door had closed. 'Are we any the wiser?'

'We know who killed Neil and his mother,' said Ben.

'But do we know why?' asked Fran.

'Ricky told us,' said Graham. 'She killed Neil by mistake because he knew she was behind the Island View development.'

'I expect she lashed out,' said Libby.

'And Pointer killed Neil's mum because – what? Neil had told her about it?' said Guy. 'But in that case, wouldn't the old lady have told the police?'

'Perhaps she thought she was protecting Stapleton?' suggested Fran.

'I think you're going to have to wait until Ian tells us the whole story,' said Ben. 'And meanwhile we've got two days of Rogation shenanigans to get through, so I suggest we all get a good night's sleep.' He stood up and held out a hand to Graham. 'Thanks for all your help, mate, and sorry you had to get involved with the ladies.' He ignored the cries of righteous indignation. 'And if you can get time off, come up to Steeple Martin on Wednesday and join in the fun.'

On Tuesday morning, the bus arrived in Steeple Martin high street to collect the Rogation Day contingent en route to Pucklefield. Simon, because of his links to the village and the Puckle Inn, was leaving the Hop Pocket in the tender care of Gwennie for the day; Ben, to Libby's surprise, was resplendent in the Harlequin checked waistcoat that Steeple Martin Morris had adopted as their costume, although he'd drawn the line at white trousers and bells; and Bethany was in full regalia, with cape and stole. Libby clambered aboard and sat next to her, their respective menfolk being further down the bus with a suspicious-looking crate at their feet.

'So what happened yesterday?' asked Beth as the bus set off amid the waves and cheers of well-wishers. 'I hear you got your man? Or woman, Ben said.'

Libby sighed. 'Nothing to do with me, really, and, to be honest, we don't know all the ins and outs, but it seems to be rather a sad story all round. The man I told you about who was possibly abusing his wife? Well, he was murdered, too, but not by his wife. And his stepson, the boy with the dog—'

'Barney,' said Beth.

'Yes, Barney, well, the murderer actually confessed to him.' Libby frowned. 'At least, I think she did.'

'She?' Beth's eyebrows shot up.

Libby nodded. 'But, honestly, I don't know much more. As soon as I'm able, I'll tell all.'

Arriving in Pucklefield, the bus parked beside the pub, and Steeple Martin Morris joined a throng of other Morris sides, including Cranston and White Horse, and, of course, Pucklefield. Beth was escorted with due ceremony to the head of the procession. Charles Bertram emerged from the front door of the pub, and with a flourish introduced, at last, the Old Rogue, whom Libby now knew to be Jimmy Bottomley.

'Bit of a disappointment, really,' Libby muttered to Simon. 'He just looks like a druid.'

'Better that than some of the old pictures,' said Simon. 'They were really scary.'

'I wonder if Nick Stapleton was ever really the Old Rogue,' mused Libby. 'Or if it was a story put about to scare people?'

'Would it really have scared people, though?' said Simon. 'People don't believe in that sort of thing these days, do they?'

'Oh, you'd be surprised,' said Libby. 'If they don't, they pretend to, and they can do some pretty horrendous things in the name of that belief.'

Simon gave her an odd look. 'Not sure I want to know,' he said.

There was a sudden bang on a drum and the Old Rogue began to speak.

'I can't hear what he's saying!' whispered Libby. 'Does Dan have to say the same thing tomorrow at our parade?'

Simon smiled. 'All written down for him,' he said, 'with a few local alterations. And he's memorised it. Look – here's the Tolley Hound.'

A figure, to all intents and purposes a hobby horse with clacking jaws, bounded out from the pub and began to run among the spectators. Libby circled behind Simon and peered out nervously.

'Never did like them,' she said. 'I think I shall like our Tolley Colley better.'

The procession set off and made its way slowly round the village. As they reached the top of the slight rise at the furthest edge, Libby was surprised to see a group of men waiting for them. The procession slowed and came to a stop. Old Rogue looked round and spoke to someone, and then to Beth.

'There seems to be some confusion,' said Simon. 'I've never seen this before.'

As they watched, Reg Fisher came forward, then he and Jimmy Bottomley spoke to the men in front of them.

'I know who they are!' said Libby suddenly. 'Look at them, Simon! They're Stapleton's migrant workers!'

'Oh, hell!' muttered Simon. 'And look – police.'

But, surprisingly, the two uniformed police constables were standing aside, and Libby could swear they were smiling.

Old Rogue turned to the procession behind him, held up his arms and said something, again, inaudible to Libby. The

Pucklefield Morris side shuffled backwards and, to murmured exclamations of surprise, the newcomers fell in behind Beth and Old Rogue. With a bang of the drum and a rattle of tambourines, the procession set off again, accompanied by the grinning policemen.

When they arrived back at the pub, Simon and Libby found Ben waiting for them with drinks.

'So what was that all about?' Libby asked, taking a grateful sip.

'As far as we can make out, they're the migrant workers from Rogation House,' said Ben, 'and they asked if they could join in. The police obviously said yes. But – no really, Lib – we don't know any more than that. They're all being taken off again, look.'

And sure enough, the group of men, all dark and roughly dressed, were leaving the pub, still accompanied by the diligent PCs, and shaking hands with everyone. And as a further surprise, a fleet of police cars arrived in the car park to pick them up. They were waved off by the assembled company with the utmost good humour.

'Well!' said Simon. 'What the hell was that all about?'

'I would imagine Stapleton's been vanquished,' said Libby.

'Probably because his right-hand man's been liquidated,' said Ben. 'And, no, Libby, you are *not* to ask Ian!'

But Libby didn't have to ask Ian, for he was waiting outside the Hop Pocket when the bus pulled up at the top of Cuckoo Lane an hour later.

'Tell me later,' said Beth as she gave Libby a farewell hug. 'I'm going to change out of this get-up.'

Libby joined Ben and Ian at the door of the Pocket, while the Morris men and the members of the choir, including Owen from Cattlegreen Nurseries, Libby noticed, filed into the pub.

Ben turned to Libby. 'Apparently, we're expected in the caff,' he said. 'Ian was sure we – make that you – would want to know, and rather than try and explain in there –' he jerked his head – 'he's

286

persuaded Harry to let us have the Geranium for a couple of hours. Fran's coming up.'

'Didn't seem fair to tell you without her,' said Ian, 'especially as it was her I asked to speak to Sylvia in the first place.' He sighed. 'I can leave you to tell anyone else you think needs to know.'

'Sounds ominous,' said Libby. 'Have you told Simon?'

'As he went in,' said Ian. 'We'll see him tomorrow, anyway.'

In silence, they crossed the high street to where the front door of the Pink Geranium stood open, albeit with the closed sign showing. Harry had already placed a cafetiere, cups and glasses on the coffee table in front of the sofa in the left-hand window. By the time they were seated and Harry and Peter dispatched to fetch wine and beer, Fran and Guy had arrived.

'I wasn't going to be left out,' said Guy. 'Coffee, please, Hal.'

Finally, they were all settled, including Harry and Peter, with their chosen beverages, and Libby was telling them what had happened earlier in Pucklefield.

'Were we right, Ian? Was it Stapleton's migrant workers?' she asked.

'Yes, you were.' Ian sighed and stared into his coffee cup. 'Those poor buggers.'

The others looked at each other in silent surprise. It wasn't like Ian to swear.

'They'd come over with a gang of people smugglers Stapleton was partially funding, and – the usual thing – then kept in appalling conditions with no pay because they were supposed to be "working off their debt".' Ian's tone put the words in inverted commas. 'Apparently he told them the locals believed in witches or something and would kill them if they tried to escape.'

'The Old Rogue?' said Ben.

'Something like that.' Ian nodded. 'So far as we've been able to learn, Stapleton was becoming increasingly irrational, and his second-in-command took over.'

'Pointer,' said Fran.

287

'Grant Pointer. And that was where Sylvia Cranthorne came in.'

'Ricky said they were having an affair,' said Libby. 'Or, actually, he said she was one of Pointer's women.'

'She was. And before becoming an estate agent she was a legal exec. Did you know?'

'No!' said Libby and Fran together.

'She was.' Ian looked grim. 'And she knew all about certificates of lawful development.'

'And forged one?' asked Harry. 'See? I said you should be looking at her.'

'She certainly helped Pointer to get one,' said Ian. 'And Neil, who you now know was Stapleton's son, worked for the business and suspected something was wrong.'

'But if he worked for the business, surely he was used to something being wrong,' said Libby.

'That I can't tell you, but Sylvia said he was trying to find out about Island View from her. He didn't tell her who he was, of course, and when she found out, she lashed out. It was all a mistake, she kept saying.'

'How did she get his body to the OB?' asked Ben. 'She wasn't very big.'

'That was Pointer. Sylvia called him to Island View, where she'd met Neil. And that was when he brought his heavies to clear the homeless from the site, while he and Sylvia dealt with Neil's body.'

'And Neil's mother?' asked Fran.

'Pointer knew about her and went to see her, because she'd been making a fuss about Neil being missing.' Ian turned to Libby. 'She was the one who broke into your friend's house, incidentally.'

'Poor woman,' said Guy.

'Pointer killed her to shut her up, according to Sylvia.' Ian drank what remained of his coffee. 'And by this time, she was panicking. And last night she arranged to meet Pointer, again at Island View.' He gave a mirthless laugh. 'He should have known better. She lashed out again.'

'What with?' asked Peter. 'Did she have a handy metal bar, or something?'

'The caravan park is part building site at the moment,' said Ian. 'There are plenty of potential weapons just lying around. We never found what she used to kill Neil Barton, but several likely items are with forensics for Pointer's murder.'

They were all quiet for a moment.

'Was Stapleton actually behind any of it?' asked Libby eventually.

'Oh, a certain amount of dodgy dealing, yes, and the people-smuggling, of course, but his hadn't been the hand on the tiller for some time. And with Pointer in charge we think the criminality was stepped up. Forensic accounting are going through the company's books and the migrant workers are all being looked after – as you saw.' He smiled round at them all. 'Sympathetically, I might add.'

'As long as they aren't bundled up and sent back to Syria, or wherever they came from,' said Fran.

They all thought about this, then Peter said: 'So the Old Rogue business was a red herring in the end?'

'Stapleton had used it in the past, we think, partially for intimidation and partially because he had rather –' Ian paused – '*specialised* tastes.'

Various sounds of distaste emitted from the company.

'So that's it, then,' said Libby. 'What will happen to Island View now?'

'And what about Ricky?' said Fran.

'Island View will be the subject of legal wrangling for some time, I imagine,' said Ian, 'and Ricky – well, he's nothing to do with us. I expect he'll go back to his mother.'

'He's going to take up his place at uni,' said Fran. 'And I don't think he wants to live with his mother. He's staying with Mavis for the time being.'

'And he can come up here whenever he likes,' said Harry. 'Good boy, that.'

'Well,' said Ian, 'I hope I've answered all your questions. I didn't think it would be appropriate tomorrow.'

'Will you be able to come in the evening?' asked Ben. 'We're forsaking Tim and having the celebrations in the Pocket.'

'I'll be there,' said Ian, standing up. 'Wouldn't miss it for the world.'

Epilogue

Steeple Martin's Rogation Day Parade went off without a hitch. Beth Cole led the procession along with Dan Henderson, dressed as a druidical Old Rogue, along with his dog Colley, wearing a special harness decorated with flowers, playing the Tolley Hound. Puckle-field, Cranston and White Horse Morris sides joined in, as they had done the day before, and the choir sang with unaccustomed vigour.

In the evening, almost everyone crammed into the Hop Pocket, where John Cole surprised and delighted the crowd by leading a singsong at the old upright piano.

'Great day,' said Fran to Libby, while John was taking a well-earned break and recouping his strength with a pint of Ben's best bitter.

'Yes, it's all worked well,' agreed Libby. 'I just wish it hadn't been a murder that sparked it off.'

Fran nodded. 'Trouble is,' she said, 'nothing you ever do these days is unconnected with murder.'

Libby gave a sorrowful nod. 'I know. Even a haircut, when you think about it.'

'True. And why were you having the hair cut?'

'Oh, yes – Colin and Gerry's housewarming party!' Libby cheered up. 'We've still got that to come.'

'And the spring play at the theatre,' said Fran.

'And the Glover's Men and their *Midsummer Night's Dream*!' Libby beamed. 'Nothing can go wrong with that – can it?'

Acknowledgements

Thank you to everyone who helped this book see the light of day: my agent, Kate Nash, Toby Jones and all the people at Headline, my family and my excellent friends, The Quayistas. Joanna Maitland, Sophie Weston, Liz Fielding, Louise Allen, Sarah Mallory and Janet Gover, who kept me going under difficult circumstances. Thank you all.